"Demon spawn!" yelled Armani Suit Guy, clutching the brass jar-thingy like it was a golden football. "Deviants! Abominations! You are the very vermin of Hell itself and destined for the lake of fire!"

"Yeah, okay, whatever," Darren said, reaching out slowly, "but in the meantime, I just have to take that little brass—"

"Abomination!" howled Armani Suit Guy, stepping back. "The Lord God will vomit you out! You and your kind!"

"Um..." Darren stopped reaching toward the brass jar-thingy and looked at the floor instead, scratching his head absently. "And exactly what *kind* would that be, pal?" He'd already started to run his tongue over his upper teeth, and Nick had known immediately there was going to be trouble.

"You vile perverts! Sodomites! Homosex—!"

That's when Darren had punched him. All things considered, it was probably a good thing. Theo had looked like he was about to throw the guy right out the window.

Other Books by Joshua Dagon:

The Fallen Series:
  Marbas the Black:
–   *The Fallen*, Fall 2006
–   concluded in *Demon Tears*, Spring 2007
  The Heir of Linos:
–   *The Beautiful People*, Spring 2008

Into the Mouth of the Wolf, Fall 2007

demon tears

†

joshua dagon

BREUR
MEDIA
CORPORATION

Published in the United States by Breur Media Corporation, Lutz, Florida.

ISBN-13: 978-0-9789955-2-2
ISBN-10: 0-9789955-2-X

Printed in the United States of America

Cover photograph: Pawel Golik
Cover design: Breur Media Corporation

BREUR
MEDIA
CORPORATION

Breur Media Corporation
18125 Hwy 41 N, Suite 208
Lutz, Florida, 33549

813-868-1500
www.BreurMedia.com

"The human and fallible should not arrogate a power with which the divine and perfect alone can safely be trusted."
– Charlotte Brontë
Jane Eyre

"Say what you will about the sweet miracle of unquestioning faith, I consider a capacity for it terrifying and absolutely vile."
– Kurt Vonnegut
Mother Night

"What glorious heresy, the children of darkness worshiping light."
– Jeff Long
The Decent

"…we were all just the way we wanted to be, dancing in the dust of the Embassy Club of our futures, in the costumes of shy children's love, and learning as only the fortunate do that God is not only the instruction of the mind but the hips in their found rolling rhythm."
– E.L. Doctorow
Billy Bathgate

To the memory of my friend and mentor

Steve Kammon

demon tears

CHAPTER I

†

Solomon's Vessel

Either how canst thou say to thy brother, Brother, let me pull out the mote that is in thine eye, when thou thyself beholdest not the beam that is in thine own eye? Thou hypocrite, cast out first the beam out of thine own eye, and then shalt thou see the mote that is in thy brother's eye.

- Luke 6:42 (KJV)

Los Angeles, California
A suite at the Four Seasons Hotel on South Doheny Drive, facing West Beverly Boulevard

†

"Don't have a stroke, Michael," Robert had told him. "It's only an executive suite."

Tilting his head, Michael tried to recall when Bishop Patrick had said that to him. Yesterday? Last week? Michael didn't know.

Bishop Michael Sigovia was confused and uneasy. Yes, the opulence of his hotel suite was disturbing, but that wasn't the problem. To boot, Robert had insisted they each required a separate suite; also disturbing, if not patently offensive, but that wasn't the problem either.

Since he'd arrived, Michael hadn't ventured near the suite's kitchenette, which appeared to have been stocked for a presidential dinner party instead of just one man. It was two days before he felt comfortable enough to use the mini-bar or its beautiful glasses, even simply for water or an occasional soda with ice. He acquired both soda and ice from the machines at the end of the hall.

The bed was delightfully comfortable and always covered with sheets as crisp and white as he'd ever felt or seen. Still, the mattress was the size of a tennis court. Michael couldn't help feeling guilty at the excess. It made sleep a challenge at times, if not firmly unachievable.

The suite was the largest in which Michael had ever stood, never mind occupied. Three enormous rooms—a living room, bedroom, *and* separate den, sweet grace forgive us, the blatant, fathomless vanity—a lavish kitchenette, marble bath with a Roman-style tub, and two walk-in closets. One closet was so large it could have held yet another giant bed, fully horizontal, loaded with linen, and still leave more remaining space than Michael's own bedroom in Athens.

Michael was surrounded by waste. He wasn't going to use the DVD player or the high-speed data port. The décor taunted him with detail the quality of which he hardly had the sophistication to note, much less appreciate. According to the brochure on the mahogany writing table, the color of the suite's carpeting was 'mauve.' Despite his best efforts, Michael could only see 'purple.'

Darkly stained, ornate, wooden molding framed the walls and ceiling. Double French doors led to a balcony complete with a beautiful, cedar patio set. One of the hotel's tropical gardens graced the view eleven stories beneath him. Michael couldn't see the gardens at the moment, though; the drapes were closed. Thank the Lord of Angels, the drapes were closed.

Don't have a stroke, Michael.

He sat on the monster bed, listening to the wind outside, staring at the lunch he'd ordered from room service, which was untouched and now, he was sure, completely cold. Michael couldn't quite remember ordering it and glanced at the herb-glazed chicken to try to remind himself. The food looked very nice and Michael thought, for perhaps the fifteenth time, that he should eat it. It too was going to waste, his lunch. He really should eat it.

Michael wasn't bothered so much anymore by the suite, or the bed, or the idea that the meal waiting for him on the small table cost twice as much as his shoes. At the moment, he was thinking about the view. Not just his own, though. Michael was also thinking about the view from down the hall, the view from Bishop Patrick's suite.

Even now, during the bright though overcast daytime, with the drapes pulled tightly closed, Michael couldn't get the picture of the gray-clouded midnight sky out of his mind, the midnight sky at which he'd stared throughout every evening during the previous week.

He sighed heavily and gazed down at the carpet; mauve or purple, mauve or purple?

Michael needed to come to terms with a couple of things. Normally, a little quiet time was all he required to get his thoughts in order. He'd been sitting on the bed since well before the sun had risen, though, and all he'd managed to do was consider that he should be hungry, then order some food so he could stare at it.

Admittedly, the task at hand did represent the accumulation of more than three decades of ceaseless effort on the part of the cardinal and his inner circle. Michael was never so keenly aware of the accrual of that time and labor until now. He'd never been so utterly enthralled by where the efforts of his life might actually have brought him. His stress was the result of a little more than that, though. Michael almost giggled.

It had been an enlightening week to say the least. Although, the most significant moment had taken place only fourteen hours ago. Michael couldn't seem to get himself to move past it. Boy, fourteen hours sure seemed like a long time when he considered that he'd barely moved at all. It wasn't a long time, though. It was the wink of an eye. No, not even that. It was the wink of a tick's eye.

Had he showered already? Michael didn't remember showering, but he must have. There was a towel on the floor and he was wearing clean socks. He really should pick up that towel.

Could ticks even wink?

One of the bigger shocks of the week was that Michael had actually bonded with Robert—and Michael didn't even *like* Robert. Actually, no one did. Ever since his unfortunate experience involving the cardinal's entire group of elder bishops—may they rest in peace—Robert displayed something of a fanatic compulsion toward his work that frankly made the rest of the council extremely nervous. After the tragic event, all the other members of the order found it difficult to be around Robert, even once he was released from the hospital and no longer required so much psychotropic medication.

Prior to Cyprus, Robert's dedication to the mission had merely been called 'notably enthusiastic.' After Cyprus—and he was able to take assignments again—Robert was described, however discretely, as 'rather obsessive.' Michael would agree, but whisper, "with the pedal to the metal toward 'clearly neurotic.' "

Robert was bound to eventually call attention to the sect, attention they could certainly do without, especially from the papacy, which was why Cardinal Matine sent him back to the States in the first place. At least, that was why they'd all assumed Robert was sent to the States.

Now though, Bishop Patrick was, truth be told, much worse. Oh, saints absolve us, Robert was much worse. 'Neurotic' didn't quite cover it anymore, did it? Michael was reluctant to use the word 'psychotic,' however, strictly for personal reasons.

Michael thought part of Robert's problem could have been living here in Los Angeles, alone day after day for the past three and a half months, waiting to be sent the tools he needed to continue. He was only human after all. Some degree of mental lapse could only be expected under such extraordinary circumstances, Michael supposed. There'd been, for example, Robert's creepy, nighttime vigil. He'd apparently sat in his darkened hotel suite each and every night for fourteen weeks, all alone, drinking Scotch and listening to classical music, meticulously scanning the sky over Los Angeles for the demon. Michael could hardly imagine it. All this time, Robert had been sitting and watching alone.

"Every night?" Michael had asked during the drive from the airport.

"Without fail," Robert had answered.

"Have you seen anything? I mean, Robert, really, how could you even hope to actually see anything? The odds have to be staggering, I can't imagine. You could sit there for a thousand years and—"

"I'll see him," Robert had interrupted. "He's here, and I'll see him."

To make a tough situation worse, Michael's arrival had been horribly delayed. Had their positions been reversed, Michael wasn't sure he'd have fared all that much better. If Robert was a touch delusional, perhaps it wasn't entirely a state brought on only by his own fixations.

Looking back, Michael wished they'd all taken Robert a bit more seriously. He chuckled at the thought, because, looking back, *honestly* looking back, after all that had just happened, Michael wished he'd become a plumber.

He certainly could have arrived sooner. Maybe Robert wouldn't have lost his mind if Michael had just gotten to Los Angeles a few weeks earlier. Robert's assertions had been such a surprise, though. No, truth be told, 'surprise' didn't quite butter the noodle; Robert's assertions were insane, ludicrous, and fanatical.

Michael shook his head, bit his lip. It was hypocritical, wasn't it? Thinking of Robert as fanatical and ludicrous was hypocritical. His claims should have been considered predictable and important: he'd apparently tracked down the very demon himself. Robert had tracked the skotos all around the world, finally finding him settled in, of all places, California. Well, ludicrous or not, predictable or not, no one had anything even resembling a plan for that possibility, nor were they very quick to develop one, which made any real efficiency, embarrassingly, beyond them.

Dear God, what had Robert expected? The majority of the council hadn't been on the job very long. Well, all right, seven years might seem like a long time, but then again, we're not talking about being a plumber, though, are we? No, we're talking about being a demon hunter, and where does one look for a rational precedent in that vocation? Hm? Neither he nor any of Michael's contemporaries had been receiving any effectual tutelage, seeing as all the council elders were gone — may they rest in peace.

Although the cardinal himself seemed to be genuinely shaken by Bishop Patrick's claims, he'd nevertheless expected action. Despite that, the rest of the secret little sect had been slow to gather and even slower to apply the resources Robert had requested. Even after all of them were finally back in Rome, the meetings could hardly be called productive. For one thing, the cardinal revealed the amount of funds he'd already been filtering to Robert, which was preposterous and still growing. Michael had felt as though they were all staring at a dam with a torpedo hole in it; everyone knew it should be fixed, but no one did anything, as they couldn't get over the fact it had happened in the first place.

It was suddenly clear to all of them: no one had genuinely expected anything to go this far or, even more fantastic, that any of them would ever actually be called to arms. With the notable exception of Robert, of course. Robert was the only one among them — besides the cardinal, let's not forget about the big guy himself, good gracious, no — who'd personally witnessed the reality of a demon. Up until last night, Michael would have added the word 'allegedly' to that observation, the same way the other bishops did when they discussed the issue; Robert had 'allegedly' witnessed a manifested demon. Things were just a tad different now, though, weren't they?

Michael giggled. Alone and surrounded by pointless indulgence, he had to press his hands to his mouth to stifle his mirth. Yes, certainly, things were just a tad different now.

All of the younger bishops, all four of them, Michael and his three colleagues, had spent years and years studying and traveling and talking and listening and boasting and documenting and lecturing and hypothesizing, all the while telling themselves that they believed. They'd been rapt in the singularity of their vocations, feeling set apart and haughty, reveling in their almost whimsical responsibilities, which resulted from their incredibly early appointments to the rank of bishop. Michael had been an exceptionally young priest at the time of his recruitment, a mere twenty-eight.

It wasn't until the call actually came, when, by satellite phone, the cardinal had uttered those simple, impossible words across countless miles, that Michael truly considered what he'd been doing with his life had any real credibility. He'd never really—not *really*—believed he possessed any special link to the Church's conception and application of demonology. It was all academic at best, perhaps theoretical, certainly speculative, but never practical, good gracious, no. In his heart, in his secret perception of himself, and even the Church, Michael was a scholar. That was all. He was an intellectual, a professor, not a ghost buster or a demon hunter, sweet grace forgive us, no, how silly.

The same thought, although never given voice between them, had been on the faces of Michael's colleagues as clear as a tongue of flame; they'd never expected to get the call either. They'd never expected to be making decisions and taking actions and working definitively toward what they'd always considered a highly engaging, exotic, all but improbable—if not flat-out unimaginable—aspect of their jobs. None of them ever believed their work would be pulled from the realm of theory and theology to lie so solidly and conspicuously in the realm of reality. None of them had ever, *ever*, expected to get the call. Not *the* call.

Expected or not, though, the cardinal had called and said, "He's found him. Robert found the skotos."

Of course the council was skeptical. Even days after they had arrived in Rome, they still held enormous doubt. They'd never been exposed to anything resembling the bizarre trappings of Robert's investigation. The council's younger members encountered demons primarily through text: fiction, legends, myths, fables, anecdotes, and scripture. Yes, Robert's recounting of the events on Cyprus was accepted as authentic, or at least coherent.

Well, Michael silently corrected himself, in the presence of the cardinal, that was, Robert's story was accepted.

Despite their educations, despite their considerable faith, taking Robert and the cardinal literally had ultimately proved beyond Michael and his peers. Michael was certain he wasn't the only one to have suppressed an occasional smirk. Even sitting in their various rooms at their various assignments around Europe, the Mediterranean, and the Near East, listening to Matìne ramble on and on over the satellite phone about what Robert found, footprints in blood, wind-blown crime scenes, baffling forensic data, and those poor, poor people with the missing strips of skin, even then, who on the council had been able to keep themselves from grimacing, pulling the earpiece away from their face, and thinking *Is he drunk?*

Michael knew the group waiting back in Rome was still smirking. He knew they had extensive doubt, because he'd had it himself. If they'd remotely considered, even for one instant, that Robert actually found the skotos—or the tangible manifestation of *any* such supernatural entity, oh my gosh, good gracious, yes—they'd have been right there on the plane as well, all of them, right next to Michael all the way.

What had they thought they'd been doing all their lives? What had they really thought of the testimonials from so many eyewitnesses around the world, not to mention Cardinal Matìne himself? What did they think had really happened to Robert and the lost senior bishops—may they rest in peace? What had they been imagining all this time? Had they secretly believed the cardinal and Robert were no more than educated liars seeking attention, maybe with just a touch of clinical schizophrenia? Had Michael and his colleagues, somewhere in the recesses of their minds, suspected that one day the entire sect would discover some illusive but rational truth?

Okay everyone, I know we've all dedicated a healthy chunk of our adult lives to the authentication and academic documentation of demons on behalf of the Church, but it turns out that the cardinal, Bishop Patrick, and all those people we've interviewed all over the world, were simply under the influence of some very bad mushrooms. Oh yeah, and all the elder bishops weren't actually killed by a demon. As it happens, they died on Cyprus in a house fire caused by some microwave popcorn. Sorry for the confusion!

Michael glanced again at the table where his lunch continued to sit. The vegetables were dried and looking slightly plastic. His glass of ice and soda had become a glass of soda and water sitting in a small puddle of condensation.

Flying to the States, Michael had expected to discover the missing component that would put all of their moderately exciting yet safe lives back into their normal routines. Before he'd landed in Los Angeles, Michael convinced himself he and Robert would simply sit together quietly, rationally review all the information, discover an overlooked—but vital—element, and all of this turmoil would dissolve like tissue in the rain.

That hadn't happened, though. And now, a week later, everything was different. Everything was different because Michael believed.

Michael believed because he'd seen him. He'd seen the skotos himself.

Don't have a stroke, Michael.

Since the day of Michael's arrival, Robert had insisted on a very specific schedule. They spent the first portion of every evening sitting inside an enormous nightclub in Hollywood, watching the young and massive crowd. The rest of the dark morning hours they watched the sky from their elevated vantage, high above the city in Robert's suite. They slept through the day, which Michael hadn't minded at all, being considerably jetlagged anyway.

That first day, Robert had taken Michael straight to a small but lavish clothing store in Beverly Hills where they spent several hours. Over Michael's stunned and increasingly agitated objections, Robert purchased an embarrassingly excessive wardrobe of contemporary outfits for him, even going so far as to insist he wear one right out of the store. Before Michael could so much as form the question of why such a thing was at all necessary, they drove straight to a hair salon, which appeared to have been constructed entirely out of marble. There, Robert arranged to have the haircut Michael had worn since he was thirteen years old quickly and totally obliterated.

Michael remembered shutting his eyes to keep from bolting from the swivel chair as almost all of his ash-blonde locks were nearly shaven off. Only a hint of his curls remained above his forehead. The change was so staggering that he and Robert, as well as the cosmetologist, simply stared into the mirror at him for several minutes. Michael thought he looked nineteen years old.

Finally, Robert had laughed with delight and said he thought the new look was perfect for their mission, a wonderful sign that God approved of Michael being chosen. Staring at himself aghast, Michael thought no one in the Church would take anything he said remotely seriously ever again.

Any dismay over all of his hair being shorn off into some kind of music-video/pornography-film style was immediately forgotten, however, due to the utter shock of discovering that the thin and graceful young girl who'd performed the hair-butchering was actually a thirty-nine year old man.

In the car afterward, Michael had expressed his alarm to Robert, who didn't help things at all when he replied, "Oh, yeah. Blair is all about high heels, latex boobs, and Botox. If you ask me, she should just have the operation and get it over with."

When they finally made it to the hotel, Robert picked out a different outfit for Michael from the bags of acquisitions they'd spent most of the day compiling and then left him alone. Michael didn't have time to take any real notice of his room, though, or to process any of his renewed shock after catching his reflection in the vanity and being abruptly reminded of what had been done to him. Before heading down the hall to his own suite, Robert instructed Michael to shower, change clothes, and be in the lobby in no more than twenty-five minutes. There was still a lot more to do. Perhaps Robert still wanted to get him a tattoo and a nose ring, Michael had thought with a chuckle.

After a brief dinner at the hotel, and an even briefer briefing — *Stay close to me and don't talk to anyone!* — they'd gone to the club. There was a line to get inside that spanned almost the length of the block, but when Michael moved to take a place at the end, Robert had seized him by the arm and yanked him back.

"Don't be an idiot," he'd grunted, looking around shamefacedly.

They'd walked right to the front of the line, where a very young man, whose entire neck seemed to have been eaten by his shoulder muscles, smiled at Robert and even opened the door for him.

"How'ya doin' Mr. Patrick?" the child with no neck had asked.

"Just great, Bobby." Robert had smiled back.

They'd just walked inside. Michael had expected to hear cries of protest from the line of people already waiting, but they apparently didn't notice.

The muscular young doorman's attention had been almost completely focused on Robert. The face atop the stack of hungry shoulder muscles grinned widely at him, only glancing at Michael long enough to slide his gaze down his body.

Had he stopped at his crotch? Michael could have sworn the muscle kid had stopped and stared right at his crotch.

Inside the front door, there'd been a small crowd of very well dressed, young, and almost unbelievably attractive people gathered around what looked like a check-in counter, behind which another very muscular young man had been standing. With his increasingly dark mood, Michael wondered to himself if Robert had brought him to a nightclub or a health club.

The stunning, smooth-skinned, thick-haired, overly-muscular young man standing behind the nightclub/health club check-in counter had looked up at them questioningly. He displayed his mildly inquisitive concern by creasing his brow with wrinkles about as perceptible as the threads of a spider web. Robert only smiled and waved some kind of card he'd fished out of his wallet. It looked like a gold credit card, but Michael hadn't had a chance to really see it.

Was that how you got into nice clubs in LA? Did you just have to prove that you had good credit?

The demigod behind the counter had smiled, his face smoothing out again like polished ivory.

"It's twenty-five tonight, Mr. Patrick," he'd said, nodding deeply in what Michael could only assume was some casual form of respectful acknowledgement. Michael had been reasonably impressed that both the door man and the check-in counter guy knew Robert's name.

And still there had been yet another very muscular young man on a stool at the end of the hall—holy God, how did they staff this place? Clones?—looking utterly bored and completely disconnected. Robert gave him some money but the boy did not express the slightest interest. He could have been a machine programmed to take the entrance fees from patrons, like a robotic Disney creation from *Great Moments with a Playgirl Centerfold*.

Robert had been given two tiny, raffle-type tickets, which were then taken away by an older gentleman standing at the mouth of a dark corridor not two and a half feet from where the tickets were issued. Robert and Michael proceeded around a corner, down a smaller and even darker hallway, and then up some stairs.

Michael had thought it made sense that the club's security personnel kept themselves in good shape, although the ones he'd seen so far looked awfully extreme. Yes, it made sense that the staff of a place such as this, with its undoubtedly unpredictable clientele, should have the physical requirements for handling trouble. Right after he'd come to that conclusion, they turned a corner and were inside the club itself, where he saw the security personnel hadn't been extreme at all. With just the first glance inside, Michael thought maybe the world's surplus of human muscle had been stockpiled in Los Angeles and the guests of this club were the trustees.

"Why are all the boys so, uh... big?" he'd asked Robert.

"Welcome to Steroid Land," was the reply.

The club, Michael thought, was utterly gigantic. Still, there'd barely been room to move.

"It'll get busy in a couple of hours," Robert had said.

Michael had just stared at him.

They didn't stay in any of the common areas. Robert had talked briefly to still another large young man, this one dressed all in black and with some kind of hearing aid, standing by an unmarked door at one end of a huge mirror. The mirror turned out to be a window through which one could watch the club from inside a special, private room. Apparently, the large black-attired, muscular, hearing-aided young man didn't let just anyone inside the special room. You had to have even better credit than usual, apparently.

Inside, Robert had immediately crossed the crowded room and sat in a small open booth along its back wall. It had a sign on the little round cocktail table that said, 'Reserved,' which Robert set aside. Michael asked Robert if he'd reserved the table, and Robert had been rather boorish about answering him.

"No, it's reserved for Cardinal Mahony," Robert had said. Then he laughed. "Of course I reserved it, you twit. I called this afternoon."

Twit?

Before Michael had a chance to be impressed with the clout Robert seemed to have established in such a short time, he learned that anyone could have reserved a booth in that room, once they'd also pre-purchased a two-hundred-dollar bottle of liquor.

So Robert and Michael had set up camp in their booth with some very expensive Scotch, and there they'd remained for the next three and a half hours.

During that first evening, Michael had witnessed a horribly large number of exceptionally young people do some very awful, awful things. First of all, the girls were barely wearing anything at all, which just didn't make any sense considering how cold it was outside. Then, as the evening wore on, some of them shed still more of what little they had on, some walking around in what appeared to be silk pants and bathing suit tops.

Eventually, the boys all took their shirts completely off and danced with the girls, sometimes more than one at a time. The physical contact between the dancers was brazenly sexual, appearing to refrain only from the actual act of intercourse itself. However, Michael never went near the dance floor in the main room, and the Lord in Heaven only knew what was going on out there.

At the center of the large private room was a lavish U-shaped couch with a large glass coffee table in its center. It was impossible to actually see the coffee table, however, as the crowd around it was constantly very dense. The milling throng in that specific area was jam-packed from the moment Robert and Michael sat down to the moment they left. Michael wondered what drew such a number of the club's patrons to that little spot. The answer horrified him.

"Oh, well, the ones who aren't talking to Missy are probably snorting cocaine," Robert had explained.

"What?" Michael's eyes had bulged.

"Sometimes, between songs, you can hear the razor blade chopping against the glass top."

"You've got to be joking, Robert! Who's Missy? Is she a drug dealer?"

Robert had laughed. "No, no, no," he said, still chuckling. "Missy is a code name for the drug 'ecstasy.' They call it 'Miss E.,' or 'Missy.' Most of their drugs have female code names. 'Tina' is crystal meth. 'Gina' is GHB. There are lots of them, from what I'm told."

Michael didn't know how long he'd sat there with his jaw hanging open.

Although they hadn't moved around the club, Robert and Michael certainly didn't go unnoticed. A steady trickle of people stopped by their table and bantered with Robert as if they'd known him for years. Robert explained that his 'cover' included the ruse of his being a high-ranking and influential entertainment industry executive, which made his work so much easier in that, "the little twits fall all over themselves to get to me. I don't have to do a single thing."

Each night had been like that, each evening exactly the same, with one remarkably significant exception.

On the third or fourth night at the same table at the same the club—the nights had all sort of melted together by then and Michael couldn't quite remember exactly which night it was—for a very brief time, a small group of almost impossibly attractive people had wandered into the special room. As soon as they'd assembled and stopped to talk to one another, Robert had gripped Michael tightly by the forearm

"There he is," he'd said.

"Who?" Michael had whispered back, alarmed.

"The guy with the wavy black hair."

Michael had looked around, at first not seeing any guys with hair any longer than his own, which was just about bald, thanks to Robert, thank you very much.

Then he saw him.

Michael saw the guy with the wavy black hair and his heart all but stopped. Michael's breathing did stop, though, his jaw nearly chipping the table from dropping so far away from his face. He'd recognized the guy immediately.

Standing in the middle of the small group, smiling and laughing casually, was a young man Michael had seen in Athens many times. He'd never paid any particular attention to him on those occasions, however, except to note his familiarity. Michael had observed him at one or two public events around the city; a gallery or museum, a boulevard or market perhaps, but Michael remembered him just the same. The man had a striking, even resplendent air about him that was impossible not to notice.

And so Michael had taken note of him again, there in the special room of that enormous nightclub in Hollywood. He'd also noticed that, despite not having seen the young man around Athens for years, at least four or five, although it could have been as many as six, the black-haired young man still looked exactly the same. Every detail of his appearance seemed to lay precisely over the one in Michael's memory to a degree that was unnerving. Certainly, there hadn't been enough years between catching sight of him in Greece and seeing him in Los Angeles that would cause Michael to have suspected anything like cosmetic surgery, but that didn't account for the fact that there was simply no change in him at all. Nothing at all; his hair was exactly the same length and even in the same style; his stature, his deportment, the utter lack of any indication of age. Aside from his clothing, the tiniest details of the man were all precisely the same, down to the very pattern in his wavy black hair as it fell behind his ears.

"I've seen him in Greece," Michael had said, mesmerized.

"So have I," Robert replied, quickly taking a hearty gulp of his Scotch on the rocks. "And in Jerusalem, Istanbul, Florence, Venice, and New York."

"You're joking." Michael had only reluctantly turned his eyes back to Robert.

Robert had leaned closer and whispered, "Plus, I've heard extraordinarily similar descriptions of young men in London, Edinburgh, Stockholm, and Amsterdam."

"You think he's connected to the skotos in some way?"

"Oh, yes." Robert had nodded slowly. "I think he's quite connected indeed. On several occasions, when I've been able to authenticate the demon's activity, I've come upon a description of that man too, in one way or another. Not always linked in any obvious way, but there just the same."

"My God." Michael had gasped.

The little group of people containing the mysterious young man hadn't stayed long. When they left, Michael asked if they should follow them, but Robert just shook his head.

"I don't want him to recognize us."

"What are we going to do?"

"I don't know yet."

They'd watched them leave. The familiar young Greek and his companions had smiled and nodded to the muscular security boy as they passed him.

"A priest, you think?" Michael had ventured, still gazing at the door even as it closed silently. "You think he's a satanic priest?"

"Well, maybe..." Robert's voice had lost a notable degree of confidence. "Either something like that, or..." He hadn't finished his thought, but just stared down at the tiny cocktail table.

"What?" Michael pressed him.

"Well... they can change form." Robert stared at the ice in his drink, absently sliding the nearly melted pieces around the bottom of his glass. "It's not beyond their power to look human, you know."

"They...?" Michael's words had caught in his throat before he could utter them.

"I suppose it's possible, that..." Robert looked up at the room's closed door and squinted, pursing his lips, shaking his head, and drawing a deep breath.

"That man? You imagine...? I mean, you believe he could...?" Michael had only been able to stammer, incapable of articulating the possibility that both of them were obviously considering.

After a short moment, Robert had suddenly taken a quick and deep breath, which appeared to wake him a notch or two.

"I suppose it's possible," Robert said.

Michael noted Robert hadn't ever actually said exactly *what* he thought was possible.

"But we made that same mistake on Cyprus," Robert had explained. "We misinterpreted everything, made a mess of the situation. That happens, you know, when you treat possibility as fact. We took some small signs, some arbitrary details, and constructed them so they'd show us what we wanted to see. It was a very big mistake. Very big. It got everyone killed." Robert shook his head and raised his drink to his lips. "I won't be so blind this time."

They didn't see the raven-haired young man again. Even so, the implications of his presence sent shivers through Michael with just the slightest thought. The very idea that they'd witnessed the actual existence of some kind of demonic cleric, perceptibly consecrated with prolonged or eternal youth for his devotion to the unholy, was altogether awe inspiring. The other possibility was just too overwhelming to even contemplate, much less discuss.

However, the most extraordinary experience of that week had been only a day or two away.

After being at the club each night until two or three in the morning, they'd driven back to the beautiful hotel on Doheny Drive, and gazed out at the city from Robert's suite. Through the open French doors, beyond his balcony and the rise of the neighboring roofs, billboards, and chimneys, they'd watched together for hours and hours, scanning the night's view filled with stars, clouds, treetops, search lights, airplanes, helicopters, birds, and mist. They'd listened to Mozart, Vivaldi, Rossini, even Copland and Gershwin. They'd sipped wine—or gulped Scotch, in Robert's case, oh, sweet grace forgive us, a heck of a lot of Scotch—discussed the weather, the news, the immorality of the city at which they gazed—Robert's favorite topic—and sometimes even basic theology. That part of Michael's time with Robert had been rather pleasant actually and, although perhaps a little indolent, was very peaceful and even a little comforting.

They'd never discussed their mission directly. During those hours in Robert's room, it was as if Michael had traveled seven thousand miles for nothing. They didn't utter a word about the cardinal's great mistake in that lovely little chapel in Rome, they didn't discuss the 'magical' artifact resting in its locked custom case behind the suite's small wooden desk, and especially not the slaughter on Cyprus of which Robert had been the only survivor—well, besides Bishop Jarvis, of course, but he'd passed away six years ago while still at the nursing home, without ever having spoken a single word during the two years between the tragedy on the island and his death.

They certainly hadn't discussed the skotos. Robert and Michael hadn't spoken about the creature for which they sat and watched the sky night after night. They didn't mention him, that was, until he flew by.

It had been just past midnight. The sky was hidden by a low and thick blanket of seamless cloud that reflected the lights of the city against its gray surface. The gray surface also distinctly revealed the shape of the huge black demon as it sailed silently through the air in the distance.

Robert had spotted him first and issued a sound that was part gasp and part moan. Michael caught the image almost immediately afterward. Instantly, his mind screamed with a deafening insistence that he was only seeing a shadow, maybe an illusion caused by some obscured aircraft. As it glided closer, though, as the details of the image slowly became clearer, such convenient explanations were blown right out of his head.

It wasn't easy to make out every aspect of the shape, but discerning all that was necessary was far from difficult. Most intriguing was that the very light around the creature, the reflected illumination from the city off the clouds and the glow of the moon behind them, was dispatched by its presence. A trail of blackness seemed to follow the flying image, like the wake of a small black boat sailing upside down along the surface of the clouds. The light disappeared behind it then swirled back into position, as though the demon flew across the expanse of a turbulent lake.

Michael thought that, had the creature been flying at a slower speed, it would not have been visible at all, but only a streak of blackness through the sky, enveloped by whatever light-sucking phenomenon surrounded him; a brief parting of the clouds themselves.

It was the very creature Michael had seen in the enormous painting hanging in the rectory hall of Cardinal Matine's chapel. It was the very creature.

In Michael's head, a frantic voice had bellowed desperately; he was, of course, jumping to conclusions. It was not the demon at all, the insistent voice ranted. It wasn't the Darkness himself sailing happily across the sky and trailing a colorless void behind him. Nope, no demon at all, sweet grace forgive us, no. It was a hang glider. There, it was a hang glider, piloted over the city by an utterly deranged lunatic, who just happened to also be dressed entirely in black. Never mind how silly that explanation was, Michael's mind was simply not ready for the possible deluge of irrationality at hand and so the mental sandbags were going up.

After all, the voice continued with whatever lucidity it could grasp, desperately shoveling psycho-sand into neuro-bags, Michael had never been in Los Angeles before and, oh, without question, hang gliding at night could be a very popular pastime in this part of the world. Yes, that's absolutely true, for glory's sake. For all he knew, there was a purple-clad hang glider just around the side of the hotel and out of view, which was, wouldn't you know, followed by a paisley hang glider sailing silently next to a neon-orange hang glider. Of course there was, of course they were only watching one wayward member of The Rainbow Brotherhood of Nighttime Hang Gliding Lunatics. This was LA, this was *Hollywood*, where these types of pointless, crackbrained activities were common all season long, oh Lord in Heaven, saints protect us, of course they were.

Demons were, after all, probably just metaphors. Although, Michael would never, ever suggest such a thing to anyone. Never mind that no one in the Church would admit it—not in open company, at any rate, or without a touch of plausible mirth in their voice, in case they had to suddenly blurt *Just kidding!* should the listening portion of their private conversation express even the slightest indignation at such a brazen display of faithlessness. Never mind Margaret Murray's *The God of the Witches*; never mind John Milton or Dante Alighieri; never mind the Gospel according to Matthew and Jesus' warning about the devil and his angels, about the goats being separated from the sheep, about curses and everlasting fire; it was all metaphor and poetry designed to communicate the horror of living without God on an emotional level with a sprawling multitude of first-century minds that couldn't even read. Never mind all of that. What it boiled down to was that demons were no more than ancient imaginative mechanisms designed to give philosophical clarity to people whose understanding of the world would never expand beyond the sands of Palestine and the shores of the Galilee. Demons were pre-history's psychiatric use of anthropomorphism. The real demons in the lives documented in biblical literature, the ones even too terrible to discuss, too horrible to acknowledge, were Poverty and Ignorance, and their all too clear and fleshy benefactors, Herod and Caesar.

The voice in Michael's head had bellowed the same stupid explanation over and over, cleaving to the last shred of disbelief as if it were his frayed and failing solitary tether to the rational world.

That can't be a demon, because demons are metaphors, and metaphors don't fly around like big black hang gliders, holy Heaven above us, no.

The final blow to any alternative reasoning hadn't come because the black shadow flew any closer. It came because the supposed 'glider' suddenly lifted its great wings and flapped them once in a tremendous sweep of sky and mist, shot up into the clouds, and was gone. With that single motion, that vast and splendid gesture, the outline of the image was uncompromisingly clear for the instant it lay against the illuminated belly of the clouds.

It was the skotos. It was, undeniably, the black demon lion with the wings of a dragon. The Skotos, the Darkness, the Gryphon of Greece, had flown straight out of legend and metaphor. It soared across the sky toward Michael, a solid and literal creature, leaving all that Michael thought he understood of reality shredded in its lightless wake.

In that moment, Michael had felt himself flying directly through the looking glass. Or had he been there all along?

Never had any experience affected him that way. The true nature of faith itself poured like fresh cement into the core of his heart and settled there, after all these years, finally at one and at rest with his soul, in a state about which he suddenly realized he'd only imagined until that instant. Reading the works of Saint Frances, Saint Dominic, Saint Augustine, and even Dante, Michael had thought himself to be in possession of a faith that, if not completely equal to theirs, was at least a prelude of theirs, at least the potential of it. He'd been wrong. Oh, Lord in Heaven, he'd been miles from it.

With that perspective of faith, however, came a flood of new questions, new ambiguities and possibilities. The Kingdom of Heaven, the realm of the Divine and the damned alike, had made its unquestionable reality known. But did the sight of the creature really mean all that much? Did every contour of the puzzle take its true form with just the discovery of this tiny piece?

The demon had flown within their view, just ever so briefly beneath the cover of the clouds, not to be glimpsed by anyone who hadn't been looking for it specifically, who hadn't been gazing at the sky for any other reason than to catch that very creature in flight.

Afterward, Michael looked at Robert, neither of them noticing their drinks had fallen from their hands, the stem of Michael's wineglass shattering and the contents soaking into the carpet along with the Scotch and ice that had poured from Robert's lowball. They'd looked at each other and suddenly Michael couldn't breathe.

Today it seemed... well, today all the winds of the world had begun to blow. Just outside the hotel, just beyond his balcony, wasn't that a heavy wind Michael was hearing?

The tiny salad on the small hotel table was holding up nicely, much better than the medley of sliced carrots, broccoli, and green beans next to the chicken. It all still looked nice, though. He thought he really should eat it.

Had the drapes just stirred? The French doors to the balcony were shut, weren't they?

The wind whistled and Michael worried he might have a stroke.

†

Bishop Robert Patrick poured himself a drink. The afternoon was barely two hours old, but he'd stopped considering such details weeks ago. Besides, Bishop Sigovia wasn't answering his phone. Robert would eventually need to walk down the hall and knock on the twit's door, make sure the twit was all right. Perhaps some Scotch would bolster Robert's patience.

Robert shook his head, put the cap back on the bottle, picked up his drink, and sat down. He would walk down the hall, he told himself, after he'd had a glass or two of patience.

Overall, Robert was pleased. Although stretched to its brink, his patience had eventually paid off. Apparently, even for Matine, replacing such a treasured artifact as Solomon's Vessel with a fake and arranging for the actual relic to be smuggled into the United States turned out to be a daunting challenge. Of course, he was no rocket scientist, the cardinal.

Robert had waited, though. Somehow he knew that the skotos wouldn't leave the city. Somehow he'd been able to calmly watch the sky as the days turned into weeks and then the weeks into months. He waited while the four pompous infant bishops gathered reluctantly in Rome at Matine's summons and then debated the authenticity of Robert's claims.

It hardly mattered. Another week or two and Robert would have gone back to Italy himself. He'd have walked out of the chapel with the Vessel under his arm. Robert had found the demon and he intended to put him back where he belonged.

A small jar of simple brass, no bigger than a bottle of soda, sat in the locked case behind Robert's desk. He'd opened the case immediately after getting into the car with Michael when he picked him up at the airport. The artifact had been there, cradled in soft, dark-gray Styrofoam, which had been molded to support its every curve as if the metal jar was made of the most brittle glass. The mouth of the Vessel had been sealed with molten lead, sealed with heat, as if it still contained its timeless occupant.

Robert had been incredibly relieved, to say the very least. It was a shocking degree of relief, really, when he finally held the Vessel, when he finally had what he needed.

The Vessel could hold demons, so the story went. It could, in fact, imprison many, many demons. How such a thing was possible was unimportant; how many angels could dance on the head of a pin?

Robert had heard the story told a hundred times by Cardinal Matine, which, after all, was his job. It went something like this:

King Solomon, through the use of a magic ring entrusted to him by an angel, had rebuilt the Temple of Israel with the forced labor of demons, which, apparently, was even cheaper than labor in Mexico or Thailand. Niké should have such a ring.

The stronger demons, however, proved very difficult to control, even with the aid of the angel's magic gift. Therefore, some of the demons that Solomon called to his court weren't sent to work on constructing the Temple's immense walls, buttresses, ceilings of domed splendor, or any of its other architectural intricacies and extravagant features. Instead, the more powerful demons were forced into brass vessels, which were sealed with lead and thrown into the sea. There they would be imprisoned and helpless, sinking into the mud at the bottom of the ocean, out of sight, mind, and concern of Solomon and the entire Kingdom of Israel.

Unfortunately, the Babylonians saw to it that the imprisonment of the strong demons within the brass jars wasn't very long at all, the idiots. In fact, Robert pondered that, in quite a few other places in history as well, they sure as heck didn't seem to be rocket scientists either, those Babylonians.

Seeking treasure, the Babylonians dredged the very seas into which it was rumored a hearty portion of the wealth of Solomon had been cast. Upon recovering a number of the brass jars, the Babylonians opened them expecting to find riches. It was well before the establishment of banks, you see, and evidently that was what people did with their money; seal it in brass and toss it in the ocean.

Nope. Certainly not rocket scientists.

Instead of jewels and gold, or even mutual funds, the Babylonians only found trouble when they opened the Israelite's own little versions of Pandora's Box.

What's in your jar? Mine just has a scary lookin' monster-thing.

Yeah, mine too.

I know! Let's open some more!

Who knows how many creatures of immense and terrible power had been unleashed upon the world? Those particular Babylonian treasure seekers had themselves perished in their boats, almost to the man, with the exception, of course, of the one or two who would eventually tell the tale.

Centuries would pass before a single empty vessel, its seal of lead long since broken and chipped away, eventually wound up in the possession of the Church.

Late in the fourteenth century, Pope Urban V decided he would test the authenticity and rumored power of the artifact.

Although unknown outside of the highest ranking clergy, an ancient ritual was performed at the request of the medieval pontiff. A man claiming to be a sorcerer was commissioned to call up a demon for the purposes of using the Vessel to capture it—never mind that such a thing was oh-so-commonly referred to as 'witchcraft.' Such observations got one into serious trouble back in those days, and so, Robert assumed, everyone had just kept their little mouths shut.

The sorcerer hadn't been asked to prove his powers. There was never the smallest mention in the story of any apprehension over the authenticity of the 'sorcerer.' Apparently, he had a very large, unique, and sorcerer-ish hat.

Four young priests were selected to accompany and assist the sorcerer in his task, after which they were to take custody of the demon—Robert always smiled at this, as it gave the definition of 'demon possession' such a fun little twist.

The four priests had been hand picked by the pope for their youth, intellect, and devotion to the Church. As incentive, they were promised the unfathomably lofty title of bishop upon their successful return.

Robert had heard the story many times and always wondered if any of the priests originally involved in the scheme had any kind of backup strategy if only half their plan worked.

Call up a demon: check. Put it in the Vessel: um... okay, um, how do you turn this thing on?

Returning to Rome after the attempt, which had taken place with the utmost secrecy and seclusion deep in the deserts surrounding what used to be Judea, the young priests had professed to the pope that the ritual was a complete triumph. Back in Rome, they presented Urban with the sealed and, supposedly, occupied Vessel.

However, after bestowing the pope with his prize, each of the men was questioned thoroughly. During the almost brutal interrogations, it was learned that only one of the four clergymen committed to the task had actually witnessed the ritual in its entirety, the subsequent

manifestation, and the containment of the entity. At varying points in
the process, all three of the other priests had fled in terror as they
individually came to comprehend the authenticity of the event.

Even after having performed the ritual, the sorcerer himself had
fled the remote canyon cave, finally toppled from his resolve by the
sight of the materialized devil. It was the last remaining priest who
ultimately faced the demon and managed to confine him to the
Vessel. Although, just *how* was never entirely understood.

Immediately following the ritual, the three trembling priests had
been gathered up and the group began the return journey. After two
sleepless days, they came upon the sorcerer. He was dead, lying
unburied in the desert, half his skin torn from his body. They'd
identified him by his hat.

The pontiff was not quick to believe the story offered by his
priests. In fact, he'd been incensed that most of them ran from the
cave before the completion of the ritual. He even went so far as to
suggest that, in his solitude, the last remaining priest could easily
have sealed the Vessel, claimed to his brethren that a true demon had
materialized and been captured, and finally attempted to present it in
Rome, sealed though empty, in order to claim success in their
commission.

Hearing this, the three who had fled turned to the fourth, accusing
him of that very deception in the hopes of deflecting from themselves
the brunt of the pontiff's disappointment.

As the story goes, the brave young priest who withstood the
demonic ceremony—whose name had, unfortunately, been lost to
history—and the capture of the demon, in true humility, made no
effort to correct Urban and refute his accusations. Instead, he gave
over the Vessel to him and his care, saying that, empty or not, such a
treasure as Solomon's Vessel should not be trusted to the unworthy
likes of a simple, country priest, and should remain instead with the
rightful head of the Church.

However, he warned Urban: should anyone ever be tempted to
open the Vessel and investigate the status of its occupancy, they
should first seek some truthful insight from the depths of their soul.
Perhaps after concentrated prayer and deep meditation they might be
allowed some inspiration from the Lord himself to guide their
decision, as opening the Vessel without the guidance of the Divine
could prove unforgivable. On the other hand, leaving the lid sealed
and keeping nothing at all inside, he'd suggested, would be much
better than removing it to determine the validity of the demon's

presence, only to bear the consequences of its release upon the world.

It was good advice. Just ask the Babylonians.

Those familiar with the story knew that Pope Urban decided right then and there, not only to believe the priest, but also to return the Vessel to him, make him a bishop, and commission him with the Vessel's eternal care. Him, and those he chose to succeed him. However, it wasn't the young man's warning that those present believed ultimately convinced Urban, but that when the priest removed his cap, they all saw his hair had turned completely white.

No further mention was made of any of the three other priests; whether they were publicly flogged, or burned at the stake, castrated, or whatever would have been the Church's regular protocol for handling loser-twits in those days.

And so it was that Solomon's Vessel was passed from custodian to custodian down through the great expanse of history. At the end of the Vessel's line of inheritance was, of course, Cardinal Matine.

Throughout the centuries, the popes had always been very aware of the Vessel and its history. They'd wholeheartedly supported the exclusive sect of Christian scholars entrusted with custodianship of the artifact and the mystery of its single demonic prisoner. By the time Robert became a member, the order was a noteworthy component of the Church's research and educational mechanisms dealing with the occult, paganism, and demonology.

Normally, very young and intellectually gifted priests from all over the world were recruited to the sect and given the rank of bishop. In this, the members had the stamina and flexibility of will to contend with whatever might arise from such a vocation, and the authority to pursue the necessary loyalties from those outside the order, with immediate compliance and without question. After all, babysitting a demon was not a job to be taken lightly.

The story should have ended there. It should have remained a lavish and exotic tale from the history of the Church. Perhaps one day the Vessel could have been displayed in a museum, maybe with a tour guide recanting the journey of the sorcerer and the priests of Pope Urban V. Crowds of the faithful could have gazed upon the Vessel itself sitting majestically on a platform of velvet and locked within a thick glass case that would rival even that of the Shroud of Turin.

The story should have been over. It certainly wasn't, though.

In 1969, after entertaining a large group of visiting dignitaries at his small but beautiful chapel close to the Vatican, after a dinner and piano performance in the rectory's adjacent hall, Cardinal Matine displayed the artifact and told its story. There was nothing unusual about that; it was what he did and what was expected. It was the highlight of the evening and a treat the Church offered only to its most prestigious guests. Although the cardinal's group was commonly thought of as 'secret,' it was hardly one that the papacy considered extreme, as Matine and the Vessel were often employed to impress and entertain a number of international notables.

The presentation of the Vessel had charmed the group, of course; it always did. There weren't many artifacts in the world that predated the Roman Empire and were still in such wonderful condition. The VIPs were even allowed to pass around the ancient and utterly priceless relic, which was the cardinal's first deviance that evening from his normal procedure, although certainly one with far less horrifying consequences than the next.

The cardinal's guests each held the Vessel, marveling at its surprising lack of weight. Everyone who ever held Solomon's Vessel made the same observation; it was exceptionally light.

Then the guests had all left and the cardinal found himself alone with the artifact, as he'd been before after countless little events on similar evenings. He was alone again, pondering the icon's ancient mystery for perhaps the thousandth time when, for whatever reason, after years and years of telling the same story, of living with the vigilant care of one of the Church's most prized, if little known, treasures, Cardinal Matine had blown the whole thing. He abandoned the most sacred vow of his post, the same vow taken and held by his mentor before him, and his before him, and so on and so on, back through time for more than six centuries.

He opened it.

Nope. Certainly no rocket scientist, the cardinal.

†

"I can't even see the menu," Michael said.

Robert tapped his fingers on the table, frustrated to still be waiting for the waiter, despite having been sitting in the restaurant since at least the end of the Bronze Age.

"Just give yourself time to adjust to the dark," he suggested. "Have a drink."

Bishop Sigovia was visibly unhappy, probably bordering on miserable. Although Robert didn't care, he also didn't blame him. It hardly seemed like Christmas time at all. The southern west coast of the United States just couldn't host any of the fundamental aspects of the season. Although the locals enthusiastically tried to instill their city with the holiday, it was simply beyond them; they just didn't get it.

Of course there was no snow, which loomed as a major obstacle for achieving any Dickens-like milieu, but that wasn't really the problem; there were countless places around the world that had never seen a white Christmas yet still seemed to genuinely revel in the celebration of the birth of Christ. Unfortunately for Los Angeles, all the expensive lights in the world, all the costumed carolers roaming the shopping malls, all the tinseled wreaths and silver painted plastic bells hung throughout the streets couldn't disguise the fact that Christmas here was just another excuse to drink heavily and buy things. Christmas's decorative trimmings should be inspired by the spirituality of the season, not the other way around.

Down the street from Robert's hotel was a billboard displaying an advertisement for a holiday recording. It featured the image of a very young contemporary female singer clad only in a Santa-esque outfit that appeared to have been designed by Queen Jezebel. That photograph, and its ludicrous visibility, aptly summed up the Hollywood Yuletide as far as Robert was concerned.

Normally, being around another member of the Church would have offered at least a little comfort. Michael was a twit, though. All the younger bishops in Robert's order were twits.

Robert had tried to make the most of the situation, to make conversation and attempt some level of tolerance. Michael made that very difficult, though. He was annoying, puerile, and far too confident. Not only that, he spoke like he had testicles the size of jellybeans.

During the long wait for him to arrive from Europe with the Vessel, Robert had allowed himself to hope Michael might also be of some genuine assistance. Those hopes were briskly diminishing. During all the nights of the previous week, listening to Michael whimper through his little scholarly opinions while Robert was trying to concentrate, the kid had only succeeded in reinforcing his twit-hood.

Now the twit was complaining about Robert's favorite restaurant. Robert shook his head. It didn't matter. He'd have to cross this place off his list completely now. If the restaurant had the nerve to charge three dollars for a glass of water, they could at least see that someone was available to bring him some Scotch when he sat down. Weren't waiting periods just for handguns? The worst part was that he and

Michael were currently the only patrons.

"Can't I just get plain pasta?" Michael was actually whimpering. "Why does everything have to have oil on it?"

Where was the stupid waiter? If Michael didn't have something to put in his mouth soon, Robert was going to stuff it with the tablecloth.

When they arrived at the restaurant, Robert had allowed the somewhat unkempt little valet/actor/whatever to park the Mercedes. However, he made it known he was more than capable of kicking the kid's skinny little ass if there was so much as a nose hair on the car when it came back. Michael had given him a look Robert could only assume was supposed to be disapproval. Yeah, well, Michael had never even *been* in a Mercedes before, much less driven or been responsible for one.

The restaurant itself was a dimly lit and somber place. Although the large windows on two sides of the building would normally have provided more than enough sunlight to cheer the room considerably, the heavily overcast sky, so dark that Robert thought for sure they'd have a torrent of rain any minute, made the day seem as dark as night. Richly stained mahogany and wallpaper the color of old rust couldn't reflect enough illumination even to reveal where the walls became the floor. The table candles—tiny electric lights designed to resemble candles, actually—gave the only indication there was any furniture in the room at all. That any employees managed to navigate the dining area without slapping a plate of pasta onto someone's head was a miracle. Robert and Michael were in a huge confessional with waiters.

Actually, the presence of waiters was, as yet, unverified.

"Robert," Michael started, folding his menu, "don't you think we could find someplace a little more, uh, illuminated?"

"I like this place," Robert said, still drumming his fingers. "I used to anyway."

Squinting across the dark room, Robert could just make out the female bartender as she talked casually with a kid in a white shirt and apron, who'd better not be their waiter, the lazy, unobservant, piece of—

"Still," Michael went on, "just a dinner salad here costs enough to feed a family of six."

Robert turned to him. "I have to keep up appearances, Michael. I've explained all this."

Michael shook his head silently.

"Look..." Robert sighed. "I'm not going over it again. If I'm seen driving through McDonald's, we're done."

The kid from the bar, who apparently was exactly what Robert had feared, finally finished flirting with the liquor-slut and decided to saunter over to find out if they were paying customers, as opposed to having come inside and taken a booth due to a sudden impulse to sit in a dark empty room and starve to death.

"How are you gentlemen—?" he began.

"Scotch, rocks," Robert blurted. He considered letting the kid know he'd been watching him waste all of their time, but decided that Michael's mood probably wouldn't tolerate it. He'd already been complaining about the prices on the menu and the lighting, or lack thereof, whatever. If Robert went off on the waiter, he might also have to order a large amount of cheese to go along with the younger bishop's inevitably resulting whine.

"What do you want, Michael?" Robert said. The apron-kid was standing there staring, an annoying smirk on his face. "Come on. Wine? What?"

"Water, please." Michael didn't even look up.

"Bring two." Robert glared at the kid. "And he's going to want a chilled glass of wine, whether he'll admit it at the moment or not. Bring him something, okay? I don't care what it is, but he doesn't like anything too dry."

The 'waiter' grinned flimsily, turned to head back to the bar and, even though his back was to them, Robert was sure the kid was rolling his eyes.

"Robert," Michael whispered, shaking his head.

"What?" Robert shrugged. "You don't like dry wines."

"That boy must think we're completely insane."

"No, he doesn't." Robert drummed the table some more. "He thinks we're two homosexuals having a fight."

"What?" Michael turned completely white. Even in the dark, Robert could see it clearly. He almost laughed.

Robert nodded, smiling. "He thinks we're a couple of homos in the middle of a tiff."

"Ah..." Michael's mouth hung open.

"Would you lighten up, please? The scripture doesn't say, 'Thou shalt not lie to a waiter as to a woman.' You don't have to march in any parades. Calm down."

"I don't believe it. He does not think any such thing. You're making that up."

"What part of town do you think we're in, Michael? For that matter, what part of the world? This is West Hollywood, California. It vies with San Francisco for the title of Queer Capital of the Universe."

"How do you know that?" Michael whispered, leaning across the table.

"Are you really so completely clueless? You'd think Athens was Amish Country."

"My attentions are with the Church."

"Yeah, well," Robert said, "this isn't Rome either, Bishop Sigovia. You are on the front lines."

"I will grant you what I saw the other night—"

"Michael, you need to realize what we're doing here. Do you think we're going to get anywhere, make any progress at all, if we don't blend in? We've got to keep everyone from feeling even the slightest bit threatened by us. It's fine to have your attentions with the Church, but right now that means focusing on where you are and what's going on around you."

"There's got to be a better way besides pretending to be..." He looked around awkwardly, then whispered, "...to be gay."

"You're going to have to get used to it."

"Now, that's just unreasonable. Whether or not you think this part of town is very gay, I'm sure two men can eat together without being on a date."

"Maybe that's true, but we need to have some kind of acceptable image if we're going to get into that private party. So, if you can think of something else, I'm open to suggestions."

"What are you saying?"

"The only plausible scenario for two men like us going to that party together, that I can think of, is the gay scenario."

"Were you going to tell me about this ridiculous idea of camouflage, or just buy me a ring?"

"Oh, for cryin' out loud! We don't have to do anything brash." Robert glanced at the ceiling, shook his head. "I think we just need to have a relatively believable back-story to keep us level during any small talk."

"There's got to be something else, some other story—"

"It's just too improbable we'd be heterosexual friends because I'm so much older than you are. I think we'd be less conspicuous if I play the 'daddy' type. You're going to have to be the 'twink.'"

Michael appeared to be having an aneurysm. Robert ignored him.

"I haven't the slightest clue as to what you just said," Michael finally managed, "but whatever it was, you can forget it."

"If you blow this, if you destroy my chances of finishing this mission —"

"You've already proven yourself," Michael huffed. "Slow down. I saw him. I believe you. Why do we have to go about posing as deviants to finish our mission?"

"This must be done quickly! We don't have any time to waste."

"How many times do I need to apologize for —?"

"Never mind that. We've got to get to him now! If we're going to make any progress, it's crucial we blend in with this environment. This city is formed of the worst abominations and we must hide in their midst."

"You can't mean that the whole city itself is somehow wicked." Michael smirked.

"What do you think brought him here? This is Sodom herself, reborn! This is not holy ground."

Michael squinted, sitting back against the booth's cushion, folding his arms. "You're actually saying that the skotos settled here because the city is sinful?"

"That's exactly why he hasn't moved on yet." Robert bit his lip and shook his head. "And you're acting like a fool. This is beneath you."

"Spare me your 'exalted prophet' routine, Robert. I'm not here to be your scribe."

"No, you're not," Robert hissed. "You're here to discredit me."

Michael's face flushed with a look of alarm that was intensely satisfying.

"Discredit?" he blurted.

"Yes, that's right." Robert nodded. "I'm not unaware of how you and the others feel. You came here to discredit my claims and then get on with the business of doing nothing. But you can't anymore, can you? You can't, and now you don't have any idea what you're doing here at all. What's worse, you don't have any idea what you've been doing with your whole, pitiful life. Isn't that the situation? Isn't that why you sat in the dark in your room all day yesterday and wouldn't answer the phone or the door? Isn't that what's happened?"

"I didn't come here to discredit you," Michael mumbled stupidly.

"Michael, I already think you're an imbecile. Don't add 'liar' to that assessment."

The waiter returned and set down two glasses of water, a Scotch on the rocks, and a wine glass filled with something chilled and pink. Robert couldn't really tell in the dark, of course, but it looked pink. How appropriate. Robert rolled his eyes.

"Would you care to start off with—?"

"He's having plain fettuccini marinara with garlic," Robert said. "Don't oil the pasta or he'll have a stroke right here."

Michael hitched in shock. The waiter also reacted to Robert's statement, but he was desperately trying to stifle a grin.

"I'll have the grilled salmon," Robert went on. "I want steamed brown rice on the side and if I taste one granule of salt, on *any*thing, I'm going to have a very unpleasant conversation with your manager."

Robert gave the kid his best attempt at a plastic Hollywood smile, but the one he got back was far, far better. Touché.

"You did that on purpose," Michael said through his teeth after the waiter left. "You ordered for me so he'd think we were... we were..."

"Fags?"

"Oh, Mary, Mother in Heaven." Michael put his face in his hands.

Robert couldn't help chuckling. He shook his head and smiled as he swallowed another gulp of Scotch.

"I'm sure you find this all very funny," Michael whined from behind his fingers.

"No, not at all. I find you funny at the moment, Michael, but all of this? No."

Michael looked up at him. "I suppose after seeing the demon flying through the clouds, I should have just forgotten the whole thing, been unaffected. I guess my need to somehow cope with this is a liability, Robert. I should have been able to immediately pour another glass of wine and then check to see who was on Leno."

"Don't be so dramatic."

"After all..." Michael stopped for a deep breath and a long swig of the wine he didn't want. "I'm sure you and Larry simply took lunch and caught a movie right after your little frolic on Cyprus—"

Robert pounded his fist on the table.

Michael, as well as the cutlery, jumped spastically. Although the conversation had resumed between the waiter and the liquor-slut, it ceased immediately and they both pressed their hands to the base of their necks in shock, their eyes as wide as cue balls. Robert gave them a glance and they immediately went back to their chat as if

Robert hadn't just slammed the wooden table hard enough to crack it.

Turning to Michael with a scowl, Robert slowly lifted his drink and took a leisurely, deliberate sip. The younger bishop stared back at him like a hapless ten-year-old about to be spanked.

Slowly, Robert set his drink down, smoothed the table linen, and licked his lips.

"Don't ever speak about Cyprus in that way again," he said. "And don't ever speak to me in that way again. I watched men of faith, faith the likes of which you will never, never in your spoiled, arrogant life, see the equal, go to their deaths for a purpose you haven't even bothered to fathom before now."

"Of course, Robert. I'm sorry, but—"

"Shut up," Robert interrupted with a livid whisper.

"Hrrg..." Michael gurgled. He didn't know what to say, apparently. That, or he was finally following instructions.

"You and the others from your class, you never had the benefit of any real guidance from the elders. I begged Matine—"

"The cardinal is an elder himself, lest you forget. I think you're forgetting a great many things, Robert."

"The cardinal is an idiot."

Michael's jaw dropped almost into his wine, but this time he made no sound. Robert supposed he was beyond even the acknowledgement of a gurgle.

"None of them would be dead," Robert went on, "none of the other council elders would have perished on that island if not for Matine's lack of faith."

Michael issued a stuttering, frustrated gasp and reached for his wine.

"Oh, I see," he said, trying to sip calmly. "Well, how enlightening. And I suppose you should be the one to be wearing his colors then."

"Don't put words in my mouth."

"Yes, well—"

"You weren't there! You didn't hear the demon howling at them! You didn't hear Brathwidth scream at each of them in turn, or watch them burst into flames from his breath alone."

"We all know you went through something terrible, Robert, but—"

"You're a sickeningly patronizing little twit, you know that?" Robert's patience was gone. "How many people have pointed that out to you in the past month? A hundred? Two? You keep track don't you? I really want to know."

"What have I done?" Michael raised his palms. "Did I ask for this somehow? Did I do something to deserve this disrespect?"

Robert clenched his fist as if he would pound the table again and Michael watched his hand with obvious alarm.

Robert contained himself, though. It was satisfying enough to see the panic on Michael's face.

"It's what you *didn't* do, Michael," he murmured. "It's what all of you neglected to do."

"We did everything we knew how."

"That's no excuse."

Michael looked away.

"We ran, you know," Robert said, gazing at the table.

"What?"

"Larry and I ran. We just left them there, we ran away while they were burning. We just turned and ran. We could hear him laughing behind us. We could hear Brathwidth just roaring with delight as we raced away and our friends burned behind us. All we could hear was Brathwidth laugh and our friends scream."

Robert suddenly thought that it wasn't dark enough in this restaurant. Not dark enough at all.

"Robert, again..." Michael sighed. "I can't begin to imagine—"

"No you can't," Robert hissed. "You can't begin to imagine what that was like. You can't know how it feels to try to explain something like that, to have to look someone else in the face and explain how three of your colleagues, your friends, were cremated where they stood and how your closest friend lost his mind. You can't imagine explaining to anyone why it was you who was the only one that seemed to have escaped unharmed, much less staring at yourself in a mirror and wondering the same thing, day after day, year after year. Nothing, none of the doctors, none of the medications, none of the therapies or treatments, will ever be able to help me do that.

"You can't begin to imagine what it's like to expect the support of those closest to you. You can't imagine thinking you'd have that support, you'd at least have that, that faith, and instead see nothing but doubt on their faces. You can't know that disappointment. You can't know how desperate you'd become to flee from those faces, to get out and back into the world, to find some proof, some justification for what you're asking them to believe and, worse, what you're asking them to do.

"You can't imagine it, so don't sit in judgment of me, you sheltered, pompous, feeble, squealing, girly, little twit. Don't assume to speak about the things you haven't taken the time to even consider

before. Don't look at me and try to hold your own. Stop trying to
gather your wits as if you were my equal. You could have all the
time in the world, but you just don't have enough wits to gather. You
can't imagine it. So, stop pretending you know anything. You don't."

Michael scowled, took a sip of water.

They sat there, in the dark and empty restaurant, looking down at
their drinks, at the table cloth, at the wall, out the window and into
the gray, lifeless day.

"Maybe I wasn't on Cyprus," Michael started quietly, "but two
nights ago I was right next to you." He leaned across the table with a
composed fury. "I was right there in the room when you saw him for
the first time. When the skotos flew out of all our limited academic
accounts and right into the sky before us. I was right there! Don't
forget that! Keep that in mind while you call me feeble. Hold that up
in front of you while you call me names!"

"Oh, I haven't forgotten." Robert shook his head sadly. "I had so
many hopes for your help. When we saw him, when he finally
appeared and, as an even greater miracle, you were actually there to
see it too, I was so relieved, so thankful. I was hoping that finally
seeing him would get through to you. I was hoping that would be
enough, and you'd be able to leave your overconfidence and
educated naïveté packed up in your room. I thought maybe, since
now you had more than just the word of the cardinal and myself to
convince you, that you'd join me and at least take a serious attitude
toward this fight. I was hoping I wouldn't be alone anymore."

"Robert, yes, I saw a flying black lion," Michael said. "I saw the
creature. It fits the description of the Darkness, and the image in
Matìne's painting."

"Then there should be no question to our purpose here or that we
must act now."

"You're not listening even to yourself," Michael whispered,
leaning over the edge of the table. "I *have* to question this. It was
you, after all, who warned me not to treat possibilities as fact."

"You *saw* it!" Robert couldn't believe his ears.

"Yes, but I didn't see people falling dead in its wake," Michael
said softly. "I didn't see it spreading plague with its breath. I didn't
see it dripping acid from its mouth instead of spit, and I didn't see it
snacking on any living children. What we saw was a miracle, it was
beyond remarkable, but don't you think we should ask ourselves —?"

"I see." Robert folded his arms. "So merely observing the very
demon itself isn't enough for you? You have to personally witness all

the details of the legends. What would satisfy you? To actually see it sitting in a schoolyard chewing on first-graders?"

"Would you just stop for one moment and listen to yourself, please? You told me you don't want to repeat the same mistakes that—"

"What more do you want?" Robert was almost shouting. "You *saw* him!"

"Robert, I've been thinking about this a lot." Michael leaned across the table at him, speaking softly and slowly, which made Robert want to deck him with the centerpiece. "It might not even be a demon, for all we know. I sat and thought about it all day yesterday, while I wouldn't answer the phone or the door. It's been tearing me apart. The real problem I have is that what we saw might not really be evil, or terrible, or any of the other things we've been told all throughout our lives. It might have nothing at all to do with any of that. We have to take the time to look into—"

"Have you lost your mind?" Robert huffed.

"Lower your voice." Michael pressed his hand slowly toward the table.

Robert could have punched him. He was glad he didn't when he noticed the pseudo-waiter and the liquor-slut watching from across the room. They'd been joined by the hostess and two bus boys. All of them were staring quite blatantly, thoroughly entertained. All they were missing was a bucket of popcorn.

Taking a deep, calming breath through his nose, Robert tried to settle himself back into his seat. After a few more breaths and a gulp of Scotch, he bit his lip and turned his head slowly toward his little audience. They scattered like roaches.

"Robert," Michael whispered. "I saw something amazing, there's no doubt. But to automatically assume that what I saw is guilty of every terrible thing in all the stories and in all the ancient legends that have been gathered for centuries from all over the world, well, I think that would be a mistake. I think we'd be jumping to conclusions. It would be the same trap, the same unenlightened mistake the Church has been making since the Council of Nicaea first closed its table."

Robert shut his eyes. " 'Blessed are they that have not seen, and yet have believed.' "

"Oh, yes, that's the way Robert." Michael shook his head and slapped his hands into his lap. "Bludgeon me with scripture. Smite me with the words of Christ. That will make all your assumptions true, surely. Bend the Word to validate ignorance. Yes, fine, that's a time honored tradition, as much as wearing that false righteousness like a costume. You are from another time, my friend."

"And your eternal soul is in mortal danger as long as you fail to realize that evil is not a philosophy for you to interpret." Robert was seething. "Evil is real and it inhabits this very city, right along with us, this very day."

"I've no doubt there's evil here. I'm sure California is a festering cesspool, just like everyone says. However, despite my 'educated naïveté,' I'd prefer to avoid adding to the problems of this unfortunate city by rushing in where wiser men fear to tread."

"Oh, yes, bludgeon me with clichés, Michael—"

"You're impossible!"

"You should go back, I think." Robert leaned away from the table, against the smooth fabric of the cushioned booth, and resigned himself.

"What?" Michael squinted, crossing his arms tightly over his chest.

"You're not going to be of any use to me here." Robert couldn't look at the twit anymore. He turned his eyes instead to the long front window and the pale gray day. "You should go back to Rome. I'm not going to stand next to you and allow you to jeopardize everything I've fought for, everything I've searched for, as you attempt to face the skotos and ask him if he's evil. He'll incinerate you before you finished your sentence, and Michael..." He stopped, took a breath. "Michael, I'm not going to explain that to Matîne again."

Robert would do this alone. Somehow, he always knew things would play out that way. He'd been kidding himself to think otherwise. Even as he sat with Bishop Jarvis in the garden of the mental hospital all those years ago, sitting there alone with him, begging Larry to help him, to speak and to give the council something to get them moving, to be a witness along side him and spark the Church into the search and into the fight, even then Robert knew.

The fragrance of pine and freshly cut grass filled his memory as he thought back to that bright afternoon seven years ago. Larry had looked right past him and said nothing. He just sat there. Robert could hardly tell he'd been breathing.

He'd been a genius, Bishop Leonard Jarvis. Before the trip to Greece, he'd been Robert's inspiration and his very closest friend, his mentor. Still, whatever line had connected Larry to his intellect, to his remarkable insights and convictions, even to any simple lucidity, it had snapped that day on the island.

After that, Robert had been alone. The elders were dead, Robert's peers were scattered and weak, the four apprentices were less than useless, the Church was clueless, the cardinal was a moron, and Larry's sanity had snapped like a dry rubber band. Robert had known then that he'd have to eventually face the skotos by himself.

It didn't matter, though. This time he wasn't going to run away. He certainly *had* learned from his mistakes and was going to stand his ground and see his mission through to the end. He was going to make his stand in faith.

Maybe he'd find out why the Lord had forsaken them to the Demon of Cyprus. Maybe he'd be allowed that before he met the skotos, the lamia, or—and this really made his stomach fall—Lilith herself.

Why did he need this twit-bishop anyway? He didn't. The Vessel was locked in its metal case, safe and sound behind the small wooden desk in Robert's suite. He had everything he needed. For the first time in his life, Robert had absolutely everything he needed.

Even among the clergy, true faith was in terribly short supply these days, it seemed. Michael Sigovia was an overeducated papal messenger; a pompous, sightless, faithless, blithering twit. Nothing more.

"I'll call the cardinal when we get back to the hotel," Robert said. "You can go home on the first flight out."

"What a simple solution." Michael was the one raising his voice now. Maybe Robert would get to punch him after all. "What a clever way to win your argument. Send me away. Too bad you can't have me burnt at the stake, Robert."

"That's really what I'm trying to avoid here."

Michael's jaw dropped in preparation of his answer just as the pseudo-waiter was setting a plate of pasta in front of him.

"I know," the kid said. "It looks fabulous, doesn't it?"

†

The mental condition of Bishop Patrick was a lot worse than Michael had first thought.

He stood by the side of the monster bed in his ridiculously lavish hotel room, staring down at his half-packed suitcase, sure now that Bishop Patrick had become not just a little obsessed, but that he'd completely crossed the border and skipped happily far, far into Dangerously Irrational Land.

Knowing Robert had lost every particle of objectivity, however, and figuring out just what needed to be done about it, were two very different things.

A headache started to form as Michael tried to organize his thoughts.

He couldn't stay here. Robert had already informed the hotel that Michael would be checking out right away. Even if he was able to get the cardinal on the phone and convince him to let him stay in Los Angeles, even to grant him a small budget, Michael still couldn't stay in the suite down the hall from Robert. That just wouldn't work.

Oh, what was he thinking? The cardinal would never consent to Michael staying in the city against Robert's recommendations. He'd certainly never send even more money to Los Angeles. Maybe Michael could get him to call Robert back to Rome instead. Then the cardinal could send Philip and maybe even Bishop Carter out to… oh, there was just no way. Michael was fantasizing.

He could go to the papacy. Michael could go to Cardinal Paccezzi, who always liked Michael, and tell him everything.

See, a few decades ago, Cardinal Matine opened Solomon's Vessel, only he didn't tell anyone about it, not even the pope, because, see, he released the demon that was inside it. He said it looked just like the painting in the hall! It was a big, giant, winged, black lion that took one look at him and then vanished into thin air. Matine's been secretly filtering enormous funds to a tiny faction within his group ever since. We've all been trying to find the demon again and get it back into the bottle. Only now Robert's on his way to losing his mind, just like Larry, and he's in LA acting as if he's the vengeance of God incarnate, and no, I don't think he's totally bonkers, because, well, I sort of saw it too. It looks like a big hang glider, only with fur!

Michael sat down. He suddenly had a terrible headache.

He was going to have to find some inexpensive motel, *very* inexpensive, where he could wait until the night of the party. He needed to somehow get into that party and make sure Robert didn't do anything insane.

Michael had no idea how he was going to do it. Without Robert, he would never have gotten inside the club, much less an exclusive private party to which Robert had been given the only invitation. Michael was frustrated enough to just say 'to heck with it all,' get on the plane in the morning, go back to Rome, and leave Robert to his delusions of grandeur.

He got up and emptied the neatly folded shirts he'd been keeping in the hotel drawers, absently packing the two-hundred-dollar Rubios that Robert had purchased for him right next to the five-dollar ones he normally wore.

The fact was that, despite his certainly having fallen into irrationalism, Robert still made a couple of valid points. They hadn't believed him about what had happened on Cyprus. Lord have mercy, how could they have? No one doubted that something horrible had happened, but there was nothing left of the elders, besides three piles of ashes that neither the local officials nor the Church ever saw for themselves. Plus, the only other witness to the event besides Robert had been so traumatized he couldn't corroborate anything and would in fact spend the rest of his life staring into space and silently drooling on himself.

Something horrible had happened, yet none of the other council members made any significant effort to find out what.

An unusually large number of senior bishops had gone to the island to investigate some explicitly detailed accounts of demonic phenomena, accounts strikingly similar to others from around the world. But this time, instead of one or two witnesses, there were seventeen individuals giving evidence about nine separate incidents that occurred within days of each other. Therefore, Matìne's elder bishops had been convinced they'd found the skotos.

The truth was that, in their enthusiasm, they'd dismissed some important details and gotten the 'Gryphon of Greece' stories mixed up with the 'Demon of Cyprus' stories and the consequences had apparently been fatal.

Michael and his young colleagues, four fresh bishops in their early thirties just getting used to the dynamics of their vocations, were not ready to be told their new positions had that level of hazard to life and limb. As far as Michael knew, no other council members, in all the centuries since the Vessel had been recovered and the order formed, had ever been killed in the line of duty. Certainly none had ever been roasted alive where they stood. Such dangers hadn't been discussed with him and were certainly not in his job description.

Yes, something horrible had happened on Cyprus. Although it was far, far easier to believe that Robert had taken a hefty blow to his mind, just like Bishop Jarvis, than to believe they'd all woken up in some modern horror movie like *The Exorcist Goes to Greece*.

But now Michael had witnessed an entity matching the common description of the skotos. Whatever it was, it looked just like the creature Cardinal Matìne insisted had popped out of the Vessel in 1969.

Falling over the edge of reason was not an improbability at the moment with all of these familiar and plausible improbabilities swirling around in his head. For the second time since he'd arrived, Michael completely understood how Robert had lost sight of the rational world. As it was, Michael had to press his hands to the sides of his head and sit down for several moments, trying to decide if he should crack the little bottle of prescription codeine in the shampoo pouch of his canvas suitcase.

If someone were hurt, though, if Robert did something stupid, something horrible, out of the drive of his aggravated fanaticism, Michael would never be able to forgive himself.

He decided he couldn't just say 'to heck with it.' Michael would stay in Los Angeles. He'd stay and he'd get into that party somehow. How difficult could it possibly be? It was at a private residence, after all. It wasn't as if the place had been designed to control a massive amount of guests every single night of the week. There had to be a way. He'd get inside, he'd keep an eye on Robert, and maybe, God willing, an opportunity would present itself for Michael to open Robert's eyes.

Michael packed. In the morning, he'd check out and leave the hotel, just as Robert expected. He wouldn't be going to the airport, though. He wouldn't be getting on a plane to go back to Rome. Hopefully, long before Robert realized that he'd never left the city, Michael prayed this whole nightmare would be over.

†

Amos had warned the people of God that the pleasures of this world would draw them away from the Lord.

Robert opened his Bible to the second chapter of the book of Amos and ran his finger down to verse six. He'd only left the small light over the mini-bar burning, as he wanted to be able to see the view of the sky over his balcony, the view of the dark and vast December sky, clear, black as pitch, with only a handful of visible stars to suggest its infinite depth.

To read, the single light behind him would be more than enough.

Thus saith the Lord, he read, *For three transgressions of Judah, and for four, I will not turn away the punishment thereof: because they sell the righteous for silver, and the needy for a pair of sandals — they who trample the head of the poor into the dust of the earth, and push the afflicted out of the way; father and son go into the same girl, so that my holy name is profaned.*

Israel had been enjoying a rather splendid economy back about seven or eight centuries before the birth of Jesus, back when the prophet Amos had shared his spectacular perception of the will of God. The wealthy people of Israel had become quite spoiled and lazy. They had time on their hands and weren't in the least bit hungry. So, of course they'd been screwing around and not paying any attention to their sworn commitment to God, which had really pissed off Amos, apparently.

They'd become slackers in the truest sense of the word. Had it existed at the time, Robert was sure Amos would have used the word over and over again.

"*Slackers!*" the ancient prophet would have cried, his finger pointing accusingly as it swept across the bewildered crowd of locals. "*You're all nothin' but a horde of frickin' slackers!*"

The chosen people had indeed been slacking off in the comfort of their promised land, their land of milk and honey. They'd been resting on their laurels and taking the grace of God for granted, the twits. The Lord had provided for them—and then some—and the Israelites had accepted happily enough.

"*Sure*, they'd said, "*we'll follow the rules. Thanks for bringing us to the Promised Land! That whole forty years in the desert thing was a bit unfortunate, but we're not bitter at all! We're just happy to be here! Oh, and by the way, thanks for helpin' us smite the Canaanites! Those psycho-twits were squattin' in our new digs!*"

The Hebrews had taken the land granted them by God and promised to honor His covenant with them in return. He'd instructed them as to how He expected them to behave and, if they could tow the line, He'd set them apart from the rest of mankind; He'd lift them up and make them special.

And, the Israelites had towed the line. At least for a while. Then they had children. They'd multiplied, as instructed, and their children had born children, and those children had borne children, and those children had forgotten somewhere along the way to fear the Lord, and then their children had never even known they *should* be fearing the Lord, whoever the frickin'-frack that was.

Passover had eventually, after the erosion of just a few measly centuries, become nothing more than a tepid ritual, Yom Kippur and Rosh Hashanah casual observances. Moses was known by the desert youths as no more than the name of a story-time hero. Abraham was as abstract and as negligible as Marduk or Ba'al, and the Egyptians were just some exaggerated fairy-tale villains: big, bad scoundrels of sloth and indulgence, wearing cloth napkins on their heads and way too much mascara, running around the fertile valley persecuting the righteous and gentle Children of God.   The Egyptians were like mythical cross-dressing boogiemen with chariots.

Oh, the irony.

In that early biblical dispensation, scripture told, the fields of Canaan had been unbelievably bountiful; the wells were full, the sun was high, and there was more fruit on the vine than could possibly be gathered while it was fresh.   In that time of blessing and abundance, while God had been smiling, content and lax in his generosity to mortal desire, a demon had seen his chance and come a-knockin'.

A demon had crept silently into the valley of the Lord, surely. His name was Iniquity, his manner languid, his speech enchanting, his presence invigorating and novel, his purpose dark and revolting, subtle yet profoundly destructive.

The Children of God had not only answered at his knocking, but they'd done so with bright, big, stupid smiles.

Why not answer? Why not see what Iniquity had to sell? Why not let him reveal pleasures the Israelites had never known, worldly luxuries that God had yet to bring forth; aromas and flavors, delicacies that were really the masks of gluttony? Why not allow themselves to be enthralled by his flattery, entranced by his charisma, and calmed by his wit? Why not share Iniquity's rage over the transgressions of the innocent, laugh at his stories of the bumbling ignorant, the feeble, the simple? Why not accept his assurances that the wealth of Israel had been earned and justified? Hadn't it? Hadn't they plowed their own fields? Hadn't they tended their own flocks? Hadn't the bounty of the harvest been the result of their own dedication, their own determination, their own labor and sweat? God did not make orange juice, after all; ya had to squeeze the frickin' things yourself, gosh-darn-it.

What value, therefore, was the allowance of God? What endowment was His favor? Was it God's hands that blistered from the plow? Was it His face that peeled from the sun?

The Lord had only delivered their forebears from the bondage of Ramses the Great, disposed of the Canaanites, and lain the world at their feet.   The Lord had only brought forth their crops and multiplied their herds. He'd only kept away the storm, the invader, and the plague. What was the big deal, anyway? The Exodus had been hundreds of years ago. How long did they all have to keep paying the bill?

Yes, we know, we know. You delivered us from Egypt a gazillion years ago, and all that jazz. Praise, praise. Yada, yada, yada.

The distant descendents of Moses had known no other way. The Canaanite valley had been theirs for more than half a millennium and all debts had surely been reconciled by then, hadn't they? Of course they had, how silly. They'd earned their leisure. They had earned the time for frivolous things; to dye their garments with vivacious colors, to adorn themselves with decoration, to garnish their houses, and neglect their labor. Why not sit down with Iniquity and hear what he had to say? Heck, why not let him bring his buddies, Complacency and Arrogance, along with him? The more the merrier! Why the frickin'-frack not?

At first, though, Iniquity had to be stealthy. When he first arrived, it was necessary he hide himself in the splendid houses among the fine furniture and brimming pantries. Nonetheless, eventually the Hebrews welcomed him somewhat openly and he simply moved in, bringing his friends over to drink and dine every night. Everywhere there was wine and apathy and gluttony and sloth.

The Israelites had been charmed and Iniquity settled in, comfortable enough amongst their leisure and their satisfaction.

Robert gulped his Scotch, shaking his head. The patterns of history were all here, all of them among the pages containing the Word of God. One had but to acquire the skill to read in order to hear His voice.

Eventually though, Iniquity presented his bill to the Israelites, as Amos had predicted, as he so gallantly and boisterously warned them.

Just as the prophet foretold he would, the timeless and stealthy demon left his bill, presenting it quietly, in the dark and still hours for the Hebrews to discover when they awoke. He left it in every house when no one was around, of course, when the wicked and the stupid were sleeping off the weight of their lust and indulgence. He unfolded his carefully itemized invoice and left it unceremoniously on the kitchen tables, a self-addressed envelope attached to it with a paperclip—or some type of scroll or papyrus-binding, whatever— they sure as heck weren't billed for their sins by e-mail, no-siree-bob.

All the households of the Promised Land had simply woken one day to find the register of their misbehavior bared as plain as day and for all to see. They stumbled into the light of the morning and found that they were going to be held accountable for their actions. Wow. What a shocker.

They'd of course been genuinely surprised too, Robert had no doubt. What was this unexpected intrusion on their lives? What was this horror lain before them detailing their indulgence? A price? Surely, such a thing as lethargy was free, wasn't it? There was no cost for willful pleasure, was there?

There was, though. Of course there was a cost.

There was a price and it was high. There was an incredible balance against their accounts, but they had to pay it just the same. They'd freely acquired the services offered by Iniquity, after all. There was no hiding that. They were guilty, having taken his offerings legitimately—and eagerly—enough. So, now they had to pay the price.

Of course Iniquity expected his due. Who offering any kind of service wouldn't? Of course there would be a cost for such hapless merriment. Nothing so amusing or so enticing could ever be free. They had danced as the piper played, and now he was holding out his hand.

The Israelites had to scramble. Did Iniquity have a financing plan? What was the current interest rate on debauchery?

Robert gulped his Scotch again. Holding open the Good Book, his finger marking the verse, he reached for a coaster on the wet bar behind him. His glass was beginning to sweat.

The people of Israel had made a meager effort to keep the laws of Moses, only just, but what was ritual without faith? What was reverence without piety?

Empty activity, that's what it was, and Amos had said as much.

"For they know not to do right, saith the Lord, who store up violence and robbery in their palaces."

You go, Amos.

Their children's children had let the sacred covenant with God fall to the wayside, and *their* children had forgotten so much that even their feeble lunges at the most casual observances were pathetic. The children of *those* children were the sorriest still, as they mistook the covenant for myth and their obligations as unimportant. Time eroded more than mountains, it seemed, and reverence for the Divine could be lost in the passing of just a few generations.

Amos had pointed out the offenses of the Children of God, and rightly so. Still, they'd banished him for it, the blind, hapless, twits.

How many generations had been custodians of the faith since the time of Amos? How many centuries had dried and shriveled the spirit of men, just as the sun had dried and cracked the desiccated land of Judea?

There were churches in Los Angeles. Sure, there were churches here, 'houses of the Lord,' or so they said. There were Christians here. There were crosses and sermons and meetings and bake sales and jubilees and picnics and retreats and chatter and ranting and babble and noise. There were cars with fish symbols and dove symbols and all manner of holy icons glued faithfully to the lids of trunks filled with beach chairs and volleyballs and kegs of beer and sub-woofers and disc-changers and water skis and plastic lawn flamingos and cases of champagne and nothing.

"They pant after the dust of the earth on the head of the poor."

Too true, Amos, you sorry, pathetic, lonely voice, you. Too true, buddy.

And to think, in the minds of the masses of these modern days, Amos was only the name of a mouse in a children's story. A story that made American history familiar instead of scripture, raising the name of Benjamin Franklin, instead of the Creator, the Lord God, Èlōhîm.

Robert shook his head in frustration and disgust. He would change it all, if he could.

He wondered what it must have been like to actually hear the voice of God. How would it be to live with the purpose of a true prophet? He wondered how it must feel to face one's destiny with such complete confidence, to have assurances from the mouth of the Almighty himself.

Robert glanced at his lowball, which was glittering with condensation and now only held melted shards of ice and tepid water. There was just the faintest line of Scotch still coloring the base. It was a depressing sight.

The ice bucket had been full not forty minutes ago, but was now considerably depleted. It hadn't yet reached the stage of water with floating ice remnants, like his poor, pitiful drink, so there was no need to walk all the way down the hall at the moment. The cubes were still relatively large. Still, they didn't have that wonderful new, dry look, like a thin coating of crisp, winter dust.

The bottle of Scotch Robert opened that afternoon was still not quite half empty, and there was even another bottle sitting next to it. The second bottle was new, a pristine and unbroken seal around its neck, which was a much more cheerful sight and almost made Robert forget about his dismal, droopy ice.

He got up from behind the tiny desk and dumped the contents of the lowball into the little bar's deep, steel basin. He dried the empty glass with a hand towel and, using his fingers to pick the best cubes off the top of the bucket's melting heap, he filled his glass with ice and then rinsed the cubes with Scotch. It was a familiar and very comforting ritual.

He sat back down and continued to consider the literature of the Old Testament and its ancient prophets. If Robert had been granted the gift of hearing the voice of God, he thought, no dissenting argument would ever touch him again. He'd never, ever again have to endure the scratch of antagonism within his mind. The whiney, delicate, and utterly fickle voices around him would be as whimpers in a hurricane; blown apart and meaningless.

Iniquity could knock until his knuckles bled and Robert would only laugh. The house of divine inspiration was wholly immune to even the most persistent solicitations of wickedness.

Whether His voice issued from a burning bush or from the softest breeze, to have heard Him speak, and then to face the world afterward, must have allowed the biblical prophets such a sense of righteousness that nothing like doubt, no such humbling human consideration as fear or insecurity, could have ever touched them. It must have been such a complete joy, such a searing and faultless satisfaction.

Robert turned the page of his Bible, a page as thin and weightless as tissue.

Although, he thought, to carry forward without clearly hearing His voice, to bring about His plan in the absence of complete and unquestionable enlightenment, to ignore the knock of temptation with only the strength of one's will, well, that was the very nature of faith, wasn't it? How would faith survive at all if there was no mystery with which to feed it?

And yet, Robert had heard it in a way, hadn't he, the voice of the Lord? He'd heard the voice of God. He'd seen the demon gliding across the sky, despite the sheer odds against such a thing, which Michael was so eager to point out—the feeble, faithless, little twit— and so willing to question. That was a true revelation, wasn't it? Seeing the demon, that was a miracle, a guidance from the Divine just as pure as the tone of His voice, was it not?

Surely, it was a sign. It was the signal from God that Robert's mission was righteous, that he was working the will of the Lord, and that the support of Heaven and all the angels was with him. Why yearn for a voice from the clouds? Why ask to hear the whisper of God's voice come forth from the breath of a gentle breeze? Why covet the same miracles given the prophets of old when he had his own new and oh-so-clear signs, signs from the holy and the damned alike?

The clouds didn't need to boom with the voice of God; they had revealed the demon and, therefore, the truth.

Robert drew a deep and satisfying breath, raising his head and gazing out over massive hotel balcony. The night sky was clear now, despite the overcast day. He leaned back in the desk chair, laying one hand on his chest, holding his drink in the other. The curtains were drawn open all the way, as he normally kept them during the nighttime hours, and he could still see a star or two in the black December sky.

Old and neglected—shunned?—memories began to seep around Robert, surreptitiously and delicately bleeding from his mind. This happened all the time, it happened in the quiet, in contemplation's stillness, but usually Robert put a stop to it right away.

This time, though, he didn't notice, or he would have immediately sought refuge from his memories. He'd have willfully brushed them back, pushed them aside, and sprinted for more comfortable ground, perhaps within the Good Book, which was conveniently open before him and always a haven from such onslaughts.

Robert wasn't looking at its pages, though. He was staring out over the balcony, out into the night, and so his memories came and took him.

Robert saw what he always saw when he wasn't carefully guarding his thoughts, when he wasn't sternly focused on the task at hand, after the enthusiasm of piety had exhausted him. It was always the Mediterranean island. The lovely island where everything had changed. Always, he saw first its more apparent and pleasant wonders; all its hostility hidden, its secret terrors waiting just out of sight, nothing showing but languid beaches, sheltered lagoons, groves of olive trees, and soothing, golden sunshine.

Larry found a beautiful place for the team to stay when they first arrived in Paphos, on the island of Cyprus. There, they could accomplish all the final preparation for their mission. A great deal of planning and coordination, which couldn't be handled from Rome, was required before sauntering up the Ezousas River to the actual site. The area was further inland from Paphos, just outside of Pano Panayia, in a small region at the foot of Mount Olympus.

Olympus. Such an appropriate heathen name for that most godless of peaks.

There had been a number of stories coming out of Pano Panayia, and further investigation only served to strengthen Peter's request to the cardinal that it was time to send a team to the island.

Quite a few years passed after the massacre in Greece before Robert noticed the significance in the patterns of the lamia and/or Lilith. He didn't know then that interest from the demon Lilith was a sign of the presence of the true skotos. She was after him too. The reason didn't matter. The evidence of her pursuit would serve as credibility toward the entity's identification.

Robert hadn't known that, though, not in time to save the cardinal's group from Brathwidth's fire.

Stopping in Paphos, on the western coast of Cyprus, had been a logistical necessity. It wasn't a huge tourist spot with the enticing distractions that such a place would be bound to contain. Far more attractive to academics, to archeologists and historians, its claim to fame being that it had been the capital of Cyprus until the time of Constantine, that most wonderful of Roman emperors, who played such a dynamic and essential role in the evolution of Christian history.

To say that Robert had been excited by the idea of being allowed to join the team would be an understatement of universal proportion. Give any teenage boy an invitation to a midnight bikini party at the Playboy Mansion and you might just get a glimmer of his jubilation.

Larry was the one who told him, of course. Robert hadn't been too young, not an apprentice certainly, he was a respected member of the order. Even so, he certainly wasn't an elder, and his inclusion was far from assured.

For a preceding trip to Pakistan, Robert had been left behind. Sure, nothing happened there, but he'd still been excluded, which was humiliating enough. The team hadn't discovered a single thing or made any progress toward locating the skotos, however. Still, Robert tried not to be too overtly buoyant when they returned to Rome in failure—he tried, but he'd been wholly unsuccessful.

Bishop Davis had suffered the cardinal's open contempt for several months over that trip's extreme waste of resources, but that was small consolation for Robert. The issue was that, while the majority of the cardinal's team flew off to the Near East toward what they thought might be the demon's recapture, he'd been casually left behind in Rome.

Larry—good old Larry, Robert could always count on him—had initially suggested Robert be allowed go with the team to Pakistan.

He was denied. Just the fact that the cardinal—actually the council as a whole, Robert discovered later, Larry being the only exception—decided Robert wouldn't have been valuable, or at all useful, well, that particular detail hit him square in the jaw.

Life did go on as usual, though. Robert poured himself into every task presented to him—and quite a few *not* specifically presented to him—determined not to let another opportunity slip by. He would mold himself into someone absolutely essential and completely irreplaceable. It was everything he wanted, everything for which he hoped and prayed; to be essential to the council, and so valuable that his exclusion from any future endeavor would be entirely unthinkable.

The opportunity came in the early 1990s. Certain reports from Greece became not only incredibly frequent but also alarmingly consistent. Robert paid very close attention to the developments of the situation; he'd had a feeling.

The reports from Greece were very compelling. Apparently, several island women, some of whom were no more than girls, the rest being married women, locals of Pano Panayia and various villages along the Ezousas River, fell victim to a dark-haired man with piercing blue eyes and irresistible charm. None of them had ever seen the stranger on the island before. Still, each of the women depicted him as being impossibly beautiful and charismatic. Their descriptions were disturbingly similar.

All the women had succumbed to the stranger and been taken by him physically. Rape was a charge of one or two of the victims, but the remaining women simply stated that the man's allure and appearance were so extraordinary, so enthralling, they'd been completely drained of any degree of self-control whatsoever. They were hypnotized in a way, although they hadn't used that word. They'd been entranced and therefore not responsible for the encounter. The word 'witchcraft' was even lobbed about.

Predictably, the husbands of the victims were enraged and demanded immediate, vigorous, and decisive action from their church, being Greek Orthodox.

The Greek Orthodox Church hadn't taken sufficient action, evidently, because some impatient individual got in touch with a guy who knew a guy who knew a guy in Rome.

According to local accounts, the married victims were just one part of the issue. The plight of the virgin sufferers was voiced with even more vehemence.

What was a small, rural, God-fearing community supposed to do when its women were being seduced by a devil? They weren't going to remain silent, that was obvious. No, they were going to cry out to the clergy, any clergy, quite loudly it seemed, and insist someone with some authority, any authority, step in and use its divinely bestowed power to relieve them of the evil curse. A conclusively demonic force, after all, was compromising the purity of the island's women.

The island's mysterious, dark-haired stranger was given, for some very odd reason, a French name by the locals. They called him "de Montleon," the Demon of Cyprus.

All of this alone would never have inspired the attentions of Cardinal Matìne and his extraordinary sect of individually selected young bishops, except that these stories were accompanied by some enticing and familiar details, such as sightings of strange animal tracks around the villages at the base of Mount Olympus. But the cincher, of course, had been the photographs. Amateur photographs were sent to Rome from a variety of sources on the Mediterranean island. A number of large, feline-looking tracks had been documented and submitted.

More alarming, though, were the pictures of charred landscapes. Images of remote island groves scarred by fire in unusual patterns were photographed quite frequently during that time. Usually, the burn patterns were in strictly long and straight lines, originating from a specific point and widened as they traveled across the countryside.

Of course, the photographic evidence could have been artificial. Some or all of the fire damage could have been the decorations of a hoax. Theoretically, any jerk with a flamethrower and either a very strange sense of humor or a serious psychological problem could have created the diagonal streams of blackened bark and scorched earth documented in the black and white glossies mailed to Rome. Even so, after seeing the pictures, added to the random victim accounts and the numerous sightings of strange animal tracks, it had been decided by the cardinal and his closest advisors that the issue merited, at least, a visit.

After papal consent had been granted, the materials were reviewed in two or three closed sessions by Matìne's council elders. One issue they worked to resolve was exactly who from the sect would best suit the needs of the investigation. Robert hadn't slept for two days in anticipation of their decision.

The situation was obvious to him: the evidence clearly showed that the skotos had retreated to the island where it attempted to lay low. The nature of a demon, however, was irrevocable, and the creature eventually succumbed to his fundamental lusts and unquenchable demonic appetites. Robert could see the truth as clearly as if he'd received a report directly from the very entity itself.

Clearly, the skotos was on Cyprus and he was having his reckless way with the women of the more rural areas. Hopefully, the council would be able to recognize what was right in front of them and every resource at the cardinal's command released upon the island before the demon moved on, before it was too late.

The skotos was on Cyprus and, as with every evil, its very nature had given it away.

Larry only had to give Robert a simple look. He knocked on his door with a tormenting subtlety, and when Robert opened it, he could tell by Larry's grin that both the elder bishops and the cardinal had approved Robert's inclusion on the team. Larry hadn't had to say a single word.

Looking back, Robert thought, of course the council included him. It was, after all, the will of God.

Cyprus was so beautiful that, despite Robert's initial consuming enthusiasm with the assignment, he had a terribly difficult time focusing on what they were doing. The enchantment of their surroundings had been almost overwhelming.

For one thing, it was exquisitely funny for Robert to be with the elder bishops in such a casual setting. Seeing senior members of the Church wearing leather sandals and khaki shorts was a little jarring.

They'd spent more than a week at that tiny inn near the beach, that secluded and impossibly lovely hideaway Larry miraculously found. Robert closed his eyes as he thought of those long ago days. They were, he considered, the last happy days of his life.

How could anyone look at a sunset dancing across the vast expanse of the Mediterranean Sea, glittering in golden shards, the kisses of angels dancing from the horizon all the way to the shore of that ancient city, and not believe in God? How could any heart not be moved by such a dazzling display of divine beauty? Robert would never know.

The Scotch might have been more than a little responsible for Robert's melancholy, but it didn't matter. He was still gazing out at the late-night, California sky, but all he could see was Larry's face, so many years ago, as he sat on the steps of their porch, outside the villa they'd shared, facing the sea from the quaint and silent shores of

Paphos. Larry looked so young, so vital, as he gazed at the sunbeams leaping along the rippling water. He'd seemed at least ten years younger. Almost all of the damage done to his features by his life of study and dedication disappeared as, together, they watched the waves break and listened to their crashing, melodic chorus.

Robert had watched him, had seen the essence of the man unburdened, unhampered by so many years of so much incredible responsibility. Robert thought he'd never seen Larry so content.

Those days of preparation had been filled with a heavenly calm, yet bolstered by a current of revolutionary energy and fanatical focus. Bishop Peter Davis was the leader of the team, eventually forgiven for his failure in Pakistan. It was therefore in his room they all met, every day after a late breakfast and jovial conversation. They'd spread their documents and maps and newspapers and scripture and research all over the tiny room where they frantically discussed their mission. The stacks of papers, open binders and books, all lifted and shuffled in the breeze from the ceiling fan; the written materials themselves brought to life just as much as the men who studied them. The team of bishops gathered, unshaven, in T-shirts, a little sunburned, and laughing and eating and drinking and arguing and resting and planning, like summertime American teenagers at a neighborhood Denny's.

"I'm not convinced Mr. Popodopolous isn't trying to steer us away from the village," Bishop Davis had offered.

Hector Popodopolous was the mayor of Paphos at the time. His office was the council's primary source of aid and information in this endeavor. Although the more controversial facets of the sect's purpose was diplomatically concealed, it was obvious the mayor knew exactly why they were there; only an idiot wouldn't have been able to connect the surge of rumors coming from the island and the sudden interest from Rome.

"We'll assure him again of our purpose," Bishop McBride had stated. "We should just reiterate and simply proceed."

Randal "Randy" McBride was a man of very few words and liked to cut to the quick of every issue. He was very difficult to speak with, as he was always interrupting and finishing other people's sentences out of his obdurate belief that he knew absolutely everything. To hear him speak, one would assume he'd decided his primary ability and purpose in life was to personally fix the whole world's problems, absolutely everyone's, all of them, everywhere.

Actually, each member of the team was a certified genius. Robert had thought that was a mistake. He thought so then, and he thought so now. With extreme intellect came extreme ego, which just about negated the benefit of having so many IQ points focused on the same task and assembled in the same room. This observation would gain horribly painful credibility as the years passed and the clarity of hindsight haunted Robert's every thought.

"He's bound to make it difficult for us to continue on the basis of our thin little cover story alone," Peter said. "The man is determined not to let—"

"He's a minor obstacle, Peter." Randy shook his head. "We don't owe him anything more than the most basic explanation. Who's paying the bills here, anyway?"

"We have Jeeps reserved for us in Panayia, right?" Larry asked, always the detailed one, always the rational thinker.

"Two," answered Bishop Chen. "Peter will drive one and I'll take the other one."

"Why?" Randy had pressed his eyebrows together. "Who made that decision? Are you two the only ones who can drive a stick shift?"

"Randy..." Bishop Chen sighed, as though he should have seen this coming. "If you want a key, just say—"

"I'd like a key," Randy said.

Bishop Chen had smiled and nodded. He was used to Randy. The many, many years they'd spent working so closely together had eventually softened Randy's abrasiveness.

Robert had really liked Stephen. Bishop Stephen Chen was not only Chinese, but also so Asian-looking that to Robert it was uproariously shocking to hear anything but Mandarin coming out of his mouth. Even after knowing him for over half a decade, hearing such a short, oriental-looking, biblical scholar speak with a massive Bostonian accent still flew well into the realm of the hilarious.

Robert shuddered at the memory. It was Stephen's face that he'd seen in the flames. He'd been the only one he recognized, the only one whose face was at all distinguishable when Robert turned for just that tiny instant, just that smallest of moments, as he fled. He'd turned and looked as he raced away from the fires and the screams, while Brathwidth sat and laughed his head off. Stephen was the only one who hadn't yet been completely consumed by fire. Both of the others had become great columns of flame. They were nothing more than faceless, shrieking infernos.

"There are four villagers I want to speak with before we try to find the site," Stephen had said, blindly setting in motion the actions that would end in his death. "I just want to confirm the story about the brass knife and the stone alter."

Robert recalled that there had been lovely white curtains covering the door leading to the old wooden deck off of Peter's room, so thin they were almost translucent. The softest breeze would lift them into the air. They'd rise into the midst of their meetings, like a woven fog, or the bodies of delicate spirits, hovering in a tranquil dance. The inn had been built only a few years after the end of World War I and looked to Robert like the set of an old spy movie. They'd lounged in wide wicker seats, behind mosquito nets in a tropical hideaway for one-eyed smugglers and international fugitives.

Robert's suite in Los Angeles, where he now sat in the thrall of his mind's wandering, had very heavy navy-blue drapes that fell from the ceiling like theater curtains. In the mornings, when he caught up on all the sleep he'd sacrificed to his mission, he appreciated their bulk, which easily kept out all of the sun's intrusive light. They never billowed, though, these heavy, velveteen decorations. It would take a gale-force wind to push them into the room. Even then, Robert didn't think it would be a very tranquil sight.

It had been the right decision to send Michael back, Robert thought abruptly. Michael just didn't understand what was happening.

Robert stared into the night, hardly noticing the vision of the Mediterranean shore fading from his mind. The memory of Larry's sunset-illuminated face retreated, giving way to the bland oak desk, the immaculate carpet, the perfectly made bed, and finally the endless winter sky. Only the streaks on the window left by the glass cleaner allowed Robert's mind any rational perspective, and kept him there in the hotel. Sometimes sanity was only possible because of the most trivial of things, as it was possible here, secured for the moment by streaks from the chemical glass cleaner; a focus, a point in reality that kept Robert's mind from flying out into the void.

The waiting was just about over. He had his invitation to the private LA bash, which he was sure the mysterious raven-haired Greek would attend. He would confront the boy there and the game would be on.

Robert could have confronted the Greek boy on so many other occasions, on so many other nights throughout the summer while he watched him at the club. There would have been no danger while they were in such a crowd. The mysterious young man wouldn't have presented any threat. Unless, of course, the mysterious young man wasn't a man at all.

That's what had stopped him. It was a very large unknown component, which was unacceptable if Robert was going to play his hand. He needed to have Solomon's Vessel in his possession before he would feel confident that he'd covered that possibility.

This was the event Robert had been waiting for all along. He could feel it as surely as he had eight years ago, when he knew somehow that it was the will of the Divine he be included on the trip to Cyprus, if only to personally witness the bare powers of Hell at work.

This time, though... well, this time things would be different.

Now, sitting alone in the lavish suite in Los Angeles, Robert wallowed in the fruits of his prayers. He realized that his request of God had been granted after all. Even if no one else knew it, even if the cardinal himself never acknowledged it. Robert had what he'd thought he always wanted.

He had become essential and irreplaceable.

CHAPTER II

†

Drugs, Idle Banter, Famous People, More Drugs, and a Big, Big Loveseat

For the flesh has desires that are opposed to the Spirit, and the Spirit has desires that are opposed to the flesh, for these are in opposition to [are hostile toward] each other, so that you cannot do what you want. But if you are led by the Spirit, you are not under the law.

- Galatians 5:17 -18 (NEV)

Los Angeles, California
Inside a limousine idling on Nichols Canyon Road, deep in the hills of Hollywood

†

Nick couldn't believe how many cars were parked along the normally quiet road leading up into the hills of Hollywood. Block after block after block after block; it was surreal. He thought the house that was hosting this party had better be huge or else the revelry sure wouldn't last very long. If there wasn't enough room to contain the noise and the crowd, there'd be police helicopters buzzing around the chimney before midnight.

At least they didn't have to worry about parking. That was something about which they never really thought anymore, being so used to limousines and all.

Tonight, the car carried only the three of them, Nick, Darren, and Scott. Theo and Eddie had gone up to the house earlier in the evening in order to 'help' Karen. Nick, however, was sure he knew exactly what kind of help the boys were most likely providing.

So, we're going to just cut up all this nice cocaine for you and then test it for imperfections. Let us know if you have any other chores in mind, like some K or some G, or something, okay? We're here for ya, babe!

Although it was much more peaceful, Nick missed them. The past fourteen weeks had drawn them all unbelievably closer.

They'd all had breakfast together that morning and then headed to Crunch for a disco-pump, followed by protein shakes at Scott's house. No one dared eat any actual food after the lunch hour had passed; later that evening, once they started talking to Missy, she might not agree with whatever they'd eaten and insist they expel it immediately, which would seriously suck. Worse, if they ate any solid foods within four to six hours of attempting to meet up with her, she might just decide not to make any kind of an appearance at all. It wasn't completely unlike her to behave like a spoiled, finicky bitch. So, if they wanted her to stay in a good and loving mood, it was wise to just stick to doing the things that usually made her happy. If Missy was going to be kept in a friendly disposition, it was always best to follow standard procedure and not risk her temper.

Nick rested his head against the long cushioned seat of the car, painfully aware that Scott and Darren were talking again, quietly together, underneath the music, obviously so he couldn't hear them. Nowadays, Nick had become their charge, and therefore not always privileged to all of their thoughts and actions. Now that Nick knew Scott's second name, the three of them had to be especially careful. Sure, he didn't know the big-momma whoop-ass name, but the name of 'Marbas' was enough to get Nick into serious trouble, should he be so stupid as to allow anything else to touch him again that might be capable of plucking such juicy little tidbits out of his brain in regard to his handsome, supernatural chum.

Although Marbas wasn't Scott's true name, the one known— supposedly—only by Scott and God himself, it was what he'd been called as an angel, by both the other members of God's entourage, as well as all the terrestrial entities. It could therefore be used to identify him and him alone to whatever cosmic power, friendly or not so friendly, might be interested. It was immense information and, as any mortal in possession of such knowledge would, Nick had to be protected. He needed some steadfast looking after, and Scott had recruited Darren to help him do it.

It was a responsibility both Scott and Darren took very seriously, and they discussed it often. There was more, though, Nick thought. Now, there was more than just the responsibility of protecting him that bonded Scott and Darren. They'd shared something, evidently, something enormous and terribly intimate. Nick somehow understood this as clearly as he understood his own language. Not that it upset him. On the contrary.

Nick came to believe that Darren and Scott had shared something simple and very poignant. Nick smiled each time he saw it. Each time he saw Darren comforted with just a glance from Scott. Each time the three of them laughed or smiled together and a single spark of secret understanding leaped between Nick's two companions, Nick saw it and it made him smile. No, there was no doubt. Darren shared something tender and fulfilling with Scott.

Whatever they'd shared, it hadn't been sexual, nothing like that at all. Still, Nick knew it was important and comforting to Darren. And, instinctively, he also knew should must remain between the two of them, between Scott and Darren. Nick knew this, and welcomed it. He had his own intimacy with Darren. They shared their own splendid and profound secrets.

At the moment, though, the smirk on Darren's face suggested he and Scott were discussing much more trivial matters. After all, it was two days before Christmas. Nick suspected their conversation had more to do with whatever obnoxious—although no doubt sweet and sickeningly endearing—surprise Darren had planned for the holiday, rather than the same tired and tedious precautions with which they'd all been dealing for almost four months now.

For Nick, the biggest question of the past couple weeks had been, 'What does one get a demon for Christmas?' Nick chuckled every time he thought about it, and now was no exception. Scott and Darren gave him a funny look, which only made him chuckle more.

What would a demon want for Christmas? Boy, that was probably a holiday dilemma that could stump even Martha Stewart.

Nick chuckled some more.

He'd agonized over that strange question for days and finally chosen a compilation of contemporary dance CDs and a collection of classic movies just released on DVD. At his house, Scott always had The History Channel playing on at least one of the televisions, only turning it off when there was a famously classic movie running, or when everyone came over in the early evening to get ready to go out. When those little pre-pre-parties were going on, Scott left the televisions off and simply had to have something mixed by Brian Ikon on the stereo. Scott loved dance music, and he loved old movies.

Scott's new place was always full of people. It was almost as though there was an official standing pre-party at his house every Saturday afternoon. Sundays, as well, would offer the delights of company more often than not; it turned out that loading into a beachside Jacuzzi with a throng of early-morning revelers — some of whom had just left the club's after-hours festivities, others arriving from a plethora of similar events — was a very popular idea. Yeah. Gorgeous, nearly naked, party boys piling into a bubbling hot tub together was a popular idea. Go figure.

Liberal as Scott was, however, bathing suits were never optional at these spontaneous happenings; he didn't want his home to have that type of reputation. Not that he had anything against guys walking around in nothing but towels — or even less — he simply felt there were more appropriate places for such goings-on.

Of course all the guys — and Karen, of course — always phoned on Saturday afternoons and made sure it was all right to stop by. Without fail, Scott simply told everyone, "Come on over! We're just picking out our pants."

The gang began arriving sometime around one o'clock every Saturday afternoon. A steady stream of pleasant and beautiful friends and acquaintances continued filtering in after that until the word eventually went out it was time to move on. Usually, the group's journey was merely from Scott's house to the club.

Although these parties were a little outside the usual neighborhood, no one seemed to mind the drive. To Nick's knowledge, traveling all the way to the beach in Santa Monica, almost right onto the sand, hadn't produced a single complaint. Such a trek traditionally prompted moans from WeHo boys, for whom anything beyond Westwood was understood to be China.

During the summer, there were also more than a few nights when Scott's house wasn't the pre-party spot at all; it ended up becoming the location of the party itself. The neighboring homes weren't close enough to be too disturbed by a moderate collection of guys and a reasonable music level. Besides, it wasn't unusual for the neighbors to either be having their own private fête, or to wander into Scott's with a bottle of White Zinfandel in one hand and a baggie full of joints in the other. After all, life was just one big party, wasn't it?

Nick and Darren spent an immense amount of time at the enormous beach house Scott ended up buying. He'd looked at about a zillion condominiums, then bought a house. Nick never saw a realtor get that close to suicide. Luckily, his commission was also unexpected, in that it came in an amount of money that could very easily feed Boston.

Scott, Nick and Darren, had argued a bit while the property was still in escrow — something around five minutes — because Scott thought the two of them should just move in with him. There were nine bedrooms in the house — estate, really — six full bathrooms and four half-baths. It had two living rooms, each the size of hotel lobbies, enough closet space to satisfy Imelda Marcos, and a kitchen that could have handled a finicky hockey team after a famine.

Still, as much as Darren and Nick each loved Scott, they didn't really want to move in with him. Ever since that disturbing weekend back in August, Nick and Darren's relationship had changed. It had become something for which Nick hadn't even allowed himself to wish and, having become so, they needed a place of their own.

Since that horrible night and the following day when Nick had woken up in his own bed, after dreaming of running rabbits, fire-breathing dragons, and even of Scott and Darren, things had begun to change, and change rapidly.

First, there was Nick's bizarre dream, in which Scott had been looking down at him tenderly, glorious enough with his gentle eyes and expressive grin, his tumble of shimmering black hair — it was a mane, really, wasn't it? Nick couldn't stop looking at Scott and thinking of that fall of thick wavy blackness as anything but a mane. Yet, there was a big difference to Scott's appearance in that particular dream — oh, yes sir, a *big* difference — he's also been outlined by two vast and glorious wings. Not the solid black dragon's wings, though. Not the great gothic flapping appendages Nick had seen the night before looming out from between the shoulders of Marbas, the Demon Lion. No, they'd been the wings of an angel, so white they were like thousands upon thousands of tiny, tiny mirrors pressed into almost liquid shapes that together created a magnificent image of glittering, cascading feathers.

Next to Scott, beneath one of his massive, shimmering wings, had been Darren. He'd been holding Scott's hand and looking down at Nick with those big handsome brown eyes of his. In Nick's dream, Darren's familiar eyes had been filled with some deep and unmistakable suffering.

After that day, after Nick woke up on that endless day, after he sat with Scott and Darren on the carpet in front of his couch and said and listened to everything there was to say, Nick had been much more clear about what he and Darren wanted, both for themselves and from each other.

The two of them spent those long, long waking hours talking about what had happened and listening to Scott describe what was conceivably yet to come. They'd locked themselves into hours and hours of talking and screaming and crying and laughing and whispering and silence. The way Nick and Darren saw the world, their very associations of reality, comprehension of existence, had been changed both dramatically and permanently.

The conversation on that day began with Scott apologizing. First he apologized to Darren. Scott reached up and took down the photograph of him and Nick on the beach, the miraculously fabricated picture of the two of them laughing together on a sunny day that had never been. Scott handed it to Darren and told him to wipe off the glass.

Darren had pulled up the bottom of his T-shirt, wiped off the frame and the glass as if cleaning it of dust, and then he'd almost dropped it. His shirt came away and Scott's image was gone. There was Nick's older brother Tom again, back in his spot, as if he'd never been replaced, as if his likeness had never been distorted underneath a paranormal smear of Scott's magical demon spit.

Although he'd been obviously shaken, Nick noticed Darren wasn't anywhere near as shocked as he thought he'd be. He certainly hadn't been completely dazed and lightheaded like Nick was on that particular Sunday. Darren held himself together and accepted the story about the alley, Nick and Scott's initial deception, Scott's flight from New York away from the demon huntress who would deliver him to The Beast, the encounter outside the club, and the consequential confrontation with Lilith's servant imp, Gillulim.

Darren had put the picture back on the bookshelf. Then they all sat down on the floor together, close together, near the crook of the sectional in an intimate huddle out of sight from the windows, out of view from the outside world.

Scott and Darren had both begged to be forgiven. Darren spoke to Nick about their own relationship. He cried and cried, burying his face into Nick's neck, rocking him with his sobs.

Scott's pain over the unforeseen developments of his situation had been so apparent, so vivid, it was agonizing to witness. He'd felt he somehow betrayed Nick and Darren both, and yet the notion was impossible for either of them to fathom.

Nick had held each of them, each in turn, each in the misery of their confessions, he'd pressed his face to theirs, squinting at his own tears and wholly unable to speak. That afternoon, tears had seemed the price of the day, a day that brought immeasurable revelation, intimate and profound acceptance, and private absolution.

After that day, that particular Sunday, a wall had come down from between Nick and Darren, a wall that, frankly, Nick had expected would stand forever, solid and impenetrable. It disappeared, though, destroyed by some revelation of Heaven. They saw each other with fresh eyes and new appreciation.

So, despite Scott's arguments, Nick and Darren had decided they needed to have a place of their own. It was obviously time.

They knew they'd spend many, many days and nights at Scott's house and in his doting and tender company—Scott still insisted upon designating one of the larger bedrooms as theirs, which was kind of cute, when Nick thought about it—but they nonetheless wanted a place that was apart and simply for the two of them. They needed a quiet space where they could lay in silence and contentment, and where they'd know nothing but each other.

Eventually, after much debate and skillfully constructed arguments, Scott finally relented. Even so, with a shrewd smile and a tone that was undeniable, he commanded there would be a compromise: he bought Nick and Darren a four bedroom condominium on the bluff overlooking Pacific Coast Highway, not ten minutes walk from his beach house.

The condo was in a splendid building. The occupants of more than half the other units were so famous there was an elevator between every two doors to maximize the privacy of the residents' general comings and goings, not to mention an army of valets and security guys—each of whom Theo didn't really like very much. He thought they were always looking at him funny.

Almost predictably, Scott's spending didn't stop after purchasing Nick and Darren's four-bedroom beauty. Two floors below and three units south was Theo's two bedroom condo—he'd have to get used to the funny looks from the security guys, Nick supposed—and another two floors below that was Eddie's.

Scott not only outright bought all three homes, he furnished them lavishly as well, regardless of the sometimes passionate objections to the extravagance of his doing so. Scott would hear no arguments, make no more further compromises, and proclaimed that he intended to purchase and furnish all three properties; the boys could choose to take possession of them or allow them to stand empty. It was up to them.

Each one had ultimately given in and accepted. Sure, they felt a little guilty, or at least considerably out of their arena as to how to behave in the face of such things, but in the end they all took the keys from Scott. What else would anyone do? Of course they accepted the gift-condos, how stupid.

Signing all the papers, when Scott officially transferred owner-ship, he'd beamed with triumph and a profound affection. Scott took enormous and conspicuous delight in the blissful chuckles and rapturous airs from all four of the other guys whenever they opened their new doors and strode happily into their scrumptious new digs.

The novelty and excitement of moving into brand-new beachside condominiums in the same building took a surprisingly long time before it so much as began to subside for the guys. Especially endearing, Nick thought, was the sparkle in Darren's eye each time he realized he need only ride an elevator for a moment or two in order to visit the homes of his closest pals.

At that point, Nick thought maybe all of Scott's urges for outland-ish bequests had been exhausted. They hadn't.

In October, for Theo's birthday, Nick bought him two very flatter-ing designer shirts and even splurged a bit in order to throw in two orchestra-seat tickets to see Toni Braxton in concert. Darren bought Theo a gorgeous leather gym bag. Eddie took him to The Magic Castle for dinner and gave him a bracelet-box filled with a green laser-pen and several hits of ecstasy—the latter being somewhat tacky, in Nick's opinion.

Scott, however, gave Theo a car. Scott had given Theo a mother-fucking car as a birthday present. Good gravy on a biscuit, talk about being shown up! Nick thought he'd been splurging when he bought the concert tickets, lord help us all.

Scott also threw a huge party for Theo's birthday at his new beach house, of course—at which an incredibly fabulous time was had by all, one of those seriously exceptional experiences they'd each remember with heartbreaking clarity until the day they died.

Karen made sure that anyone who was anyone made at least a casual appearance at Theo's party, which included no less than the likes of Vivica Fox, Alyson Hannigan, Christina Aguilera, Will Smith, and Ben Affleck. The private event took on an almost mythical air when it was described repeatedly during the coming months and years to the masses of those unlucky enough not to have attended.

Theo had gotten seriously and appropriately schnocked, been attended to by several of the finest and most incredibly beautiful men to ever walk the planet, and afterward wasn't able to knock the smile off his face for so long that he expressed concern it might cause him to wrinkle prematurely.

The official *Theo Ramon Birthday Bash!* was an unquestionably important local event. However, earlier that afternoon, just the five of them had all gathered privately at Theo's condo for a small celebration, a little party just for the family. After singing Happy Birthday in a number of lovely but random keys, Scott brought them all out to the parking garage to see Theo's stunning new Porsche Turbo coupe. Watching his two hundred thirty-plus pounds of muscle behind the wheel of the sleek little sports car was very nearly funny, but somehow deeply gratifying at the same time. When he spotted the coupe, Theo appeared as though he suddenly couldn't breathe or speak and would simply break down and cry. Nick couldn't blame him, what with the condo, the furniture, and now the car. He was obviously having significant trouble figuring out exactly how to process it all. Nick thought, all of them were having the very same trouble, really.

Theo had been horribly stunned. Even after the condo and all the other lavish treatments Scott showered upon them, somehow the car was over the top. So, Theo stood there, stunned, in the echoing cement-covered parking lot, overwhelmed and motionless.

Tenderly, Scott had taken Theo by the chin, looked him square in the eye, and said sternly, "Sweet pea, don't you even lose one moment of contentment over this. It's a drop in the ocean for me, as easy as a greeting card, and I assure you I want nothing in return but that you are good to all these people here that love you. You be good to this family that you've chosen, but most of all..." Scott paused. He took a breath, licked his lips, and sighed. "Most of all, Theo... well, Theo... most of all you just be good to yourself."

At that, Karen—who'd been speechless right along with the rest of them from the second they walked away from the cake, into the parking garage, and were confronted by the sight of the car and it's ridiculously enormous bow—immediately burst into tears, which were accompanied by some very loud sobs. Nick put his arm around her, even though he was only about a hair away from exactly the same thing himself. It was about time things started going right for Theo. It was about motherfucking time.

Although he didn't buy her a car or a condo, Scott and Karen still clicked deeply and immediately. When he wasn't with the other guys, he was skipping all over town with her, loading his trunk with dresses, shoes, and jewelry that Scott spontaneously decided had been destined by the Omnipotent Fashion Forces of the Universe to be worn by Karen, and Karen alone.

Over dinner at Mark's in late October, Karen remarked to Scott that, although she was probably going to be getting him something along the lines of a sculpture or painting for Christmas, something to just touch his home with a hint of the affection and gratitude she felt, if he happened to be wondering at all what he should get for her, he might look into something on the more practical side, such as a closet the size of a parking structure.

To top it all off, Scott mentioned he'd like to take them all traveling. The gang talked casually about places they'd like to see. They dreamed together about seeing the gay delights of Sydney in February and of Montreal in October, of wandering the streets of Amsterdam, cruising the seas to Alaska, of standing beneath the confetti in Rio de Janeiro. Scott smiled wordlessly while Theo and Eddie bantered about the sights of Athens and the beaches of Míkanos and Kárpathos. New York came up once or twice, but the idea of Miami, Fort Lauderdale, and South Beach won out each time instead. The thought of Fat Tuesday in New Orleans had inspired a gasping, silent contemplation, and there was much ado about frolicking in the clubs of Minneapolis, Chicago, and Dallas. Of course, plans for weekends in San Francisco, Palm Springs, and San Diego were rolled around as recklessly as marbles on a summer sidewalk.

They chatted about renting enormous cars, convertibles in the tropics and Pathfinders in Aspen, maybe twin Jeeps in Maui. They would travel the country and the world, insisting upon balconies facing the sunsets attached to open suites with mosquito nets over the beds, mountain cabins with steaming hot tubs surrounded by snow, luxury suites in Las Vegas with mahogany floors, bearskin rugs before real fireplaces, and views of each different city glittering in the night far below them like God's own colossal pinball machines.

The delights of their fantasies went on and on, but no one suggested any dates, called any travel agents, or pulled up any vacation web sites. After all, they'd only just settled into their lovely new coastal homes. Each of them was far too contented simply lounging together on their own private balconies to suddenly pack up and start gallivanting around the world. They'd been too satisfied to wander around Los Angeles in Theo and Scott's new cars, careening through the twists of Mulholland Drive and inching along with the traffic on Sunset or Hollywood Boulevard; to laugh with Karen and Eddie while they tried to mop up Theo as he dripped ice cream down his chest in Venice Beach; to stroll in the early evenings down Santa

Monica's beach boardwalk, loitering behind Nick and Darren, watching them holding hands, in envy and adoration of their devotion; to see the sun ignite both sky and ocean as they all relaxed in the calm silence of the California dusk on Scott's gargantuan deck, silently at ease together, happy enough beneath just the blanket of the shoreline breeze.

Why should they run off into the big, wide world just now? They were young, there was chilled wine and sliced fruit on the deck table, fresh air clearing their thoughts with the sweet scents of the western American coast, the blissful comfort of each other's arms, and the soft strength of each other's familiar shoulders. What more could any of those far away and exotic places possibly offer?

The summer had stretched out into fall with such a wave of sumptuous fantasy and emotional contentment it was all they could do not to lose their minds in happiness and disbelief. It helped Nick and Darren to be able to trudge up the little shoreline hill to their condo, shut their door, pour some wine, and rest in a meditative stillness, clearing their thoughts of underlying fears, settling their hearts through the song of the crashing waves across the street and the soothing familiar rhythm of each other's breathing. They could smile at each other between tender kisses, easily and with reassuring frequency.

For some reason, Darren didn't make baby lion noises anymore when he slept, but he'd toss and turn unless he could drape at least his hand over Nick, if not both an arm and a leg—it was getting cooler at night, so having a six-foot-three human heater sprawled on him every evening wasn't keeping Nick awake so much anymore.

Even so, while Eddie and Theo seemed to be slowly giving themselves permission to revel and thrive in their new and sumptuous lives, Nick and Darren weren't above asking Scott for a tiny bit of additional help. He had those striking and magical blue eyes, after all. Why not put them to good use? There was also Nick and Darren's need to deal with the not-understatedly-colossal realities of their situation, and sometimes a journey to lose that anxiety, a dip into the crystal pool of Scott's supernatural gaze, was a welcome and cherished relief.

Nick couldn't help smiling with the stream of charming memories. Scott and Darren were still lost in quiet conversation on the far side of the limo, which Nick noticed had begun to slow. Maybe they were stopping. Even so, they still couldn't get out and go inside; divine illumination or not, Darren certainly wasn't going to walk up the street to this party as if he'd driven there himself and parked four blocks away behind some dumpster. As usual, Darren wanted to wait until the limo could get to the very steps of the path leading to the house's front door. Right now, there was just too much of a crowd and jumble of cars jostling for position on the slender residential street for their driver to get any closer.

The event Darren produced at the club back in November had been such an outrageous success even Karen was shocked and impressed. Max immediately gave Darren two more dates after the New Year, and if those events went over well, he'd promised Darren the Saturday before Memorial Day.

Certainly, Darren was a rising star, and he still wanted to put forth at least a reasonable effort to maintain his still-burgeoning, super-glam image. So, stepping out of the limo in front of the crowd was a must. However, Darren had recently proclaimed that he didn't care anymore what people thought in regard to his relationship with Nick.

"It wouldn't matter to me," Darren had said one night back in September, nodding his head and pouting confidently, "if the people who don't already know about me find out. I'm cool with that."

" 'The people who don't already know?' " Scott had smiled. "You mean both of them?"

At the moment, Darren and Scott appeared to be having the time of their lives. Less than an hour ago they'd been laughing together when they left the house. It was going to be a good night. Nick closed his eyes and tried not to think about all the other things that were happening. He wanted to be able to enjoy Karen's party.

Nick began to meditate lightly, the way Scott had taught him, clearing away clumps of excessive thought like brambles of weed. Shallow meditation was a very useful trick, once he'd gotten the hang of it. Although, even shallow meditation had taken quite a long time to achieve.

It had become very, very necessary for Nick and Darren to learn as much as they could about the realities of their situation—with the exception of any of Scott's more dangerous names, of course. In Darren's case, there was only the revelation about Scott's casual, mortal name, derived by Nick from 'Exousia Skotos.' Helpfully, though, Scott had elucidated on that detail a bit. He explained that 'Exousia Skotos' was a Greek phrase meaning *out of the darkness*, or *that which comes from the darkness*.

As Scott explained how his most common name might be trans-lated from Greek into contemporary American English, Nick kept thinking of the strange dream he'd had on that first early Sunday morning. As he listened to the variations of terminology and the effect of semantics, it occurred to him that something coming out of darkness didn't necessarily imply evil. It could just as easily refer to emancipation from darkness. It could imply an escape from darkness and into light. Perhaps some ancient Greek clairvoyant had named Scott not as a creature born of evil, but as one who'd been freed from it.

Nick was thoroughly captivated by the whole myth of history. Mortal history: the product of the mesh of religion and sociology and psychology and biology and geography and politics and culture and assumption and corruption and ignorance. The supernatural enchanted him as well. He poured himself into book after book about demons, the occult, and the mystical. However, Scott nearly laughed himself into a coma whenever Nick opened his mouth to share even the smallest bits his newly acquired 'knowledge.' His well-intentioned if mis-focused academic efforts, therefore, had been shelved.

Scott just couldn't be more amused at the way humans all over the world and all throughout history couldn't help but take the simplest stories and embellish them into profound sagas that were laborious, loaded with rigid mortal sensibilities, and incredibly complicated.

The first thing Scott made sure to point out was that, with the exception of the angels and God himself, every sentient immortal entity was of the same substance; demons, devils, vampires, goblins, ghouls, genies, dragons, fairies, elves, pixies, on and on and on. Every one of them. Included too was every single ancient god ever noted and named. Even, to Nick's absolute delight, gargoyles.

It didn't make any sense to study the particulars of zombies or mandrakes or sprites or leprechauns; they were all the same thing: immortal, terrestrial entities of varying size, appearance, age, and power. The inconsistency of description, character, and origin was due entirely to human perception, which was heavily influenced by everything from religious politics to changes in the weather. The same entity witnessed by one community in one part of the world might be called a 'god,' in another a 'demon,' and in still another a 'banshee,' or their linguistic equivalents, and so on and so forth, et cetera, et cetera, and so the story goes.

Unfortunately, an incredible amount of lore was no more than customized fabrication for the purpose of manipulating the loyalties of, what Scott called, "the continuously growing masses of the uneducated."

"A demon by any other name, you know, and yada, yada, blah, blah, and blah," he'd chuckled.

In the seventh century, for instance, Scott explained, two very powerful demons, Astaroth and Sargatanas, practically destroyed the English countryside while engaged in quite a heated disagreement. Their conflict eventually escalated into massive physical combat on several occasions. They even went so far as to fight in their most monstrous forms, battling with the utmost extremes of their considerable power, which included spewing streams of flame at each other over the hills and through the damp forests of ancient Britain. They were seen by more than one mortal while in the throws of their anger, eventually giving some potent assistance to the rising legend of dragons.

Scott himself had been seen on many occasions flying in his true form through the skies of the Mediterranean, the Middle East, and Europe. His own image had been morphed in the minds of more primitive communities and he believed he was normally depicted as a dragon, when he was seen from far off. Though, after being witnessed more closely, it was the legend of the griffin that got the glory. Sometimes Scott was referred to as a griffon or a gryphon, but it was all the same; it was all him, morphed by embellishment and the passing of the centuries. To his knowledge, however, regarding an actual griffin, no such creature ever existed. Exactly how and why the eagle's head and wings were assigned to the legend, Scott didn't know exactly, but presented a fascinating theory involving strange fossils and misinterpreted archeological evidence.

In the midst of all this, Scott pointed out, there were two truthful understandings that seemed to stream through just about all the tall tales, exaggerations, overstatements, and embellishments. There were thin threads of truth that had been remarkably preserved through time and the development of human thought: one was the core teaching of human experience, which was to love each other, and the other was the existence of the nemesis of that imperative, which was the Beast.

The problems of language and superstition had taken their toll all over the world, to be sure, but some reality of varying degree was found at the heart of a thousand stories from a thousand civilizations. Stories that told of the need for human compassion toward each other, and of the Beast, although in a thousand guises, and his eternal and angry obsession.

The truth was, Scott explained, that an angel of God who'd been jealous of what was granted to humanity fell from Heaven when he attempted to acquire the same consideration.

"He wanted to be worshiped just like God, right?" Darren had asked, completely enthralled.

"No," Scott had explained. "He wanted to have *choice*."

The living souls on the earth were allowed to choose what kind of relationship they would have with God, if any at all. It was a concept as unknown to the angels as wind to a fish. When the mightiest of the seraphim first recognized this, his sudden understanding brought down upon him a discerning attention from God.

Scott didn't know exactly what had happened between them at first—it was all just angel gossip really—but supposedly God and his seraph were able to initially work things out and everything was fine for a while. The seraph contented himself merely to be the only one of all the angelic spheres to understand the existence of choice and its denial to the entire host. It wasn't until he turned the idea around and attempted to put the notion into practice that the real trouble began.

When Heaven's brightest angel made his first decision, the instant he moved in an action formed of his own will and not in the sole interest of God, either directly or otherwise, he discovered the ramifications of an existence independent of the Divine. The angel's form, his very substance, changed in such a way that the environment of Heaven could no longer sustain him.

"Just thinking about taking an action, something that might be outside the will and purpose of God, was what caused the transformation," Scott had explained. "It triggered the mutation of the angel's substance. The bindings of God's realm dissolved and released him. And so he became the first of the Fallen."

"Like, right through the clouds, or something?" Darren had been really getting into it.

Scott smiled affectionately. "Not literally. Yes, I'm using very common terms and images to help you understand these ideas. But really, it's just a representation of what happened, not what literally happened."

"Um... okay... what?"

"Well, see, essentially, you don't need to think of an 'angel' in terms of Judeo-Christian tradition. I know I'm using that terminology, but anything else would be even more confusing."

"Oh, okay." Darren had winked at Nick, who smiled, shook his head.

"Bear with me." Scott had closed his eyes, nodded. "In truth, angels do, more or less, resemble the standard, human notion. An angel's fundamental nature, though, is much, much larger, but has suffered from human perceptions. Even the most enlightened clairvoyants throughout history tended to associate the visions they had with the teachings of their culture, teachings that were fundamentally limited."

"Clairvoyants being…"

"Well, you know, prophets and the like."

"So, they didn't understand what they saw?"

"Well, that's not really it either."

Darren had huffed and chuckled, which he often did when he was confused.

"Stay with me, big guy," Scott had said. "See, even the most gifted clairvoyants, the ones capable of the most transcendent thought, weren't able to completely divorce the things they saw, the glimmers they were allowed of Heaven or angels, from the facets of their culture. Clairvoyants born and living within Christian environments interpreted their revelations according to their prevailing worldviews. In other words, truth was filtered in with myth and superstition. Every culture has done it to some degree throughout history. Factor in the compulsion to organize and explain and what you get is terminology and doctrine, which becomes tradition, which then becomes literature. Boom, boom, and boom. See? Revelation mixes with culture and suddenly we have *The Celestial Hierarchy*. From that we have Dante's *The Divine Comedy*, and Milton's *Paradise Lost*."

"Uh… oh… kay."

"You don't see it?" Scott had looked shocked. "Of course we're going to *use* the names and terms from those works! Of course the angels themselves are going to happily adopt the names they're given by humans! Of course! Duh!"

"Huh?"

"Clairvoyants, those with clear sight, they glimpse what is divine and name it. Thus there are 'angels!' See? Okay… am I speaking French?"

"Oh!" Nick had laughed. "You are such an ass! Don't start that shit again."

"Even demons do it," Scott went on, smirking. "As a joke, the court of the Beast is named after Dante's fictional, frozen lake, Cocytus. See what I'm saying? It's all just human terminology that represents truth.

It's not literal truth. The Beast didn't literally 'fall.' "

"I'm kinda lost," Nick had said. Actually, he might not have been completely paying attention. The three of them were in the hot tub, of all places, and Darren was reaching for the cooler on the deck and, well, Nick's concentration could only be stretched so far.

"Yes, I'm not surprised." Scott had smiled, following Nick's gaze.

"What?" Darren looked genuinely confused when he'd turned around.

"Wait, wait!" Nick was going to interject some of his new 'knowledge.' "Didn't Satan have that conversation with God about Job? Weren't Satan and God in Heaven when they had that lil' talk?"

"Very good, Nick!" Scott had beamed at him.

Nick had nudged Darren happily.

"But now consider what I've just been explaining to you" Scott had continued. "And..." He waved his hand in the air expectantly.

"Oh, my god..." Nick's eyes had bulges.

"Go on..." Scott nodded at him, smiling.

Nick grinned. "Satan isn't really the name of the Beast."

"He shoots! He scores!" Scott had laughed, raising his arms.

"What?" Darren's mouth dropped open.

Scott laughed and laughed. "I'm sorry," he chortled. "You should see your face!"

"Okay, very funny," Darren was splashing water all over Scott, who only laughed harder.

"Ha, ha, and ha," Darren chanted, still splashing Scott. "Shut up now. Shut up, shut up." *Splash. Splash.* "Who the heck is 'Satan,' then?"

"Satan," Scott said, settling himself on the lip of the Jacuzzi, "is not the name of a single being."

"I got it! I got it!" Nick had chimed in again, encouraged by his recent success. "There's more than one devil!"

"Sure, okay." Scott nodded, shutting his eyes. "That's very close, but not quite what I'm talking about."

"You shut up too." Darren splashed Nick, who splashed him back.

"Satan is a Hebrew word that translates roughly to 'adversary.' It comes from Shatan, which is 'accuser,' but I don't want to get too mired in etymology."

"Eddie-who?"

"Basically, anyone who stands in the way of another's will is his adversary, and therefore Satan."

"So, the Beast *is* Satan, then, right? What?" Darren had looked really puzzled.

"All right, I suppose in a very general sense, that's true." Scott had nodded. "But 'Satan' isn't his *name*, and the Beast was certainly not the entity that challenged God in the story of Job."

"Who was it?"

"I don't have a clue." Scott shrugged. "But it wasn't the first of the Fallen. It wasn't the Beast."

"*Any* adversary is a Satan?"

"Not *a* Satan, but Satan, yes. It's not a proper name, but something one would call someone who stood in their way. King Solomon had quite a bit of trouble from Hadad and Rezon, and referred to both of them as 'Satan.' Even angels have been called Satan."

"Oh, my gosh." Darren shook his head. "Angels that haven't fallen? That's fucked up."

"No!" Scott laughed again. "Remember, Satan just means 'adversary,' so it doesn't necessarily carry an implication of evil with it every time it's used. Well, at least that used to be the case."

"People just went around calling other people 'Satan' if they messed with them?"

"Sure."

"Oh, okay." Darren had given Nick another funny look. Nick splashed him.

"Darren," Scott said, "God sent an angel to stop Balaam from going somewhere that He'd told him specifically not to go. The angel He sent to block Balaam's path was called 'Satan' because he stood in Balaam's way, not because he was evil. Certainly not because he was evil, because it was God himself who'd sent him to do it."

"Who's Balaam?"

"A prophet." Scott took a sip of beer. "He's dead. You wouldn't know him."

"You're such a comedian," Darren said sarcastically. Though, Nick had been laughing his head off.

"Jesus even called Peter 'Satan,' " Scott had said. "When Peter suggested to Jesus that he should try to avoid being killed by the Romans, then Peter became an adversary to God's plan. 'Get thee behind me, Satan.' That's in Matthew's gospel. He was talking to Saint Peter when he said that."

"All right." Darren nodded. "So 'Satan,' doesn't refer to the Beast, like it's his name, or anything."

"Weeell…" Scott smiled. "In a way it does, but see, that idea is counterproductive to what we've been discussing—"

"I'm about to drown you." Darren had crossed his arms and smiled. "You know that don't you? You don't have to hold my hand and read my mind to figure that one out, right?"

They'd sat in the water until they were human prunes and Scott tried to explain all he could. He said that after the Beast found himself outside of Heaven, and realizing what the simple act of making a choice had done to his very form, the first fallen angel became consumed with anger. From that moment, his overwhelming purpose was to reveal the possibility and power of choice to the other angels. He would reveal the notion of choosing whether or not to serve God to the very creatures created for just that purpose. Simply understanding the possibility would be enough to transform the essence of the Heavenly host. Throughout the spheres, from angel to seraph, grasping the concept produced a fall. In this way, the Beast would raise his army. On earth, he formed his legions of terrestrial demons. Out of Heaven, though, came his real power, a legion of the Fallen.

Not to forget, through the Beast, the notion to choose not to serve God would also be presented to humans as well.

"After all," Scott had said, sipping his Corona, "it wasn't just a piece of fruit that made the downfall of Adam and Eve possible for them. It was choice."

So it came to pass that what had first happened to the Beast eventually happened to all of the angels who contemplated, with his help, the notion of choosing their own paths. They were the angels, changed by choice and consequently ousted from Heaven, the immortal terrestrial entities would eventually come to call 'the Fallen.'

"At first he thought they could help him," Scott had said. "At first the Beast instigated their choosing, simply by revealing the possibility to them. He did it believing they'd understand and then join him. He was sure they'd understand and then share his anger and resentment. But a good deal of the time, the Fallen ended up angry and vindictive, not toward God, but toward the Beast for having pulled them into such a hopeless and futile position. They rallied openly against him. So, one by one, the Beast has hunted and destroyed us. Most of us, anyway."

"How could he destroy all of you guys?" Darren had asked, his testosterone showing a little. "I mean, can't all of you gang up on him?"

The idea had provoked Darren visibly, which Nick thought was actually kind of sexy.

"Yes." Scott nodded. "Those of the Fallen still standing against the ambitions of the Beast could band together to fight him. It would be a noble effort, but undoubtedly futile. The word 'great' hardly touches the degree of power at the command of the Beast."

"So, he's one big, bad, motherf—"

"Yes, yes, yes, blah, blah, blah." Scott rolled his eyes, finished his beer, and waved Darren off with his hand, who grinned and splashed him. "Certainly, yes, a final, massive battle against the Beast would be very righteous and spectacular. Unfortunately, it's just not an action that would really affect him. It's been tried, though."

"You're kidding!" Darren blinked. "What happened?"

"A seraph by the name of Anat fell from grace about a thousand years after my own fall. She didn't last long, even though she was very powerful. She realized her mistake right away and set to work learning to use her new resources to bring about the destruction of the Beast."

"New resources?" Nick said.

"Magic," Scott had answered. "In falling from grace, none of us lost very much of our instinctual understanding of the functions of the universe, its various energies, and how to manipulate them. That's what mortals eventually called 'magic.' The Beast himself taught his army of terrestrial demons. He taught his fallen angels and his earthly demons both how to use the correct language along with a mortal voice to cast the most powerful spells."

"Mortal voices?"

"Mm hm. The major spells require humans to chant them. That's where the relationship between witches and familiars comes from. The relationship would eventually be called 'witchcraft.'

"What Anat did after she fell was to develop ten spells that would specifically hinder the power of a demon. Those spells could be used by another demon, but each of them required the help of a human. It's all really intense magic.

"Of course, learning this, the Beast immediately proclaimed that just so much as having knowledge of The Spells of Anat would mark a demon for destruction. It didn't take long, maybe a year or two, and the Beast had hunted Anat down, and sent her into oblivion.

"She was barely on the earth for a decade. Her spells were written down, but the book was lost.

"Less than five centuries after her destruction, The Spells of Anat were discovered by a modest member of the Fallen, an archangel by the name of Linos. Having your very same idea, Darren, Linos took The Spells of Anat and called others of the Fallen to him, rallying them into a force against the Beast. The little band was doomed, though. There were only ten of them when the Beast discovered the plot. Each member of Linos's group had been attempting to memorize all ten of The Spells of Anat, but they'd only had time to commit a single spell to memory, although different ones for each, before the Beast found them. The battle was terrible but brief. Five escaped. Five went to oblivion, along with the spells they'd memorized, now lost forever. The book, you see, containing The Spells of Anat, was also discovered by the Beast that day, and reduced to cinders with a single grunt from his snout."

Nick and Darren learned a great deal in the past few months—no small amount of which while in the Jacuzzi. Scott also told them about his personal history. It was the Cliff Notes version, of course; four thousand years is a heck of a lot of time.

How Scott originally came into being as an angel was a complete mystery. While in the service of God, he'd never considered such a question. After he fell, access to any dependable answer was utterly beyond him.

Scott didn't know the exact year, in mortal terms, that he fell from grace. However, Abraham had already passed God's baffling test of faith, but Moses was yet to be born.

When Scott went into detail about a particular experience, it was upon reaching a time in his existence that he considered his darkest. He happened to be in Europe in the Middle Ages, at a time when society had become, to say the least, disheartening. To top it off, the fourteenth century was devastated by an event set in motion by Scott himself.

Believing he was bringing about an end to a holy war, Scott had used an aspect of his power with which he'd been, to date, completely unfamiliar. He'd been aware that his abilities held the potential, but he'd never attempted it: he caused an illness.

The idea of 'sorcery' or 'witchcraft' to contemporary ears, especially English speaking ones, has associations far closer to the fictions of J. R. R. Tolkien or J. K. Rowling. The reality of it, the very essential basis for its legend, though, was far less charming. During the turmoil preceding the Age of Enlightenment, a favorite tactic of demons was to offer humans access to certain supernatural secrets. One of these secrets was how to summon and direct the power of other demons, even some of the oldest and most powerful. All one needed was the demon's name. *The* name. Its big, momma whoop-ass name. Such was the very basis of true sorcery.

Somewhere along the line, Scott's true name had, evidently, been discovered. The indignity of being subjected to such a thing was made far worse by the fact that the individual who found himself in possession of this knowledge also happened to be privy to a couple of additional magical secrets as well. He'd been quite an accomplished sorcerer indeed. Specifically, he'd been able to manipulate Scott's very perception of reality. The sorcerer knew a spell that was capable, for a time, of creating a false perspective in the mind of its victim, a perspective that could essentially shape the very worldview of anyone, even that of a demon. Scott explained that it was similar to hypnosis, although much, much more powerful. Someone under the influence of such a spell was considered to be 'enthralled.' The victim retained the fundamentals of their character, but key beliefs could be directed by the witch or sorcerer; trust became suspicion, tolerance became cynicism, indifference became rage.

Scott had been the strong-arm for the sorcerer's will and, believing he was acting in the name of righteousness, brought forth a sickness upon the world. The infection, which Scott had summoned, exploded completely out of control and spread ruin far beyond even the most misguided intentions of the sorcerer himself. Scott, at the direction of a zealous medieval sorcerer, had used his divine powers to cause a disease that would eventually be called The Bubonic Plague; The Black Death.

Even as the illness swept across the known world, carried by vermin, Scott had remained within the grasp of the sorcerer's ill-gotten magic. By the time Scott realized what he'd done, the plague was well beyond his ability to stop.

Had Scott known how to destroy himself, he'd have done so. After the plague, even the Beast himself hesitated to obliterate a potential powerhouse like Scott; he might be of use.

Scott became desperate. The best action at hand had been to merely allow himself to phase out into nothingness, which wasn't really a solution at all, since he could be called back into being. Nevertheless, exhausted and miserable, he'd cast himself into the void, praying as he went, asking God to grant him this last request: that he be allowed to remain in limbo for the rest of time.

Apparently, God hadn't thought that was best. Scott's fears of being called back by anyone with the correct knowledge were well founded. Still, upon being summoned again into the mortal world, an unexpected opportunity had presented itself and Scott had taken it. Without hesitation.

Scott had been offered a much better place to hide. He'd been shown a place where he'd be out of the reach of mortals and immortals alike; they could call his true name until their tongues fell out and he could not be summoned back.

That refuge, though, proved to be much more fragile than he'd hoped. After an exile both torturous and somehow reviving, his sanctuary had been broken. Quite recently, as a matter of fact.

Exactly how or why he'd been brought back into the world was, until much more recently, as nebulous as Scott's initial creation. He'd eventually discovered the specifics by accident, after a chance meeting with someone who knew the details. Specifically, after that person had unknowingly shaken Scott's hand.

The experience of his release, at first, was like waking from a very deep sleep and any actual consciousness had remained, for a time, a bit elusive. He didn't know the exact date and neither did his unknowing resource. The year, however, was 1969.

Scott had gone first to Greece, having encountered a scholar who was surprisingly familiar with ancient history. The man had been a comfort and a friend. How many hours the two of them spent talking alone about the evolution of human history, Scott couldn't say. To him, the time was immeasurable and, as with all such memories, should remain so.

The man had also surprised Scott with his knowledge of Scott's demonic nature—once that tiny, little detail was inadvertently revealed—yet he'd somehow been able to consider Scott without the usual heavy burden of conditioned associations. He had his share— all humans do—yet remained remarkably unaffected by them. Scott's friend shed academic and theological misconceptions with no more effort than it took him to crumple a flyer left on his windshield.

In a way, Scott had been enthralled all over again. They would sit sipping tea—or wine, depending upon the hour—and tirelessly analyze the most obscure scraps of history. Those were days and hours of almost hedonistic indulgence. Of course, Scott was an incredible academic resource, having himself personally witnessed a significant amount of mortal history. Still, even the vast stretch of his ancient experiences had, in their quiet, private study, become but a single petal within an entire bouquet of dazzling color, which was the whole of world history. Scott's experiences, after all, took place like everyone else's: at a specific time and in a specific place. Meanwhile, the vast majority of the events of the global community developed without his witnessing them.

Eventually, after acquiring significant international renown—with not just a little assistance from Scott—a professional move from Greece to the United States became more and more attractive. Scott therefore accompanied the now world-famous historian to New York City. He stayed with him there, enjoying every moment and feeling wholly unworthy. Scott remained with the historian until his death.

On that subject, however, Scott could say no more. Not that there wasn't more to say, there certainly was, and it was important Nick and Darren heard it all. Scott couldn't, though. Each time he tried, his lower lip covered his upper, his brow furrowed, his head shook back and forth in a quick and subtle denial, and his eyes welled with tears that would stream into unremitting trickles.

Scott, despite being an immortal entity of formidable power, would become physically unable to speak. At such times, Nick would kiss him on the forehead, wipe his face with his fingers, kiss him again, even a third time, and say, "Tomorrow then. Tell us tomorrow."

Scott would nod, convinced he could finish his task the next day. After four millennia of every extreme of joy and pain, he just needed one more day and he'd be able to speak about this most recent agony. One more day, and he could tell Nick what he needed to know.

Scott would cry silently, pressing his face to Nick's. Nick would run his fingers through Scott's hair, and hold him until his face was dry.

Their days and nights, Nick, Darren, and Scott's, were ornamented with divine enlightenments and the perks and pleasures of loving and living freely.

Nick's agent called in early September and the result had been an ad campaign for a rising European designer. The magazine spread was so effective it was expanded, running internationally and eventually resulting in a series of billboards, one of which prominently donned the intersection of Sunset Boulevard and Crescent Heights. That alone almost catapulted Nick into near supermodel status. It didn't, however, because Nick just didn't feel like traveling. "I'm completely available," he'd say to his agent, "as long as the work is within forty miles of Los Angeles." Still, the calls kept coming and coming. Eventually, Nick's agent developed a nervous disorder that ultimately required hospitalization. Nick was beside himself with guilt until he discovered that such conditions, within that particular vocation, were devastatingly common.

Nick's contract with the agency would be up for renewal in March. Nick was seriously considering allowing it to expire. Although the job had turned out to be much more successful, not to mention lucrative, than anyone ever expected, it also reminded Nick of all the aspects of his industry that seriously pissed him off.

Darren had produced two major circuit events, one of which being his long-awaited date at the club. Darren worked ceaseless hours promoting his parties. When he had an opportunity to spend an evening with Nick at the condo, he usually fell asleep in Nick's lap before the ten o'clock news. Nick would have complained, but Darren was so intoxicatingly happy that saying anything would have been unthinkable.

While they were working, while they were spellbound within the activities they'd chosen, Darren and Nick skipped the weekend parties. Missy and Gina were neglected. Still, Nick and Darren knew the girls would forgive them. Even after being denied and disused, they would undoubtedly be even happier to hang out with them whenever the boys got around to it; absence makes the heart grow fonder, you know. Missy and Gina would patiently wait to party with the guys as soon as the business of living allowed.

The business of living, however, included Missy and her crew less and less and less. Scott, after all, had been very clear with both Nick and Darren; there were far more important considerations at hand.

Scott was assiduous with Nick and Darren's education. He wasn't able to answer every question, although he did his darnedest.

"Just keep in mind," he'd said, "faith and understanding will manifest in increments."

"What does that mean?" Nick asked.

"It means keep your eyes open." Scott had nodded gravely. "Everything you've learned, everything you've seen and experienced, especially you, Nick, will affect the way you perceive the world. You're going to notice things that before were invisible to you. You'll see things, hear things, smell things, touch things, that until you were made aware of their existence through me, you were completely unable to see, hear, smell, or touch."

Scott had shown them all he could with what materials were available. Even in what he called "terribly flawed" contemporary English translations of the Bible, the theme was repeated over and over: one could choose to love one's neighbor, and therefore God, or one could choose another path, and perish. It was the brazen theme in almost every story told to massive numbers of whole generations over countless centuries.

Scott made a noble effort to explain the effect of thousands of years of semantics, tradition, and simple human sensibilities on the many, many renderings and versions of scripture, but even that most human process of developing communication could take years to fully appreciate.

"It's a shame," he had said on a local outing quite recently. They'd been loitering in the isles of A Different Light Bookstore on Santa Monica Boulevard on a clear November evening, thumbing through the pages of works on theology, spirituality, religious history, and social philosophy — revisiting their conversation was pretty much automatic whenever the three of them were alone. "It's a shame so many people are so afraid of the idea that the word of God might not be so strictly black and white, that they might have to work a little bit to find it."

"Or," Darren had said, "that they might not be able to exclude whoever they want from their idea of loving their neighbor."

"That too, yes. But Darren, my love..." Scott had given him a reproachful glance.

"What?"

"Whether or not your observation is accurate, keep in mind that it doesn't allow *you* to make any exclusions in that regard either."

The picture Scott painted, the gaps he filled, the misconceptions he corrected, certainly brought with it more than a little hope. Nick got the sense of some possible achievement, some hidden illumination, just waiting to be found. At the same time, it chilled him to remember that Scott's original transgression against the Beast had been enlightening a human soul.

There were still a thousand questions Nick wanted to ask, a thousand possibilities were grappling with a thousand assumptions, but now was the time to put them away. He wanted to settle his mind and his fears and enjoy the night and the company.

"Hey, are you awake?" Darren looked at him from across the limo, grinning, raising his eyebrows like he was Groucho Marx. "Think we should drop?"

Nick grinned back. "That's the way, baby."

The limousine was only a few yards from where Darren would allow them to emerge from it. He pulled his little black plastic box from its hiding place in the interior of the car. Inside it, he kept all the necessary drug paraphernalia: a small mirror and razor blade, two full bullets of coke, a dosing vile for GHB, and the little plastic baggies filled with any surpluses—except the G, of course, which was in a plastic container hidden between the liquor bottles in the tiny bar. Since moving to the beach, their indulgences with these substances had certainly become less frequent. Tonight, though, had been marked on the calendar for months, its indulgences planned meticulously. Tonight, each of them knew, would be special.

Nick was only going to take one hit of ecstasy. Missy was making something of a reconciliation with his body chemistry. Perhaps his alterations of perception over the past several weeks had something to do with it. Perhaps his tolerance had abated as a result of his overall decrease in use. Perhaps the local chemists were using a new and improved formula. Who knew? Who gave a rat's ass?

The music coming from the house was audible from inside the car, but just barely. There was an incredible din from the throng at the house, inside and out. Whoever owned this place must have had a very, very good relationship with their neighbors.

Although there'd been no incidents like the one on that particular Saturday night back in August, when Nick was held hostage by a smelly, overgrown imp in the back streets of Hollywood, he'd been shaken by the experience, more so than he'd admit. Nick's behavior was noticeably affected. He never shook anyone's hand anymore, or touched the shoulder of a gabbing club patron to let them know he was squeezing past. Nick watched every move he made and didn't care what people thought of it. Nick wouldn't touch anyone he didn't know intimately. No more hugs for casual acquaintances; no more laying his hand gently on someone's arm as he leaned closer to hear them in a noisy crowd; no more throwing a leg or an arm over any non-established members of their social group while they lounged on the loveseat in the VIP room, tangled in a jovial human mesh, cooling off and catching their breath until they heard a song that would send them all back down to the dance floor. It was a shame, really. Human contact was, Nick quickly discovered, very important. His retreat from even the most informal touch made him feel more than a little isolated.

Darren and Scott certainly did their best to make Nick's social life easier. They kept people away from him as if they were actual bodyguards and Nick was Britney Spears at a frat party.

Even though the car had stopped, the driver was waiting for Darren to buzz him before he got out to open their door. Darren took his time handing Nick and Scott their pills. They shared a bottle of water and took care of business. After which, Darren hid a bullet of coke and an eyedropper filled with G on his person in their usual strategic places. Once all the supplies were secured, he buzzed for the guy in the cab to come around and open the door.

Darren got out first, followed by Nick, who liked to watch the crowd when they saw Scott step out. Scott really was such a striking, masculine image that even the more seasoned observers of beauty, who, over the years, had developed the intricacies of subtlety and discretion into an art, couldn't help but allow a conspicuous slip of restraint. Nick pitied the poor chumps with less experience, who just outright stared in a manner well beyond a mere slip of discretion. Those sad souls had their hands full just trying to remain conscious.

Regardless of age or gender, status or experience, everyone noticed Scott. He was simply enthralling.

†

"I've been expecting you," she said, letting go of his hand.

"You have?" Michael raised his eyebrows. He'd never seen this girl before in his life. If he had, he was sure he would have remembered her. She was incredibly beautiful with her long and glamorous stream of dark brown hair, her green eyes and flawless skin.

"Oh, yes." The alluring young woman smiled, nodding.

"Oh. Um—"

"Now, you understand that this party is very private and I know you don't have an invitation. So, what you'll need to do is just go inside, turn right down the first hall, and wait for me for just a moment near the room at the far end. I'll be right in."

Michael had no idea for whom this woman mistook him, but he intended to take advantage of his incredible luck. With an expression he prayed was one of ordinary confidence and not absolute surprise, he nodded at her and went up the cement steps and into the house.

†

Robert trekked up Nichols Canyon Road from where he'd parked on Hollywood Boulevard. He may as well have walked from the stupid hotel; he'd had to park halfway to Beverly Hills. Robert grunted and shook his head. This town was incomprehensible.

It felt good to be walking, though. Driving up and down the street, passing the billowing crowd in front of the party's address several times, just trying to find a place to put the Mercedes, had seriously irritated Robert. He didn't want to turn off the street and park on another residential lane that might have had even less lighting. Eventually, he opted for a spot on the boulevard and hoped the high visibility would help protect the car.

The Mercedes was insured, of course. He knew if it was stolen or vandalized it wouldn't really affect him or what he was doing. Still, the simple idea of being victimized was unacceptable. Becoming a statistic of Los Angeles was not an attractive idea. It was enough he had to register at the hotel. Worse that he had to give his name and vital information when he leased the car. All that was bad enough. Robert didn't want to give the city any more. He didn't want to leave any mark on this place, any trace he'd ever been here at all. He would provide no more information about himself than was absolutely necessary. He wanted to completely avoid becoming enmeshed with the city's sub-dynamic current, even if it was as a victim, even if he had nothing to do with creating it. No, filling out a police report, answering someone else's questions, that wasn't going to happen. Robert was only passing through, just doing his job and then getting out. He wasn't going to let the city affect him.

He felt inside his jacket pocket for his invitation, and then his right pants pocket for his keys, just to make sure he hadn't locked them in the car—he'd never done that in his life, but it couldn't hurt to make an effort to be aware of everything. He reached up and touched the stiffness in his hair; Blair had styled it earlier. Robert wasn't used to wearing even as much as a little hairspray, much less the quart of gel Blair had happily squished onto Robert's head.

He thought the hair style looked good, though. Blair had told Robert he looked very Russell Crowe-ish.

Wearing a casual suit, in conjunction with his stylish do and carefully adopted deportment, Robert was sure he would again be able to easily pull off the 'industry executive' charade, and therefore avoid any unwanted scrutiny.

A dark blue Volkswagen Jetta sped past him toward the party for the third time. It was filled with young men who appeared to have twice as much gel in their own hair. They were obviously looking for a place to park. Robert shook his head and smiled. Good luck.

He was close enough to the house to hear the chatter and the music coming from inside. The blue Jetta that had just passed him was stopped momentarily behind a long black limousine. The Jetta was waiting for some southbound traffic to go by before it could go around the long car and head back up into the hills, continuing its parking space quest.

The door to the limo was standing open. Robert was just close enough to see the three men that got out. It was some of the same little group he'd seen several times at the club. And with them, the raven-haired youth from Greece.

Robert stopped walking. He would wait until the men went into the party and then follow at a discrete distance. Things had just gotten very interesting.

Robert absently touched the object hidden in the low inside pocket of his blazer. The artifact, lying on its side at the bottom of the lining, shouldn't be noticeable at all if he kept the jacket unbuttoned.

Then, out of habit, Robert craned his neck, scanning the sky for flying lions.

†

Private parties weren't really Eddie's thing. He understood the allure of the exclusivity and all the hype and all that, but to him it was a little dull.

Looking around, he could tell that Karen and Laura had decided on the usual two-pronged Hollywood approach regarding the invitations: Step one: personally offer invitations to the physically-elite, motivating their attendance by promising a night of schmoozing with the industry-elite. Step two: call the industry-elite and let them know the party would be filled with the physically-elite. Classic.

Someone once told Eddie that, when casting the film *The African Queen*, Humphrey Bogart was told that Katharine Hepburn had already agreed to do the project, and Hepburn was told that Bogart had already agreed. Eddie supposed those sorts of manipulative maneuverings were only considered sleazy if they didn't work. Otherwise, they were simply clever and creative.

The two-pronged Hollywood approach had obviously worked here; there were plenty of both Hollywood social castes. That was very important at an event like this; there had to be balance. The industry-elites didn't particularly enjoy speaking to each other, much less *looking* at each other. To maintain a pleasant, festive atmosphere, it was imperative to have plenty of highly distracting physically-elites roaming around in very, very tight shirts.

The danger was that, if they weren't sufficiently distracted, some of the smarmy, pompous industry-elites just might gaze right at another smarmy, pompous industry-elite and have an epiphany; they just might recognize *themselves* staring right back. Such profound personal enlightenments could potentially cripple the entire Hollywood machine. You'd have smarmy, pompous industry-elites recognizing themselves in each other and, consequently, running all over town committing suicide.

For some reason, no one ever seemed to worry about the physically-elites looking around and noticing anything. Hm.

Here and there throughout the room Eddie observed several tiny clumps of players standing around in teams, ogling the eye-candy. Sandy Gallin was never far from Bill Samath, and David Geffen always had a yes-man or two nearby. There were also quite a few major celebrities roaming around, but what Eddie found entertaining was watching the up-n-comers attempt to court all of the money and power in the room.

Eddie grew up with money and was very used to it. He rolled his eyes and set down his now-empty glass of soda. He'd grown up around more money than he would ever admit to anyone, and it most definitely did not impress him. Let the actor guys fall all over themselves.

It was nice to live at the beach, in the condo Scott bought for him — certainly since Eddie might soon be cut off financially by his father.

Mostly, Eddie enjoyed being so close to the guys and the nearly giddy spontaneity it added to their lives. The extravagance of the gifts from Scott, however, didn't touch him in the same way as he could tell it touched the other guys. Eddie had a much better understanding of the manner in which people with a lot of money thought about their wealth. The gifts actually sent up more of a red flag than they produced gratitude. Still, Eddie couldn't quite place Scott with either the industry-elite or the physically-elite, even though he unquestionably rocked the whole fucking boat in both categories.

The real shocker, the gesture that had knocked Eddie right off his moorings, was what Scott said to him the day he gave him the condo keys. Eddie still hadn't told anyone else about it. Not even Theo.

"I want you to feel comfortable here," Scott had said as they opened the door and walked inside for the third time — it was the first time since the decorating was completed, though. "I want you to absolutely know that you don't owe me a thing for this."

Eddie had started to speak but Scott silenced him.

"Just listen," he'd said. "I don't expect you to completely take my word for it. I'd bet such things hold very, very little water with you. So, instead, I want to give you this."

Scott had handed Eddie yet another key.

"This opens a safety deposit box," Scott explained. "Inside it is a small book containing the account numbers and contact information for four or five equity accounts managed in the European and Asian markets. Together they're worth somewhere in the neighborhood of nineteen million dollars."

Eddie had suddenly felt as though his face was made of cement.

"I know this may seem a bit cheesy..." Scott squinted. "...and it might just be an idiotic attempt to smother a fire with turpentine, but it's the only way I could think of to put my money where my mouth is, so to speak.

"If at any time, any time at all in the future, you even so much as slightly feel that I've implied you owe me anything more substantial than a smile and a nod for buying this place for you, I want you to take this key, claim the money, and do whatever you want with it. Take Theo, take Nick and Darren, and go anywhere. Take yourself and them far, far away. Don't even say good-bye. I'm sure the value of the accounts will increase, though I can't say to what degree, but this is my collateral for your confidence. This is the balance-weight I'm hoping will put your suspicions at ease and let you simply enjoy your home. Because, that's what this is now. It's your home. You're struggling to figure me out, I know. Just the same, I want to take every step I can think of to ensure you enjoy all of this."

Eddie hadn't known what to say. What could he have said? The answer never came to him.

He'd made some calls, gone through the Internet a bit, done the math, and checked on the accounts, which turned out not to be worth nineteen million dollars. They were worth twenty-one million. What the heck did all this mean?

Here's a condo and a ton of expensive furniture for you with no strings attached. Oh, but just so you feel comfortable that there are no strings attached, here's twenty-one million dollars as insurance, with no strings attached.

It wasn't until he was seventeen that Eddie was able to realize all the trimmings of his life, all the luxuries and entitlements his parents made available to him, weren't anywhere near free. In fact, they were miles and miles and miles away from free.

He'd realized that, in return for all the clothes, all the sports cars, all the trips to Aspen and Palm Springs and Fort Lauderdale and Maui, the bedroom with the massive entertainment center and computer equipment updated every other month, and the unending flow of simple, mindless cash, Eddie was expected to adhere to a way of life that was completely disconnected from his own sensibilities. He was expected to follow the narrowest path, to avoid all personal desires, and turn every aspect of his character toward the very specific goals outlined for him by his family.

He'd tried at first; he liked his cars and his home and all the money. He liked all the popular kids and all the parties and all the unrestricted carousing. At first, he liked it all very much. How fucking stupid, of course he liked it. That such things weren't a fundamental necessity of life had never even come close to occurring to him. However, the novelty eventually began to wear off. Just a little at first, but that was all it took.

When Eddie sat with his father one day, during the summer after his junior year in high school, when they reviewed the college courses Eddie was thinking about taking, and his dad had changed each and every one of them, Eddie began to realize his life was not his own. He started to see that maybe everything his parents had ever provided for him, from his first pacifier to his first car—a blue convertible Camaro—came with some very heavy strings attached.

Eddie had finished high school and went on to college. But he'd taken the courses he originally wanted. His father threw a horrible fit and threatened to take away Eddie's car. So, Eddie simply gave back the Camaro. That was one account Eddie no longer had to settle.

As for the pacifier, his dad was just going to have to send him an invoice.

Each year at school it was something else. His father invoked every threat he could, even including expulsion from the family altogether, but Eddie hadn't budged. He'd lost his allowance, his spring and winter trips, his credit cards, and his apartment. The next thing on the chopping block was his tuition and then his inheritance.

Looking around, watching the crowd at Karen's party, recognizing all the smarmy, pompous industry-elites as they ogled all the pathetic, transparent physically-elites, who were nudging each other around trying to get close to the smarmy, pompous industry-elites, Eddie knew he'd made the right decision. He'd been increasingly panicked over how he would handle things when his dad stopped paying his tuition, but giving in would never be an option. No one owned him, and no one was *going* to own him. Not ever.

So, here's twenty-one million dollars, just to prove I don't own you.

Eddie shuddered.

"You look a little glum." Karen came up from behind, handing him another soda.

"I'm cool." Eddie smiled, taking the drink.

"Where's Theo?"

"He's still out on the patio, I think."

Karen nodded. "How many admirers?"

"Four or five." Eddie laughed.

"Has he gotten to the 'Madonna at the Hard Rock Café' story yet?"

"Probably.   I think he should just be finishing the 'Leonardo DiCaprio at Gold's Gym' story."

"Has he done any coke?"

"Hello?"

Karen nodded again. "So, he'll be going into the 'Patti LeBelle at Pavilions' story, and then the 'Jordan Knight at IHOP' story, of course."

"Of course."

"I'd say you have at least forty-five minutes."

"At the very least."

"Why not mingle?"

Eddie snorted a laugh.

Karen frowned. "Sweet cheeks, what's going on?"

Eddie looked down at his new soda and bit his lower lip. "Karen," he started, "what's Scott's last name?"

"Ooh." Karen raised her eyebrows, gazed at the ceiling. "Um... okay, I know this one."

"I don't think you do."

"Oh, sure I do. It's um, it's..."

"Well, *I* don't know what it is, at least."

"Wow." Karen shook her head. "Some fabulous couple of friends we are."

"He's given us everything."

"I know, I know," she nodded. "You'd think we'd at least know his last name."

"So..." Eddie sighed. "What do we do now?"

"Well, I suppose we could ask Nick or Darren what his last name is—"

"No, no!" Eddie laughed. "I mean, now that we have everything. What do we do?"

Karen just looked at him, then pouted and raised her eyebrows.

"Because," Eddie said, bringing the glass of soda to his lips, "I sure as shit don't know."

†

"I think you might have me confused with someone else," Michael said.

"Well, young man," she said, closing the door behind her, "in just a moment you're going to wish that was the case."

Michael cocked his head in confusion. Why had she called him 'young?' She couldn't be any older than twenty-five.

"I don't follow you," he said.

"Ah." The dark-haired beauty smiled at him, nodded. "You will, Michael. You will."

†

Nick guessed the party would be swarming with A-list club-people. He was correct, and then some. The place was swarming with the triple A's, and that don't mean the fuckin' auto club, baby.

It might have been silly and irrational, but somehow it felt satisfying and a little safer to be in the pseudo-familiar crowd and yet outside the club itself. The shindigs at Scott's house never reached even a fraction of this pulsing mass. If this was only a promo-party, then on New Years Eve, they were going to need a much bigger club. Nick wondered if maybe they should move Los Angeles's biggest party to Las Vegas.

Nick had been back to the club several times since the incident with the imp/gremlin/smelly little fairy. Still, at first, it took Scott and Darren quite a while to talk Nick into it. He didn't want to ever go back. Even after they convinced him, Nick almost had to be sedated before he could make it through the front doors.

After having no problems on his first evening back, and not encountering anything scarier than a very heavy Asian drag queen named Empress Ambient, it got easier and easier to allow himself to enjoy the club again, more and more, a little each time. Scott thought it was important that they took back the club for themselves. He was relatively confident there wasn't another entity of any significant power in the area who could keep them from having a normal — although cautious, let's not be stupid — social life.

Scott never fully explained what he'd done to the imp. Nick had seen Gillulim run into the night and Marbas flying after him, but nothing more.

When questioned, Scott had simply answered, "He's no longer a threat."

"You killed him, or whatever?" Nick whispered.

"No, that's not my way." Scott had leveled his eyes at Nick and shaken his head slowly. "You need to trust me, Nick. Although I didn't destroy him, Gillulim won't ever be a threat to either of us."

Once or twice, though, despite the return of some relative comfort and security for him at the club, Nick thought he'd smelled something funny. It wasn't exactly the odor he'd experienced so intimately—gag!—while in the clutches of the putrid little gray demon, but it was similar. Nick never caught the odor for more than a second or two. But on a couple occasions the smell seemed to be wafting around Karen somehow. Although certainly not all the time—a massive relief, hello, praise the Saints in Heaven, praise, praise, sing halleluiah!

Nevertheless, Nick had noticed it.

Looking at Scott during those moments, Nick had never seen so much as a twitch of concern, not for an instant. Scott never appeared to detect anything more dangerous than Ponytail Guy's rancid cologne. So, the funny smell must have been Nick's imagination after all.

This change of venue, even with the ensemble of regular A-listers, went a long way toward allowing Nick to relax. Darren and Scott were right next to him, and he could just feel Missy gathering herself up and getting ready to make a lovely and grand entrance.

Nick smiled.

†

Darren let go of Nick's hand. He maneuvered himself so that, as they stepped into the entrance hall, he was between Nick and the encroaching multitude. Scott, Nick, and Darren smiled in near comic unison at the growing number of familiar faces. They exchanged the normal pleasantries with the horde of club regulars they all knew intimately: *hug, hug, smooch, smooch, smile, smile,* "You look great!," *grin, hug, wink,* "Cool pants, babe!," *hug, smooch, hug, hug, kiss, kiss, giggle, chuckle,* "Did you get your hair cut?," *laugh, smile, smile, kiss, smooch, giggle, giggle, hug, touch, touch, pat, pat, smile, smile,* blah, blah, blah, yada, yada, yada, et cetera, et cetera, and so on, and so on.

Once the entrance hall had been successfully navigated, Darren let out a breath of relief and took Nick by the hand again. My god, those queens could be annoying. Darren wondered for a moment how funny it would be if everyone was only going through those grotesquely girly-affectionate greeting rituals because they thought it was what everyone *else* expected.

Scott followed as they stepped into the master living room. The house was huge and gorgeous. It had three stories and a basement; full tennis court; a hot tub the size of a pool, bubbling with water, though empty of people, at the moment; a pool the size of Lake Ellsinore—complete with floating candle decorations that someone had obviously stolen from an episode of *The Love Boat*—*gag, gag, barf*; a library the size of, well... of a library; and a stuffed moose head, mounted and hanging in the main living room, which looked real enough, which couldn't actually be the case, because it would have just been, in the words of one guy who was, let's call it, 'very in touch with his feminine side,' "So tacky, oh goodness Becky, yes!,"—clutch the pearls, *tsk, tsk, grimace, grimace.*

The house belonged to "a local acquaintance of Lauren Isseroff," and no one seemed to know any more than that. Fair enough.

Although Darren was still riding high from his successful event in November, looking around this party, he couldn't help but notice the little green-eyed monster sitting on his shoulder, suggesting something was terribly wrong. How the hell did Laura Shah-na-what's-her-fuck manage all of this?

The house was so filled with stars it looked like a Malibu block party. The AAA-list element made itself immediately apparent. He wasn't certain at first, but after a moment or two of disbelief, Darren realized that one of the guys on the couch near the patio door was motherfucking Lance Bass.

And, good-gravy-on-a-biscuit, it sure-as-shit didn't end with him.

Laura Shah must be the world's primo party-promoting goddess. If Darren got through the evening without sneering at the little whore, much less publicly tripping her, he'd consider himself worthy of sainthood.

He took a deep breath, closed his eyes, and slowly exhaled. He did not at all like how he was feeling at the moment or the brazenly shallow thoughts running amuck between his ears. Missy had not yet made her appearance, and he was more than a little suspicious that his irritation had much more to do with his customary anxiety over her arrival than just some professional jealousy.

Darren grunted, turned to look at Nick, who cocked his head and threw that little you-didn't-forget-how-fucking-cute-I-am-did-you? smile at him. Darren couldn't help but grin. Instantly, life was good again. Amazing how that worked.

The air was heavy and stimulating. Incredibly rousing dance music threaded through the crowd. Karen had mentioned that she'd actually booked Brian Ikon to spin. The famous DJ's equipment was hooked up to a good number of extra speakers brought to the house. Darren made a note to remember to get Karen to take them up to see him. He and Nick already met Brian Ikon a couple times, but Scott would like that.

Darren looked around for Eddie and Theo but didn't see them. Karen wasn't in sight either, which was weird, because she'd told him that if she wasn't at the door, then Laura would be, and Laura would tell them where to find her.

Laura hadn't been outside, though. The entrance doors were only guarded by Bobby and one other Security Guy who Darren didn't recognize.

It wasn't that big a deal. Darren had just been hoping to get into the V-VIP room right away. Not that there was any shame in hanging out in the common areas apparently; if Lance Frickin' Bass was doing it, then whoa-nelly-momma, they could sure-as-shit do it.

Darren wasn't as nervous anymore while in a crowd with Nick as he'd been back in late August. After finding out about everything that had been going on, Darren's only over-the-top reaction, surprisingly enough, was one of intense protection of Nick.

Boy, you'd think Darren would have been agitated. After finding out he'd been spending time with who he thought was his boyfriend's cousin, his new chum, but in reality was an ex-angel fallen to earth and running amuck since before Moses. Darren had been hanging out with a demon who changed into a giant black lion with wings the size of trampolines. You'd think such a thing would make a guy a little agitated.

Darren had been agitated, actually, but thought he'd managed to hide it well enough. After all, hiding what he was really thinking and feeling was a skill he'd been developing for a couple of decades. It was tough but he managed it. He managed to keep from fainting the second he'd cleared the magic spit off of Nick's photo. Darren was evidently stuck in an episode of *Buffy the Vampire Slayer meets Queer as Folk*.

His own alarm aside, Darren needed to keep his wits about him. It was impossible to know for sure if everything he was being told by their new friend was true. The guy *was* a demon. It could all be an intricate but charming construction of fascinating fibs.

Nick believed him, though. Nicky trusted Scott completely. So, until such time as he was given a reason to do otherwise, Darren would trust him too.

Scott, and even Nick himself, had seemed to find Darren's deter- mination to protect Nick so "cute" they'd stand and just stare at him with these stupid grins on their faces, like they were his motherfucking aunts at his high school graduation, for crying out fucking loud. Those little smirks actually pissed Darren off a slightly. They made it seem as though he wasn't being taken seriously. Well, maybe he wasn't.

If Darren decided to show a little temper over it, Nick and Scott even thought *that* was cute, which just made things worse. So, they'd all stand there in the kitchen, Darren getting more and more angry, Nick and Scott thinking it was just the fucking cutest thing they'd ever seen, until Darren either threw his hands up completely, or screamed, or both. Every time, though, before he knew it, they were all suddenly laughing, and the whole peculiar thing just seemed so damn silly there was no way to deal with it at all. Not with a straight face, anyway.

Seriously, though. For all intents and purposes, the reality was that Darren and Nick had befriended a gay fire-breathing demon. Even now, Darren smiled just thinking about it. How the fuck could they *not* laugh?

Come to think of it, Darren thought, Scott never said anything about being gay. Scott sure said a lot, but never that he was gay. Sure, there was that shit the first day they'd met when Scott talked about having a boyfriend, but that was all tangled up in the cousin story and all of that crap, so...

Nope. Scott had never said he was gay. 'Course... he'd never said he wasn't.

Now, Darren, Nick, and Scott were drifting around the main living room, floating from group to group, getting their bearings on the party. They would continue like that until they landed in a spot where they all felt comfortable throwing out the anchor.

Nick was very good at avoiding physical contact with people he didn't know. So, Darren wasn't really worried about that, even in the crowd. The other partiers sailed by and touched him all the time, but Scott had explained that that didn't count; Nick had to make a conscious decision to allow himself to be touched. Sure, there were rumors spreading here and there that Nick was a major snot-rag, seeing as he refused to shake hands—or hug or kiss or smooch or fuckin' bitch-slap or any of the other common physical greetings within their hollow little A-list community—with anyone he didn't already know very well. That sure didn't bother Darren, though. Let Nick be the one with the stuck-up-dick-head reputation for a while.

†

"I'm only going to allow you this single opportunity to give me what I want," she said.

Michael barely heard her.

"If you refuse," she went on, "I'll force it from you. You have this single opportunity to give me what I need without suffering."

Michael was desperately trying to understand what was happening. He'd merely been trying to be polite, merely following the young woman's instructions. All he'd done was wait for her like she'd asked. He'd planned to simply explain that she'd mistaken him for someone else. His only concern at the time was that she might, as a consequence of his honesty, ask him to leave.

The moment she'd walked in, though, she said things that just didn't make any sense. She'd called him by his first name, which completely shocked and silenced him. Michael had tried to say something while he struggled to grasp what she was saying, to discretely discover how she could possibly know to call him that, but he'd only managed to stumble and stutter out fragments of words in his alarm. While he'd struggled for something to say, she'd laughed.

Hearing her giggle at him, suddenly thinking he might be the butt of some joke, some manipulation, he'd found his voice. It even abruptly dawned on him that maybe Robert had discovered Michael hadn't left the city. Maybe this girl was instructed to watch for him and keep him contained.

"That's quite enough," Michael had managed. "I'll have you tell me exactly —"

But that was all she'd allowed him to say.

The woman simply lifted her hand. She lifted it toward him in a gesture of amused annoyance, as though she were merely swiping a gnat from the air. With that subtle gesture, she'd projected a power at him that was anything but subtle.

Michael was lifted off the floor completely and thrown backward through the air. He slammed against the far wall, connecting to it solidly and painfully. His head hit the wall, against the canvas of a mounted painting, with almost shattering force. Instead of bouncing off the wood and plaster behind it, he had stuck there, like a magnet to a refrigerator, as though the decorative paint were the glue on some human-sized fly-paper.

He'd been completely unable to move, even to so much as turn his head. Just filling his lungs with air, the effort of pulling his chest and abdomen away from the wall to simply breathe, took a staggering effort. It felt as though gravity itself had been re-focused horizon-tally, pressing him against the wall, and that its force had been unbearably magnified.

Now, the young woman was standing only a few inches from him, muttering about how he was supposed to give her something.

"Around here, I'm called Laura," said the beautiful young woman. "Although, my name is Shehlá."

She was whispering and smiling seductively. Michael merely looked at her. None of this made any sense. His head was a boulder of pain. He tried to turn his face. He felt the paint beneath his head as it cracked and flaked against his skull.

"Someone like you, my dear young bishop," she said, "might best know me as Lelia. Ring any bells, doll-baby?"

Michael caught his breath at the familiar name. The young woman laughed again.

"The Hebrew is *lyl*, or *lylh*," she explained. "It could be translated as 'night,' in case you've forgotten that day in class. I've been called by many other names, of course. Inanna, Ishtar, Lamia, Lilith, Venus, it goes on and on, I won't bore you. Don't be confused, however. Although the mistake has been made in the past, I am definitely not Lilith. I *am* trouble, without doubt, but I'm not the demon you'd know as Lilith. I am not the Night Hag." She laughed a little. "Not just yet, anyway."

He struggled through a single breath. Only moving his eyes, Michael looked down at her. She was beautiful, as he'd noticed right away, but something was changing. He scarcely detected it, but there was a slight shift taking place. The woman all of a sudden looked ashen and worn, her skin less radiant, less youthful.

And what was that smell?

He recognized the name, Lelia, from *lel*, the entity mentioned in the Tanakh. Also, he noted that she referred to herself as a demon, flatly and casually, but those were the last completely sane thoughts that ever passed through Michael's mind. Everything after seemed to disintegrate, thankfully, into nothing.

"If you still have the presence to do so," the woman continued, "you may want to whisper some thanks to your God. Thank Him that it isn't Lilith standing here with you now. Your timing isn't all bad it seems. Another week or so and you would have faced the mother of the Legions herself. She defines suffering in such a glorious way, I can only hope to one day comprehend it myself."

Michael tried to pull another breath into his lungs and felt the weight of mountains against his chest.

"Go ahead then," the woman said. "I'll allow it. Send your thanks to Heaven. Make amends and whisper your little prayer, doll-baby. Whisper it while you can."

"What do you want?" he heard himself ask.

"Look into my right eye," she answered flatly. "Look and understand that I am a demon of the earth, a huntress of the highest caste within the Legions of his most glorious immortal majesty, Yetzer Ha'ra.

"Gaze into my eye, and then, doll-baby... then I need you to freely and knowingly grant me the power of your human soul, without reservation, without repentance.

"Do that, and I shall not tear the skin from your body, piece by piece, as you scream from your very bowels for me to show a mercy that I do not possess."

†

"Why do I get the feeling that everyone in town has seen your new place but me?" Troy asked.

Theo smiled. "Hey, I asked you to walk up and take a look a month ago, but you were too interested in all the guys hanging out in Scotty's kitchen to—"

"Okay, you were taking a whole tour group up there, and you know what I mean, big guy. I want a *private* invitation."

"Are you drunk?"

"Oh, heaven help me, if it were only that simple."

Theo smiled at him. "What're you ridin'?"

Troy tried to remember everything he'd swallowed, snorted, and smoked since he arrived at the house, and couldn't quite.

"Do you know what 'speed-balling' is?" he asked. "I'll give you a lil' hint. It doesn't mean 'having sex really, really fast.' "

"Don't you just love this house?"

Troy giggled. This was going to be a typical Theo conversation.

"Sure," he said. "I suppose if one wants to employ an enormous maintenance staff, and have a mortgage that's roughly the size of the yearly budget of, um, like... Minnesota, then I'd say this would be the perfect place to live."

"I'd love a place like this."

"Tired of the beach paradise already?"

"No, no." Theo shook his head. "I love it. I mean, I can't even believe I, like, *live* there, you know?"

"Yeah, well, neither can anyone else, baby."

"But, someday, maybe I'll be able to..." Theo glanced around, at the awning, the patio furniture, toward the distant tennis courts and pool. "I don't know. Maybe I'm dreaming."

Troy giggled, stirred his drink. "Ya think?"

"Did you see Janet Jackson? She was just sitting there in the library. I couldn't believe it. She is so fucking hot."

"Honey, it's okay, just tell me," Troy started. "Really, I won't say anything. About your new condo, who the fuck did you fuck to—?"

"I am so in love with Peter Jamison."

Troy rolled his eyes. "Who?"

"Peter Jamison. He's that guy in the white shirt over by the barbeque." Theo pointed for Troy.

"Yes, dear." Troy nodded. "He's lovely."

"Have you talked to him? He's so nice."

"The guy's a dick."

"What?"

"He bought an eight-ball of Tina from me yesterday afternoon."

"Okay, yeah, well, so did half the town, so um..." Theo shot Troy his Am-I-the-Slow-One-Here? smile.

"Sure, okay." Troy grinned back. "Normally, that doesn't make someone a dick, but he tried to pull some shit about some ecstasy not working, and thought I should give him some kind of a credit, or something, and oh, my god, what am I? Rite-Aid? Please, Becky."

"Peter owns four clothing stores."

"He screws everything with teeth."

"You think he's a slut?"

"Theo, honey, he fucks every boy in LA as soon as they're on the latter side of puberty."

Theo laughed, shook his head. "You don't know that."

Troy rolled his eyes again; they were real acrobats today.

"Anyway, I think he's really hot." Theo was staring across the patio at the muscular, gorgeous, well-dressed jerk/chicken-hawk.

"Whatever you say, baby." Troy gazed down into his drink. "I'm sure you won't have any trouble with him."

"No?"

"Well, you have teeth, don't you?"

"Did you get your hair cut?" Theo was suddenly gazing at the top of Troy's head. "It looks really cute."

Damn, if this boy's attention deficit disorder wasn't working some holy overtime...

"Oh, my god, baby, do you need a bump?" Troy was tired of

talking. "Because, I think I'm in just fucking *dire* need of a big, fat, motherfuckin' bump. Of just exactly what, I am, as yet, undecided."

Troy didn't wait for Theo to reply. He grabbed his wrist and pulled him along. They pressed through a clueless cluster of kids who somehow didn't realize they were idling in the doorway to the kitchen, then scampered across the tile and into the dining room, around the enormous table, and into the side hallway, where there was a short line for one of the bathrooms.

The door opened and two girls and a guy strolled out—golly, what could they all have been doing in there at the same time? *Sniff*—stopping for a moment to smile and giggle at a young redheaded guy at the front of the line, who'd been waiting there with his little girlfriend.

Troy grabbed Theo and took advantage. There were several colorful exclamations as Troy pulled Theo inside with him, ahead of everyone who'd been waiting. The exclamations became great and boisterous huffs of disbelief as he slammed and locked the door. There was some heavy knocking and yelling, but neither he nor Theo seemed to even notice, much less give a hairy hooch.

"What 'cha got?" Theo smiled, bouncing his eyebrows.

"Well, I might just talk to Kelly, I think," Troy said, fishing around in his world-famous fanny-pack, "and light up the psychedelic bitch with some fabulous cola I just got from that oh-so-beautiful of far-fabulous foreign countries, Miami. But you can do what you want, baby. I've got Tina, if you'd like to talk to her."

"Some lit-up Kelly sounds like fun to me, baby, baby." Theo's smile got even broader, which made Troy laugh.

"Yeah, Kelly does sound like fun, don' she?" he said. "I don't think Tina would be a good idea right now. That horrid clit might put me into an even worse mood."

Troy pulled three long, glass vials from his fanny-pack, each with a different color cap. He put the one with the red cap back inside.

"What's wrong with your mood, honey?" Theo asked.

"Oh, jeez, nothing." Troy tapped out a healthy bump of K onto his hand and held it up to Theo's nose.

"Okay." Theo pressed a finger to one nostril to close it, stooped, and expertly sucked the K off Troy's hand. Not a granule was left to tell the tale.

"It's just all this crap," Troy said, tapping out another bump and offering it to Theo. "All these perfect boys roaming around, I feel like I'm invisible."

Theo quickly eliminated the second bump, sucking all of it up his nose in a single, decisive breath.

"You're not invisible," Theo said, tilting his head back, snorting again loudly. Every seasoned drug-snorter knew enough to continue dragging a lot of air into their noses to help attain all the lagging residue.

"I mean, it's just like that Peter Jamison guy..." Troy tapped a bump for himself and snorted it. "He just ambles around as if he's the lost love-child of Isis and Jesus."

Troy tilted his head back and, like the trained professional he was, gave his sinuses a good, long, cleansing sniff.

"Maybe you just caught him in a bitchy mood yesterday," Theo suggested.

"Yeah, that's it." Troy rolled his eyes, tapping out another bump of K. "Do you want some coke too, baby?"

"Hello?"

Troy giggled. "Well, you'd better do a water-bump or you'll just end up walking around with huge drug-boogers."

Theo nodded and smiled, went to the sink and turned on the faucet. While he was wetting his fingers, Troy snorted his second bump of K.

"He didn't seem stuck up to me," Theo said, lifting his wet fingers to his nose and sniffing loudly.

"Well, jeez, look at you, baby." Troy capped the vial of K, put it in the fanny-pack, and picked up the vial with the blue cap. "Standing next to you, I don't think anyone could pull off being stuck up."

"Are you saying I'm a bitch?" He moved away from the sink so Troy could get to it.

"Oh, come on, Theo, I don't mean it that way. You're not like him." Troy turned the faucet back on and did two very thorough water-bumps. "You're nice."

"Peter's just a guy, Troy."

"Yeah, well..." Troy laughed. "So is Dylan McDermott."

"Didn't you faint the night he came to the—?"

"Okay, we really do not need to go there, honey." Troy opened the blue-capped vial and tapped out some very chunky cocaine onto the back of his hand. He cursed himself for not having ground it up better. "Just do this one bump, babe. I think it's really packed. It's more like a fat line that's still all bunched up."

"Okay." Theo closed one nostril and snorted hard with the other.

"I just think all the beauty-boys could be a little more humble and sensitive, you know? Like Nicky."

"What's so special about Nick?"

"Oh, jeez, Theo—"

"He's just a guy too, Troy."

"Hardly." Troy shook his head, tapping out another hefty bump of coke for himself. "Besides you, Nick is one of the only muscle-boys that isn't so shallow and stuck up that he's blind to his own insecurities. I hate being around all these nasty gym-bitches who think they're somehow superior people because they get through three sets of bench presses twice a week."

"You hate being around them, and yet..." Theo moved to the door, cocked his head, looking meditative. "...and yet here you are."

Troy'd been in mid-snort when he realized what Theo had said. He had to stifle a shocked laugh, but couldn't control his breath, and still blew the chunk of cocaine all over the bathroom.

He and Theo both burst out laughing.

"You will *not* be getting all insightful around me, you snatch!" Troy said.

They howled.

"You just ought to be more tolerant and forgiving, my friend," Theo chimed.

"I oughtta to kick you in the balls, bitch, is what I oughtta do!" Troy laughed, tapping out another bump and quickly sucking it into his nose before Theo could say anything else that might be wildly out of character. "Shit, Theo. You do a big bump of coke and suddenly you're Dr. Phil."

"Are you ready to face the world?" Theo smiled at him. "Because you're starting to bore me."

Troy laughed again, nodded. Smiling, Theo opened the bathroom door.

They stepped out into the hall, still chortling, and faced the angry line. Young Redheaded Guy was just returning to the scene with one of the Security Guys—who Karen had brought with her from the club— trailing lazily behind him. It was just Bobby, and Troy gave him a little smile. Bobby frowned at them, tapping his foot like he was someone's mother. Young Redheaded Guy looked very pleased at that.

Then Bobby, Theo, and Troy all burst into a riotous laugh, to the utter horror of Young Redheaded Guy.

"Life sucks, don' it, kid?" Troy sauntered past them, slapping Bobby on the fanny as he went.

†

Robert almost tripped over a power-cord that had been hastily laid between a sofa and one of the temporary speakers. He was watching the progress of the black-haired Greek boy as he moved through the crowd with the other men.

Unlike the Greek boy, the men with him were only familiar from the club. Robert hadn't seen them in any other city and there hadn't been any descriptions that fit them from any other sources either.

The tall one looked somewhat formidable. It seemed as if he was suspiciously scanning the entire crowd, looking for something, cautious of some danger he suspected might be present. Robert instinctively stationed himself close to a corner around which he could duck if necessary, trying to remain inconspicuous. The shorter guy walking around with them didn't seem to be in as high a state of alert as the tall blonde. Maybe he and the black-haired one were both...

Wait a minute...

The tall guy and the shorter guy were holding hands. Robert smirked.

Each time he'd seen the Greek boy at the club, he'd been with these two other men. Now they were sauntering through this party holding each other's hands. It wasn't really a shocking development, or even one that might be completely unexpected. The homosexual element in Los Angeles had simply been a peripheral component to Robert's mission until now.

Were they just acting? Was it the same kind of camouflage that he'd suggested to Michael? Was it a rouse to bring the unsuspecting into their grasp by displaying such a provocative deviance so publicly, so brazenly? Robert shrugged, supposing it made some sense. What better way to make the sinful feel comfortable around them than to so flagrantly advertise the indulgence of such a mortal sin?

Of course, they really could be queer. That'd be a hoot.

Robert had seen quite clearly, during all his stake-out time at the club, that homosexuality was as stagnant an element of this city as arrogance and selfishness.

†

"Now there's a pretty boy." Nick smiled at Eddie as he ambled over to them.

"Hi, baby." Eddie smiled back and wrapped his arms around

Nick's waist, resting his head on his shoulder, hiding his face against his neck.

"What's wrong, honey?" Nick asked.

Eddie didn't answer. He just shook his head a little, pressed himself closer to Nick and held him tighter.

Nick gave Darren a questioning look, who shrugged.

"Have you seen Missy already?" Nick whispered down to him, kissing him lightly on the cheek.

Eddie nodded. Nick and Darren exchanged a knowing look.

"Where's Thelma?" Darren asked.

"Mm mm," Eddie shrugged, still pressing his face to Nick, who held him, swaying gently with the music.

Missy was beginning to walk herself all over Nick as well, and Eddie felt very good in his arms. He took a deep breath, closed his eyes, rested his cheek on Eddie's, kissed him lightly again, and rubbed his back. Eddie moaned. Life was made for moments like these.

"I'm going to take Scott upstairs and introduce him to Brian Ikon," Darren said. "Why don't you and Eddie sit down. You look like you need to cuddle for a bit. We'll be right back."

Nick wasn't going to argue. It sounded like a great idea.

†

The tall blonde and the Greek boy/supposed-demonic-cleric/possible skotos crossed the room toward Robert. His stomach sank sickeningly as he thought, at first, they'd made him. Then he realized he was standing between them and the stairs, which must be where the two were headed.

Stepping quickly out of the way and around the corner, slightly inside the hall along the side of the banister, Robert watched from a relatively safe position. They came around the sofa, pressed themselves through the crowd with smiles, polite touches, and an occasional "Excuse me," approaching the bouncer who'd been stationed at the base of the stairs.

Robert noticed a lot of the same security personnel from the club working throughout the house. Apparently, someone didn't want all the Hollywood derelicts wandering around up on the second or third floors.

Outside, the security boys supposedly insured that only the invited guests were admitted the party. If that was the case, the bouncers had done a miserable job. Those guys were so clueless they let in anyone wearing matching socks. That, or so many invitations had been given out it hardly mattered. With the number of people who'd shown up, all that was missing was a Ferris wheel and some bumper cars. Judging by the sounds coming from further down the hall, Robert had clearly stumbled into the Tunnel of Love.

Approaching the stairs, the blonde guy smiled and tossed a common, contemporary-American silent slang greeting, the Quick-Upward-Nod, at the black-attired bouncer, who smiled and quick-upward-nodded back. Still smiling, the bouncer and the blonde guy exchanged words.

Although only a few feet away, Robert still couldn't hear a single thing they were saying over the music. There were two speakers within a ten-foot radius of the base of the stairs; eavesdropping was out of the question. The music's volume was undoubtedly at club level and, in the small space, Robert was genuinely surprised the guests on the first floor weren't forced to communicate using flash cards.

Whatever the blonde guy said to the bouncer, it was quick and effective. The bouncer nodded — the normal way; downward first — the blonde guy and the boy from Greece were allowed to bound happily up the stairs.

Robert smirked again as he noted that, now, they were also holding hands.

†

"Oh, jeez, look at us." Darren stopped just as they reached the door to the DJ room.

"What?" said Scott.

"We left Nicky downstairs alone."

"Arg." Scott closed his eyes and shook his head with an aggravated grin.

"We'll just be a minute, though, right?" Darren offered. "He's with Eddie. I don't think anyone will bother them."

"True. Though, we'd really hate ourselves if..." Scott grimaced, shook his head and sighed.

Darren nodded. "Probably. But why don't I introduce you to Brian really quickly, and then I'll run back down? You can stay and hang out as long as you want. I'm sure Brian will like that."

Scott thought a moment, then nodded. "Okay."

†

"I'm sorry, sir, I don't care who you are," the arrogant bouncer-twit said. "No one is allowed upstairs."

Robert's eyes bulged. "I just saw you let—!"

"I'm going to ask you to step away now. Maybe you could go get a nice drink at the nice bar and have a nice relaxing time out on the nice patio with all of these nice people at this nice party, because, if you stopped bothering me, it would sure be nice."

Robert took a very deep breath. "Yes, how nice for you."

The bouncer-twit smiled back and blinked sarcastically, making Robert completely understand spontaneous violent expression.

"Before I do, however," Robert said, quickly trying to manufacture a story that had even the slightest possibility of affecting this person, who had surely heard it all. "I wonder if you'd just give your boss a short message for me?"

The bouncer-twit stopped smiling.

"Please just let Ms. Alanson know," Robert said, "that Bob Patrick from Fox had to leave and therefore won't be able to meet with the gentlemen she begged him for a half-hour on the phone this afternoon to come out and meet. Please let her know that, as I'm not going to wait for twenty minutes to get into a bathroom downstairs, and as I'm not going to take any more shit from some punk bouncer-twit, who maybe should have finished high school before moving to Los Angeles to become an actor, and who is now taking the opportunity to assert the only form of power he will ever experience in his sad, sad life by denying me access to a simple fucking bathroom upstairs, I'm going to go home and piss there. Can you retain all of that in your feeble, twit-memory? Is that too much for you? If so, just tell her this. Tell Ms. Alanson that the favor for which she asked me is not going to happen anytime before our solar system's sun burns itself out."

At that, Robert grinned, blinked back at the bouncer-twit, and turned to leave, instantly happy he hadn't chosen to hit the boy.

Robert felt radiantly good all of a sudden. Alarmingly so, truth be told. Oddly, he no longer cared that he hadn't been allowed upstairs. Not in the slightest bit.

He'd barely started to take his second step toward the front door when the security-twit grunted behind him. Robert heard such a miserable grunt of anguished frustration that he almost felt pity for the poor, dumb guy. Almost.

"Sir," came the bouncer-twit's voice, an octave lower than normal, so beset with pain it fell audibly to the carpet and rolled there like a bowling ball.

Robert stopped, smiled to himself, habitually applied a modest effort to conceal his triumph, and turned back to face the bouncer-twit.

"Yes?" he said, trying not to be too overtly buoyant at his success. He tried, but was wholly unsuccessful

"Please don't take too long up there," said the bouncer-twit, stepping completely off the stairs to allow Robert up.

†

"I can't find Laura and I'm beginning to enter Bitch Mode," Karen said, sitting down next to Nick and Eddie, who were lounging comfortably in a loveseat roughly the size of a pontoon boat. "She promised me I wouldn't have to do anything at this party, but that's hardly going to be my experience if no one can find her. I swear, if one more snooty circuit-brat asks me where I've set up the VIP room or when I'm going to open the upstairs, I'm going to stuff a cheese-log up their ass."

"Yeah, gee, cheese-logs." Nick smirked. "You might as well stuff 'em somewhere. No one's actually eating them."

"I might be able to handle Bitch Mode for a minute or two, but if I get knocked into Total Bitch Mode, there's bound to be some buzz-kill, which will knock me clear up to Super Snatch Bitch Mode, and if that happens, we're all going to be sans a heck of a lot of cheese-logs."

"Speaking of buzz-kill, could we dispense with the party-food imagery?"

"This is just unacceptable." Karen shook her head.

"I think things look like they're going pretty well," Eddie offered.

"Thanks for your support, luscious." Karen patted him on the arm. "No offense, though, but you're clueless."

"What?"

"So, just tell me if you spot Laura, okay? She's wearing an off-white strapless, gorgeous, thing by Vera Wang, and that gorgeous flowing hair of hers has a little extra body ruffled into it, and she looks just so much better than me, so when you spot her, hit her with something really heavy, *then* tell me."

"She wasn't at the door when we got here," said Nick.

"Obviously. Look over there." She pointed for him. "Look at the chick in that yellow, um... that yellow, like... thing. Okay, she was *sooo* not invited. I do not know who she is, probably someone's maid who was, I don't know, like, walking past the house to the bus-stop, or something, and thought she'd just mosey into my party and go right up to Matt Damon and just, like, talk to him."

"At least he's smiling."

"Wait. There's more. You see, someone's going to have to take a scouring pad to the chopping block in the kitchen tomorrow. There's cocaine and Special K and who-knows-what-fucking-else being chopped up on it as we speak. I keep walking through there and all those oh-so-discrete club-kids keep pretending nothing's going on and trying to stand in front of all their big fat lines as if I won't see them. Oh, my god, Mary, what am I, blind? What? Am I supposed to think they're baking breadsticks and they've just lined out all the flour?"

"They didn't even offer you some?" Nick smiled.

"No!" Karen raised her palms and shook her head. "Can you believe the etiquette of children these days? Were they raised in a barn?"

Eddie shook his head. "Club-kids are just rude, man."

"Oh god, and I made the mistake of going out into the garage." Karen covered her eyes with her hands. "Some asshole got sick while he was in the kitchen, I guess, and at least he made it out to the garage before he puked, but that's as far as he got, because it's all over the hood of that Jaguar in there."

Nick winced.

"And do not," Karen continued, lowering her voice, bending down to them furtively, "and I mean *do not* go down the hall to the guest bedroom, unless you feel like getting pregnant. Also, along those same pathetic lines, there's already two people in the study who are unconscious from doing too much of something, I don't know if it was alcohol or Gina." She pressed her hands into a prayer position. "Oh dear, me oh my, lordy, lordy, please, please, please God, *please* don't let it be both."

"Hey, you can't control what people do."

"Sure, sure. Oh, and what's-his-name is here. You know, that guy Theo introduced me to a couple months ago, the guy who's an agent for the Treasury Department."

"At least he's not DEA."

"No. At least there's that. At least he'd have to find more than five kilos of coke before the policies of his specific division of law enforcement compelled him to do anything."   Karen sighed. "Motherfuck, I am so very fuckin' screwed if he goes out to the pool house."

"You need a cocktail, baby."

"So, do you see? Do you see? If fucking Laura were doing her fucking job, I wouldn't be sitting here freaking out over Mr. Treasury Department stumbling upon the snow bank out in the pool house, or the messes in the kitchen and the garage, or Miss Tweety-Bird over there sneaking in and talking to *my* celebrities."

"Hey, baby, you really should relax." Nick patted Karen's hand. "Things are not that bad. First of all, Mr. Treasury Department is so high on K, I don't think he could *find* the pool house. Also, that guy is not Matt Damon, but a damn remarkable look-alike, so I can't fault you for freakin' over that one and, really, if it's just one crasher, then, really, baby, there's—"

"It's not just one, sweetums." Karen sighed and put her hand over her face. "There's been a leak for at least a half-hour or so from the size of the gaggle of bitches out on the patio, who are currently accosting Brenden Fraser."

"Oh, my god, you're right, that is serious." Nick's eyes bulged. "Someone let in *Brenden Fraser*?"

"I know, I know," Karen said, giggling. "It's all fallin' apart, ain't it?"

"Well..." Nick smiled. "You could always just watch the door 'till Laura gets back."

"See, though, see..." Karen huffed. "See, I'm not supposed to be doing any of that shit. We had such a great time getting everything ready, my babies and me, even though we were really, really busy helping to sort of kind of partly watch Laura supervise all the people doing the work."

Eddie giggled and snorted.

"And here I am," she went on, "stressing out."

"What about Brad and Bobby and all the Security Guys?"

"I had to leave Matt and Brad at the club. I brought Bobby, and he's great, but he can only do so much, and the rest of these guys are relatively new and inexperienced. They're just for show, mostly."

"Just the way you like 'em."

"Hush now, puppy."

"Well, what do you need, baby?" Nick offered. "If there's anything I can do, let me know, and Darren just went upstairs for a second—"

"Oh, no, no, no!" Karen shook her head. "That's another thing I wanted to avoid."

"We're not *that* high."

"Well, then you'd better get to work on that, because as soon as I find Laura and rip her a new one, I'm comin' back to get in on this. Troy took good care of me too, babe. Just because he's in love with you doesn't mean you're the only one—"

"Troy's what?" Nick squinted at her.

"Oh, god!" Karen covered her mouth and screamed into her hands.

"What?" Nick sat up, which prompted Eddie to make a frustrated *Hhgrmph* sound.

"Nothing!" She shook her hand at him. "Sit back down! Nothing! Sit down. You're ruffling Eddie."

"Are you okay?" Nick raised his eyebrows at her, settling back into the monster love seat.

"Yes, of course. I think I just saw Anna Paquin fall into the pool, that's all. She's such a mess."

"If you say so."

"I'm going to go help." Karen turned to leave.

"Hey, Karen," Nick called after her. "Please don't go get a cheese-log, but where *is* the VIP room?"

"That's it!" she hollered back at him, laughing. "You're gettin' one with nuts in it!"

†

"Excuse me," the tall formidable-looking blonde said on his way back down the stairs. He was alone, though, as he pressed by Robert and smiled.

Yeah, Robert thought. Definitely queer.

So, that meant that, now, the black-haired Greek boy was alone somewhere either on the second or the third floor. All Robert had to do was find him.

†

"I have to sit down," Troy said, ambling up to Nick and Eddie's opulent nest of fluffy arm rests and buttoned cushions. Theo danced along behind him.

"Karen said that you're in love with me," Nick blurted.

"Nick, honey," Troy said, wedging next to him snugly, on the side not currently covered by Eddie, "who isn't?"

"Whatever!" Nick laughed. "She was serious!" He tilted his head. "Was she serious?"

Theo walked up and crossed his arms. "Where am I going to sit?"

"Just sit down on the carpet." Nick spread his knees. "You can lean back right here, baby." He patted the edge of the seat's cushion.

Theo turned and, with surprising grace, lowered his immenseness down in front of the other three.

"I don't think I can sit here for long," he said. "Kelly's got to move, you know."

"Where's Kelly?" Eddie perked up.

"Troy," Nick said, "she was serious. She tried to cover it, but then someone fell into the pool and I think she had to, like, go save her."

Theo started waving frantically at someone across the room. "Billy Warlock! Hey Billy!" he shouted, then turned back to the three guys stuffed into the over-stuffed loveseat. "That's Billy Warlock, from the first season of *Baywatch*." He turned back and waved and shouted again. "Hey Billy! How'z it goin', baby?"

The Might Be Billy Warlock Guy looked over at them for a second or two, grimaced, and then hurried into the kitchen, glancing back and grimacing once more.

"Have you ever actually met him, Theo?" Eddie asked.

"No."

"Troy," Nick whined, "was she fuckin' with me?"

Eddie lifted his head off of Nick's shoulder. "When did Kelly get here?"

Troy unzipped his fanny-pack. "I've got you covered, baby."

People were walking by in front of them, wandering in clumps in all directions. Theo pulled his knees up to his chest, nodding, slapping his thighs in time with the music, smiling at the people who smiled down at him, raising his eyebrows at the people who frowned, laughing with the people who tripped over his boots.

Troy whipped out his vial with the green cap and tapped out a bump onto his hand. Nick looked around nervously, but no one seemed to be paying the slightest attention.

"This is Princess Kelly, right?" Eddie leaned across Nick and lowered a nostril to the back of Troy's upheld hand.

"Duh."

Sniff.

"Nick?" Troy raised his eyebrows at him.

"Hello?"

Another bump was produced. *Sniff.*

Darren appeared abruptly.

"Hey there, studly," Theo crooned, gazing up at him, grinning.

"Oh, I wish I had a camera," Darren said, smiling down at Nick, who was still sucking Kelly residue up his nose.

"Troy's in love with me," Nick said. Troy laughed.

"Nick, handsome," Darren said, sitting down next to Theo, "who isn't?"

✝

"Oh, my god, there you are," Karen said, breathing a melodramatic sigh, reaching out and grasping Laura by the hand.

Laura hadn't seen her at first, apparently, because her reaction to Karen was almost violent. She pulled away from her quickly, snapping her wrist from Karen's grip with an angry twist. Her expression looked like a mixture of disgust and... well, something else, Karen couldn't quite tell. But she'd almost thought it was fear. Laura had reacted as though a spider landed on her hand and started scampering up her arm.

She shot a glare at Karen, it was irate and horrified, but softened instantly, so quickly, in fact, Karen wondered if she'd even seen it at all. If she had, then surely it hadn't been as intense as she'd thought, had it?

"Karen, I am so sorry," Laura almost whined, her face immediately taking on her timid — and oh-so-very-very familiar — Sorry-I'm-Late smile. "I'm on my way out to the front right now. I just talked to Neal and Randal and they're going to go sweep out some of the trash."

"Fine, fine." Karen waved her off, a little shaken by Laura's first reaction. "Just don't go chat with Nicky Reynolds... 'cause I've been talkin' bitchy about you."

Laura laughed heartily — a little too heartily? — widening her eyes and covering her mouth.

"I am so high, honey," Karen said, eager to refocus their interaction. "I saw this girl in yellow pedal-pushers, for motherfucking crying out loud, and I just lost it, you know? I've done a quarter of coke, dropped Missy, only one, though, I think..." She pouted for a second, thinking. "Yeah, only one, and Troy started introducing Kelly around the second he walked in, and let me tell you, darlin'..." She shook her head vigorously. "None of that, *none* of it, is at all compatible with any-fuckin'-thing in yellow pedal-pushers, okay? Make a note, honey. That's a very important life lesson."

Laura laughed and slapped the wall.

"You look incredible, by the way," Karen said, stepping back to take her in. "Jesus, Mary 'n Joseph, I hate your guts. Honey, what have you been doing and why aren't you sharing it?"

"Oh, you know," Laura said, smiling at her, "it's just the same old eternal-youth secrets. A good mudpack, some moisturizer, a blood sacrifice to the Morning Star, a half-hour on the treadmill, blah, blah, blah."

"A what to the star of who?"

"Where's Miss Pedal-Pusher? I'll send one of the boys right over with a dustpan."

"I don't know for sure." Karen rolled her eyes. "But she's attached to a striking Matt Damon look-alike."

"Oh, great."

"This is blown out, baby. This party is rocking the world. How did you do this? I'm stunned! I mean, I knew you'd peppered the town, but crap Laura, this is out of control. I thought Lauren wanted something subtle, something surgical, something very target-glam, just to seed the clouds, you know?"

"I just hung up with her. That's why I wasn't at the door."

"What?" Karen frowned. "What time is it in New York?" She looked at her watch, "Oh, my fucking god, it's five o'clock in the morning in New York."

"Karen, doll-baby, now I *know* you're high." Laura shook her head. "It's Saturday night-*slash*-Sunday morning in New York City, and we're talking about Lauren Isseroff. Do you need me to do the math for you?"

Karen grimaced, pretended to bite her nails. "She was just finishing a gig, huh?"

"She was *right in the middle* of a gig, my love." Laura smiled. "Her girlfriend answered the cell-phone. They were in the booth, so I didn't get to speak with her for very long. She was so funny. I think she's higher than you are right now, frankly."

"Girlfriend?"

"Mm hm." Laura nodded

"Oh, yeah." Karen smirked, waved. "Of course. Is… um…" She tilted her head, crossed her arms. "So is she like…?"

Laura giggled again. "What? A lesbian?"

"Yeah."

"Oh, my gosh, I don't know!" Laura laughed and gave Karen a strange look. Karen suddenly wondered why she even cared.

"Lauren's thrilled that so many celebs showed up," Laura offered. "You can't buy that kind of buzz."

"Right, honey," Karen said, still reeling from the possible lesbian business.

Boy, Karen always thought of herself as progressive, as so ultimately accepting that she didn't need to strive to be any more
accepting. She was a little shocked at the possibility that she would
be so, well, shocked.

"Most of the really big celebs were just here for the first couple
hours, though," Karen said. "They've since trickled on to the next
spot. I saw Colin Farrel, but I don't think he was here for more than
forty-five minutes."

"That's fine," Laura said. "They were seen and that's what we
wanted. It doesn't matter now if there are any stars at all at the New
Years party."

"No more celebs?" Karen mock-pouted.

"Well, after tonight, we don't really need any really big ones.
We'd be fine if the biggest star that showed up was Rick Springfield.
Word will get out about this turnout, and that's all that matters. The
crowd at the club on the night of the event will be so tight that fuckin'
Mark Wahlberg could walk through it, naked even, and it would
never amount to anything more than an unsubstantiated rumor."

"My dear, if you get Mr. Mark Wahlberg to walk through the
party, even just in his underwear, never mind naked, I'll double your
fee."

"Don't challenge me, Karen." Laura suddenly grinned with so
much slyness, so much creepy wiliness, Karen actually shuddered.
"You have no idea what I'm capable of."

"I guess not." Karen panted, her hand laying absently on her
chest. "I guess not."

†

Robert didn't mind so much anymore that he hadn't been able to
find closer parking. He'd been lucky in other—and much more
important—ways.

Not only was Robert's hunch correct about the mysterious Greek
boy also attending this party, but the Almighty had even allowed
Robert's arrival to be timed in such a way that he actually saw the
guy stepping out of his limousine. As if that wasn't enough of a
miracle, he'd also been able to monitor him after they were all inside
the house without being detected, even contained by the crowd. He
was able to follow him upstairs after getting past the security-twit,
and then locate him, alone no less—well, without his normal brood,
at any rate—in the most secluded area of the party.

Each incident revealed the righteousness of Robert's path. The

Divine was at work, and Robert was His instrument.

It hadn't taken long for Robert to locate his quarry. Walking down the hall toward the stairs to the third floor, he'd seen him easily enough as he passed the open door of one of the house's smaller rooms.

Hardly anyone else had been allowed up to this level, and those who had were all clustered inside the same small room, which was the first door on the right as the hallway bent left at the top of the stairs. It also held an incredible amount of very electronic-looking equipment; the makeshift DJ booth, obviously.

The room appeared to Robert, in the instant he'd been able to glance inside as he walked by, to be a small study, something completely divergent to the character of the house, probably decorated as an afterthought.

Robert saw a small, black leather couch against a far wall, a beautiful coffee table of stained oak and polished glass, large and vibrant paintings, and luxurious drapes of the darkest scarlet.

There were two very comfortable looking chairs, in addition to the couch, but no one was sitting down. Seven or eight people stood in the room, all packed in a cluster behind a single man, who was holding one side of a stereo headset to his ear, manipulating a panel of controls in front of him; the DJ himself, of course.

Everyone was smiling and bouncing happily to the music's rhythm. The black-haired Greek boy was standing on the far side of the temporary DJ booth, smiling, contentedly watching the DJ work. Had he glanced at the doorway at that moment, he would have seen Robert walk past, barely a half second pause in his stride, as he discretely looked in on the little group.

The sight made Robert's heart pound. He slowed his pace near the end of the hall, listening for footsteps behind him. Had he heard any, he'd have continued around and up the second flight of stairs, which he could see at the end of the hall, rising to the third floor inside a narrow passage to the right. Instead, Robert turned around and positioned himself as if he'd just come down, in case anyone should wander by. If they did, he'd simply start walking back the other way, toward the first floor stairs, as if he'd never stopped in the hall and was merely on his way down from the top floor.

It was a shaky position in which to wait, but he needed a moment to think. What Robert really wanted was an inconspicuous place to stand, someplace out of the way, where he'd be able to see if the boy from Greece left the DJ room. There really wasn't much chance of finding such a place, though. Not knowing if there was actually anyone on the third floor, he didn't want to sit on the stairs around the corner, peaking down the hall like a child waiting for his parents to go to bed. Anyone coming down the stairs would see him immediately and surely wonder what he was doing. He absolutely did not need that kind of scrutiny. That would be bad.

The pulsing, driving beat, could be heard clearly —*felt*— as it rose like a tide up the stairs from the dense party on the first floor and flooding down from the speakers set up on the third. The DJ was working in the only room on the second floor that had any speakers. Robert felt a little detached as he stood away from it, alone in the hall between the first floor, where the main body of the event milled and gushed, and the third floor, where he assumed a private area had been created; a secret, reserved place for the late-night VIP's to retreat after the gathering eventually disintegrated.

Robert's palms were actually sweating and he realized he could hear himself breathing. He might have just snorted a big bag of cocaine or something, he thought, from the way his heart was pounding. All the gel in his hair was slowly being diluted with the same heavy, anxious perspiration that was covering his hands and running down his back.

Robert suddenly realized he didn't even have a cross with him. Dear Lord, what was he thinking? He hadn't brought his Bible, a crucifix, or even a vial of holy water! Not that he was sure they'd have helped, but he wasn't sure they would have been entirely useless either.

He supposed it didn't matter, though. Robert straightened his jacket, pulling it down to correct the fit, and felt the press of Solomon's Vessel as it lay against his thigh inside the lowest coat pocket.

A burst of voices coming up the stairs startled him. Robert bit his lip and forced himself not to burst into a run, gouging visible grooves into the paint on the wall's corner, where he was absently gripping it. He realized, though, that it was only a small group of girls, bantering loudly — probably drunk, the witless whores — with the security-twit.

The bouncer-twit hadn't let witless whores upstairs, it was just their shrill little slut voices that were wafting up into the hall. Even that realization was a small relief. Robert's heart was still racing and he couldn't seem to slow the pace of his breathing no matter what he tried. It made him think of the depictions of childbirth he'd seen on television.

Just breathe deeply, he told himself. *Inhale, two, three, four, five, six, seven, eight, exhale, two, three, four, five, six, seven, eight.*

The technique didn't seem to be helping him physically, but at least it gave his mind a moderate alternative focus. Something other than the fact that the room a few feet away contained an authentic demonic cleric or, God have mercy, the actual demon itself.

Inhale, two, three, four, five, six, seven, eight.

There really wasn't any other place to go, nowhere to wait and watch inconspicuously. He could only pray that no one saw him standing in the hall, sweating and breathing heavy like some drugged-out stalker in an Armani suit.

If only the Greek boy would come out of the room. The last hurdle, the final unknown element assaulting Robert's mission was, at the moment, whether or not he'd be forced to go downstairs again before the Greek boy got tired of the DJ room and went back to his friends.

The voices at the bottom of the stairs were constantly deceptive as to whether or not anyone was actually ascending. Robert shuddered a little at each loud laugh or shout. He had to force himself not to bolt away, to hold his position until he was certain he was actually about to be seen.

At least he could see the hallway clearly, allowing him ample warning if someone was coming out. No one had, though. Yet.

He didn't know how much longer he'd be able to handle this kind of anxiety. He'd never imagined there'd be this much stress. Robert needed help, and so, of course, he prayed.

Inhale, two, three, four, five, six, seven, eight, please, God, please give me strength, exhale, two, three, four, five, six, seven, eight, oh, dear Lord, please, please, please don't let me faint, two, three, four, five, six, seven, eight.

On the island, back near Pano Panayia, they'd carelessly wandered away from the ruined stone alter, zipping their notebooks into their backpacks, putting away the cameras and maps and ambling back toward the village road, disappointed after having finally found the site and discovering that it harbored no further clues.

Bishop Davis had been horribly quiet. Of course he was quiet, it was Pakistan all over again, wasn't it? He'd been so sure they were going to discover something valuable at least, if not how to find the very creature itself. The walk back to the Jeeps, after they'd all agreed there was nothing there, must have been horrible for him. It was bad for all of them, but for Peter especially. After all, he would have to face the cardinal for the second time and explain that a team under his leadership had failed.

And then they heard the voice.

Are all of you looking for little old me?

The voice had seemed to come from nowhere. Robert could still hear it, the transient voice in the woods. It had a slightly British accent and was quite jovial. Almost mocking. He remembered how they'd stopped at the sound, looking at each other to see if anyone else had heard the melodious voice echo through the trees.

Are all of you looking for little old me? the voice chimed. *Why, I don't think I've ever been so flattered.*

Even then, even during the instant all five of them realized they'd heard the same thing, even looking at each other with so much disbelief and terror crashing together inside of them that the very strength of those emotions cancelled each other out, disbelief and terror so strong they suspend all panic, all rationality, for that bright and eternal instant.

Even then, Robert hadn't felt the way he did now.

He hadn't had this kind of horrible physical assault; the sweating, the racing heartbeat, the shaking. He was shaking fairly visibly too, he realized. Lifting his fingers in front of his face he watched them tremble and couldn't steady them. There hadn't been this feeling of isolation or imminent doom.

Of course, on the island, he hadn't been alone.

Inhale, two, three, four, five, six, seven, eight, please, God, give me strength, a whole lot of strength, please, please, exhale, two, three, four, five, six, seven, eight, oh, dear Lord, don't let me have a heart attack or throw up, two, three, four, five, six, seven, eight.

Robert was standing in this dim hallway, in the belly of this impossibly immense house—it could have been a hotel, for God's sake, it was so stupidly huge—surrounded by the height of every human indulgence that plagued this sorry, pathetic, sinful city. Michael hadn't understood and so Robert had sent him away. He'd been right to do so, hadn't he? Michael would have only gotten in the way, or worse.

Robert understood, though. Robert had been given his perspective by the Lord himself, hadn't he? This was the right place to be and the right thing to do. Certainly it was.

He was an intelligent man, Bishop Robert Patrick, a *very* intelligent man, a genius some had even said, and still this western American city baffled him. The people here suffered from the same illusions that had hidden the light from mankind since Adam first skipped through The Garden, and yet these people were more blinded by it than any other modern community on the face of the planet. They were highly educated, deeply motivated, impossibly beautiful, devoutly disciplined, and yet all of it, every extraordinary gift bestowed upon those who settled here, was focused toward goals that would yield them nothing. They spent their entire lives chasing prizes that, once attained, surrendered only emptiness.

He'd listened to them for so many weeks, the Hollywood crowd; the young, the slightly older, the rich, the struggling, the desperate, the confident, and the downright freaky. They all ranted and raved about this and that and who was wearing what and which show someone had produced and which asshole had screwed what peon out of what credit and which studio was green-lighting whose stupid, baseless, wasteful piece of garbage and all about how so-and-so was attached to what project and why what's-her-name had been cast in what role and so didn't it just figure that what's-his-face would say all that shit about who'z-its? and why they would stick to only doing partial nudity, they were artists, after all, and why would their agent even bother to call them if the stupid part was only at scale? and wasn't it sad that that chick everyone knew had blown her own brains out? though of course she had, they weren't surprised, because she was just so whacked out of her mind on coke and what's-his-face had been pumping her for months anyway, promising this and that, but never coming through, which he did all the time and how could she have not known that, was the dumb bitch deaf? and that was just the breaks, that was just life, that was what went on, the law of the jungle, and you just had to keep your eyes open, you just had to know your shit, and if you knew your shit then you'd be just fine, by the way, do you know where I can score some blow?

It had all fascinated Robert—charmed and intrigued him too but he'd never admit it, oh, Saints in Heaven, no—listening as children of Hollywood rifled off name after name. They told him what star had talked to them at what party. Then, if they thought he was still listening, they'd drop a hundred more names as easily as loose change. So many names of so many players, producers and directors, casting agents and writers, names of fashion designers that would tumble out of everyone's mouths as effortlessly as though they were spitting out a tasteless piece of gum, even from those who could barely afford a pair of *Cherokee* shorts from *Target*. They all knew who was on top, which designer purse would make them glamorous and which would make them a joke, whether a button-down short-sleeved silk shirt would best display their muscles or whether they should go with the V-neck cotton sleeveless muscle-shirt by J. Barnett and just wear that black leather-cord necklace with the topaz charm set in plated silver that brought out their eyes so gosh-darn well.

Everything hinged on all of that, you see. The expanse of eternity rose and fell with the image of the day. With *their* image of the day.

They'd all been enthralled, of course. They were under an evil spell. Iniquity was alive and well and had found his way to the City of Angels where, apparently, he'd completely run amuck, undaunted and unchallenged. Amos wasn't here to point him out, after all. Good God almighty, they hadn't had anyone with a clear vision to point the way. There was no prophet living in LA to enlighten the children of Hollywood to their wickedness, Lord help them all.

A barrage of laughter riffled out of the little room, knocking Robert back into himself. Just a minute or two had passed while he'd allowed his thoughts to consume him, but it didn't matter. No one had seen him standing there and, most important, the Greek boy hadn't left the room.

Robert's pulse was still driving at an amazing pace. A lock of his curly brown hair had fallen and he swept it back with a sweaty, shaking hand, back into the mass of his sculpted designer hairdo where it stuck into place in the sticky, stylish mess of gel and sweat.

The same song was playing. That was good. Robert hadn't zoned out so long that a significant amount of time had passed. He was still okay.

Inhale, one, two, three …

A rise of cheerful banter pressed out of the little room and Robert looked up. The young Greek boy/satanic priest/human-shaped demonic-entity was backing out of the doorway, waving and smiling to the tiny crowd of DJ groupies.

Just a half a second passed before the Greek boy turned to head back down the stairs, not even casually noticing Robert standing lifelessly at the other end of the hall.

"Excuse me," a voice said from somewhere and Robert suddenly realized, with not just a little surprise, it had come from him.

The raven-haired man turned around easily enough, his jet-black eyebrows rising in an expression of casual curiosity over eyes, which were so blue they were almost luminous.

He looked at Robert for a moment, no recognition crossing his face, no malice appearing as he gazed at him, waiting for an explanation for Robert's pensive call.

Robert opened his mouth but nothing came out.

This whole sorry business had all been a terrible waste of time. This poor kid was just a local party boy who happened to resemble someone Robert and Michael had vaguely remembered seeing in Greece. His resemblance was striking, but that sort of thing happened all the time, and it most certainly did not mean that this person was some kind of immortal entity, roaming the earth and wreaking continental destruction. He was an innocent boy, enjoying the perks of his youth, and Robert needed to leave him alone.

"Are you okay?" said the poor guy who strikingly resembled someone Robert had seen in Greece.

Robert could only nod.

A simple and pleasant smile spread on the young man's face and he nodded back.

"Good," he said. Then he turned and started back down the hallway toward the stairs.

There was much more light coming up from the first floor, and it illuminated the retreating figure from the front, rendering him to Robert as a walking silhouette, growing smaller as he strode away along the hall.

"I'm looking for the skotos," Robert heard a confident voice, which sounded incredibly like his own, call out down the hall toward the diminishing silhouette.

The dark shape stopped in its tracks, as motionless as the shadow of a statue.

Robert grinned.

CHAPTER III

†

Enthralled

For they shall eat, and not have enough: they shall commit whoredom, and shall not increase: because they have left off to take heed of the Lord. Whoredom and wine and new wine take away the heart.

- Hosea 4:10-11 (KJV)

Los Angeles, California
The den of a large, private residence on Nichols Canyon Road, just north of Woodrow Wilson Drive

†

"It's so fucking hard to find cocaine anymore," Great Hair Guy said, leaning against the considerably sized arm of the loveseat, on the fireplace side, not the patio door side. He was wearing some cream-colored DKNY pants that Nick hadn't ever seen before—or he would've purchased them—which looked exquisite on him, accentuated as they were by the fact that, although he was large and muscular, his waist was the size of a champagne bottle.

"I know a guy," Baby-Faced Boy offered, nodding, pouting with a delectable cuteness. This guy was probably the only person at the party who was young enough—*looked* young enough?—to get away with wearing shorts in December, which was difficult even in California. He was swathed in Abercrombie & Fitch from head to toe and it should have looked silly, a catalog fall-out, but didn't at all. He was sitting on the carpet between Theo and Darren, both of whom were mesmerized by him, enthralled merely watching the beautiful boy roll a joint. Nick wondered if this kid was old enough to drink. Actually, he looked as though it were possible he wasn't old enough to legally view adult films.

"How nice for you," Troy smirked. Eddie giggled and snorted.

"Did you see anyone fall into the pool?" Nick looked up at Huge Pectoral Man, who was standing on the patio door side of the loveseat. He just smiled back down at him. Huge Pectoral Man wasn't as pretty as most, but he'd obviously been visited by the Human Growth Hormone Fairy and, consequently, small motor vehicles could have been parked on his shoulders.

"Okay, so, I almost didn't even come out tonight," said Sexy Buzz-Cut Boy, who appeared to be at least old enough to legally purchase beer, but not so old as to be eligible for lower car insurance. Also, his skin had yet to be too adversely affected by the fact that he either visited two tanning salons per day, or lived in a house with no roof.

Sexy Buzz-Cut Boy was sitting next to Theo and kept laying his hand on Theo's thigh. "See, like, I gave my friend a wad of money to get me an eight-ball of coke, right? Only, he had to go through his friend, who goes to her dealer, then she gets my coke, and she had to give it back to my friend. Sounds like it'd be pretty fuckin' easy, right? Only they get into this big fight, right? So, of course the cunt wouldn't see him or even speak to him, right? Even though she's got my motherfucking cocaine, I mean, what a bitch, right? So, like, that was eight fucking weeks ago! Eight weeks! Fuck, I could have found four or five motherfucking dealers on my own in that time, right? I mean, fuck! So, like, I almost didn't even come out tonight, but he finally got it from the snatch, and I picked it up and he was all, like, 'she's sorry it took so long,' and crap and shit, but I just told him to tell her that if she couldn't do a favor for someone, then don't, like, offer to do it, right?" Sexy Buzz-Cut Boy's forehead wrinkled up in a questioning and oh-so-unflattering expression of angst.

"Did you just, like, tell a story?" Troy said.

Eddie snorted.

"I liked the story," Darren said, nodding. "It was clever and well developed, but I really think you should add a lot more derogatory expressions about women. I mean, you hardly used any."

Laughter.

"Yeah," Eddie said, "and put in a car chase."

"Yes!" Darren yelled, pointing at Eddie. "I was just thinking that! Your little story really needs a lot more low-class, vulgar expressions about women, and a good, long car chase. That's a hit, baby!"

Darren and Eddie did a high-five.

"Car chases are cool," Baby-Faced Boy added, licking his newly-formed joint.

The four boys had started out all by themselves, simply lounging quietly in and around the big, big loveseat they'd found in the corner of the main living room, waiting for Scott to come back downstairs, comfortably watching the sizeable crowd swirl before them. It didn't take long, however, for the tide of high-glam partiers to rise and cover them. Nope, not long at all.

"I don't think anyone fell in the pool," said Great Hair Guy, smirking. He was the lightest, most natural-looking blonde Nick had ever seen; his ruffled locks were nearly white. It was striking and unnerving at the same time. Nick knew that Darren was a natural blonde, of course, but his hair was a much more common yellow-gold, a little darker at the roots and the back of his neck. Great Hair Guy had creepy, golden eyebrows and a retro-seventies cut of white-blonde locks that probably earned him the undivided attention of everyone in his company, if not modeling contracts that could easily pay for homes on each appropriate continent. Incredible as he was, his aesthetic glory was almost common among those present, which was probably a respite that was more than welcome. With the utter absence of arrogance, Nick knew the feeling.

"Oh, no." Nick shook his head, looking back up at Great Hair Guy, trying not to stare at him too obviously. "Karen saw this famous chick fall into the pool. I don't remember who it was, but I was right here."

"They should have a dance floor," said Huge Pectoral Man, gazing out the glass doors at the multitude gathered on the patio. "I've done way too much K to just stand, or sit, or walk around. Someone should have set up a dance floor."

"I think you're lookin' at it," Theo said.

"So, dance, baby." Troy smiled. "I doubt anyone will complain."

"Troy," Nick said, suddenly looking at him. "Are you in love with me?"

Missy, it seemed, had completely taken control of Nick's mouth.

"Okay," Sexy Buzz-Cut Boy said, folding his arms, looking around at all of them, "how many people here do you think are on drugs?"

Darren laughed, rolled his eyes. "How many people are here?"

"I don't think any of the stars are on drugs," Sexy Buzz-Cut Boy said plainly, obviously pleased that his stupid question had brought everyone's attention back to him. For someone in Tom Ford pants, Donald J. Pliner shoes, and who looked like James Marsden's prettier younger brother, he was a transparently insecure little guy.

"Yeah," Darren chuckled, "'cause, you know, stars never do drugs."

"Because," Nick said, still looking at Troy, ignoring the peripheral goings-on, "like, I wouldn't know how to handle that."

"I wish I could say that shocked me, precious." Troy laughed. "Golly. I really do."

Baby-Faced Boy finally lit his joint and took a couple of drags, appearing very much as though he'd never done it before, coughing a bit with a mouth-watering loveliness, if such a thing was possible while coughing. Though, judging from the captivation it stirred within the group, it was most certainly a possible thing.

The joint was passed on first to Darren, who didn't partake but passed it instead to Orange Lipstick Girl.

Baby-Faced Boy scooted very close to Darren. Darren's eyes widened a bit, then he looked up at Nick with a playful grin that said, *Are you seeing this? He's hitting on me! This little baby boy is actually hitting on me! Isn't this the cutest fuckin' thing you've ever seen?*

Nick smiled and almost laughed, because he thought he should want to kick the kid in the head. He didn't want to, though, and was having a tough time deciding if that was a good or a bad thing.

"Do you need anything else, baby?" Troy nudged Nick. "You know I can probably cover you. If you need anything, that is."

Nick looked at him again.

"I know that, sweetheart," he said. "You know something..." Nick nodded, smiling. "I know that."

Troy smirked for a second, then blushed, looking at his hands and fumbling with the zipper on his fanny pack. Nick chuckled and kissed him on the cheek.

"Okay, knock that shit off." Troy smiled, and blushed harder.

"I have no trouble stocking that shit," Great Hair Guy said. "I know at least two guys that can score me some very high quality blow."

"Tell it, chil'," Theo sang, suddenly Aretha Franklin. "Move with the groove, baaybeee."

"What about GHB?" asked Huge Pectoral Man.

"That's easy to find," Sexy Buzz-Cut Boy said. "But it's really wicked."

"Mm."

"My friend wrote this, like, little pamphlet thing called *GHB and You*. He's so worried we'll fuck up on it he wrote this, like, whole little book-thing."

"You're kidding."

"No, no! He did. It's cool. Complicated, though."

"Complicated?"

"Yeah." Sexy Buzz-Cut Boy nodded. "Oh, my god, yeah. You have to be, like, a genius to use the stuff."

"Hm."

"Yeah, man, fuck it. I ain't no genius. I never touch the shit."

General nodding. Pause.

"I don't know how you can even *do* coke, I swear to god!" Baby-Faced Boy shook his head, laughing like he'd said something ingeniously funny and nudging Darren with his shoulder.

"Coke makes me crazy," offered Huge Pectoral Man.

"Crazy, baby," said Theo, nodding to the music, gazing across the room at no one in particular. He was flirting with the entire party.

"You have to do so much, though," said Eddie. "I've got to go through a hefty line or two before I even feel anything."

"I know," huffed Huge Pectoral Man. "It's like Chinese food. A half-hour later and it's as if you haven't snorted anything at all."

"I was off of coke for almost six months, after I got out of rehab," Great Hair Guy said, taking a drag from the community joint. "It was hell. I didn't do anything."

"Except for weed and booze," said Troy.

"Right. Except for weed and booze."

"I got so used to whipping out my bullet every twenty minutes trying to stay high on coke," Huge Pectoral Man said. "Then, one time, at San Diego Pride, you know, at that cool Zoo thing they have…"

More nodding.

"…well, I'd just done a couple bumps on the side of the dance floor and my friend was looking behind me and his eyes got all huge and I said, 'the Security Guys are watching me, aren't they.' He just gave me this look, and I knew they were. I knew they'd seen the whole thing. So, I walked straight into the crowd, didn't even turn around. I just marched straight into the heart of the dance floor, then twisted and turned until I knew they'd never find me."

"They never found you?" Nick smiled, raising his eyebrows all the way into his hairline, which made his scalp tingle. Missy was running all over him and singing the sweetest song at the top of her lungs. She was a glorious diva, that Missy.

"Oh no, silly boy," said Huge Pectoral Man. "If you've seen one shirtless party-man on drugs, you've seen 'em all. How the holy-heck were they going to single me out in that mass of sweaty skin?"

Theo sat up abruptly, straining to see through the glass doors onto the patio. "Is that Jude Law?"

Darren turned his back to the front of the loveseat and dropped his chin to his chest. That was his intimate way of telling Nick that he wanted him to rub the back of his head. Nick smiled and ran his fingers up into Darren's hair.

Darren moaned. Baby-Faced Boy batted his gorgeous, green eyes, looked at Nick and grinned.

"Incredible party last month, by the way, Darren," Sexy Buzz-Cut Boy said.

"Thanks," Darren answered, head down, eyes closed, almost purring.

"I was sitting behind the back-bar and everyone on the couch was saying what a great party it was."

"Were you in a K-hole?" Darren asked.

"Okay, well, um… yeah, but I could still tell it was, like, a way-sweet evening, man."

"I had to save this guy from drowning in his own hot tub that night," Great Hair Guy said.

"What?" Baby-Faced Boy squinted back at him. "You're kidding!"

"Huh uh." Great Hair Guy shook his head. "I went to this guy's house with him after the party and he talked to Gina right before we went into the hot tub."

"She crossed him over?"

"Whoooaa, yeah. At first I just thought he was only goin' a little swoopy from her, but then he slumps over and he's out cold, just floating in the water on his face."

"Oh, my god…"

"I had to drag his knocked-out ass onto the deck. That's not as easy as you'd think, all that dead weight and stuff, and all wet on top of that."

"Wow."

"Total buzz-kill. The worst part, though, was being shit-ass bored until he woke the fuck up. Of course, he didn't even realize what had happened."

"How long was he out?"

"Ten. Fifteen, maybe."

Sexy Buzz-Cut Boy smiled and slapped Darren on the knee. "Man, the club was at capacity, man. I'll bet you made bank!"

"Bank, baby," Darren purred, not raising his head or even opening his eyes. Nick put both hands to work on him, tickling his scalp with tiny circles. Darren groaned deeply, tumbling out some vague vocal sounds that slightly resembled, *Ooooh, myyyy gaaaaaaawwd!*

Nick pressed his fingers harder onto Darren's head, who gasped and swooned. Missy had come to power. She was ruling and there was joy throughout the land.

"I had to wait in line a half-hour," said Sexy Buzz-Cut Boy.

"The member's line, right?" Huge Pectoral Man said.

"Of course," Sexy Buzz-Cut Boy sang, suddenly a raging queen.

The music coursed its way around and through them all, some of it from the speakers, some of it the happy din of all the beautiful people, resplendent, immaculate, and careless.

†

"You can't possibly have any idea what you're doing," the dark-haired Greek boy said quietly.

Robert stood between him and the closed door. He'd locked it behind him as he followed the guy into the room, even though he hadn't yet determined if such a move was really a very good idea.

They'd found an empty bedroom on the second floor, one of the house's many enormous features. He'd followed the Greek back down the hall and they'd wandered right into the Presidential Suite, it seemed.

Upon hearing Robert blurt the word 'skotos' down the hallway, the guy obviously thought he needed to find a secluded place where whatever was going to happen next would be less likely to make a scene. It would have been bad for both of them to cause a commotion or call so much attention to themselves that they ended up on the morning news or, more likely, some ultra-pathetic, daytime talk show.

"I'm not going away," Robert answered patiently, surprised at how calm he sounded. Then he realized that he actually was calm. Well, calm*er* anyway. His palms were dry. His heart wasn't hammering in his chest—at least it had come down a few settings below 'Crack Addict;' now it was beating somewhere around 'Too Much Espresso'—and his hands were as steady as he could have hoped they'd be, under the circumstances. Compared to the way they'd shaken in the hall, now his hands were as steady as a surgeon's.

"I've been looking for the skotos for over a decade," Robert said, "and I know you can help me."

The man from Greece shut his eyes.

He was wearing a pair of forest-green canvas pants and a very tight V-neck T-shirt that, although incredibly flattering, actually looked sort of cheap. His shoes, on the other hand, were dark brown leather ankle boots with beautiful silver buckles, which Robert recognized as Tanino Crisci and knew they cost just under a thousand dollars. He was mildly alarmed that he was beginning to recognize which designers were responsible for which pair of expensive shoes, but dismissed it as benign.

Whoever he was, the Greek boy had become quite acclimated to the local culture. That was brazenly obvious. He could have been any one of the multitudes of male supermodels or soap opera heartthrobs that infested the city like rampant bacteria.

The young man's face was expressionless and seamless as he stood across the room in the relative quiet, breathing silently, appearing to resign himself to the unavoidable.

"I can't help you," he finally said, opening his eyes and looking at Robert plainly.

"I'm not going to go away," Robert repeated, meeting his gaze, enjoying the power of the moment. It was a temporary power, undoubtedly, but Robert pressed into it anyway, not thinking about what he would do if his temporary power suddenly ran dry. In that instant, Robert realized, he didn't really care. He felt good and left it at that.

"This is a very bad idea," said the boy from Greece. "Believe me, you're in way over your head, my friend."

"I don't agree."

The Greek boy smirked. "Are you so sure you know everything that you need to know? Do you have every piece of the puzzle? Are all of your puzzle pieces arranged so tightly in their correct places that you're willing to risk so much?"

Robert's stomach sank a little.

Well, um, actually, no. That would be a very big, fat no.

Robert didn't falter, though. All signs had lead to this moment. With or without the crucifix in his hand, he had everything he needed. He could feel the weight of the Vessel against his leg where it hung inside his jacket pocket. If this guy was only a guy, then he certainly wasn't going to murder Robert right there in some random guest room. If he wasn't just a normal guy, then Robert was prepared.

And, of course, he had God. Oh, right, don't forget about Him. Robert had everything he needed, which included the presence and approval of God to such a degree that it went, of course, without saying.

"I know enough," he said.

The guy just stared at him for a moment, looking at Robert as if he'd asked for nothing more than the time. Then he smiled slowly.

"Those are some truly famous last words, my friend," he said. "I've heard them many, many times."

The boy's smile was subtle but haunting, lifting the corner of his mouth just the tiniest little bit. It was enough to send shivers up Robert's spine. He just about shuddered visibly. This guy, whoever—*what*ever—he was, obviously knew how to play his cards. He knew how to chip at the cornerstone of Robert's resolve and had gone immediately to the task.

"I'm not your friend," Robert said, willing his muscles to remain still, his lungs to work at a steady and even pace.

"Really? How nice of you to clarify that for me."

The guy was so composed, so mild with his tone. It was irritating and Robert was beginning to feel the stirrings of a little righteous anger.

"I'm not keeping you from anything important, am I?" Robert tried to lay his sarcasm at the same level as the Greek boy's.

"Oh, no," the Greek boy said. "I've been hoping all night that some loony-toon would pull me away from the party and threaten me."

"I'm not threatening you."

"You are, though," the boy said, his tone slightly lower, almost sad. "Unfortunately, I'm afraid you are."

"Maybe you could just answer a couple of simple questions for me and then we can both be on our way."

The Greek boy actually rolled his eyes. Robert gritted his teeth.

"You can do that much, can't you?" Robert said, trying to remain blasé, though it was obvious even to him that he'd fallen a little south of it.

"You hardly want to ask me just 'a couple' of questions," said the boy, mockingly, "and I'd bet every dime to my name that your questions are far from 'simple.' However…" he flashed his serious look again, "…as for when it is that I can be on my way, you really should be very, very careful of the kind of assumptions you allow to influence your actions."

"It sounds to me like you're the one who's doing all the threatening," Robert noted. "What was that, the fourth time?"

"Bishop," the boy said blandly, "I wasn't the one who requested this meeting."

At the sound of his title, Robert's lower lip dropped as if to allow him to respond but was held back by his jaw, which may have locked up because it knew he didn't *have* any response. It was expected that there'd be a few unforeseen components to this endeavor. This first one, though, was a whopper.

"Yes, I know who you are, Robert," the Greek guy closed his eyes again and nodded patiently, as though speaking to a toddler. "I was quite happy, back out in the hallway, because I thought for a moment you'd come to your senses and decided not to take any action after all. I saw you outside, watching me get out of the limousine. I saw you downstairs, watching me there, too. I've seen you at the club, many, many times. And of course, I've seen you in New York, watching me, and in Greece, where you were also watching me. Frankly, I'm a little surprised you chose this particular time to confront me. What made you finally decide to stop watching?"

"You disappeared," Robert heard himself say. "While I was in New York, you just disappeared." He hadn't really expected to say anything at all, but hearing it, he was glad his voice was level and flat, which was at least some consolation to help offset his shock. His heart had been kicked back up past 'Crack Addict' and was frantically hammering away, now set on 'Hummingbird.' He willfully resolved himself not to divulge any physical sign that the boy had caught him off guard. He needed a poker face.

"I know I disappeared," said the Greek boy. "Rather suddenly, too. It was not my doing. Although, there are a great many things for which I am credited..." The boy leveled his eyes at Robert sternly. "...that were not my doing."

What was this? An allusion? A suggestion toward some defensive explanation? Why was he being so casual, so condescending?

"You're going to feel very silly in a moment, Robert," the boy continued. "I'm afraid you're going to feel quite foolish."

"What are you talking about?"

"You shouldn't have come to Los Angeles."

"I saw you at that club."

"Of course you did." The boy shut his eyes, nodding, pouting a little, the patronizing little twit.

"Don't be so cocky," Robert blurted. "There were giant, bloody, lion tracks in an alley up the street. You could have saved us both a lot of time and just put up a billboard."

"And how did you hear about the tracks, Bobby?"

"Don't call me 'Bobby,' you twit."

"Of course." Blink, nod, pout. "Did you see the tracks on the news? Did Katie Couric mention them after she finished up with the day's mundane highlights?"

Robert smirked at the guy's inane question. "Did you think they'd go unnoticed?"

"Tell me why you're standing here," the boy said. "Tell me who you think I am."

"Why am I going to feel foolish?"

"Begin at the beginning, Robert. Who do you think I am?"

You're a minion of hell! Robert wanted to scream it at him and call down the wrath of God into this very room, to see the Lord bring forth a whirlwind of fire that would consume this abomination where he stood.

The Greek boy was looking at him playfully, which made Robert furious. He allowed himself to wet his lips and take a calming breath.

"You're someone for whom I've been looking," he said finally.

The boy smiled. "How typically vague."

Robert heard himself grunt in frustration and was even angrier for letting it slip.

"I just think that since we're here," the Greek boy said, ignoring Robert's huff, "we need to at least be on the same page if anything is going to be accomplished at all."

Robert squinted. This was a trick. This was a deceptive maneuver, otherwise the boy would have offered nothing but denials or simply left.

"Believe me," Robert said, trying to keep the vehemence out of his voice and actually managing it, though barely, "whoever you are, I'm ready for you."

"Yes," said the boy, as blandly as ever. "I'm sure you think so."

"This is not a game."

"Okay, well, I've been trying to make sure you understood that."

"Then I think we're about as 'on the same page' as we're going to get."

"Who am I, Robert?"

"If you're asking me whether or not I know your name, it's simple enough for me to admit that I don't."

The boy sighed. It was large and very breathy, almost an irritated huff.

"I don't know your name," Robert admitted again. "But I'd like to know how it is that you know mine."

The Greek boy grinned.

"First of all," he said, "you may call me Scott. Everyone does."

"Scott?" Robert almost twittered. "What kind of stupid —?"

"You were expecting maybe 'Mephistopheles?' "

Robert grunted again.

"Second," the boy said, "as a gesture of good faith, if I may use the term, I'll tell you how I know you're name. It's quite simple, really. I met Bishop Carter while I was in London."

Timothy Carter. One of Bishop Sigovia's little colleagues, one of the new brood. Tim had studied in London for a time, Robert knew. Though, he also knew that he'd been on a strictly academic trip and didn't have any official objective that was at all related to the skotos. At least not directly.

Still, Robert's sources had documented that this Greek boy was also in London for a time. These were secular sources; completely maintained by Robert alone and independent of the Church. They wouldn't have known anything about Bishop Carter and wouldn't have reported any connection. Robert had no way of recalling if the timelines of Tim's trip and the sightings of this Greek boy — *boy?* — would have supported his claim.

It was possible, however. It was absolutely possible.

"I don't know Bishop Carter very well," Robert said, frantically trying to figure out how to keep his voice flat. His heart was racing up again, trying to break his ribs. "But I know that he wouldn't have told you, or anyone else, anything about me at all."

"It was quite inadvertent, I assure you."

"Nonetheless, I don't see —"

"That's all I'm going to give you in that regard," the Greek boy interrupted. "Whether you want to accept the fact or not, your time here with me is very, very limited. So, there you are, that's how I know your name. Take it or leave it. Despite what you may be thinking, you don't have very long to do whatever it is you're hoping to do tonight, and something tells me that you don't want to waste this brief opportunity discussing the likelihood of the little encounter I had with Tim."

However much he hated to admit it, that was true enough. Even so, Robert's curiosity was almost unendurable. Whatever had happened in London, there was a young bishop waiting back in Rome who had quite a lot of explaining to do.

For the moment, that would have to wait.

"And your name?" Robert asked.

"I just told you. It's Scott."

Now Robert rolled his eyes. "That's all?"

"You know," the Greek boy — 'Scott' — shook his head, squinting a bit, touching the bridge of his nose as if he had a headache, "I've gone through all of this stuff so very recently, and I'm just not in the mood —"

"I'm looking for the skotos," Robert interrupted. "That's all I want right now."

Scott sighed again. "That's not an insignificant request."

"Nevertheless."

"You know..." Scott cleared his throat. "...I can completely understand your feelings. 'Bishop Bobby' just doesn't have that 'big-important serious-sacred-guy' sound to it."

A soft rumble of footsteps passed outside their door heading toward the first floor stairs. Just two or three people going back down to the party, either not noticing the closed room or not caring. Muffled voices rose briefly as the little group passed the open DJ room and shouted pleasantries.

Robert didn't take his eyes off of Scott. They just stared at each other. Maybe this Scott-person was waiting for Robert to pick up the ball and lob it back. He didn't. He held his tongue and was glad for it because it was Scott who finally broke the moment.

"Why?" he asked.

"What do you mean, 'why?' " Robert almost whined.

"I mean, why are you looking for him, for the skotos?" Scott explained. "What are you trying to accomplish?"

Robert wasn't sure how to answer. The question both shocked and comforted him. Little Timmy couldn't have told this guy too much if he didn't even know why Robert was looking for the skotos.

"So, you admit you know of him then?" Robert wanted to slap himself. Even he thought he sounded stupid.

"Must you be so redundant?" Scott rolled his eyes yet again. "Didn't you establish that little fact back out in the hallway?"

Yes, of course he had. The instant the boy — Scott — had stopped walking away down the hall, Robert knew he'd hit his mark. Maybe he was just trying to confirm it again for the benefit of a more cogent part of his mind.

"What do you know of him?" Robert asked.

Scott cocked his head. He revealed a slight puzzlement but was otherwise unmoved. "I have no idea how to answer that question."

That was going around, apparently.

"Actually," Scott said, "I have no idea where to start. Can you perhaps be a bit more specific?"

"Is he still here?"

"Still?"

This was not going well. That had been the second stupid thing Robert said in as many minutes. He felt like someone who'd been trained to operate an automobile by a team of professionals only to fail the test for his driver's license. He'd gotten into the car with the DMV employee, confident and well prepared, turned on the engine, activated his turn signal, and then promptly lunged into traffic and hit a police car. No, not going well at all.

"I saw him," Robert admitted.

"You're joshin' me!" Scott laughed.

"No." Robert frowned. "No, I saw him, almost a week ago, flying over the city."

"Get the fuck outta here!" Scott was howling.

"What?"

The Greek boy stopped laughing with a heavy sigh and just gazed at Robert, slack-jawed.

"You're telling me you actually saw —?"

"Yes!" Robert hissed.

"Please excuse me." Scott chuckled some more. "I'm just amazed, that's all. Really, that's amazing!"

"Yes, thank you. It's amazing. Now is he still here?"

"Well," Scott said, chuckling again, pressing his eyebrows together, "if my guess is correct as to what you mean by 'skotos,' and if that then refers to what you saw flying over the city, then I suppose the answer is yes."

Robert registered surprise before he could stop himself. Stunning. There was no hesitation before he answered, but Robert still didn't know if Scott had meant that the skotos was here in Los Angeles or here in this room. He was going to have to be careful with the way he worded his questions. It was sort of like finding a genie in a lamp and having to phrase the wishes very specifically; you might ask the genie to make you famous, then *poof*, you're a serial killer.

"Now see, Robert," Scott said, "do you see how many connections you forced me make all on my own. Have you begun to notice the number of assumptions you might have made that are responsible for bringing you here before me? Doesn't that bother you at all?"

"I saw what I saw," Robert huffed.

"I think it's time for you to answer one of my questions now," Scott said.

"What?" Robert raised an eyebrow.

"I've already asked you several, but let's begin with the first one. Who do you think I am?"

It would have been nice to shoot out a simple answer as quickly as Scott, but that wasn't going to happen. Some pros and cons needed to be weighed. Of course, Robert had thought about this many times before, he'd weighed as many pros and cons as he could find, but he also realized that 'thinking about' and 'actually experiencing' were two different things. Reading about parachuting, learning its facets academically, and even talking to seasoned sky divers, couldn't possibly prepare a person to cope with the facets of their own character they'd never known were there. Facets that suddenly sprang to life once they actually faced the open door of the airplane. Such things were always unpredictable and unknowable.

Even inside the sturdiest shark-cage, how many divers didn't have to work diligently to keep themselves from puking their guts out the moment before they were lowered into the ocean with a great white or two casually drifting around? The teeth of the shark may be designed only for eating, but how many of those divers still looked into the water and somehow saw the shark clearly showing off a big, sharp, and knowing smile?

Well, here he was; Robert was standing all alone in this little room, face to face with the enigma from Greece. The airplane door was open, the clouds were zipping by, the instructor was shouting at him to jump, and Robert was suddenly glad that Scott was so emotionless; he could have, after all, been showing off a big, sharp, and knowing smile.

Robert decided to turn on his engine again, activate his turn signal, look for police cars, and then just go for it.

"I think that you're the skotos," he said, his heart fluttering like a punctured balloon.

"You think I'm 'the Darkness?' " Scott asked, smirking.

Robert took a labored breath, then nodded. "Yes."

"I see." Scott folded his hands in front of him. "If you really mean that, then I am not."

"Of course I mean it," Robert smirked back.

"However," Scott lowered his voice again, "if what you meant to ask was whether I'm 'exousia skotos,' then you just might be in business."

†

"You two are in love, I can tell," observed Sexy Buzz-Cut Boy.

Darren had taken Troy's place on the love seat after he'd gotten up to speak with someone standing in the bar line. Surprisingly, Darren was able to wedge himself sideways into the gap left by Troy, who was a considerably smaller person, and when Nick shifted just the tiniest little bit in his direction, the result was a heavenly connection.

Darren, Nick, and Eddie lounged together in the loveseat as though it had been custom designed for the three of them. Darren and Nick could lean slightly toward each other and Eddie seemed entirely content to rest his head on the back of Nick's shoulder. Of course Missy was pressed in tightly between them all, relentlessly caressing and elating them toward a severe and inevitable extreme.

Darren's head could easily rest on the back of the chair while he looked at Nick. Both of them had a free arm to touch each other's face, run a finger down each other's arm or chest, or just mesh their fingers together while they both watched their own hands, entranced by the sight and beset by the rampage of feeling as their fingers entwined.

Missy was apparently very aware of their love, and she obviously approved. The diva was still singing, only now a choir had joined her, and, almost frighteningly, the orchestra was still just getting tuned up.

"That's so sweet," Sexy Buzz-Cut Boy observed solemnly. He had evidently taken his share of illegal compounds and was consequently captivated by the sight of Nick and Darren.

"Are they boyfriends?" whispered Baby-Faced Boy. Nick couldn't see him but thought that he might be attempting subtlety, maybe leaning over to Theo.

"Duh," Nick heard Theo say, and smiled. Darren smiled too.

Although it had only been a few weeks since they'd indulged, Missy seemed to be working very nicely for both of them, as if they were her special project. Nick was looking at Darren, absently listening to the conversation around them, but completely engrossed by this man that lived with him, that shared his home and everything else.

Good lord, things had changed in the last three months.

Nick knew there were moments best left unanalyzed. It was never a good idea, for example, on nights such as these, to consider how much emotion was the result of Missy's enthusiastic power and how much of it was the pure result of their own lives.

In the end, it didn't really matter anyway. No matter how many drugs ran rampant through their blood, no matter what chemical composition affected their emotional responses, it was impossible to manufacture love out of nothing. No mere drug could produce the attachment, sweetness, and comfort that came with a shared history. Especially one that had been so hard earned, one into which they'd so deeply invested their hearts.

Sure, there were some very powerful chemicals out there. There were compounds that could affect their brains in such a dynamic way that they'd easily make them believe they were in love with a coffee table. Such a thing would have been completely confusing and rigidly temporary, though. That was certainly not the case here. That wasn't at all what was going on at the moment.

They'd both taken a hit of ecstasy in the car, a single dose, one that came from a batch that had yet to prove itself. Happily, the pill's effect was more than what they'd hoped; their senses had been heightened exceedingly, their skin became almost unbearably over-sensitized, their emotions strongly uninhibited. All of these things were enveloping them. More than that, it was happening while they were in each other's company, which was the single most heavenly aspect of living that either of them would ever know.

Still, Missy was only enhancing things, bringing to the surface the deepest considerations of their devotion, the most elusive points of their commitment. Miss E was only a light. She was a powerful blaze shining behind a tapestry that had already been woven, illuminating nuances of beauty and profound texture that could only be possible within threads that had already been sewn together meticulously, strong and steady, carefully and painfully, over time. Nick had read somewhere that the only thing that ever gave anything any real value was time. Who said that? Florence Scovel Shinn? Anthony Robbins? Stephen Covey?

What difference did it make? Missy was talking. Missy could easily take them. Though, she could merely bring them to a place they'd already found. Once there, she happily emphasized and detailed a lovely and blissful passion they'd already claimed.

"What's up, baby?" Darren grinned.

"Have I told you today?" Nick grinned back, running a finger along Darren's ear.

"I don't think so." Darren moved his face closer to Nick's, smirking playfully.

"Really?" Nick smiled. "I could have sworn—"

"Say it anyway." Darren smiled back.

Nick closed his eyes, feeling the brush of Darren's breath across his nose, his chin, his lips. "I love you," he said.

The words were timid and fragile; meant for Darren's ears alone.

"I love you too," Darren said. He pressed his lips to Nick's, tenderly sweeping his fingers down his cheek, running the tips along the line of his jaw and settling them underneath his mouth, ready to hold Nick's face to his, to keep him from moving away before he was finished.

They'd both be giggling any second, knowing that if they'd been witnessing this behavior by anyone else, they'd be retching.

They'd had many, many moments like this without Missy's help. The darkness in the late hours at their beachside home provided a haven for these Hallmark moments. They joked and laughed about them a little bit while the sun was up, but once the lights were out and they'd settled underneath their heavy winter comforter, only the whisper of low tide around them, it all seemed so perfect. No words were too sweet, no touch too soft. Nothing was trivial in the dark.

Still, here in the press of all these people, surrounded by the sound of all these voices, Missy had compelled them despite the audience.

Although they probably couldn't make out the words of their conversation, Nick knew the boys seated around them were watching, each of them attempting some sincere discretion. Nick barely registered them and decided not to be self-conscious. Still, he couldn't help wondering, just a little bit, what they thought.

Whatever it was, it would have been interesting and nothing more. Nothing could have made Nick turn his eyes away from Darren's. Even knowing they might be acting a little too smoochy, he didn't want to stop. Anyone glancing at them for even a second or two, who also had so much as a casual acquaintance with Missy, would know exactly what was going on and why these two beautiful boys just couldn't seem to control themselves. Their little public display would be quickly tagged and shelved. It was nothing new.

Darren sighed and closed his eyes. Nick shifted so that he could see the rest of the room and Darren could settle easier against him. Both of Nick's hands were free now and he held Darren's with one and massaged his palm with the other. This was another little trick that knocked Missy into an uproar. Darren purred.

Nick easily remembered all the years before Darren. Being single and gay in Los Angeles wasn't an entirely unpleasant way to live. There was always something to do, someplace to go, something rambunctious and enticing of which to be a part. He'd never been short on friends, or attention, and so Loneliness had easily disguised himself behind a very big smile. Nick hardly knew he was there at all.

Nick used to travel a lot. New York was a very common destination, as well as Miami and Chicago. He'd spent a lot of time in London and a little in Paris. The opportunity to model in Tokyo had come up a couple of times, but there always seemed to be something in the States that was comparable at the same time. It was such a hassle to go all the way to Asia anyway.

For Nick, though, the really big money came from commercials; he seemed to snag a lot more jobs doing peripheral work for television ads. He rarely landed contracts that put him on mainstream runways or in print. His look and presence were much more natural, evidently, for selling shampoo or deodorant on TV. That meant hanging out in LA more often than not.

Until his recent adventure with the billboard campaign, he never got close to scoring the big contracts. No one ever wanted to put him on a poster, he never even came close to a magazine cover, and, unlike one or two of his casual professional acquaintances, no one ever thought he was worth fifty thousand dollars a day. That might have been for the best. Who knows where he'd be if the spotlight had hit him that hard? Probably dead by now, he thought.

Whenever the work did take him out of town, it was very easy to slip a little club-hopping into the itinerary. As long as he attended to the business at hand, was punctual and attractive when he had to be in front of a camera, it didn't matter what he did with his down time.

What difference did it make if the job ended on Thursday and he didn't get back to LA until the following Tuesday afternoon? The flights were cheaper if he stayed over a Saturday night anyway. It was cost effective. Besides, it wasn't as if there'd been anyone sitting at home waiting for him. No one had been waiting at the apartment, maybe putting away the laundry and getting ready to open a beer on the couch and watch a rerun of *Will & Grace*, maybe emptying the dishwasher to make room for the soon-to-be messy dinner plates and burning some reduced-fat Pillsbury biscuits in the oven. No one had been waiting to ask him what he'd done with himself during the three or four extra days he'd stayed in Chicago, in Minneapolis, in Fort Lauderdale. No one would ask, or care, how he'd spent his weekend and whether or not he indulged in anything carnal. Why not run amuck? Why the fuckin' heck not?

One or two phone calls were always enough to insure that his trips were enjoyable. Someone always knew how to find the best parties and usually the same person was able to handle the acquisition of any necessary supplies. After all, it was far from unusual that the visiting talent would request assistance of that nature. Nick thought it was almost unbelievable the way the local studios and agency offices were prepared to handle any and all desires, esoteric as they might be. From what he was told by just about every production assistant between New York and San Diego, by comparison, the arrangements that Nick discreetly requested were tame to the point of being boring. It made Nick wonder what kind of little extras the fifty-thousand-dollars-a-day guys were requesting. Drunken sheep?

On most of the out-of-town jobs, another guy from the cast, or even the production crew, would be a local resident and more than happy to show Nick around. That was always best. Nick always had the best time when he was provided with a local guide.

Every city had its A-list and at least one dazzling space in which they could be displayed. Every A-list club pulsed with the young and the stunning and the wealthy and the radiant. There were so many types of spaces, with raised dance floors and spectacular lighting and dazzling architecture and luminous hideaways. Why should Nick worry that he couldn't remember which club was in what city or what hotel was closer to which airport or who he'd met or how long he'd danced or what landmark he'd planned to see but didn't quite get around to seeing or how many pills he'd taken or whether the line of powder in front of him was cocaine or crystal or what time he woke up and if he still had his watch or his wallet after he literally crawled out of the cab and staggered back up to his room?

It didn't stop once Nick got home. Nope, there were too many events and too many wonderful experiences that he might miss if he stayed at his apartment and let the parties rage on without him. Besides, there was no one to whom to answer. Nick's apartment was empty and silent. No one would shake their head at his excesses. There was no one to ask him to stay home and just relax, to tell him that it was okay to just watch television on a Saturday night and argue over whether it was going to be *Law and Order* or *20/20*. The idea that falling asleep on the couch with his head in someone's lap— maybe with *Saturday Night Live* finishing its last sketches in the background—would be equal to a night of rampant frivolity in the most exclusive Hollywood clubs might have seemed like an unlikely possibility. Still, Nick always suspected that it was not only possible, but that the former would outshine the latter drastically.

Until Nick had both options, it was easier to handle the down time when he was in a crowd. Loneliness was still always very close at hand but at least, within Nick's frenzied life, Loneliness wasn't so easy to spot.

Eventually, Nick still spotted him. Back at the apartment, even with the stereo playing, even making phone call after phone call, laughing it up, bantering for who-knew-how-long with whoever answered their phone about who-knew-what, it was impossible not to see Loneliness sitting there, maybe on the couch, maybe slouching on the ottoman, waiting patiently for Nick to quit ignoring him.

It appeared that Scott wasn't the first demon Nick had known. No, there had been quite a few others, Loneliness only being the one with whom he was most intimate.

At first, Nick had little hope that Darren might be the one who finally sent Loneliness packing. In fact, for a significant amount of time during the beginning of their relationship, Darren had strictly followed Standard Jerk Procedure. Nope, Nick had known that Darren wasn't going to dispatch Loneliness any time soon. At the time, Nick saw quickly enough that it would have been terribly difficult for Darren to accomplish such a job, what with his head being so far up his ass and all.

Still, they'd endured. Exactly how was yet another item that Nick had no intention of analyzing too closely. They'd survived together, even through some remarkably miserable times, long enough for a fallen angel with wavy black hair to come along and slap them both hard enough to knock a little perspective into those thickly embittered heads of theirs. Whatever was going to happen next, at least they'd been given that much. At least they'd had the chance to recognize some of the things they'd let themselves overlook. At least they'd seen that what they meant to each other was the cake and everything else was only frosting.

So, Nick had finally gotten rid of Loneliness. Okay, so maybe it was with the assistance of another demon, but that wasn't so bad. Scott was a much better conversationalist than Loneliness, not to mention far more attractive.

Nonetheless, not all the other demons had been so efficiently dispatched. Although he didn't come around as much, Indulgence hadn't moved too far away. The twins, Insecurity and Arrogance, were behaving in a much more acceptable manner, but they were sly little rascals; Nick couldn't keep his eyes on them all the time, and it was difficult to notice when they might be up to something. The biggest nuisance was Complacency, who always seemed to be lounging around. He was quite a squatter, that one.

Missy and Gina still kept in close touch, but they weren't really demons, were they? No one was very happy with Tina anymore and it was extremely rare that she was invited to anything. She was just the most glorious fun for the first few hours, but then she became alarmingly bitchy and it was damn near impossible to get her to just go away. Of course, Kelly was just so much fun that it really wasn't a party without her. If Kelly was a demon, then she was the Miss Congeniality of demons. Sure, she was a little gloomy the next day, but give her a couple of Percocet and usually she didn't let herself become a burden.

The more Nick thought about it the more sense it made. He'd been coping with demons in his life for years and years. Some really nasty ones, too. Why should it be any more incredible that he met a big famous one? Sure, Scotty had been responsible for bubonic plague, The Black Death, which had wiped out a third of Europe's population in the fourteenth century, but he'd really just been the instrument of some very fucked-up human ambitions. He'd behaved according to the sensibilities of the individual to whom he'd been bound at the time. He was an immense power that had been within the control of current societal influences. So, how much of that atrocity did he own? How much unhindered perspective could he have been expected to have? He wasn't all-knowing. There was only one with that feature and that responsibility. What was Scott really guilty of? Contributory negligence?

And Scott hadn't just shrugged his shoulders once he realized what he'd done. He'd paid for his ignorance. He'd paid a very high price, that was undeniable.

Demons, demons, and more demons. Everyone could tell you about the ones they had to deal with every day. It was all some people ever talked about. *I'm coping with some very serious demons right now.* Was that so rare? Maybe run-ins with smelly gray imps the size of Elijah Wood weren't all that common, but weren't all the rest of them just as dangerous?

Maybe the Beast had already won over more souls around the world than anyone would ever guess. Maybe he was going by a new name these days. Maybe he was much more visible than anyone thought and they just referred to him by his current handle, which wasn't what people thought it was; it wasn't Satan or Lucifer. Nope, the name of the Beast was Corruption.

It was, after all, dependent upon people knowing what to watch for, what signs might reveal the influence of an ancient and malevolent force.

No wonder Scott was hiding out. Maybe a shack at one of the earth's poles would have been a place more suitable for keeping his considerable power away from the influence of flawed, mortal minds. How boring would that be, though?

Nick looked down at Darren's hand, which he was still massaging with his own. He sighed, frowning.

Where was Scott anyway?

†

The sound of more footsteps out in the hall reminded Robert of where he was and the fact that he really didn't have very long to wrap this up. The patter of people walking back and forth on the other side of the door had become louder and more frequent.

Eventually, notice would be discretely passed among the more distinguished guests that there was a private room on the third floor and that it was now available. After that happened, the sound of footsteps along the hall carpet would become constant. Then it was only a matter of time before someone who knew better realized that the door behind Robert wasn't supposed to be closed. There'd be a knock, maybe an embarrassingly boisterous inquiry, and then, regardless of whatever cosmically momentous moment might be taking place in this room, the jig would be up. This event, cosmically momentous or not, would be at an end.

"Exousia skotos?" Robert repeated. "Um... 'exit the...' no... uh, 'of the darkness?' "

"*That which comes from the darkness.*" Scott grinned at him. "It's a very old nickname."

"What's the dif—?"

"There is a *world* of difference!" The sentence was so vehement, guttural, and menacing, it was almost a growl. Before he could stop himself, Robert took a step back.

Scott's voice hadn't been any louder than before. In fact, it might have been softer, but it was as though it had shifted pitch, become dark and harshly resonant. He may have moved his head, because Robert thought he saw Scott's tumble of black hair shift for an instant, but his face hadn't moved. His hair looked somehow longer, fuller—

bigger? — which must have been some trick of the dim lighting.

And, were the lights actually dimmer? Had there been a surge or a pulse in the electricity within the house? The single bulb in the tiny lamp on the otherwise empty nightstand had flickered, dimmed. Now, it seemed to be slowly recovering, as though a drain on the electricity had caught it. It might not have been enough for Robert to notice had it not happened right when Scott spoke so angrily, as if it was a visible punctuation for his words.

Robert could smell something too. What was that? Although faint, it was very familiar and somehow comforting. Wood burning? A campfire?

You're going to feel very silly in a moment, Robert.

There wasn't very much space between Robert and the locked door. Especially now that he'd backed up a step or two. If anything happened, would he have enough time to turn around, unlock it, pull himself back far enough to get it open, and get out into the hall?

"Excuse me, then," Robert said, wondering silently why the thought of the closed door had abruptly become so front-and-center. "I suppose you could look at it that way. 'Out of the darkness,' might be in reference to something separate, something other than the darkness itself."

There was no change in Scott's expression. Yet, a small degree of calm was suddenly discernable, not on his face or within his composure, but in the room.

"Please," Scott began, his voice normal again, no dark menace, no dimming bulb in the lamp, "pay attention to what you're saying, Robert."

"My Greek might not be as solid as it used to be," Robert offered, hoping that, along with his name and title, Scott didn't also already know Robert's grasp of Greek was just a hair above pathetic. "But are you trying to say that this distinction over the creature's name is really all that important?"

"Isn't it, Bobby?" Scott smirked. "Don't you think a name is a crucial part of someone's essence? Don't you think so, Robby-Bobby?"

Greek was widely considered a very important language to any biblical scholar, as was Hebrew and Coptic. Latin came in handy when attempting to understand Christian history, but it wasn't at all necessary in regard to primary source materials, the oldest surviving documents. To Robert though, considerations regarding the original languages were interesting and might have offered some additional dimension to the scripture, but the English translations were still very meticulous and very clear. They were still the word of God.

Now that he thought about it, 'exousia skotos' might have been familiar. Maybe 'skotos' was an abbreviation. Maybe someone in the sect had gotten tired of all the syllables and simply cut it down, as those who repeat something over and over tended to do. It could have happened so long ago that no one even remembered the full name.

But what difference did that make? It was still the same demon to which the name referred. They could have nicknamed him 'Frank' and it wouldn't have changed anything. This was all a pointless diversion.

I'm afraid you're going to feel quite foolish.

"Words are so important," Scott said. He hadn't moved. His hands were clasped in front of him and he had the posture of a flagpole. "Really, I can't stress that to you enough. Just the tiniest misinterpretation can have, over time, the most profound effect. Communication is the key to everything. Fuck that up and what is there?"

Was Robert supposed to answer him? Again, his lower lip made a valiant effort but was unsupported by the rest of him.

"Chaos, Robert," Scott said. "Chaos is the result of miscommunication. Chaos doesn't have as foreboding a character as Armageddon, but it's one of its primary elements."

"Why are you telling me this?" Robert asked. "Are you the demon or not?"

"Wow, that was ballsy." Scott smiled. "Did some testosterone just kick in or did you take something more interesting?"

"You're stalling."

"Maybe."

"Why?"

"Because I'm trying to figure out if you really know what it is that you're asking me."

"How stupid do you think I am?"

"Let's not—"

"Are you the demon?" Robert almost shouted it. If there hadn't been a party going on in the house, anyone in the hall would have heard him quite clearly.

Scott smiled again. "Which demon?"

Stalling and more stalling. Why was Robert waiting? He had the Vessel, he should use it. If there wasn't a real demon in the room with him, then he'd find that out very quickly.

"I think you know exactly which demon," Robert said, trying to figure out how he was going to discretely reach into his lower inside jacket pocket.

"I have a very good idea, yes," Scott said. "What does he look like?"

"What?"

"You said you saw him. So, what does he look like?"

More stalling. Robert wasn't going to go for it; wasting this time trying to describe the demon he'd seen in the sky, trying to explain that it perfectly matched the image in an old painting. He wasn't going to fall into repeating accounts he'd heard from other eyewitnesses either, only to be given another lecture about interpretation. Of course, he hadn't actually seen the demon escape from the Vessel when Matìne opened it and therefore couldn't personally attest that it and the skotos were one and the same. Was that what Scott wanted him to admit?

"Robert?"

"I think you know perfectly well —"

"Is he a black lion?"

"What?" Robert's heart stopped for an instant. It plummeted from 'Hummingbird' to 'Rock.'

"This demon you're looking for, the one you saw flying over the city, does he resemble a black lion?" Scott repeated.

The room was deadly silent. The music outside became a muffled hum.

"Yes," Robert whispered.

"Does he have wings?" Scott asked, mildly monotone. "Do they look like dragon wings? Is he black all over, except for his eyes, which are blue, like mine?" Scott leaned a bit closer, opening his eyes into wide, exaggerated orbs.

Robert took another step back.

You're going to feel very silly in a moment.

"Does he have a wavy black mane?" Scott asked. "Is the hair of his mane really black and really wavy, like mine?" This time he did tussle his hair a bit. "That would be sort of silly, don't you think, because who ever heard of a lion with wavy hair, right?" Scott smiled.

Wrapping his fingers around the seam of his jacket, down at the lower corner, beneath the last wooden button, Robert opened it as if he were just going to casually slip his hand into his pants pocket. He was almost certain the movement would be noticed, but Scott's eyes never left his.

Robert looked at Scott and wondered it he'd intentionally referred to his own hair as a mane.

"This demon-lion," Scott pressed on, "does he breathe fire and spit acid? Can he assume any human form he chooses and will he teach that skill to a witch or sorcerer? Does he teach humans how to change shape? For a price, of course?"

Robert didn't speak. He watched Scott instead, waiting for a moment when his body would allow him to reach into his blazer and bring out Solomon's Vessel. He couldn't tell if it was a total lack of courage that kept him from doing so or if it was something else. Curiosity, perhaps?

"Robert..." Scott shifted his head. "...is this demon capable of either causing or creating illness? Can he inflict disease upon those who deny him and cure it for those who pay him homage?"

"Yes," Robert heard himself whisper.

"Does he live on the flesh of the innocent?"

"What?"

"Does he eat children, Robert?"

"I—"

"Because, as you know very well, I'm sure, these demons, they all have some very quirky appetites. This one in particular, the black winged lion, the demon you've been spending so many years chasing around the world for whatever reason, does he have the nasty little habit of gorging himself on children? Has he been known to seek out the innocent flesh he needs to survive among the very, very young?"

"Yes."

"Can you blame him? Really, when you think about it, can you blame him? Don't you think it would be incredibly difficult to find innocent flesh among adults? I mean, seriously. Especially in this age and in this part of the world. Wouldn't you think that would be an extremely difficult hunger to satisfy? Everyone is so utterly corrupted, don't you think? It's really the children who are the only source of innocence anymore, isn't it? Don't you think so?"

"Yes."

"So, that's who you're looking for, right? That's the demon you've been working so hard trying to find?"

"Yes."

"You're looking for the black lion with the wings of a dragon who's brought nothing to the world but disease and suffering, the familiar of witches who teaches them to change their shape in order to better seduce and entice the innocent, who breathes fire and drools acid, who gorges himself on the flesh of children? Is that the one? Is he the goal of your quest?"

"Yes."

"Really?"

"The very one."

"You're absolutely sure?"

"Where is he?"

"Well…" Scott raised his head, inhaled, took a step back. "I can't help you then. I don't know very much about that particular demon at all. I certainly don't know how you can find him."

"What?"

"But if you do ever find him, please let me know, because I'd really like to kick his ass."

"You'd like… what?"

"You see, he's been giving me a very bad name, this acid-spitting, child-chewing demon you're looking for." Scott took a step toward Robert and, as he did, the small bed in the center of the room slid across the floor away from him. There were no casters on the frame and its posts made a dry rasping sound as they skimmed quickly over the carpet.

Robert jumped and stared stupidly at the bed. It pressed itself against the wall and yet didn't seem to be finished moving; the posts were still vibrating violently. If not for the very thick carpeting, they'd have been making some serious noise. Even so, the thump of the frame against the wall must have been heard outside. Someone had to have heard it, surely.

"What are you talking about?" Robert's hands, he was happy to notice, were fumbling with the inside pocket of his blazer. That was good. He'd bring out the Vessel now. It was time. Obviously, this was the time.

With a massive effort, Robert ripped his gaze away from the still-jittering bed and put them back on Scott, meeting his stare, promising himself that he'd keep Scott's focus while he worked at opening his pocket.

He looked at Scott, and unexpectedly heard the voice of Brathwidth.

Are all of you looking for little old me?

As he realized what was happening, as it sunk in that this was exactly what he'd asked for, he began to pray. He didn't ask God to

smite whatever entity was currently staring back at him. He didn't
beg for a pillar of fire to destroy this thing that called itself Scott,
didn't thank Him for finally revealing this entity. He asked Him
instead for help with the stubborn button on the lower inside pocket
of his blazer.

"Well..." Scott spoke, only it was with his other voice now, the
deep bass that rattled the air and Robert's bones. "My suspicion is
that your demon really doesn't exist at all. I think he's only the
fabrication of some very vivid, but malicious and stupid, imagina-
tions. Why they should create such a fiction and then spread their
stories as fact is beyond me. However, those elaborations have done
me great harm over the centuries."

"Oh, my... over the... What? Oh, God..."

*Are all of you looking for little old me? Why, I don't think I've ever been
so flattered.*

Robert's hands were still fumbling with the button on his pocket.
Why had he even buttoned it up in the first place? What was he
thinking, that the Vessel was going to jump out of his jacket and run
down the street?

He wasn't making any progress at all toward getting his pocket
open. He had no more conscious control over what his hands were
trying to do than he had of the way his legs had backed him up
completely against the door. He wished he could flip himself around
and get out. The door was locked, but he felt like he could walk right
through the wood if he had to, if it came to that. As it was, he had no
real control over himself. All he could manage was to pray for help,
beg God to help him with his button, and simply watch Scott as he
slowly walked toward him. Each approaching step was ridiculously
slow and deliberate.

Now that the bed was pressed against the wall, it created a surprising amount of space in the already large bedroom. When Scott
took his next step, the bed flipped up onto its side and then slid up
the wall, pressing into the ceiling, the pillows and blankets pinned to
the wall, the simple wooden frame exposed with its posts, no longer
vibrating, poking straight out into the room as if they were nothing
more than four places on which to hang one's hat.

Scott's brown leather Crisci boot came down onto the carpet
again. With this next step, a small chair that had been sitting in the
corner near the room's door, right next to where Robert was
standing—cowering?—rolled up the wall and pressed into the corner.
He flinched and, although he'd resolved himself not to look away

from Scott, glanced up at it briefly. The chair was stuck there, where the walls and the ceiling met, as though it had been bolted in place.

"If there really is no such creature as the one I just described," said Scott, his voice becoming even lower, softer and bigger at the same time, "then my quarrel would be with those who have associated my image with the responsibility for such atrocities."

Scott's hair was longer now, Robert was sure of it. His blue eyes were shining brilliantly, as if the brain behind them had become a harsh and powerful light.

"Your image?" Robert heard himself croak.

"Oh, yes," said Scott, but they were barely words. He was growling now, his voice was a heavy rumbling purr. "Yes, my image. I am the black lion with the wings of a dragon. I am the one demon with the power to cause or cure illness, but the rest is nothing more than legend, myth, and fable."

He took another step and the single light, which earlier had merely dimmed, now flickered madly for a fraction of a second before it went out completely. It didn't matter, though. The lamp was sitting on top of a nightstand that swiftly shot up the wall like the weight of a carnival game when a very strong man has hit the lever with his wooden mallet. The entire lamp shattered, but no pieces fell. The shards of painted ceramic, along with the crumpled lampshade, were either pinned by the nightstand or they were as magically lodged to the ceiling as the chair in the opposite corner.

The room was now almost totally dark, but enough light was coming through the large window behind Scott for Robert to see what was in front of him. Enough light filtered in through the window to still make out the approaching figure and Robert wished there wasn't any light at all. Pitch blackness would have been less frightening.

There was a bit of light, though. Robert could see quite clearly, actually. It took just a very short moment for his eyes to adjust, but when they did, Scott was gone. In his place was a lion.

The animal was enormous. It stopped walking and sat on its haunches, barely fitting between the floor and the ceiling. The creature would have been only a silhouette in front of the window, if not for its gleaming blue eyes. They glowed like lonely Christmas lights. All around the eyes, illuminated in a soft, almost tranquil circle, was the face of the lion, covered in short, jet-black fur.

Robert's hands gave up. The Vessel was still locked away in his jacket pocket by a large wooden button that, despite his prayers, he'd been unable to manage. His hands fell absently to his side.

Then even the meager light from the window began to weaken as though the moon were on a dimmer. Robert would get his wish, apparently. The light from the world outside faded slowly, then was completely obscured as the creature sitting in front of Robert abruptly extended its wings.

Now, there were only the eyes. Just the eyes.

†

"Look, um, dude," Troy said, trying not to seem flustered, but it was very difficult to balance one's deportment when so many other influences were vying for control. "I've been here since before the party started. Dude, I'm helping, dude. Dude, like, I'm helping Karen."

The Security Guy didn't react. He seemed exceptionally grumpy.

"I just want to see if she's upstairs," Troy explained.

"You need to step back."

"What?" Troy winced. Yeah, this guy was grumpy. Too bad. It might have been easier to get by him if he'd been more like one of the other dwarves, perhaps Doc or Sneezy or Bashful.

Troy twittered to himself, then wiped furiously at an itch deep inside his nose.

"I think you need to step away and go back to the party," said Grumpy.

This was not acceptable. This was total crap and totally stupid and didn't Grumpy know who Troy was?

"Buddy…" Troy grinned. Kelly and Missy were grinning with him, shaking their heads inside his own head. Poor stupid Frumpy or Grumpy, or whatever his fucking name was. "I really don't want to make a fuss, but this course of action you seem to have chosen isn't, um…" He glanced at the ceiling, back at Frumpy the Security Guy, "it isn't, um, how do they say it in France? Um …wise."

Frumpy the Security Guy took a breath and rolled his eyes.

"You know what?" Troy smiled at him.

Frumpy just stared back, frowning.

"I think you need to take a pill."

"Now who's being unwise?" said Lumpy or Frumpy or whatever the fuck his stupid name was. He cocked his jaw and crossed his arms over his big, big, lovely chest. Yeah, he was Lumpy all right.

"No, seriously." Troy reached for his pocket. "I mean literally, whatever. Listen Lumpy… I mean Lovely Lumpy, whatever, listen, you need to take a pill." He pulled a little, tiny-weenie, gray baggie

out of his pocket. "And, you lovely, lucky, lumpy boy, I just happen
to have one for you."

†

Robert couldn't see anything anymore, other than those giant,
shining, blue eyes. All the light from the window was obscured by
the form of the demon, which had crept forward in the dark until its
eyes were only two or three feet from Robert's own, so close he could
feel the animal's breath against his shirt, could hear the rustle of the
wings as they tried to find enough space within the room to stretch
out. There wasn't nearly enough space, though, and the enormous
wings nudged and bumped the walls, hit the open drapes, rattling
them on the polished wooden rod over the window on the far side of
the room. Robert could hear the giant knuckles of the wings as they
scraped back and forth across the ceiling.

"Don't you feel just a little silly now, Robert?" the demon said.
The eyes moved slowly back and forth as the thing was no doubt
shaking its head, expressing its heartfelt disappointment. The smell
of an ocean-side campfire was very strong. "I tried to warn you. I
tried to point out that you'd stepped into a room all by yourself with
someone you suspected might be a demon. What the heck were you
thinking?"

The demon's pupils alone were the size of quarters. As it spoke,
its breath pelted Robert's face. It was hot, like the first waft that came
from an oven when its door was opened to check on a batch of
cookies.

"You weren't thinking at all, Robert," the demon said. "If you had
any kind of plan, I think it was corrupted by your own shortsighted-
ness. It was flawed from the beginning. What possessed you to take
this drastic step? What are you going to do now? Are you going to
bless me to death?"

The light from the creature's eyes was bright, but they only
illuminated a small portion of its face. The light didn't even reach the
end of the animal's nose, which was now only an inch or two from
the top of Robert's chest. He could hear the rustle of the mane, but
couldn't see it; Robert would have to take the creature's word that it
was wavy and black. The darkness around the animal's face seemed
to eat even the illumination coming from its eyes. Surely, the demon
wouldn't see Robert's hands should they try again to bring out the
Vessel.

"So, here we are." The demon was only whispering. Still, it was a frightening sound. "You've found me. Only, I'm not the monster you've been chasing. As a matter of fact, as the years go by, I become more and more convinced that the creature you think is roaming around destroying the world is nothing more than an imaginary scapegoat, perhaps created by your superiors. What do you think?"

There was no way Robert could answer him; he could barely breathe. Surely the demon could hear his heart since now it was set on 'Kettledrum.'

Meanwhile, without what Robert would have considered a conscious directive, his left hand had crept inside his coat and was working at the button holding his inside pocket closed.

"You see," the demon continued, "I don't spit acid. Never have. That's really sick, actually, and I have no idea where or how that part of the story popped up. Yes, I can assume a human form, but only one, which you've seen, and I wouldn't have the foggiest notion how to teach anyone else to do it, whether they were a witch or not. Also, I've never eaten even so much as one child, much less gorged my way through whole crowds of them like all those stupid stories say. I've never eaten anyone for that matter. Actually, I don't even like red meat. Chicken and fish are okay, I guess. Really, though, there's just so much crap in beef that I really can't enjoy it anyway. Buffalo is good, but I've only had that once. It was in a burger I had last month at a restaurant down by the beach."

The button was covered in sweat from Robert's fingers. He was having trouble grasping it. He took a deep breath and wiped his fingers on his pants.

"Now, as for the disease thing..." The word 'disease' was very guttural and feline sounding, as though this giant lion had been smoking for forty years. "It's true that I've brought about plagues, but there's quite a bit more to that story."

Once his fingers were dry, Robert still had to fold over the seam of his coat to wipe the sweat off of the button.

"For instance," the lion said, "I've cured far, far more illnesses than I've ever created. And the ones I have brought about were, I assure you, quite unintentional."

The smell of an ocean-side campfire was so strong that Robert's eyes were watering as if from the smoke. It was very hot, standing there between the door and the nose of the demon. Sweat was running down Robert's face. He could taste hair-gel at the corners of his mouth.

"Robert, I'm going to explain something to you, only because I think it's a very valuable piece of information that you'd never get from any other source. I'm going to explain this, and then I'm going to eat you."

Robert gasped and would have slammed himself back against the closed door if he hadn't already been as flat against it as he could have gotten without cracking his skull on the wood.

"Just kidding." The demon chuckled softly. "I told you I don't like red meat. Ooh, I'm sorry!" The eyes moved away a bit, squinting. "I didn't mean to frighten you *that* much."

Robert had no idea what the demon meant until he felt the liquid warmth running down his leg.

"That was mean of me," the demon said. "Really, I'm sorry. That was out of line. But what can ya do? I am a demon, aren't I?"

More soft chuckling.

"The thing is," the demon went on, all business again, "it would take far, far too long for me to explain enough about my situation for you to comprehend exactly who and what I am. There's nothing I can say in the space of the few moments we have here that would do any good. Suffice it to say that you've stumbled into a situation that is quite a bit bigger than yourself. It's quite a bit bigger, in fact, than the feeble excuse your oh-so-mighty church has given you to justify the fact that you've wasted your life romping across the globe trying to catch an illusion."

Now that both the button and his fingers were dry—unlike his crotch—Robert tried again to get his pocket open.

"You're fumbling around in something that is none of your business," the demon said. "Now, that wouldn't be too horribly awful, except that you're stupid bumbling will most likely also affect some people about whom I care very deeply."

Robert held the wooden button between his thumb and middle finger, pulling at it, trying to bring it to an angle that would allow it to slip through the sewn opening in the fabric.

"What you need to know, Robert, is that demons really have no power of their own. This is an important little detail for someone like you, so pay attention. Demons are completely unable to sustain their existence without the help of at least one mortal soul. Are you listening? There *will* be a quiz."

In the dark room, Robert nodded. In his jacket, the button slipped away from him. In his mind, he screamed, *Fuck!*

"Not only that," the demon continued, "but the power derived from the human soul must be given to the demon. It cannot be taken without the mortal's expressed consent."

Gripping the button again, Robert felt the opening in his jacket lining with his index finger and tilted the button toward it so that he could line them up.

"Of course," the demon said, "the human can be forced to give up their soul's energy. They can be compelled to relinquish the divine power of their souls to a demon. Intense physical pain is a very common tool in that regard. Humans are normally very squeamish about being tortured."

Robert gasped again.

"Don't worry." The demon shut its eyes briefly, then shook its head. "I've never done such a thing and don't have any intention of starting. There's no need to pee all over yourself again."

Robert closed his own eyes for a moment and swallowed hard. Once he opened them again, the demon went on.

"What I'm getting at," it said, "is that the power I need to exist has always been given to me freely. Always."

The button slipped through the buttonhole and Robert's pocket was open. Trying not to appear too visibly relieved, and sending a silent *Thank you!* to Heaven, he slipped his hand inside and closed his fingers around the slim, cold, brass jar.

"However," the demon whispered even softer, "that's very rare behavior for an entity such as myself. In fact, there is another about whom I think you should be far more concerned. She's here in this city, right now, and she's been forcing innocents to give her their power. She's been torturing them, tearing off their skin, preying on innocent children, subjecting them to unspeakable pain until they relinquish to her the power of their souls. She's been topping off her demonic gas tank that way so often and gaining so much strength that I'm not sure I can stand against her. Indeed, she almost destroyed me once already. She's not one of the Fallen, but she's discovered how to feed herself so efficiently that her power has become quite remarkable. I think she's planning something hideous. I think it's in both our best interests to pay close attention."

"What?" Robert breathed the word heavily, hoping it would cover any sound that might be made as he tugged the Vessel free from his jacket's nylon pocket.

Preoccupied as he was, Robert still heard the giant lion's words. The demon was speaking of the lamia, of course.

It made perfect sense. All this time, all over the world, reports of the female demons mingled with details of the skotos. They'd been difficult to distinguish at first, but after a time, it had become obvious that the Church wasn't the only entity interested in finding this particular demon. For some reason, Lilith was after him too.

Robert lifted the brass jar, slowly sliding his fingers around the lid to keep the metals from clicking as he opened it.

"She's the reason I left New York," the demon said. "Actually, 'left,' wouldn't be the correct way to describe my exit. 'Dragged away by my hair,' would be far more accurate."

Robert silently lifted the lead seal off of the ancient brass jar. He would secure this demon with the magic of Solomon's Vessel. Then, maybe he'd be able to face the lamia. He'd never considered it before, but the Vessel was in his hands, was it not? He had it, after all this time. He held it before the very creature it had imprisoned for so many years, and it was very capable of holding more than one demon. After all, that had been its original purpose, to hold a multitude of demons. Big ones too.

The lamia would be next. Robert would find this other demon and contain her as well. After which, who knew? Lilith might just be on her way too, mightn't she?

"You met Simon, didn't you?"

"What?" Robert squinted at the glowing blue eyes.

"In New York, you met Simon Frey, didn't you? You remember. He was the professor from New York University. Simon Frey? Come on, Robert, I'm fairly sure you spoke with him at least twice. Professor Frey?"

"Yes," Robert admitted. "Yes, I remember him."

While he'd been in New York, Robert attended three or four lectures on church history and contemporary scriptural analysis, hermeneutics. All the new-fangled academic developments had been nothing but a big load of horse-pucky, though. One of the speakers at one of the symposiums had been Professor Simon Frey, an expert in first-century Mediterranean sociology — something indirectly related to Jesus' understanding of his own divinity, like the pre-Easter/post-Easter theorem, very Marcus Borg-y. His proposal had been just as whimsical and ultimately ridiculous as all the rest, but Robert had spent a few minutes speaking with him afterward. It had been entirely accidental; they'd bumped into each other while grabbing cups of hot tea and a couple of the sugar cookies set out for the conference attendees. They didn't talk long; just a minute or two of polite jabbering. Even so, Robert had liked him immediately and been unable to bring himself to inform the professor that he thought he was full of crap. Only about two weeks afterward, they'd bumped into each other at another symposium. This time, both men were only there to listen, and both had agreed the speaker was full of crap.

Professor Frey was a shorter man, very thick gray hair that he kept meticulously combed — probably in the same style he'd had since the nineteen forties. He wore large and thick glasses as square as televisions, and sported a nose that looked like it could open soup cans. He'd been nice enough, and, after a rather pleasant hour or so over some herbal tea, Robert no longer considered him a complete idiot.

Although Robert had personally seen the young black-haired Greek boy in New York City, he'd never seen or associated him with Professor Frey.

"She took him, you know," the demon said softly.

There was only silence in the room for a moment, neither Robert nor the giant winged monster were even so much as breathing.

"I'd been staying with him," the giant winged monster said quietly. "I came back to his home and found his body lying on his dining room table. He had a very beautiful antique table, the kind that's been polished so much it looked as though a thin layer of glass had been lain on top. He loved that table."

"What happened?" Robert asked, still holding the open Vessel beneath the demon's chin.

"She was sitting right there. She was picking something out from under her nails while she sat in one of his dining room chairs. She was waiting for me."

"She killed him?"

The demon's eyes closed and the room went black. "Yes."

†

The DJ room actually looked a little boring. Standing in the hall, not having gained even enough interest to enter the room, Troy waved a dismissive gesture at absolutely no one, turned to the empty corridor, and took a sip of his rocks margarita. Now, he wondered if the tequila was a very good idea, considering how much interaction he'd been having with Ms. Kelly. He hadn't spoken to Ms. Gina at all, who would have certainly not approved of any alcoholic consumption — she was *really* bitchy that way. If he'd talked to Gina, he'd surely already be on his face. How did Kelly feel about it, though? She was a depressant too, wasn't she?

Troy squinted down the hall toward the third floor stairs. He wanted to find the VIP room.

Margaritas were Troy's favorite alcoholic treat. Was there anything else in the world like a margarita? That sweet, ripping tanginess that blazed one so quickly and so deeply into the Land of Joy?

The hallway was dark. No wait, it was lighted. No wait, it was dark. No wait, it... Troy shook his head. What? Was he blinking?

What was this in his hand? Why, it was a lovely, lovely, limey margarita! How fabulous! Sippy, sippy, sippy!

Troy managed three steps before the wall had to reach out and steady him. He licked some salt off of his upper lip, nodded an appreciative grin at the helpful wall, and continued toward the stairs at the far end of the hallway.

Those stairs were really far away. He needed one of those scooter-thingies is what he needed. My god, where was he? Buckingham Palace? Why was the fucking hallway so long? Troy looked around, assured himself he hadn't abruptly gained consciousness while lost in some hotel—he really hated when that happened—and, after noticing that the doors were all open and didn't have numbers on them, eventually continued in the direction of the third-floor stairs. The wall only had to hold him once more for a very brief moment while he regained some balance. Nodding, mouthing a breathy *I'm good, I'm good, baby* at the wall, Troy ventured forth.

†

"There was blood everywhere, all over his table, soaking the rug and dripping off onto the other three chairs. She was sitting away from him, against the bay window, waiting for me to come back. Professor Frey was lying on top of his table. Almost all the skin on his face had been peeled off. His ears had been ripped off. There were very deep wounds down the front of his torso."

Robert just stared into the blackness.

"He must have held out for a very long time," the demon whispered, its eyes still shut, allowing the darkness to envelope both him and Robert alike. "He must have tried to protect me until his body just couldn't handle the pain any longer. I know she must have done a great deal to keep him alive and awake, so that he could suffer. He was an old man, though, and there are limits even to her magic."

"She tortured him?" Robert whispered into the dark.

"Yes." The eyes opened. Great lumbering tears had welled behind the demon's lids and now they spilled over, running in tiny rivers down the black fur. "Still, he won. She couldn't beat him. He endured and wouldn't relinquish anything to her. Finally, though, before I could…" The great lion's breath actually hitched. "…before I could get back, his body had just given out and he died. He died protecting me. I should have been there to protect him and yet he gave his life so that I would be spared. He died in agony at the hands of a demon. He died because I led her to him and allowed myself to be distracted. I allowed her access to him and she tortured and killed him in his own home trying to get to me. She tried, but she gained nothing. In the end, Simon was very strong. Stronger than her and me combined, it would seem. He was a man of spirit who understood love and purpose. Ultimately, she could never have taken him."

The demon stopped, its eyes fixed behind Robert, beyond him and far away.

"I swore I'd never put anyone in that position again," it said. "I swore it, and even as I burned within her breath, even as she brought me to the brink of complete destruction and showed me the abyss, even as she shrieked and tore at me, rattled me over the edge of oblivion itself, I was happy that I was weak. I was glad I'd be destroyed and no other innocent would suffer for my protection. I would never love again, but that was a small price to pay for depriving the Beast of his pleasure. I would fall. I would fall again, but it would be for the very last time."

The shining blue eyes snapped back to Robert. He jumped and had to grasp the Vessel to keep from dropping it.

"But I was not destroyed," the lion whispered, barely loud enough for Robert to hear, despite almost being pinned at the end of its nose. "I survived and escaped. I hid from her. I hid in the darkness like a coward, rather than facing the destruction that should have, by divine providence, befallen me. I should have perished that day. I should have been weakened and destroyed, if not for a random turn of fate and the fumbling of yet another innocent. I should have fallen into the abyss but was saved by the favor of a childish beauty. A beauty who screamed with his very soul for my help. He'd been beaten too. Not by anything as brazenly demonic as a Legion huntress, but beaten and ravaged just the same. He screamed for help, and so I gave it. I gave my help and my love, again, though I swore to the peaks of Heaven itself that I would never repeat that mistake."

The tears were flowing clearly and freely down the face of the demon.   Was there such a sight anywhere in history, anywhere between Heaven and Hell that was any more of a paradox?

"I fell again," the demon sighed.   "To the voice of this beauty, and within the very sight of the Divine himself, I fell again and gave what I'd promised I would keep to myself.   I failed him, this beauty who screamed for help.   Though, in his innocence, he doesn't see it."

More tears.   The lion closed its eyes and there was blackness.   He opened them and fixed Robert in his gaze.

"I will not allow the minion of the Beast to use another innocent soul to get to me, Robert."   There was, for the first time, Robert noted, real vehemence in the creature's voice.   "I will not allow yet another to suffer for my weakness, suffer so that the demons of the earth can control my power.   If I must destroy you here and now, if I must incinerate you until not even the marrow of your bones remains to mark your existence, if I must myself face the very flames of Hell for doing so, to protect the innocent soul that is now in my care, I will do it.   I will not allow your blundering to call the attention of the Legions to me.   I will destroy you first, and without so much hesitation as could be considered by the tiniest thought."

There was a soft, padded-thud sound, and Robert thought for a moment that someone had knocked at the door.   The sound didn't come from the door, however.   It came from the floor.

It was the Vessel.   Robert had dropped it.

†

This was just unreasonable.   This was a dream-hallway, the kind that kept growing longer and longer until you realized it was a dream-hallway and then started having a much more reasonable dream, something involving Heath Ledger and Jake Gyllenhaal in a bathtub.   Except, this dream-hallway just kept going and going and going, long after Troy realized it was just a dream-hallway, and he kept waiting for Jake and Heath to show up, or someone equally delectable, yet the scene didn't change.   The hallway stretched on and on and on and on and Troy wondered for a moment if he was even still walking and realized, not with just a little amusement, that he was not.

Silly me, he thought, slamming into the opposite wall as he propelled himself forward, hardly aware of the indignant huff the snooty fucking wall blew at him, the bitch, as he almost cracked his head on a black, metal photo frame.   Walls could be such bitches.

This whole fucking party was full of bitches.   Glam-bitches and muscle-bitches. All over the motherfucking place, nothing but the finest, most glorious muscle-bitches ever to draw breath. No, that wasn't completely true. Theo and Nicky were here, and they were just so *not* bitches, but Eddie was with them, who was sweet at times, but really just far, far too beautiful to be so authentically nice. So, he must be a sub-surface bitch, which was even worse than an overt muscle-bitch, wasn't it?

And Darren. Then there was the big and lovely Darren Jacobson. Motherfucking, asshole, Darren "My-God-Aren't-I-Just-So-Fucking-Perfect?" Jacobson. Darren "Of-Course-Lil'-Nicky-Reynolds-Is-My-Boyfriend-And-Not-Yours-You-Stupid-Skinny-Troll" Jacobson.

Troy waved a silent apology at a poor innocent light fixture that he'd somehow knocked clean off its mounting. Poor little thing, hanging by its little wires. Poor little, pathetic thing. Probably from Home Depot, poor, ugly thing.

†

"I have so much more respect for you now, Robert." The lion had stepped back and was looking straight down at the carpet where his eyes were illuminating the Vessel in their soft, blue glow. "Really, big guy, I can't tell you how relieved I am."

The Vessel was laying on the floor where it had thumped softly after slipping through Robert's fingers. The demon was just staring at it, as was Robert. The Vessel had slipped out of Robert's hand. He was holding it, right in his hand, right beneath the demon's head, right under the creature's chin where he even felt the sweep of its heavy mane across his fingers. Robert didn't speak. He'd dropped the Vessel and now it was on the floor. He was looking right at it. It was on the floor.

"You'd really thrown me for a loop, at first," the demon said, still looking at the fallen brass jar. "I didn't want to kill you, but I couldn't help thinking that any man who'd march into an empty room, alone, with someone he was fairly sure was a demon, had to be completely out of his mind or dumber than a can of soup. Either way, I was trying to decide if it would be too dangerous to let you go away breathing."

If Robert just dropped to the ground, could he grab the Vessel before the demon swatted his head off?

"See," the lion continued, "I really couldn't afford to have a loony-toon, especially a stupid loony-toon, running around drawing attention to me. Even as I was trying to explain things to you, to maybe find out just how deeply you'd moved into Fanatical Land, I couldn't get past the fact that you were standing here in front of me, even despite what you went through on Cyprus, which would have meant that you'd learned nothing at all, and that's a very, very dangerous kind of person."

Robert looked up and the demon met his eyes.

"Oh, yeah, I know all about Cyprus, Robert," the demon said. "I met Bishop Carter, remember?"

If Robert just collapsed his knees, really, really, abruptly, could he snag the Vessel before one of those huge paws batted his head off of his shoulders as easily as a titanium driver knocked a golf ball off a tee?

"But here you are," the demon went on, "with Solomon's Vessel in your pocket. I'm very impressed. Really, I am. You had a plan after all. Good for you!"

What difference did it make? What difference did anything make after this instant? Robert might as well take a chance and attempt to retrieve the Vessel. The demon was going to kill him anyway.

Just in case, though, Robert reached behind him, easily found the knob that had been poking him in the back, and quietly unlocked the door.

Without thinking about it for another instant, Robert's knees buckled and he fell to the carpet. He landed right on the Vessel, which slammed into his hip painfully, but he tucked his hands beneath his stomach, grabbed it, and rolled. He slammed into the wall in the darkness, not even a quarter of the way through his tuck-and-roll. He rolled the other direction and was at least able to get to his knees. With lightening reflexes, he thrust the Vessel out toward the demon.

Robert was very pleased to see that the demon had retreated several steps back into the room; the eyes were a little more distant, smaller glowing blue orbs in the blackness. And he was also quite happy that it hadn't knocked his head off.

"You're really spry for your age," the demon said, sitting somewhere near the center of the room. "What are you? Fifty?"

Robert grimaced and stood up, feeling the Vessel in the dark and finding that the open end had been facing the wrong way.

"I should have known you had the Vessel with you. I should have figured it out. That would be the only reason you'd have ever allowed yourself to face another demon. It never dawned on me that you guys wouldn't realize the thing doesn't work."

"What?"

"Well, the jar doesn't really do anything," the demon explained. "It'll hold a demon, of course, a whole crowd of them. Any brass container will hold demons, but you need the Key to force them to go inside."

Robert closed his eyes.

Call up a demon: check. Put it in the Vessel: um…, okay, um, how do you turn this thing on?

"But how —?" Robert heard himself croak.

"I was very tired and I needed a place to hide," the demon explained. "No, Daniel didn't have the Key. He faced me alone, with only his faith to protect him. The sorcerer fled the instant I appeared. Poor Daniel was left to face me on his own."

Daniel. So that was the name no one had bothered to record and no one could remember.

"We had a very pleasant conversation," the demon said. "He was terrified at first, so I spent some time calming him down. I was trying to find out how the sorcerer had learned my name, but Daniel didn't know. He had no idea how I'd been summoned."

Robert closed his eyes and dropped the useless jar back onto the floor.

"Anyway, we came to an understanding," said the lion. "We were going to help each other. He needed to bring a demon back to Rome and I needed a place to hide. It was providence."

Robert heard another thump on the carpet and realized he'd fallen to his knees.

"I went into the jar, Robert." The demon looked down at him, not without sympathy. "The Vessel's first custodian didn't cast me into it. I went into it willingly."

†

Suddenly the hallway was very dark and Troy couldn't see the stairway anymore. He had no idea which way to go, which way would bring him to the quiet and, as yet, secluded private quarters on the third floor. He needed a quiet, out-of-the-way place, away from all the muscle-bitches for a while, away from Darren Jacobson while he made googly-eyes at Nicky, with whom Darren also got to sleep every fucking night, totally naked probably, and wasn't that enough? Did he have to google-eye Nicky right in front of Troy? What an asshole.

The hall was so dark. How was Troy going to find his way? Then he remembered to open his eyes again, and *presto!*, there was light in the world.

Troy started again toward the silent stairway, pushing himself away from the wall, which was becoming irritated at having to keep holding him up. Fine, fine. He just needed to get to a nice, long, comfy couch upstairs where he could lounge against the armrest and pretend to be lucid.

He heard something of a ruckus suddenly. It came from one of the rooms near the third-floor stairs. The door was the only one in the house that was closed. The ruckus was very brief and then he heard whispering.

What was going on? Why was this door closed? None of the other doors were closed. Why was this one closed? Did it have a room number on it? Nope. Was something fabulous going on inside this room? Were there muscle-bitches in there? Were they reveling in the perks of their muscle-bitchiness? Were there glam-muscle-beauty-boys behind this door, possibly losing themselves within the transcendent heaven offered only to them due to their flawless, physical magnificence?

Troy opened the door.

†

Drops of music were floating out onto the patio toward them. Nick opened his mouth and inhaled in a long hungry gasp. Drums thumped. Rifts of tambourine and splintered bamboo leaped and danced. Snares and muffled cymbals cleft to the edges of his shoulders. Darren's hand pressed warmly at the base of Nick's neck, his nose brushing Nick's forehead. An electronic flute sang in glorious streams, ringing over them, melting into the walls and blending the air and light into a liquid blanket. Nick tilted his head, pressed his lips to Darren's chin where an almost undetectable stubble clung to them. He brushed back at them playfully with his tongue.

Maybe they hadn't needed to start bumping up with Kelly, but now that she was here, she was absolutely shameless.

"Oh, my gosh, there you are," Karen's voice came rolling out of the house.

Darren was shifting. Oh, crap. Darren was moving, turning himself within Nick's arms, turning toward the sound of their friend. She didn't sound happy. She was slightly out of breath and maybe even a little annoyed. Crap.

Darren craned around to look toward the open glass doors. Nick leaned over a bit from where he sat against the red brick barbeque, straining to see around Darren, who was leaning against him. He saw Karen as she pushed her way around Great Hair Guy, who looked over at her absently.

"Oh, you guys came outside," she said, brushing a hair off her forehead. "That's nice. It's nice out here."

"Are you all right?" Darren asked, his chest vibrating beneath Nick's fingers.

"Sure," she smiled. "No. I mean, I don't know."

"What's going on?" Theo asked. Nick turned to smile at him. Theo sat up. He'd been almost flat on his back in a padded wicker lounge chair.

"Well…" Karen was breathing heavily, as though she'd been running. Nick turned his head. He watched her brush more hair out of her face. "I'm not really sure."

"You're that chick," Sexy Buzz-Cut Boy said, pointing at her. He'd been leaning against the patio table, unsuccessfully hitting on Theo. Nick was amused he was pointing like that, adroitly displaying his limitless class. "You're that manager chick."

Nick smiled, shook his head, raised his eyebrows. Sexy Buzz-Cut Boy was so sad.

"Oh, dear god." Karen rolled her eyes, put up her open palm toward Sexy Buzz-Cut Boy. "Have another bump, sweetheart."

"Karen?" Nick pushed himself up off the lip of the barbeque. Darren stepped aside, letting Nick stand.

"It's probably nothing." She shook her head. "Laura's handling it."

Eddie got up from where he'd been slumped in his wicker chair and went to sit with Theo. He moved Theo over in the lounger and laid his head on his chest, sighing, closing his eyes. Theo shifted so that he could hold Eddie and also face Karen, eyes wide, grimacing, pouting.

"Karen," Nick said again, "please tell all these people who it was that fell into the pool."

"Ha!" Karen blurted, quickly covering her mouth.

As the evening progressed, the party's main body had all moved into the living room and the kitchen. A large portion had already left, which included a good number of the celebs, to pursue other glam-spots and photo ops. The boys had decided that the patio, after being relieved of its crowd, looked rather pleasant, and so retreated outside.

The change of venue was refreshing, and Kelly had been invited out with them to share the mild winter night.

Sexy Buzz-Cut Boy patted Theo on the thigh. "She's that manager chick."

"Where's Laura?" Darren asked, looking at Karen, patting Nick on the stomach to assure him he hadn't been forgotten. Nick flexed his abs. Darren loved it when he did that.

The music was subsiding, falling back into the house.

"She's handling everything," Karen said. She brushed at more of her hair, although Nick couldn't see any of it hanging in her face. "Everything's peachy." Karen thrust out her bottom lip and blew at an invisible strand.

"Cool," Darren said, stepping toward her, reaching back for Nick.

"Why isn't there a dance floor?" said Huge Pectoral Man, standing at the glass doors, watching the mill of the people inside.

Nick let Darren pull him closer. He was still aware of the wonderful music playing in the house and whispering around them, slipping out from inside the building. It lifted as he stood, a rising mist that swirled thickly just below his chin. There were people talking loudly in the living room. They were all lovely. Their conversations were buzzing together and melting into the music, in tune with it, enshrouding him, collecting in warm, soothing waves that swept through the room and out onto the patio. Everything was flowing together like a great heaving breath.

Somewhere, he thought he could hear Karen talking.

"It's just that there's this door," said a beautiful woman who looked just like Karen. She was pointing into the living room with one hand and holding her hair in place with the other. "There's this door, and it's closed, and Laura doesn't seem to care." She released her hair, which fell and danced like golden wisps of smoke around her face.

"Hey, Karen," Nick chimed, hearing his own voice join with the great heaving, magical breath. "Hey, Karen, Karen. Hey, baby, Karen, baby, baby, Karen, Karen."

The beautiful woman looked at him, grinning. "What, honey?"

The light from inside the house was shining through her loose blonde hair like a glowing aura. He loved her, this beautiful woman with the shining aura-hair who looked just like Karen. Nick loved her.

Darren turned his head, grinning too, swinging Nick's hand in his, which felt really good. Nick felt *really* good. Nick loved Darren too.

Nick loved Darren, and it was, at that moment, like a bright light into which he couldn't look. He couldn't look into that love at the moment. He'd cry if he did and that would be really embarrassing.

"Hey Karen, you know Troy? Well, he's in love with me." Nick smiled at the beautiful golden-aura woman who looked just like Karen.

"I know, baby." She closed her eyes, shook her head. "I'm the one that—" She stopped abruptly and covered her mouth, her eyes opening very wide. Darren burst out laughing.

Darren was so handsome and big. He was big and handsome and when he laughed his face lit up and his chest heaved and it made Nick smile. Nick loved Darren.

The beautiful woman looked at Darren and they both laughed together, sharing some little secret, something old and sweet. They were laughing together, being beautiful together. Nick smiled. When they stopped, the beautiful woman reached over and held Nick by the chin.

"Sweet, sweet boy," she said, "everyone loves you. You're just so nice and so pretty, it's impossible not to adore you."

Nick squinted. What was she talking about? What was the beautiful Karen-woman talking about?

"Where's this door?" Darren asked, looking mildly concerned and gazing into the house as though the mysteriously closed door would be just a few feet away.

"Down the hall." Karen waved at the living room, toward the first-floor hallway, grasping her hair again into one big-wispy-golden-luminous ponytail.

"Let's go," Darren said, starting toward the glass doors, pulling Nick behind him.

"We'll wait here," Theo said from behind them. He was resting back onto the wicker lounge chair. "We're gonna stay out here and watch the fort."

Without opening his eyes, Eddie shifted himself so that he could lay across Theo, who put his arm over Eddie's shoulder and kissed him on the head. They were both so pretty. Nick loved Theo and Eddie. Nick thought Theo and Eddie should love each other, which they did, but not in the special way Nick was thinking, only in the kiss-on-the-head way. That was okay too, though. Nick loved Theo and Eddie.

Most of their early little impromptu gaggle had already been swept back into the tide of the party. Baby-Faced Boy didn't even look back as he was pirated away into the house with Orange Lipstick Girl and Huge Pectoral Man. Sexy Buzz-Cut Boy and Great Hair Guy were shanghaied by a giggling group of twenty-ish-looking thirty-somethings who'd flashed some extra large vials of white powdery substances and then disappeared into the kitchen, perhaps to make more lines on the chopping block.

Darren pulled through the gigantic living room. Over his shoulder, Nick watched Theo, now alone outside with Eddie. Theo stretched out his legs, crossing them at the ankles, made himself comfortable, kissed Eddie on the head again and smiled at Nick through the open glass doors. Darren had apparently brought Nick inside at some point. Nick could tell because the music was much louder.

They stepped carefully around a group sitting near the fireplace, underneath the alarmingly authentic-looking mounted moose-head, and made their way to a spot where they could get through the crowd and to the hallway, between an off-white upholstered swivel-chair and a tall brass floor lamp.

Nick watched the floor lamp. He was certain it was about to be knocked over by the guy currently swiveling in the chair with two smiling women in his lap. He had one leg extended to allow enough room for both girls to sit with—on—him, and his black leather boot was swinging closer and closer to the lamp.

Darren pulled Nick steadily along, following Karen through the crowd, on their way toward the front of the house.

They passed between the chair and the lamp without incident. Nick smiled at the two girls sitting on the guy's lap. They smiled back. One waved. She was very pretty and Nick waved back. They were sharing something, Nick and this pretty, pretty waving girl. He had no clue what it was, but it was sweet, and so he waved back, happily sharing whatever moment he and this girl were having. No questions asked.

They'd only just passed through the dense portion of the lounging crowd when a large Security Guy came bustling out of the darkened hall. He was moving with a purpose and Nick felt an immediate sense of alarm, not so much from the brisk stride of the huge, black-attired young man, but by the horribly sober expression on his face. Actually, his expression had been more than just sober, more than just uninvolved. It had been scared. Something had happened. Something very serious had happened.

Nick had a sudden cramp. There was an odor wafting out from

the hallway. It was very heavy and very damp, ripe and sickly sweet. His stomach curled up just as his nose caught the first assault.

He pulled his hand away from Darren's and wrapped both of his arms around his stomach as the cramp shrank into a tight, horrible pain. Squinting, turning his head and gritting his teeth, Nick fell to his knees. The smell was slamming into him, knocking the breath from his body and ripping across his face like a sour wind.

"Nick?" Darren said as their hands were pulled apart. He turned to him with a look of puzzlement that immediately became panic. He reached down and grasped Nick by the shoulder, coming to his knees beside him, holding him at the back of his neck, grasping the base of his head.

"Nicky!" he shouted in an urgent whisper. "Nick, baby, what's wrong? Baby? What's wrong?"

Nick opened his eyes and just looked at him. Couldn't he smell it? It was horrible. Couldn't Darren smell that awful, rancid odor?

"Baby?" Darren grabbed Nick by the chin. "Baby, what's wrong? Are you sick, Nicky? Do you need—?"

Darren didn't finish his sentence because he was almost knocked over by a woman with long flowing brown hair. She was striding after the Security Guy with just as much, if not more, imminent purpose.

The odor hit Nick like a wall. It was coming from the woman with the flowing brown hair.

Nick immediately knew, however, she was not a woman at all.

†

Troy turned the knob and swung the door completely open.

There wasn't any light in the room and it took a second before Troy's eyes could adjust. When they did, he saw a man in a beautiful Armani suit crouched on his knees just a few feet beyond the threshold. Past him, a giant black lion with massive leathery wings sat facing the door. Troy was wrong about there being no light. The giant lion's eyes were glowing.

"Hi, Troy," said the giant black lion.

Troy didn't respond.

The big, black lion looked puzzled for a brief second, then glanced down at itself.

"Oh, shit!" it grunted.

†

"Ooh, Darren, what are you doing on the floor?" Laura stopped and reached toward him.

Darren saw Nick suddenly retch. He fell over, holding himself up with one arm while he held his other hand to his face. He was making a frightening sound, like he was throwing up backwards.

Darren's stomach felt like a brick. His own breath had caught in his throat. Completely forgetting about Laura, he grasped Nick by the shoulders.

"Can you breathe?" Darren tried not to scream, but motherfuck, Nick was scaring the shit out of him. Oh, holy-fucking-fuck! Was he going to have to call an ambulance? One hit of Missy and two bumps of Kelly were hardly an overdose. Still…

Nick shook his head. No. He couldn't breath. Sweet-Jesus-in-the-morning, Nick couldn't breath.

What was he supposed to do? Should he make Nick stand up or lie down? Nick hadn't eaten anything, so he didn't need the Heimlich-maneuver. What the fuck was going on?

"Baby, can you stand?" Darren was impressed with the command in his own voice. He was crapping his pants, but damn if his voice didn't sound just like he had everything under control.

"What's wrong with him?" Laura began to squat down toward them.

Nick let out such a breathless, heaving screech that Laura and Darren both pulled away from him. With what looked like a massive effort, Nick reached out and slammed the palm of his hand into the padded shoulder of Laura's silk jacket, shoving her away from him.

"Oh, my god!" Laura squealed, falling back on her ass. She was clutching at her neck as she bumped her head on the back of the swivel chair. The guy doing all the swiveling, who was somehow oblivious to the fact that Nick was choking to death right behind him — maybe it was the two girls on his lap, which might have been, understandably, focus stealing — didn't feel Laura hit the chair, evidently, because he just kept on swiveling, happy and oblivious.

The chair's movement threw Laura over onto her face, closer to Nick. He screeched again, and threw himself up and away from her, flattening his body against part of an open closet door. It slammed shut beneath his weight with a hearty bang. Thankfully, no one was hanging anything up or reaching into the closet at that moment. They would've lost an arm.

With the bang of the closet door, everyone in the living room and the visible portion of the kitchen immediately stopped talking and were looking at Nick, their jaws slacked, their drinks aloft, some eyebrows furrowing, some foreheads wrinkling, the party music throbbing around them stupidly.

The swivel chair was now motionless.

"You fucking asshole!" Laura bellowed, pushing herself up from the floor.

Nick was hacking dry, grinding heaves and frantically clawing at his throat.

Karen came running out of the hallway, into which she'd continued walking, not having seen Nick go down behind her. She went right to him, slamming down onto the carpet on her knees and taking his head in her hands.

Darren and Laura both got to their feet, facing each other.

"What the motherfuck is wrong with that butthole?" Laura screamed at Darren, pulling her dress back down into place.

"Laura, I don't know," Darren said, instinctively placing himself between her and Nick. "I don't know, but I think you should just leave."

"What?" she screamed. "This is my fucking party, you idiot!" She pointed at him and stepped forward. Darren could hear Nick behind him, grunting and coughing. He glanced back and saw him crawling down the hallway with Karen scampering after him on her knees.

At least he was breathing. At least Darren could hear Nick gasping in wheezing drags of air.

"I don't know what shit your little boyfriend has been slamming, Darren," Laura said, taking another step toward him, "but I suggest you contain him right now, or else get the fuck out!"

Darren stood his ground. He casually turned to face Laura and to better block even so much as her view of Nicholas. He pulled himself up, all six-foot-three, two hundred thirty-five pounds, which towered over the tiny little banshee currently waving her finger at him. He clenched his teeth and exhaled loudly through of his nose. Laura dropped her finger from in front of his face.

He stooped slightly, widening his eyes and pursing his lips at her. Then he squinted, took a breath, and said slowly and simply, "Go."

Laura lowered her eyelids to a contemptuous half mast. "If you even think for one second—"

"I'm not *asking* you," Darren growled.

"What?" she huffed.

"You have exactly one second to leave this room before I split your face open with the back of my hand."

"Fuck off!" she actually rose up onto her tip-toes to scream it in his face.

What happened next was far too fast for Darren to have made any calculated decisions. One instant Laura was spitting her curse in his face, and the next, Darren was dragging her out the front door by her throat.

CHAPTER IV

†

Demon Blood

For their power is in their mouth, and in their tails: for their tails were like unto serpents, and had heads, and with them they do hurt.

- Revelation 9:19 (KJV)

Los Angeles, California
The first-floor hallway of the private residence on Nichols Canyon Road

†

"Nicky!"

Karen waddled on her knees down the hallway after Nick, who was crawling away frantically. What the heck was wrong with him? For someone practically flat on his belly, he was really bookin'. If he got any farther away she'd have to stop to get back on her feet and then sprint to nab him.

Whatever she did, she couldn't let him get down to the end of the hall. No, that would not do at all, not one little bit. Nick wouldn't want to see what Karen had been told was in the farthest room of the first floor hall. The fact was that Karen most certainly did not want to see it either.

Besides, she had to get Nick—not to mention all of the other guys—out of the house and far, far away before the police got there. She didn't know how long she had; Greg had just gone into the study to make the call. She'd sent her security guy, the one who found the body, to call nine-one-one, and now she had to get the boys out before some cranky detective decided that everyone at the house should have their urine tested.

"Nicholas Charles Reynolds!" Karen bellowed as loudly as she could while huffing across the carpet on her knees, which was not at all easy. "You stop your little ass right where you are right now!"

To Karen's quite immediate surprise, Nick stopped even before she'd finished her sentence. For a very brief second, Karen thought that Nicholas had actually heard her. Good. She could catch her breath. She even rested a hand against the wall to do so. That was her mistake, really.

Nick lifted his head, like a deer hearing a rustle in the grass, then sprang to his feet—agile little cuss, he was—and bolted back down the hall, now fully up on both legs. Karen had half an instant to take action, which was barely enough time to bulge her eyes. She realized Nick hadn't heard her yelling at him and, as she was still on her knees, she abruptly also realized that he was not going to see her either. She was half her usual height, stilled and stunned directly in his frantic path.

There wasn't much space between them, but there was enough for Nick to gain speed. He struck her at full throttle.

Nick's torso connected with Karen's head first, then it was just bedlam. She fell straight back onto the carpet, lifted up slightly by the force of the impact. That was probably a good thing, as it allowed her legs to straighten themselves out in the other direction rather than snapping under the pressure of her instantly flattened body, which might have popped off a kneecap or two, shooting them both down the hall like bloody, white skipping stones.

Nick toppled over her, yet was still frantically trying to scramble away. His legs were pumping, even as Karen screamed and struggled to hold onto him so he wouldn't scamper up and slam a knee into her face. She did the only thing she could think of to keep Nick from killing her in his panic. She pressed her head to his stomach, wrapped her arms around his butt, clasped her hands to each of her opposing elbows, and held on for dear life. Shutting her eyes and holding her breath, Karen tried to turn herself into a human anchor. She only hoped that Nick calmed down enough to realize she was attached to him.

Whenever Karen had asked Nick to help her with some physical task, such as carrying a box for her or putting a new bottle of water on the cooler in the office, he'd joke that his muscles were only health club muscles. Everyone would smile and laugh when Nick pointed out that his physique's purpose was limited to exhibition; nothing actually worked. Well, whatever it was Nick had in those sculpted legs of his, at the moment, they were easily draggin' Karen's ass across the carpet. She was getting a rug burn on the back of her shoulders, which was going to be just so difficult to explain.

Nick was huffing in frantic bursts. "Huh, huh, huh, huh, huh!"

Finally, still screaming, Karen kicked her leg out from beneath her and, finding some leverage against the wall, threw Nick onto his back. She immediately pounced on top of him. He tossed her off easily — those muscles were most certainly *not* just for show — and she landed on her butt. They sat there for a second, facing each other, sitting square on their asses like toddlers on a kindergarten floor.

Nick was looking right at her but not seeing her at all. Karen saw that he was about to get up again.

"*Niiick!*" she screamed, so loudly her throat burned.

It worked, though; he stopped and looked right into her eyes, suddenly aware of her. Nick didn't seem to know exactly who she was, but at least he saw her.

"We've gotta go!" he panted. "I've gotta find him! I've gotta find him and we've gotta go! We've been so stupid! I've gotta find all of them and we've gotta go! We've gotta go now! All of us! I've gotta find them all and we've all gotta go now all of us have to go right now we haffta —"

"Honey, I know, I know!" Karen tried to reassure him. "We'll go, sweetheart, all of us!"

" — go right fucking now!" Nick suddenly screamed. "I don't have Scott and I have to have Scott and we've got to get the fuck out of here and I need Darren don't you fucking understand where's my Theo because he's got to come and I need to have Eddie with me and Scott has to take us away I've got to get Scott away —!"

Karen slapped Nick hard across the face. Why the fuck not? It worked in the movies. Her palm stung, but slapping him had been — though she'd never admit it — faintly satisfying. Her shoulders really hurt from the rug burn and, besides that, the little prick was pissing her off.

Nick gapped at her. He didn't speak or move, he just stared at her. And then his eyes softened and his shoulders slumped.

"Oh, Karen," he said. "It's all my fault!"

With that, Nick began to sob.

†

The big black lion raised its paw and some brisk, invisible force pulled Troy into the room. He stumbled but stayed on his feet. Then he fell over the guy in the Armani suit.

The door slammed shut behind him and everything was blackness.

†

Darren had Laura out over the threshold before she could get her balance. Laura might have gotten her feet back underneath her, but when they passed over the doorstep, she lost any possible leverage.

Darren just kept walking. He wasn't squeezing hard enough to keep Laura from breathing, just enough to keep her from going anywhere. She was holding onto his hand with both of her own and clumsily staggering backward, still too astonished to start screaming again, which was surely next.

Several yards down the front walk were two Security Guys. Unfortunately for Laura, they'd wandered down toward the street in their boredom. One of them, Darren saw, was Bobby.

They were staring at Darren as though he had two heads. Well, at the moment, technically, he did.

"Hi, Bobby," Darren said, dragging Laura backward down another step on the long cement pathway. "This bitch needed a walk."

Going down one more step toward them, Darren suddenly stopped and thrust Laura off to the side and into a bramble of acacias.

Bobby and the other Security Guy did exactly what Darren prayed they would: they went to her immediately.

Before she was able to bring the pitch of her screaming back down to a point where the guys could understand what she was saying— Darren heard it clearly, however: *"Not me, you idiots! Him! Fucking get him! You morons! Get the fuck off of me!"* —Darren was back inside.

He barely made it, though. The whole raging assemblage of the party was streaming out of the house. He was almost washed back down the walkway with them. Back inside, Darren saw rivers of people flowing out the front, the side, the back, and the garage doors. Obviously, they weren't just going out to see the results of the drama that had just occurred. They'd been affected by something else.

They were escaping.

†

Troy was pushing on the floor, except that the carpet felt like fur. He was trying to stand, but his feet kept swishing through nothing at all and he had no idea if he was lying down or standing up or upside down or floating in the air or falling through space or what.

Somewhere off, just a bit away from him, he could hear a man moaning. He was fumbling with something, mumbling over it to himself.

"Which end is the... this is where it's open, so, I should..." the man's voice mumbled, "...okay, so, if I point this... maybe... okay, he's got to be lying because..." the voice trailed off until Troy only heard the sound of the man's frantic breathing.

"Troy, be still," a deep, soothing voice said. "Just relax, Troy. You're okay. Everything is okay."

That had to be a lie, though. Everything was most certainly not okay. The carpet felt like fur, and it was really pliant. It was motherfucking breathing, if you could fucking believe that shit. There was a hot vent open somewhere. Troy kept trying to close his mouth, because his jaw was beginning to ache, badly, like after a night on crystal with someone who really liked to be blown, but he couldn't seem to manage closing his stupid mouth. It was stuck, and hot air kept pulsing out of some vent and making him sweat.

The other breathing sound, the man's breathing, from somewhere in the dark room, was becoming more frantic. Troy felt a wall of fur press against his back, only this fur felt much more flat, and much more like carpet, and it wasn't at all pliant, and he pressed his head back into it, which gave him a small comfort, but nothing more.

The blackness was actually swirling around Troy's head as if he were in the eye of a tornado of tar. Even as he pressed himself into the fur/carpet, the sheer lack of light raced in a streaming circle around his face. It was spinning at an incomprehensible speed and he wondered for a moment if the circle of blackness was somehow connected with the universe itself and, if so, what the fuck a giant black lion had to do with the entire universe.

Troy was able to think that maybe three margaritas hadn't been such a good idea after all. That his indulgence with a larger excess of designer chemicals could also have been a facet of his mental state was, at that moment, a consideration outside of Troy's capacity. After all, he *needed* those chemicals so he didn't suffer too much while he was around the muscle-bitches. Troy always suffered when he was around muscle-bitches.

The world was blackness, it was caught within a hurricane of nothingness, and Troy could not for the life of him remember if he was wearing any shoes. This was the muscle-bitches' fault, of course.

The chemicals were his refuge, his trump card. Tina, Kelly, and Missy could not possibly be to blame. Not them. Not the magic wonder women. No, it was the alcohol and the muscle-bitches, surely.

Alcohol, like muscle-bitches, sucked.

✝

The music hadn't changed and there was no stirring in the air on the patio, but Eddie still opened his eyes. He'd been so content for such a long time, it was puzzling to think what could have pulled him away from such a state.

Glancing up, he saw that the party was over. However, his eyebrows rose in surprise, as this party was ending in a hasty, fast-forward manner. People were pouring out of every exit like water. Eddie had never seen such a thing.

✝

Karen held Nick while he cried. She held him, even as she watched all the people quickly stream out of the house. She had a very clear view of the front entrance hall and gazed at the mass of the exceptionally young and well dressed as they pushed and ambled nervously out of the building.

She was glad, though. The police were already on their way. It was a great relief that so many innocent lives would not be ruined by... well, by whatever the fuck had happened.

Comparatively, it was of little weight that whoever, *what*ever monster was responsible for the atrocity at the end of the hall might also be slipping out of the house right along with the innocents. Karen supposed it was a lesser of two evils, that such a monster was allowed the opportunity to flee while she took the time to tend to her boys.

Karen had no idea what was wrong with Nick. That was also an issue of little weight. She would comfort him silently as long as he needed her. If the police showed up before she had a chance to evacuate the guys, so be it. She'd handle it.

Karen knew what it was like, you see. She had a unique understanding of the priorities a person should have in regard to the people they loved. She would stay with Nick until he was calm. She would not ask any questions and, come what may, she'd keep him safe until he didn't need her anymore.

With someone in her arms who needed her, someone she loved with such a clean and simple ease, how could she act in any other way?

✝

"Go out the back way!" Darren commanded.

The now-sparse stragglers who'd been heading to the front door didn't question him. They just turned and headed for the exit in the kitchen. They didn't seem to know exactly what had happened, as even Darren didn't know what had happened. They just knew that everyone was leaving in a hurry and odds were they wanted to be with them.

After the largest press of the crowd had gone through the front door, Darren could see Bobby and the other Security Guy. They were struggling like salmon to move against the current of people and get back into the house and to Darren.

Locking eyes with the Security Guy he didn't know—Darren didn't want to throw his contempt at Bobby; he liked Bobby—Darren closed, locked, and bolted the door. As an after thought, he propped a chair beneath the doorknob the way he'd seen in an old episode of *NYPD Blue*. It couldn't hurt and it made him feel better.

Darren was glad he'd done it when, not thirty seconds later, he heard Laura screeching some very filthy curse words outside the door, as well as the telltale jingle of a large set of keys.

†

"Look at me, Troy," said the deep, soothing voice.

Troy looked but there was nothing there. Everything was black.

"Troy, look at my eyes."

And there they were; big, blue, glowing eyes. Two of 'em.

"Troy, look at me."

Troy tried to say that he was looking already and to shut up but Troy's mouth had slipped off somewhere. His mouth had probably fallen off while he was trying so hard to close it. Troy'd never be able to find his poor mouth again in the dark.

"Just look at my eyes, Troy," the voice said, "but try to focus on the left one."

†

Theo was sitting up too. Both he and Eddie were staring through the sliding glass doors at the alarmingly empty living room. Actually, they were staring through the living room at an even more puzzling picture.

Why was Darren barricading the front door of the house?

Eddie looked at Theo, who was already looking at him with an expression of severe concern.

Without saying a word, they both got up off the lounge.

†

"Is he okay?" Darren stooped down to where Karen and Nick were huddled together in the hall.

"I think so." Karen nodded.

"Darren?" Nick looked up.

"Yeah, baby. I'm right here."

"Where's Scott?"

"I'm right here." Scott's voice startled them.

Darren turned and saw Scott standing at the base of the stairs.

"What happened?" Scott asked, looking around.

Darren could only stare at Scott blankly. Scott was wearing a completely different outfit than when they'd arrived.

†

"Are there a lot of people upstairs?" Karen got up and approached Scott. Darren would take care of Nick, who'd released Karen at the sound of Darren's voice and gone to him like a magnet to a refrigerator. Karen was not at all insulted. Not the tiniest little bit.

"There's a modest crowd upstairs," Scott said, frowning at the empty living room. "And I think the VIP room was discovered before you'd planned."

Karen's stomach sank. What the fuck had happened with Laura? Why had she been screaming at Darren?

Karen turned back to the guys on the floor. "Darren, what happened to Laura?"

"I threw her out," he said, not looking up.

†

Darren wrapped his arms around Nick's waist, which was awkward because of how they were sitting on the floor in the hall. Nick crumpled against him.

Karen had started to explain what she knew to Scott. However, she didn't have a chance to even begin her second sentence.

Darren had just wanted to look into Nick's eyes and ask him if he was all right. He'd just wanted to see his face and maybe get a glimmer of what was happening to him. So, he'd tried to put his hand beneath Nick's chin and lift his head.

That was when Nick started to scream.

†

The skinny kid was wearing Salvadore Ferragamo and Hugo Boss.

He had straight auburn hair, which was very short in the back but with long bangs that he had to keep brushing out of his face. Robert was sitting close enough to see the Hermes Paris label on his watch. The skinny kid had money.

Clutching the Vessel, watching the skinny, rich kid intently, Robert breathed through his nose, silently picturing himself bursting to his feet, tossing the skinny kid against a wall, and making a dash for the stairs.

Although its only lamp was ruined, there was light in the room again. At some point, Robert had realized that he could see glimmers of silver illumination shining on the brass jar. He'd looked up to see the demon, back in his human form, although naked.

Scott was sitting on his knees, opposite this skinny, rich kid, whispering to him gently, grinning and whispering, words of comfort, no doubt. The skinny kid had been nodding and holding the demon's hand.

The room's furniture had been slowly sinking back to the carpet as though they'd simply been tossed into a pool and were settling down through the water. The room gently refreshed itself. The show was over, apparently, and the next group would want to see it all from the beginning.

All the furniture had slowly drifted away from the ceiling and settled back onto the floor. Though, the bed didn't slide back into place, and the lamp on the night stand was still flattened beyond recognition, its wires hanging out like veins.

"He'll be right back," the skinny kid repeated. "Just chill, dude. Scott's gonna go find some clothes, but then he'll be right back."

The kid couldn't weigh any more than one-twenty or so. If that. Robert really should just get up, push him aside, and go.

Robert sat where he was and gripped the useless artifact. Next to him, Robert noticed a single, leather Crisci boot, its silver buckle missing, its stitching shredded.

†

"Did you touch her?" Scott asked.

Darren was fighting back tears. It was all he could do to keep himself from rushing back to Nicky and begging to be forgiven, to plead with him, anything to be able to comfort him, to not have failed him again.

Despite that, Darren could see Nick had already calmed a little. Karen had rushed back and was holding him.

Darren just tried to touch him and he'd screamed. Nick screamed and Darren had thrown himself away, instinctively removing whatever threat Nicky had detected, even if that threat had been him.

"Oh, god, Scotty, I…" he managed, still staring down at Nick and Karen.

"Did you touch her?" Scott repeated.

Looking at Darren with confused puppy-dog eyes, Karen mouthed a silent *I'm sorry!* Darren watched Nick bury his face against her.

He looked at Scott.

"Yes," Darren admitted. "I touched her."

†

They must have passed out. If he'd been wearing a watch, Theo could have just looked to see how long he and Eddie had been allowed to crash on the patio.

Theo hated when that happened. Passing out wasn't at all like going to sleep. If he just went to bed and to sleep, Theo still woke with some sense of time passing. If he passed out though, it was as if he'd blinked his eyes and a fraction of his life just disappeared. That must be what had happened here. He'd passed out. Eddie passed out right along with him, apparently, and everyone had just left them alone.

It was still night, but the party was completely over. Eddie opened the patio door and Theo followed him back into the house. He could have sworn it had been a good party but, if that was the case, it certainly wouldn't have completely emptied out before the sun came up. It must not have been that great. Maybe he shouldn't feel so bad about missing most of it.

†

"Where is she?" Scott asked.

"She's outside the front door," Darren said. "I locked it."

"That won't hold her."

"Bobby and some other security guy are with her. She has her keys, but she might send them to go around the house.

"Who are you talking about?" Karen asked from the floor. "Laura?"

Scott looked at her and put his finger to his lips. She looked confused, but stopped talking.

The music was still playing and that was all they could hear. It was an enormous sound.

Scott turned to the coal-black speaker that was closest to them. It was set up near the closet door. He put his finger to his lips again, gave the speaker a stern glare, and said, "Shh."

The speaker went silent.

"Oh…" Karen started, cocking her head and grimacing at the sound equipment. "Um… ho… um… okay."

Scott turned to the two other speakers near them and, each in turn, shushed them into silence.

Another speaker in the kitchen was still working, but it wasn't nearly as loud. Now Darren could hear the frantic jangle of keys and the faint clatter of the door and doorknob. Someone was violently trying different keys, thrusting them at the locks over and over.

He could hear a woman cussing loudly.

"She's still there," Darren said.

"We have to get everyone out of the house right now," Scott said. "We have to get to those people upstairs."

"Okay." Darren looked through the living room toward the patio and was relieved to see Theo and Eddie coming inside. "Maybe she hasn't sent Bobby or the other dude around the back."

Scott shook his head. "I hope she has."

"Why?" Darren asked, but he knew.

"Because any second now she's going to get tired of bothering with those keys and just get inside her own way. Then she'll kill both of them for having witnessed it."

†

Eddie stepped between an empty swivel chair and a floor lamp. Darren and Scott were looking at each other with such pale expressions that Eddie's stomach cramped. He'd thought something had gone wrong with the party, but the expression on their faces told him it was far worse than that.

When he saw Nick and Karen on the floor, he felt suddenly very sick.

"What happened?" he asked.

Scott turned to them abruptly, his expression changing from white fear to something almost like determination.

"Do you trust me?" Scott asked, shifting his eyes from Eddie to Theo.

"Oh, my god…" Theo said. Eddie guessed that he could sense it too, the desperation that was vibrant between Scott and Darren.

"If you trust me," Scott went on without an answer, "then just listen. We have to do this very rapidly, I'm sorry. You have to make a very quick decision and I can't tell you why and I can't tell you what might happen because of which way you end up choosing. There might be answers I can give you later. But then again, there might not."

Eddie just looked at him. Theo didn't say a word.

"I am a fallen angel," Scott said, "and I need you both to allow me the essence of your souls."

Karen gasped in a squeaky mouse pitch.

"Darren," Scott said, turning to him, "you too."

†

She would have gotten up and screamed at all of them. Karen would have screamed for someone to please explain what the fuck they were talking about, but Nick was still clinging to her. Darren had thrown Laura out the front door—Karen wasn't too horribly upset about that for some reason, really—and Scott was afraid she was going to kill Bobby and Glen.

Huh?

Now, Scott was claiming to be a fallen angel, which would have made her immediately suspicious that he'd just been rockin' really hard on whatever it was she'd seen so brazenly chopped and lined up earlier in the kitchen. Karen would have instantly thought that, but three twenty-five thousand dollar speakers had just quieted themselves because Scott told them to shush. Motherfuck if they hadn't.

Karen had never hallucinated before. That was something very difficult to accomplish from cocaine alone, and she'd only done cocaine tonight, right? Where the fuck was Troy?

Darren was nodding solemnly at Scott. "Whatever you need," he said.

When Scott took the two steps that put him in front of Darren, Karen was able to see Eddie and Theo's faces. She was immediately relieved to observe that they looked as though they were just as flabbergasted as she. Their expressions were horribly lost and confused. At least Karen wasn't the only one who was utterly stunned by Darren and Scott, who were bantering together as though they'd just shared a magic mushroom salad.

Scott touched Darren's chin, tenderly and briefly, sighed, then put his arms to his sides.

"What do you need me to do?" Darren asked.

"Nothing," Scott said, "just look at me." He smiled. "Maybe tell me that you trust me and everything's going to be all right."

"I trust you." Darren nodded. "I trust you, Scotty, and everything is going to be just fine."

Karen was all gasped out, which was why she didn't make a sound when Scott's eyes began to glow.

†

It was a very pleasant feeling, actually. Despite having benefited from the wonders of Scott's eyes on several occasions, Darren had never done this before. Scott had never asked him for anything.

At first, Darren felt exactly like he did on the days when Scott's eyes had simply given him a little boost. Scott provided a magical little boost on the days when the world at large was added to the pressure of the impossible circumstances that had taken over their lives. Whenever it overwhelmed him, Scott sat Darren down, held his hand, smiled, and said, "Look into my eye. The left one."

It hadn't happened all that often, but sometimes Darren's best efforts to keep a positive perspective seemed to crumble in a way that was beyond his strength. It was a last resort; he and Nick did yoga and meditated and practiced two or three other methods by which they could cleanse their minds. Those things worked quite well, but when they didn't, when they just weren't quite enough, Darren had a choice: suffer, or go to Scott.

Now, though, Scott needed him. He needed whatever comfort and support Darren could supply. Well, Darren certainly wasn't going to say no.

At first, he felt the familiar release of tension, which was absolute and immediate. As usual, Darren could feel knots and stress quickly slip away. Each time it happened, he'd been surprised at just how much crap he was carrying around with him. This time wasn't any different.

Then, Darren felt a tiny and measured divergence. Darren could barely describe it. The difference was like that of waking to a purpose as opposed to settling in to comfort. It was like reading to his nephew instead of watching television. It was like shopping with his mother on a Sunday instead of napping with Nick. It was like surprising Nicholas with dinner instead of taking his time at the gym. It was mild and serene, languid and enticing, and yet a little electric and stirring.

Whatever the divergence, whatever new thing Scott was doing, it was utterly lovely, simple, and there was nothing to it.

†

First Darren, then both Theo and Eddie stood before Scott and gazed into his eyes. Karen was absolutely astounded. None of this made any sense at all.

The party was over, that was for sure. Considering what had been discovered in the downstairs study, crammed behind a sofa and soaking blood into everything, she didn't think ending the event completely was a bad idea at all.

The police were the next issue. The motherfucking police were on their way and Karen hated having to deal with them. No matter the problem, even if it was just a stubborn club-kid making a scene or a clutch of beer-zombies beating each other up, the police always treated her as though she'd started it, as though she'd sent out gold-leaf invitations to all the low-IQ locals saying, *Please come to the club and act like an idiot! You get a dollar off well drinks in the front lounge if you start a brawl! Two dollars off if someone is hospitalized!*

Karen ran a nightclub that sold alcohol and created a place for people to let loose. So, of course the police spoke to her as though it was her fault when one or two patrons made poor decisions. If the police had to take three people away in handcuffs, suddenly it didn't matter that there were two thousand more who didn't cause anyone else any grief at all. There were always thousands more who were able to control themselves, despite whatever they put into their bodies, and it always made Karen shake her head in wonder. It only took the tiniest fraction of the crowd to ruin it for everyone else.

Well, now she'd hear the same song and then some. After all, Karen had thrown a party and, this time, someone was dead. So, of course, the police would treat her as though she'd planned the murder as entertainment.

Karen shook her head and held Nick. She held onto Nicky because he needed her to comfort him. She'd gotten up and left him with Darren but that hadn't worked. Nicky needed her.

The party was over, some poor soul was dead, and now Scott had gone crazy and was flashing his neon-electric contact lenses at her friends.

She turned to Nick and saw that he was much better. In fact, he looked rather calm.

"I think it's going to be okay," Nick said when he saw her staring. "Maybe everything's going to be fine."

"What is he doing?" she whispered. "What's Scott doing, Nick?"

"Scott's okay, Karen. Don't worry. You'll see. I think he might be able to get everything under control."

†

While Scott was looking at Eddie, Darren took Theo's hand.

"I'm sorry, Thelma," he said, stepping closer, touching his chest. "Maybe we should have told you."

Theo shrugged, smiled.

In the next instant, the world went crazy. Theo was knocked into Darren as an explosion ripped into the living room from the entrance hall. All two hundred forty-plus pounds of him were slammed into Darren faster than he could blink. The blast sent a pulse through the room, along with a deafening crack of wood and glass. Debris flew in a stream behind them; a mist of wooden splinters and plaster and dust. A good portion of the house's entryway, the huge oak door, as well as the chair Darren had positioned against it, were blown apart into nothing more than flying toothpicks.

†

When the entryway blew up, Karen didn't scream. Maybe Nick's calm tone had soothed her own nerves. Maybe watching the obvious trust that Darren, Theo, and Eddie were giving to Scott, with absolutely no questions asked, had quashed her anxiety. Maybe it was all of that, but Karen wasn't panicking. She thought that, by all rights, she should have been panicking. She should have been blithering her fucking head off. Still, when the foyer blew up, she didn't scream. Her heart leaped into her throat, her eyes nearly bulged right out of her head, and all her internal organs tried to rush out through her ass, but she didn't scream.

After the blast, Nick jumped up off the floor, still grasping Karen's hand tightly. "I think we need to get upstairs," he said with a firm voice, motioning toward the other guys.

No one spoke. Amusingly, dance music was still thumping through the living room. Party on, baby.

No one moved. Everyone appeared to have been stunned into statues. They all gazed toward the entryway, slack jawed and silent.

Karen heard a horrible hissing sound come from the house's entrance, a labored, breathy expulsion of air. Following it, something massive and black flew into the room and bounced with a muffled thump onto the carpet. Watching the object land, Karen saw that it was Bobby. His head had been turned completely around on his shoulders. As he lay on the carpet on his stomach, his dead eyes still stared at the ceiling.

Karen heard another angry hiss come from outside and another body flew into the house. It was Glen, who, she could tell from the way his limbs were flopping around the rest of him, was also dead. Karen couldn't see if he'd died in the same manner as Bobby, but she didn't want to see.

"Fuckin' crap!" Eddie screamed.

Karen jumped to her feet next to Nick.

"Scott!" she yelled. He turned away from the bodies to look at her. "Don't you need me too?"

"Oh yes," Scott said, nodding his head in relief. He stepped over to her, looking ashen and on the verge of tears. He touched her face. "Oh, may all the blessings of the Divine touch and keep you, yes. Thank you, Karen, yes!"

†

If there'd been time, Nick would have kissed Karen full on the mouth. As it was, his adrenaline rush had barely cleared away enough of the chemical fog for him to fumble out his warning.

"Scott," he stammered within his quickly returning lucidity, "is there time for that? Maybe you should do the eye-thingy with Karen upstairs."

Whatever was coming in through the ruined entry hall was making an awful lot of racket. Huge chunks of debris were still flying into the living room. With a metallic jangle, what looked like the crumpled remains of a security gate whistled through the room and hit the drapes, sticking there, black shards of iron piercing the drywall like spears. Following that, a shattered cluster of wood and plaster flipped like a lost plane propeller and shattered half the sliding glass door leading to the patio.

"Why is she doing that?" Darren screamed. "Why doesn't she just come inside?"

Scott turned away from Karen. "She doesn't want to crawl over anything sharp," he said simply.

Crawl? Nick thought.

"Everyone go upstairs," Scott said, taking a step toward the front door hall. "You've got to make sure you get everyone who's still up there out of the house."

"You're coming too, aren't you?" Nick almost pleaded, even as he moved with the group to the base of the landing.

Scott didn't answer. Instead, he faced away from them, lifted his right hand, and splayed out his fingers.

"Hach li dach nà lé kah!" he said. It wasn't Scott's voice that issued from his body, though. It was the thundering bass-tone of Marbas.

As he spoke, white-blue light leaped from his spayed fingers and shot through the air in a circle, disappearing into the floor, walls, and ceiling. Behind Nick, Karen made a little squeaking noise.

Eddie croaked, "Holy..." But then said nothing more.

Scott turned back and looked at them all where they stood, dumbfounded and rigid as mannequins at the base of the stairs.

"Why are you still here?" he asked stupidly, looking a little frightened. "I don't know if that will hold her."

The hissing from around the corner sounded immense and violent, like a leak in some enormous hydraulic machine. And it was getting louder.

Nick noticed that the pieces of broken door and wall flying from the entrance and through the living room were getting smaller.

"Please go," Scott said.

Abruptly, the flying debris stopped. So did the hissing sound.

"Darren..." Scott whispered. "You've got to get to the second floor, warn all those people upstairs..." He shook his head, unable to finish.

Darren nodded at him, turned, and bounded up to the second floor. Theo and Eddie followed him.

"Nick..." Scott looked at him.

"What is that sound, Scott?" Nick asked.

Scott stopped and looked at the floor, listening. Karen stepped next to Nick, taking his hand.

There was a grinding of wood, some brief snaps and splintering, but it was almost lost beneath the sound of a sleek, steady rustle. It sounded to Nick like the dragging of the heavy canvas he and Darren had put on the floor when they'd painted their bedroom. As they'd pulled it across their hardwood floor, it made that same dry, steady rustle.

Then they heard the hissing again, only very soft and in rippled bursts.

It was a giggle. Something was giggling. Some horrible *thing* was just tickled pink.

The face on the creature that came around the corner looked strikingly like the woman whose odor had knocked Nick on his ass. The face was that of Laura Shah.

A fresh wave of the reek thudded into Nick and, had he eaten anything that evening, it would have flown out of him. He grasped his stomach as the stench caused another painful cramp.

As it was, Nick was almost knocked forward into Scott as Karen's body fell onto him from behind. She'd fainted.

The thing was actually more snake than woman. Much more. It was the color of dark brown leather. Ripples of luminous green ran over its shining skin as it slithered along, reflecting the sparse house-party illumination. It was impossible to tell just how long it was; most of its body was still twisted out of the house. Where the animal should have had its head, was instead the torso of a woman. The gleaming skin of the serpent ended just below her breasts and then swept up beneath her armpits and over the back of her head, ending above her eyes, where her eyebrows should have been. The creature's arms waved through the air. The woman-portion of the thing was easily kept aloft, higher actually than Laura would have been in a standing position, while the bulk of the creature slid into the room, making a dry, steady, rustling noise as it moved.

Once it made its way into the house, the torso turned to face Scott. Nick was just lifting Karen, still unconscious, into a sitting position on the stairs.

Seeing Scott, the snake-woman's eyes shone a sickening green and the hood of a cobra spread out behind her. The cobra hood was wide and shimmering with searing green patterns running thickly down its length, which was more than twice as long as the human portion of the thing.

The animal pulled still more of itself into the house, curling a mass of thick brown-green tail beneath it. It rose up until its head almost touched the high, vaulted ceiling.

"There you are," it said, looking down at Scott. It had stopped hissing completely and the voice was entirely human. It had a very feminine, melodic quality, and was even pleasant.

"Indeed," said Scott. "You've grown, I see."

"You have no idea," said the snake-thing.

"What are you doing here?" Scott asked.

"I live here."

"Liar." Scott's tone was bland, conversational, all anxiety either gone or hidden. "I would have smelled you the moment the slightest breeze crossed the miles between us, oh rancid one."

"You are unfamiliar with the perks of real power, Marbas."

Scott shrugged. "You're still lying. What are you going to tell

Lilith when she sees what you've done to her house?"

"I'm tired of this game."

"The centuries have robbed you of your senses a bit, Shehlá. I think you need a nap."

"Where is Gillulim?" the snake snapped. Nick's mouth went dry at the name.

"I sent him back to his master, of course," Scott said, huffing as well as any teenager saying *Well, duh.*

"Of course you did." The snake-lady appeared almost pleased. "How typical of you, Marbas. Did you send him back to her in ashes, as you did Coronus? Did you completely reduce him to cinders to relay your message to her, or did you merely remove his tongue, as you did to my Vinkah?"

Scott tilted his head, squinted his eyes. "Why are you feigning this interest?"

"Suffering always interests me," the snake grunted. "His especially."

"No doubt."

"Maybe you showed some originality then. Perhaps your magic only returned to Lilith the tongue-less head of her minion? Perhaps only his head-less tongue?"

"No." Scott shook his head slowly. "Gillulim was unharmed."

"He escaped you?" The metallic-green scales that served as the thing's forehead rose in surprise.

"Again, no." Scott lowered his head while he shook it this time, probably closing his eyes as well, but Nick couldn't see his face. Surely, Scott was purposely drawing out the conversation, stalling. "I thought my message to Lilith would best be conveyed by the words of the imp himself."

The snake squinted, shaking its human head. "Now you are the one who is lying, fallen one. You haven't spoken with the voice of an angel since before the rise of man."

"Perhaps," Scott said. "Though, tell me Shehlá, how can you claim to understand real power when you have *never* spoken with such a voice?"

"My voice holds enough power." The snake-woman coiled tightly in defiance. "The winds have always risen at my call. How would wings add to the spell of my tongue?"

"Command the breezes then, if it satisfies you," Scott answered calmly. "Call to the storm, if that's all it takes to please you."

"I move much more than the air, skotos."

"You're voice is of that which is beneath the earth." Scott spoke very slowly. "You are below even the crust of man. Even the lowliest mortal cry will still find the attention of the Divine. Whereas, to the likes of you, His ears are eternally deaf."

"Your lips are full of mortal praises because your cheeks are still wet with their kisses." The snake-thing began to hiss again. Maybe it was showing some irritation. When it said 'kiss,' it sounded as though the word had at least twenty more *S*s than necessary.

"Who has been enraptured here, fallen one?" it asked, whipping its body through the room. "Was such simple beauty the only spell? Has the great Marbas fallen again to the charms of a youthful, beautiful human? History is such an easy circle. Did I weaken you so as this humble youth captured you so effortlessly?"

"That could be." Scott pouted, nodding. "Still, whatever his magic, it's well beyond you, serpent."

"It isn't, though." The serpent hissed an acid giggle. "I have but to take him apart to find it."

"You wouldn't find anything." Scott glowered. "It wouldn't be the first time."

"Oh, but the searching is so much fun."

"You don't have the power to reach him, Shehlá."

"You do not stand above me!" The snake hissed again, angrily swaying from one side of the room to the other. "You are a demon! No more! You have been placed upon the earth! You have been cast out! You are exiled here beside me! More than your wings have been stripped of light!"

"I've been placed upon the earth, yes." Scott nodded. "But my belly will never know the dirt as intimately as yours and, although you believe you've glimpsed power..." He smiled. "Nothing you will ever possess will lift you away from the dust."

"You are bound to this place!" The snake swayed across the room, faster and faster. "You are no better!"

"And yet," Scott said, very softly, "the company of the clouds has never been denied to me."

With a scalding hiss, the snake struck. It was too fast for Nick to see. One moment it was swaying in a wide, hypnotic arc, faster and faster across the room, and then it was no more than a streak, a brown-green haze.

The snake-demon never hit its target, though. Whatever spell Scott had cast before the creature entered the house stopped the monster cold. It hung suspended in the air, its eyes bulging in surprise and anger, its fangs not two feet from Scott's face. The length of the monster shook suddenly with violent spasms and its mouth gaped in a silent scream. A second later, it was over.

The woman's eyes ceased to shine. They rolled back into its head. Scott stepped out from beneath it just as the torso fell to the carpet with a sickening slap.

Scott turned to Nick, sweat beading across his face. "We have to get Karen to wake up. I need her right now."

Even as he was speaking, Scott's image began to shimmer. His wavy black hair was writhing with life and seemed to be growing. His eyes were shining like sapphire beacons.

"Try to wake her up," the voice of Marbas issued out of Scott in a rumbling growl. "I'll be right back. I just have to go outside and set the street on fire."

†

It must have been the look on his face. The second Darren entered the little makeshift DJ room, each of its occupants saw him and then suddenly looked sick.

"Oh, my god," one little redheaded guy gasped. "What happened?"

"You've all got to get out of the house right now," Darren said. "I think I saw a stairway out back that leads to the upper deck over the wooden awning. You can probably get to it through one of the rooms on the second floor and then go down to the backyard. Whatever you do, though, don't go to the street out front. I don't care if you have to hop ten fences for half the night to avoid it. Believe me, you don't want to go that way."

"Shit!" a very busty blonde girl huffed. "The cops are downstairs, aren't they?"

"Yeah." Darren nodded. "Yeah! That's it!"

Maybe they'd heard the noise when the entrance hall had been blown apart and maybe they hadn't. The music was unbelievably loud in the tiny DJ room. Maybe everyone was so fucked up that they'd faintly heard the ruckus and chalked it up to some extreme party rowdiness. Darren didn't give a shit either way. He just knew they all had to get out. They all had to get out so that he wouldn't have to worry about them any more and he could concentrate on getting Nick and all of their friends safely away.

He'd bounded up the stairs and was already halfway down the hall before he noticed that neither Nick nor Karen had followed.

Darren had to swallow a burst of temper. He would just have to trust that Scott could handle the situation in the living room.

Darren sent Eddie and Theo up to the third floor to sweep the VIP room. He hoped they'd find Troy up there or that he had already left.

✝

"He's not supposed to leave." Troy pointed at the older guy in the nice suit. "Scott said so."

Theo had let Eddie go up to the third floor by himself after they'd opened the bedroom door and discovered Troy.

"Vermin!" the older guy said. "You are vermin! Minions of the damned one!"

"Sure, whatever, dude," Theo said. "But if Scotty thinks you should wait here, then you're not goin' anywhere, buddy. Sorry."

✝

The DJ himself actually knew exactly how to get to the second floor patio deck and, consequently, the stairs at the back of the house. All the party-kids followed him hastily. No doubt, each of them was silently devising a plan to get away. Some would call cabs or friends from their cell phones and arrange to be picked up on some distant block. They'd either share their rides with the rest of the refugees or loan them their phones so they could make their own arrangements. Later, they'd each judge at what point over the weekend it might be safe to cruise back to claim their own cars. The 'lucky' ones, the ones who'd found parking close to the house, might have trouble doing that once there was a significant police presence.

Whatever their plans, Darren knew these people well enough. They'd leave this party, and in a hurry, but they weren't going home. Nope, they were going to the club. They'd all go straight to the club, to either listen for gossip about this mega-bust, or to spread it.

The flurry of people passed an open bedroom door, where Theo stood watching them file by. A second group, much smaller, came down the stairs at the far end of the hall and immediately followed the first directly into the room across from the stairs. Eddie came down behind them and turned to Theo and Darren.

"I told them the DEA had knocked down the front door," he said. "I don't think there's anyone else up there."

"Troy's in here." Theo motioned to the room behind him. "He's watching some guy."

Darren rolled his eyes. "Of course he is."

†

At least all the music had stopped, which probably meant that Darren had been able to clear the upstairs rooms.

"Karen…" Nick gently lifted her back into a sitting position and tried to figure out how he was going to move her over next to the wall. If he could scoot her next to the wall, then maybe he could prop her up. He couldn't take his eyes off of the motionless demon, though. Prone like that, it might have looked as though some poor woman were being eaten by a giant anaconda, if not for the thick strip of snake skin that ran from the top of her head and straight down her back. Unconscious, the cobra hood had retreated into that broad scale covering over her spine. Just below the rib cage, all human traits vanished. The rest of the creature was only the thick trunk of a serpent. From a distance, the snakeskin running from her forehead, over her skull, and down her back might just seem to be her hair, perhaps very wet and combed straight. Nick was quite close to the snake-woman, however. The brown-green scales were more than apparent.

Nick just wanted to get Karen—not to mention himself—up and away from the thing as quickly as possible. He didn't think it would wake up. Scott wouldn't have left them alone with it if his spell was all that temporary. Still…

"Karen… baby…" Nick whispered, lifting her gently. He was happy to see her turn her head on her own and even wet her lips.

"Ungoh," she said.

"That's right, baby." He gently brushed some hair off of her face. "It's time to wake up now."

"Is the party over?" she asked dreamily.

"Come on, gorgeous." Nick got to his knees, lifting frantically, trying to get his elbows beneath her arms. "We've got to get upstairs."

"For a second, I thought…" Karen turned her head and looked down at the dead-looking snake-lady thing. "Oh, my god!" she shrieked, leaping up and knocking Nick back against the wall. "I knew it!"

Karen tried to muffle her own high-pitched screams with one hand. She stood there for several seconds, screaming, muffling herself, and pointing down at the snake-thing. Very briefly, she stopped screaming to breathe. Then she shrieked, "Oh, my fucking god, I knew it!" She started to scream again.

"What?" Nick was trying to stand up. "What did you know?"

"That's Laura!" she shrieked at a decibel worthy of jet aircraft. "I *knew* there was something totally wrong with that little bitch!"

†

"Who are you?" the formidable-looking blonde guy asked. It was the second time he'd posed the question and Robert could have sworn he'd answered him.

"Nice suit," said the shorthaired, smaller, muscular kid.

"He's not supposed to leave," the tall skinny kid repeated. "Scott said so."

"Why not?" asked the formidable-looking blonde.

The skinny kid shrugged. "Hm mm."

"Troy..." The blonde lowered his eyes at the skinny guy. "Are you all right?"

The skinny guy—Troy—smiled. "I am at peace and my mind is in balance."

"Oh, Becky," chuckled the shorthaired, enormous, muscular kid.

The blonde squinted at Troy. "What?" he asked.

"I am at peace and my mind is in balance," repeated Troy. "Everything is going to be just dandy. This man is not to leave this room until Scott returns. I am at peace and my mind is in balance."

"Um... okay." The blonde guy's eyes widened and he nodded very slowly. "That's very good, Troy."

Both of the shorthaired, muscular kids, enormous and smaller, looked at each other and giggled.

"It was the demon," Robert heard himself say. All four of the young men turned to face him. "The demon touched his mind somehow."

"Scott?" asked the enormous, muscular boy.

Robert nodded slowly. "The demon that all of you have called into your lives. He touched him. Call the demon what you want, but it touched the mind of your friend. And so, just like all of you, he's been enthralled."

†

"Something's burning," Karen said.

"Well, um, Scott told me that he was going outside to set the street on fire," Nick offered. "I think he wants to slow down the police."

"No." Karen shook her head. "It smells like a camp fire. On the beach, maybe. It smells like the beach, and a fire..."

"Oh!" Nick smelled it too suddenly. He smiled. How could he

have missed it? "That's Scott. Well, I mean that's Marbas, actually."

"Who?" Karen squinted at him.

"Nicholas?" A very deep voice rumbled to them from around the corner, outside the house's ruined entrance.

Karen's face turned white. "Who is that?"

"That's him." Nick nodded gently. "It's Scott, only it isn't. It's who he really is. He's a fallen angel. He's really a fallen angel. Marbas the Black."

The voice of Marbas called again. "Nick?"

"Scott?" Nick called back.

"Yes. It's me."

"What's wrong?"

"I cannot change."

"What?"

"The spell has spent me already. I am too weak to..." Marbas didn't finish.

"Oh, boy," Nick whispered.

Marbas called again, "Karen?"

Karen's face lost even more color. Nick nodded at her gently. "It's all right," he said.

"Um..." she croaked. "Scotty?"

"Oh, Karen..." Marbas sounded lost, broken. "Oh, my dear beautiful girl, I am so sorry."

"Why?"

"You were not to see this. You are a pure and radiant blessing and I have brought only this curse to you."

"Scott, honey..." Karen shook her head, gazing past Nick at the debris littering the floor. "You haven't brought anything. This fuckin' snake-bitch has been working for me for a very, very long time."

"Shehlá."

"Who?"

"The snake-bitch," Marbas whispered from his hiding place around the corner. "Her name is Shehlá. She is a very ancient demon, called into being long before even the pyramids stood. Called by the words of men and through knowledge revealed to them by bitter angels. Bitter, raging angels, cast out of Heaven."

"Wow," Karen said, a little color returning to her cheeks. "Okay, so she's how old now, really?"

"I don't know, precisely. Seven or eight thousand years, I think."

"You don't say?"

"I'm going to need your help with her, Karen."

"Scotty, honey, you just have to say the word and I'll help you mop the floor with her." Karen looked down at the unconscious she-demon with disgust. "Good god, I thought she was only, like, twenty-nine, or something."

"Karen," Marbas called again from around the corner. "Karen, listen to me. Shehlá is very, very powerful. It took much more strength than I thought I would need to cast the spell that subdued her. Right now, I cannot ask for more energy from Nick or any of the others. I need your help. Without you, it'll be a day or two before I can recover. I need you."

"Name it, baby."

Nick grinned. That was the Karen Alanson he knew and loved.

"Karen," Marbas said, "I am in my true form, and I need you to face me. I need your trust, and I need you to look into my eyes."

Karen swallowed. "Is that going to be a really big deal?" She looked at Nick. "He says that like looking into his eyes is going to be a really major deal."

"Make no mistake, my love," Marbas warned, "I am a fallen angel, called a demon by the sons of man. I am Marbas the Black. I am That Which Comes From the Darkness. I am Midnight and I bear the Wings of Shadow. In my ignorance and in my fumbling to find a place to rest and be at peace, I have brought death and pain to this world. You must know this as you look into my eyes. You must understand my failings, and know that I am not pure."

Karen glanced at Nick in alarm.

Nick kissed her on the cheek and whispered into her ear. "I can't help you. I've given him all I can."

"There may still be peace for us all, Karen," Marbas said. "Although, you would only be accepting the hopes of one who has failed again and again. Even so, in the face of my own arrogance, beneath the weight of the same mistake I've made over and over since I fell from grace, I am asking for you to allow me this last chance to redeem my form from the darkness itself. That, and to spare those I love from the agony I have created.

"I am asking for the allowance of your soul. I am asking you to do what none of the others have done before you. I am asking that you gaze into the revealed eyes of Marbas the Black, the eyes of the winged, demon lion, unhidden by magic or transformation, and doing so, freely grant me the power of your mortal soul."

Karen looked at Nick. "Lion?"

"Big, big cat." Nick nodded. "Really, really huge kitty."

"With wings?" She grimaced.

Nick nodded again. Then he took a breath and lowered his eyes. He didn't want to influence her any further. Karen had to decide for herself. He didn't want to indicate with even the most inadvertent glance how she should decide. He never thought that, to help them, she'd have to face Marbas himself.

Scott's near-angelic human image had always softened the reality of his existence for both Nick and Darren. Now, Eddie and Theo as well. Karen, though... it seemed she would have to face the demon revealed.

Karen took hold of Nick's hand. He looked up at her despite himself. She didn't appear lost, though. She didn't look as though she needed the slightest guidance.

"Tell me his name again," she asked quietly.

"Scott's name?" Nick whispered.

"Yes." She nodded. "Tell me how to say his other name again."

Nick nodded back. "Marbas," he said. Then he added, "It was his name always. Even before he fell. Marbas was his name while he was still an angel of God."

"Nicky," Karen barely whispered, "are we gonna, like, go to Hell for this, or something?"

"Karen, I don't know!" Nick whispered urgently, shaking his head. "Good fucking grief, have you asked yourself that question before today? I mean, have you ever asked yourself that before? What the fuck do we know about shit like that! That's Scott outside! I don't know what all of this crap means, and I don't know who's going to Hell, or whatever. All I know is that Scott is outside and he needs us. He's never done anything to hurt any of us. What do we fucking know about fallen angels, or about what people call demons, huh?"

"I just mean..." She shook her head, lowered her eyes. "I don't know."

"You do whatever you need to," Nick said softly, touching her arm. "All I know is my life is better because of him."

Karen nodded, threading her fingers through Nick's.

"Maybe he's totally fucked up a lot of shit in the past," Nick went on, "but we're not angels either, Karen. None of us. What do we fucking know about demons and Hell? Really? What does anybody *really* know?"

A breeze rushed through the ruined house, carrying dirt and bits of plaster from the destroyed entrance hall and sweeping it out the shattered patio doors. The smell of a campfire was very strong.

Karen looked past Nick. "Marbas," she called. There was confidence in her voice.

"Karen..." came the soft response.

"I have to propose a condition."

There was no answer. Karen gave Nick a quick look and then went on. "I'll help you, I'll do what you want, as long as every ounce of energy, or whatever, that you take is only used to fix this mess. You have to promise to fix this mess and to protect these boys of mine."

"That is not so much to ask," Marbas said.

"Well..." Karen swallowed. "...and also to do away with this nasty thing laying on the carpet."

Nick looked up at her, a little startled.

"You've gotta get this thing out of our lives forever," she said. "I want you to promise me that this, whatever the fuck this snake-bitch-thing is, this thing, will never, ever, never, never show its ugly fucking eight-thousand-year-old face anywhere near me or any of my boys again."

Distant sirens were just becoming audible. The scent of a burning campfire was beginning to mix with the distinct odor of scorched tar and rubber.

Marbas had indeed ignited the very street, it seemed.

"I have to ask you to do that stuff," Karen called out. "I'm sorry."

Marbas was quiet for only a very brief moment.

"If you're asking me to destroy her," he called back, "then that is a very significant request."

Karen didn't answer.

"There would be consequences," Marbas added. "Grave consequences."

Karen swallowed. "You need to promise me that you'll get rid of this thing, Scotty. It's been using me. It's been using me and hurting a lot of people. People I care about."

"I understand, Karen. Believe me, I do. It still may not be wise to destroy her. Karen, you need to trust me. I will take care of her. I will use what power you grant to me to see that she does not hurt you or anyone else again. It might be very difficult, but there's a possibility that I can do that much."

The sirens were getting louder. It sounded like more of them had arrived. The horn of a fire engine joined them.

"She really hurts people, Scotty," Karen said. "There's some poor man in the back room right now. She did terrible, terrible things to him. She ripped him apart. And I think she killed someone else I knew. I think—"

"I know what she does," Marbas said.

"You have to make her go away!"

"Karen..." Marbas said gently. "I have to know what she knows. I have to take from her all that she has stolen from so many innocent souls. I need to make her relinquish what she has stolen. I promise you, my love, if she does not do as I command, then I will destroy her. You should not question that. The demon lying before you will give me what I ask or I will destroy her utterly.

"Still, her knowledge is valuable. Being so, I will offer her much more mercy than she has ever offered those she found within her grasp. I have to offer her the hope of her continued existence in return for what we all need from her."

Karen started to cry and Nick put his arm around her.

"You have to make her go away," she said, squinting, wiping at her face.

"I will do that," Marbas said. "I promise, I will do that much for you, my love."

Moving away from Nick, toward the front door, Karen wiped the tears from her face. "I trust you, Scotty. I trust that you'll take care of us, me and my boys. I know you love them."

"I love you just as much, beautiful woman."

Karen sobbed.

"You need be their strength now, Karen," said Marbas. "And mine."

The sirens were still blaring outside but didn't sound as though they were getting any closer. They'd been stopped by the blaze in the street, by the demon fire.

Karen nodded to herself, to no one, wiping at her face.

"I'm here for you Scotty," she said. "I'm ready."

†

Darren left Theo and Eddie in the giant bedroom. They could take care of Troy and the Armani-Suit-Guy. There hadn't been any noise from downstairs in a while and he was becoming very, very anxious. As soon as Darren heard the sirens, he knew it was time to find out what was going on.

When he reached the bottom of the stairs, Darren saw Scott on the floor, he was naked, stooping over some naked woman, who was apparently being eaten by the biggest snake he'd ever seen. Darren's jaw hit the carpet.

"Darren," Karen called to him quietly. She was standing very close, just a few feet from the bottom of the stairs.

Both Scott and Nick looked back at him.

"Everything's under control, big guy," Scott said. "At least for right now. Is there a back way out of the house?"

Darren nodded numbly. He was still staring at the snake-woman. Scott was trying to roll it over onto its back. With a very guttural grunt from Scott, the snake-thing twisted, and the woman part of it flopped over onto its back, tits dancing like firm, Jell-O volleyballs.

Karen had been standing in a sort of daze, leaning against one of the swivel chairs. She pushed herself away from the furniture and walked over to Darren.

"There's so much we don't understand," she said quietly, resting her head on his shoulder. He put his arm around her. "There's so much to this world and this life that just passes around us, unnoticed, unrecognized. We just go on and on, laughing and thinking that we're a huge part of it all. But we're not, really. None of us. We're just embers from a larger fire. Just sparks flying through a vast inferno. Just sparks."

"Oh, my god..." Darren said. " 'Embers from a larger fire?' What the fuck did you guys do to her?"

"Nothing." Nick shook his head, grinning. "She helped us, that's all. She looked into Scott's eyes... no, I mean, she looked into the eyes of Marbas, and she helped us."

"Nick," Scott said. Darren tried to pretend he hadn't noticed that Scott wasn't wearing any clothes. "Nick, I'm going to need to cast a couple more spells. They're going to be some whoppers."

"Oh boy." Nick sighed.

"Listen..." Scott looked down at the snake-woman. "I've got to get both this demon and myself back to my house before I can do what Karen has asked of me. To do what must be done, I have to get her back to my house. You'll need to hurry back there as well."

"All right." Nick nodded.

"First, though," Scott said, "you should make sure that Troy gets home. I've cast a spell on him and he needs to be at his own home when it wears off. Take him straight home. He won't remember anything."

"You put a spell on Troy?" Nick asked.

"He sure did," Darren said. "He's all, like, sober and shit. It is way totally spooky."

"You have to take Troy home very quickly," Scott said.

"Okay." Nick nodded again.

"Then the rest of you have to meet me back at my house. All of you. Eddie and Theo too. It's very important. We have a lot to discuss. There's a lot of work to do and everyone needs to be prepared."

"I'll bring them," Nick said.

"Darren..." Scott suddenly looked at him.

"Yes?" he answered.

"There's a man upstairs. Troy is watching him for me."

"We've met," Darren said, shutting his eyes, nodding.

"He has something I'll need."

"All right."

"You'll have to bring him along with you. Bring him to the beach house. He may object to that." Scott sighed. "He may object somewhat strongly."

Darren took a deep breath, stood up very straight. "That won't be a problem."

Scott grinned. "He has something with him, something crucial. This thing, it's a small, brass jar. You'll know it when you see it. Make sure you have it with you when you bring him. It's essential you don't leave it here. Then you've got to get the guys out of this place and back to my house. The police must not see you."

"You need me too," Karen said. It wasn't a question.

"Yes, of course, beautiful woman," Scott whispered. "You will be their strength now, their heart, more than ever before."

"I'm with you, baby."

"You know, though," Scott said, lowering his eyes at her, "that you can't leave with us, right?"

Darren was startled. "What do you mean? She's got to get out right now! She's got to come with us right now!"

"No, no!" Karen touched him gently on the arm. "It's all right, Darren. Scott's right. I have to be here when the police finally get through. I've got to be here to explain what happened."

"Are you insane!" Darren couldn't believe his ears. "What the motherfuck are you going to tell them?"

"Oh, my god, Darren," Karen said. "It's really not that big a deal."

"What! You're out of your fucking mind! They're going to arrest you!"

"Why?" Karen said patiently. "It's not *my* fault that Laura Shah was dealing drugs out of this house and that some wacko mobster-dudes came and wrecked her world."

Darren stepped away from her as his understanding slowly dawned. "Oh, my holy… " He shook his head and gaped.

"Look, Darren, honey," Karen explained, "maybe back in Salem in the seventeenth century you had to accuse someone of being a witch to ruin their life. Nowadays, it's much easier. You just accuse them of being involved with drugs. Bada-bing, bada-boom. Buh-bye. Guilty or not, buh-bye."

Darren's eyes could not have been any wider. "Karen Elizabeth Alanson…"

"Just look at these bodies, Darren." She gestured behind her. "Oh, my god, these poor men. Who will ever believe that I could have done such a thing? No, it's okay. I'm going to be fine."

"Oh, dear god," Darren said. "Oh, my holy god, Karen—"

"It's so simple, really," Karen said. "It just came to me a few seconds ago—"

"Karen!" Darren looked at her urgently. "They're going to know that you've taken drugs yourself. They're going to test you! They'll make you pee in a cup and they'll find—"

"No, they won't," Scott said, shaking his head firmly. "I took care of that."

"Darren, we don't have time for this," Karen said. "I love ya, honey, but knock it off and get my boys out of here."

"You are a scary, scary woman."

"Darren, sweetheart," Karen said, "I don't know what just happened between Scott and me, but whatever it was, it was right and it was good. That's Bobby over there, Darren. This fucking snake-thing twisted our little Bobby's head nearly off. I think I may just be in shock right now, but it won't hold my tears away much longer. I can feel it. That's our little Bobby-boy laying broken over there and, by the time the police are able to get here, I'm going to be a blithering, hysterical woman. That's all they're going to see."

"You're a scary woman," he said again. "A scary, impressive woman."

Karen reached up and kissed him on the chin. "You never have to worry about that, baby doll," she whispered. "As long as you don't ever piss me off."

"Scotty," Nick said. "Are you going to be okay? I mean, on your own with this, whatever-thingy, and everything?"

"Just hurry, Nick," Scott said. "I'll be fine. But you have to prepare them. You need to make sure the guys are ready to see me as I am. The spells I have to cast, they're going to take a great deal of effort and I won't be able to hold my human form when it's done. It might be as long as a day before I can phase back, and we don't have that much time.

"You'll find me in the basement. Down beneath the kitchen, in the basement. It's the only space in my home where I can sit in my true form with any comfort. You'll find me there."

"Okay." Nick nodded again, then looked back at Darren. "Did you know he had a basement?"

They both looked back at Scott, just standing there a moment, watching him, transfixed. They watched him for a moment longer, very briefly, before Darren took Nick by the hand and led him to the stairs.

"Give me just a minute, Karen," they heard Scott saying behind them. "I just have to cast this first spell and then we'll go over your story very quickly. We're going to make sure the police don't detain you for too long."

Before they went up, Darren and Nick stopped and looked back toward Scott once more, somehow unable to leave him. Karen had taken a seat in one of the swivel chairs, resigned. Scott was already hard at work, mumbling down at the fallen creature in some ancient language.

They watched as Scott raised his hand to his mouth. With a quick and practiced motion, he sliced open his own thumb with his teeth. Then, with his blood, he quickly drew a strange symbol on the forehead of the unconscious snake-demon.

At that, the boys rushed up the stairs. They didn't need to see any more.

CHAPTER V

†

The Bishop's Rage

If a wise man contendeth with a foolish man, whether he rage or laugh, there is no rest.

- Proverbs 29:9 (KJV)

Santa Monica, California
The basement of a private residence on Palisades Avenue,
south of Fourth Street

†

He was in Hell. That was the first thought blossoming in Robert's head when he began to swim back up to consciousness. The formidable-looking blonde had punched him in the face and, instead of just knocking him out, the punch had killed him.

All around him was a vast darkness. He was lying on what felt like a very thin layer of carpeting, which was just barely covering some kind of flat, hard surface, like rock. Robert never considered that Hell might have some kind of carpeting or any other such mortal adornment. His thoughts, though, were like slim streams of smoke, taking brief and almost meaningless shape before blowing immediately back into nothing. It was these thin streams of thought that gave him all of his perception at the moment, if it could truthfully be referred to as such. The thin streams of perception were suggesting to him now that maybe the demons had done some decorating.

Gaunt wisps of awareness or not, Robert knew there were demons nearby. There were demons around him in the vast darkness. Oh yes, there certainly were.

Robert lay on the thin carpeting, in the near darkness, staring across the space before him. There were two recognizable items within his view: the back of the giant black lion and, behind him, a very, very beautiful woman. She was sitting silently in a chair, as if in a trance, nude but for a dark blue sheet wrapped around her. The beautiful woman had a weird, red tattoo in the center her forehead.

The winged lion sat just a few feet away, his back to Robert, his wings partially spread. One of them had knocked over what Robert decided looked like a patio chair. Apparently, Hell had thin carpeting and possibly also patio chairs.

Through his slim veil of consciousness, Robert tried to note the rest of his surroundings but could see nothing else. There was so little light; all he could make out was the demon, the beautiful woman, the patio chair, and the seemingly infinite darkness surrounding all of them. It could have been anywhere, really. All Robert knew was that the demon-lion was very near.

He watched as the demon flexed his great black wings. Robert could also hear his voice. He could hear the demon-lion's unmistakable voice, rumbling around him. It rumbled and echoed.

In an abyss? asked a tentative wisp of awareness. *How could there be an echo in a lightless abyss?*

The sounds mixed with a number of other voices, also coming out of the darkness. The lion was far from alone. There must be many demons here then.

Robert shut his eyes and tried to listen. It was then that he realized his hands had been tied behind his back. Consciousness slipped closer, wisps of awareness became plumes, and he tried to understand more of the situation. He was lying on the ground, on a thin layer of carpeting, in a very dark place, with his hands tied behind his back. Was this really Hell? If so, why would the demons bind him in this way? He tried to move his legs and realized that his ankles had been bound as well. Were the demons afraid he'd run? Where would he run? That just didn't make any sense.

Robert tried to lift his head, which was a mistake. Any plumes of thought, thin or otherwise, were blown apart by the shift. His skull suddenly ached horribly and he was aware of a blunt pain in his nose and cheek. He could taste blood. The darkness began to swirl again. The voices became distant and liquid.

Before he slipped away again, Robert had an instant of hope, a single surviving wisp of understanding. Maybe he wasn't dead after all. Maybe the formidable-looking blonde guy had indeed only knocked him out. Maybe, instead of lying bound upon the carpeted patio rock of Hell, he was merely drifting within his own consciousness.

Robert let his head rest back down against the thin carpeting as, once more, the darkness took him away. He dreamed about a wide, turbulent river. Its water was the color of Scotch, roaring over enormous boulders of ice.

†

"Is he awake?" Darren asked, pointing at the man they'd tied up.

Nick looked across the floor at the guy in the Armani suit lying near the far wall in Scott's basement. It looked to him as though he was still out cold.

Darren must have really whacked the guy a good one. Nick had never seen Darren's temper flare so quickly or strike so surely. He also had no idea that Darren could knock a guy so utterly unconscious with just one punch. He hadn't really had much choice, though. The Armani Suit Guy just wouldn't give up the brass jar-thingy.

"Look," Darren had said back at the house, "I really need to borrow that thing, or else all of us are going to be in a very deep pile of shit." Darren seemed to be at least attempting patience with Armani Suit Guy, despite the blaring sirens down the street, which were totally freakin' everyone out.

"Demon spawn!" yelled Armani Suit Guy, clutching the brass jar-thingy like it was a golden football. "Deviants! Abominations! You are the very vermin of Hell itself and destined for the lake of fire!"

"Yeah, okay, whatever," Darren said, reaching out slowly, "but in the meantime, I just have to take that little brass—"

"Abomination!" howled Armani Suit Guy, stepping back. "The Lord God will vomit you out! You and your kind!"

"Um..." Darren stopped reaching toward the brass jar-thingy and looked at the floor instead, scratching his head absently. "And exactly what *kind* would that be, pal?" He'd already started to run his tongue over his upper teeth, and Nick had known immediately there was going to be trouble.

"You vile perverts! Sodomites! Homosex—!"

That's when Darren had punched him. All things considered, it was probably a good thing. Theo had looked like he was about to throw the guy right out the window.

Thinking back, Nick was pretty sure that Darren had most likely made up his mind to kick the shit out of the crazy guy right after all the 'vomit you out' stuff. Crazy Armani Suit Guy was so busy screaming about perverts and sodomites he didn't notice when Darren hauled back. His eyes only widened with understanding during the split second immediately before Darren's fist slammed into his face. That was all it took. The guy went down in a heavy Armani heap.

Nick always knew that Darren had a mild violent streak. It was an insecurity thing, maybe mixed with a testosterone thing, he thought. Darren had been arrested once for punching out some guy at *The House of Blues*, who, Darren later explained, was touching Nick too much.

Now, Darren had already lost his temper with the she-demon snake-thing—although he hadn't known it was a she-demon at the time—and removed her physically from the house.

And now this. Nick loved his boyfriend, but he thought Darren really needed to chill out.

Still, Nick smiled to himself; one punch, baby. Pretty studly guy, that boyfriend of his. One mighty punch. Even Theo had been impressed.

"He was close to being awake just now," Marbas said, nodding toward the unconscious man. "Only for a moment, though. He's unconscious again."

They were all standing in the basement of Scott's beach house. Frankly, Nick hadn't known that Scott even *had* a basement. It was just a big empty space—*huge* empty space, really—carpeted with a cheap, gray floor covering and illuminated by some very cheap-looking floor lamps.

Probably some mega-store fodder, Nick thought. Troy sure didn't stock shit like that at his shop. Nick guessed why Scott hadn't invested in decoration or better lighting in his basement: only Marbas spent time down there and no light survived for long in his company.

The door was at the top of some wooden stairs, which also looked pretty cheap. This was a thriller-movie basement, Nick thought. How appropriate.

Scott's basement had a very damp smell. Basements in LA were exceptionally rare, especially in homes near the ocean. On the beach, anything below ground level was going to be very difficult to keep dry, and would probably always have a mild fungal odor.

The ride from the house on Nichols Canyon had been filled with a frantic briefing. Mainly, Nick tried to explain to Theo and Eddie all the things that had happened since his initial alley encounter with Marbas the Black, the Gryphon of Greece. In dutiful detail, he told them of their very first encounter, way back in August.

Man, August seemed as though it had been at least a gazillion years ago.

In the car on the way to Santa Monica, Nick had tried to explain to Eddie and Theo why no one said anything, why he, Darren, and Scott kept the entire amazing story to themselves.

"We would've believed you," Theo had said, sounding very disappointed that he'd been left out.

"That wasn't the problem, big guy," Nick explained. "Scott could have proven all of it to you pretty easily. Probably just by spitting on something. But it wasn't a question of whether or not you guys would've believed any of it."

"I don't understand."

"Think if it this way..." Darren had touched Theo on the knee. "You know how it is when you're out and about, and you meet some new people, people who seem to be pretty cool?"

"Okay..." Theo nodded, listening.

"Well," Darren continued, "do you ever wait for a little while before you just blurt out to them that you're gay? Do you ever just wait to see how cool they really are before you test their coolness with that info?"

"Yeah." Theo had nodded again slowly. "I do that. Yeah, okay. Go on."

"We would have eventually told you everything," Nick said, "but we were still pretty bowled over by the whole idea ourselves. None of us knew what was really going on or how we should be handling it exactly. Not even Scott."

"He just wanted to try and rest and maybe find a little peace," Darren whispered. Nick had looked at him, surprised by the sadness in his voice. "Theo, I think that Scott just wanted to try and enjoy a little bit of his existence. Maybe we didn't tell you guys, Nick, Scott, and me, maybe we kept the secret from you so that it might be easier to give Scott what he seemed to need so badly. He's given us all so much, and I think that was the only thing he really wanted in return. He just wanted to be one of us, even if it was only for a little while. He just wanted to count himself among us, to be around people he loved, and who loved him back. He wanted to feel human, and normal and... well, I think that maybe he just wanted to feel loved. He wanted to feel like the rest of the world didn't judge him harshly because of things they didn't understand. He just wanted a little peace."

Nick didn't speak, didn't add anything, only looked at Darren a moment.

"Well," Eddie said, "we might have been okay with it, though. I mean, I don't know, we might have been okay. We wouldn't have just sent him away." Eddie was silent a moment, then shook his head solemnly. "I don't think we would've done that."

"I don't think so either, baby," Darren said. "But we just didn't want to blurt it out at you too soon. We just wanted to make sure that you guys were going to be okay, that's all. Just like when you meet new people. It's not like you're ashamed of who you are, or anything like that, but you still wait anyway. We all do. We wait for just that right moment, just that right, comfortable moment, when we think it would be okay to reveal who we really are."

They'd all sat quietly in the back of the limousine while Nick recounted the whole story, starting with him running into the alley to be sick and right up to the snake-thing destroying the house in the hills. No one questioned him. No one raised an eyebrow. Eddie and Theo understood. Not only that, they didn't seem like they were all too sure they'd have done anything differently, if their places had been reversed.

Now, Eddie and Theo just wanted to learn as much as possible so they could try to help Scott. They didn't care what kind of major eternal trouble into which he might have gotten them. They just wanted to do whatever was needed to help him.

When the guys first left through the back of the house on Nichols Canyon, Nick hopped over a couple fences to make sure the police hadn't yet spread completely around the neighborhood. Theo and Eddie carried Armani Suit Guy, and Darren called the limo driver with his cell phone.

It hadn't been difficult to get the driver to bring the car around to the street on which the little group waited to be picked up. Apparently, the driver had his own stash of recreational chemicals with which he'd been indulging, in his solitude, to a degree appropriate for one who didn't expect his clients to be needing him any time soon. That, plus the additional happenings at the house to which he'd no doubt at least a partially witnessed, left the driver in no condition to consider the strangeness of Darren's request.

By the time Darren got the driver to pick up the car's phone, he was completely wigged and, high-paying clients or not, quite possibly thinking about driving off to more understandable surroundings and leaving them all behind. They were really very lucky he hadn't come to a decision and driven off as soon as he saw the fire.

The first sign of trouble, though, Nick thought, would have been the mass party exodus. Nick could only imagine the expression on the limo driver's face as he looked up from his portable coke-mirror, the straw perhaps still hanging from his nose, and watched the steady stream of young, pretty party people suddenly heading for the hills.

Then there was the fire, of course. It probably stunned the driver completely. The sight of it must have been incredible, to say the very least.

Scott told them that he'd ignited the street with his breath, but that the fire was not natural. It burned at his command, with flames rising to an impossible height. Anyone seeing it would not have been able to explain why it was there or what, exactly, it was burning. It was just *there*, right smack in the middle of the street, like a dancing orange and yellow wall.

The limo driver must have been dumfounded. Then, the line of police cars, sirens blaring, had raced past him. Apparently, it hadn't yet occurred to him to do anything, to make any decisions regarding whether or not to pull out of his dark parking space and risk calling attention to himself.

Once Darren had him on the phone, though, the driver was remarkably open to some decisive instructions. Certainly, right about then, the limo driver had been pretty ripe for someone to tell him exactly what it was he needed to be doing. He was very receptive indeed.

When he'd pulled up to where the five of them waited with their unconscious chum, three blocks from all the hubbub, he didn't get out of the car to open their door, or so much as look at them. Actually, that had been fine, considering the limp, human bundle they had to somehow get into the back of the car. The driver seemed to be dealing with his own issues and wasn't about to make things worse by glancing out the window.

They'd quickly dropped Troy off at his building. He insisted he didn't need anyone to make sure he got upstairs.

"I am at peace and my mind is in balance," Troy said, smiling, waving at them from the sidewalk.

When the guys reached the beach house, Darren tossed a few fifty-dollar bills at the driver and sent him on his way. The look of relief on the driver's face had been both vivid and comical.

They'd all helped to carry the man in the Armani suit into Scott's house and down into the basement, each one looking around nervously at all the other dark houses on the beachside street. Although they knew that, even if someone had seen them, it wouldn't have been the first time Scott's neighbors witnessed listless bodies being carried from out of the back of limousines. This was still very early Sunday morning, in Los Angeles County, after all. The residents of Scott's beachside community were no doubt quite familiar with the sight of one of their neighbors returning from an overly festive blowout. They weren't alien to witnessing figures in the darkness stumbling out of their haphazardly parked cars, maybe ralphing in the bushes or even the street or, as with Armani Suit Guy, being carried. In fact, it wasn't uncommon for the folks on Scott's street to open their doors to retrieve the Sunday paper and see one of their neighbors lying across their own front porch, not having entirely made it over the threshold. Sights of that nature were common in this part of the world and didn't bother anyone. No alarms would be raised. Life was one great big party, after all.

Once the guys got inside Scott's house, they all struggled to get the unconscious man down the stairs and into the basement. The lamps in the basement weren't much help; it was as though the light itself was being consumed by the darkness beneath the house.

Nick looked over again at the man they'd kidnapped. It dawned on him suddenly that this whole mess might be getting a bit out of control.

Now, sitting and listening to Marbas, it became clear that things had been a bit out of control for a very, very long time.

"He'll be awake again soon, ," Marbas said. "It won't be long."

"Do you come down here a lot," Theo asked, "to like, stretch out?"

The giant, black lion cocked his head at him. "Not that much. That's not something I need to do very often."

Both Theo and Eddie had been utterly enraptured by Nick's story. The whole time he'd been talking to them in the car, they'd each had the look of first-graders hearing about Santa Claus. Nick tried to describe Marbas and use as much detail as possible. He'd warned them about how Scott had driven people crazy with only the sight of him. So, the guys all needed to be ready. They didn't want anything like that to happen here. Everyone needed to be ready to see him.

Happily, no one went crazy. Everyone had certainly gasped, though. Loudly.

The image out of the darkness stunned them into a stark and reverent silence. Even after just seeing him as he faced Karen at the house, Nick couldn't help but be overwhelmed once again by the majestic sight of the mighty demon-lion. After they'd heard his deep, thundering voice coming out of the basement's blackness, telling them to put the unconscious Armani Suit Guy over against the wall, the four boys had just stood together at the base of stairs, their eyeballs the size of dinner plates, watching.

Marbas had walked out of the dense shadows like Aslan out of Narnia. He sat before them, bowed his head, and spread his great, black wings as though in welcome.

"Holy motherfucking crap," Eddie had gasped.

"Indeed," said Marbas.

†

Darren was thunderstruck by the sight of Marbas. It almost made him forget that he'd probably broken every bone in his hand.

"It might be almost a day before I'm able to assume human form again," Marbas was saying. "In the meantime, there're a few things that you all should know."

The basement only seemed to contain some mismatched patio furniture and not much else. In the very dim light, Darren recognized the remnants of past barbeques and evening gatherings on the beachside deck. Nick and the other guys were arranging them so they could sit and listen to Marbas. Holding his injured hand, Darren moved to pull up a chair next to Nick.

"You should let me see that, Darren," said Marbas.

Darren stopped and looked at him. The huge lion was staring at his hand.

"I..." Darren swallowed. "I think I broke something."

He knew this was Scott. In his head, Darren knew the giant blue eyes that were gently staring back at him were Scott's, but he still felt a harsh grip run through his stomach and up into his throat as his reason fought his fear.

"I can help you," the lion said.

Darren looked down at his swollen, throbbing fingers. There were two small but deep cuts on his knuckles where they'd probably connected with some teeth. Almost his entire hand was turning a sickening blue-black. The pain was intense. "I think it was, um," he said, "when I, you know, um, punched that guy in the face."

"That would be my guess as well," said Marbas.

Darren stood staring down at his hand as he held it with the other, but didn't move.

Marbas whispered, "I'm not going to hurt you, Darren."

"I know." Darren closed his eyes and nodded.

"I made Nick a promise on that first day, remember? Even if I had not, you would have nothing to fear from me."

"I believe you." And he did.

So, why wasn't Darren going to him?

"I'm sure everything's fine for now, Darren," Marbas said quietly. "When you're ready, I'll help you."

"I'm ready," Darren said. Though, he knew he wasn't.

"I know this is a lot."

"I don't know what's wrong with me."

"It's all right."

"I mean, Eddie and Theo, they haven't known about you all summer, and they're handling this all pretty fine, I think." Darren looked up. "I've heard Nick describe you all summer. I've listened to you tell me all about demons and angels and all sorts of shit. You told me all about stuff that I certainly could have gone my whole fucking life not ever knowing existed. I've heard it all, so why...?"

Darren looked at the floor. He shook his head.

"Acceptance, Darren," Marbas said, "is not such a simple trick as most would like to believe."

Darren was very glad suddenly that his back was to Nick and the guys as he felt his eyes well.

"I've accepted you, though," he said.

Marbas didn't answer. When Darren ventured a look, the lion was watching him silently, tenderly.

Darren was still astounded by the vision before him. The light from the meager floor lamps skipped across the creature's huge wings, making ripples of shadow. The lion's fur was a dense, pure, matted black, without shine or contrast. Only the dimension of the creature exposed its shape within the battle of the light as it was consumed by shadow. As much as Darren had conjured him in his mind, as many times as the image of Marbas had flown through Darren's imagination while Nick told the story of their encounter again and again, Darren still hadn't fathomed the sight. Now, with Marbas actually in front of him, it seemed Darren's heart couldn't reconcile reality with his eyes and his mind.

"Eddie and Theo," Darren whispered, looking down again at his hand, "they're not freakin' out."

"Are you?" Marbas whispered. "Are you 'freakin' out?' "

Darren looked up at him again, and then nodded slightly as a single tear ran down his face. "What's wrong with me?"

"Nothing at all," Marbas said.

"I do trust you," Darren whispered.

"Darren..." said Marbas. "Don't try to fight yourself. The true sight of me is not a minor issue."

Darren stared silently back at the great winged lion. In the basement, the darkness itself seemed as though it was swirling around the creature like mist.

Watching Marbas, keeping his eyes locked to his, Darren crossed the few feet between them. He could feel the demon's heavy sigh touch his shirt.

"I do trust you," Darren whispered again, sweeping his injured hand tenderly along the lion's jaw. It was a gesture Darren thought would force his own courage to the surface. He would prove to himself that all was well. He'd never trembled so violently in his life, though. He was sure that, even several feet away in the darkness, Nick could still see him shaking.

Marbas lowered his eyes and tilted his great head affectionately against Darren's touch.

Darren smiled. "I trust you, Scotty," he said again.

Marbas looked up at him, nodded, and then took in a great breath. Instead of sighing heavily, which Darren was certain he was about to do, Marbas released his breath in a tiny stream, a slow, slow, breeze. His breath was no longer hot, but cooling, chilled and sweet smelling, like incense made from the dried essence of pears and grapes. Tingles rushed from Darren's chest around his torso and through his body, more violent and exhilarating than any drug, more consuming than Missy in her most supreme moments.

Finally, his lungs empty, Marbas leaned back away from Darren and closed his eyes.

Darren wasn't shaking anymore. He was warm and at ease. Marbas opened his eyes and Darren saw that there was nothing to be said. He nodded to him anyway, and couldn't help but grin. Marbas nodded back.

With the same grin on his face, Darren turned back to the guys and sat down next to Nick, who put his arm around him.

Darren smiled, happily flexing his fingers. The pain was gone. Looking at his hand, there wasn't even the slightest bruise showing, and the cuts on his knuckles had disappeared.

"I'm going to wake up the man behind me in a moment," said Marbas, addressing them all. "First, though, we should discuss the demon, Shehlá."

"That's Laura, right?" Eddie asked.

"Yes."

"What's the deal with her right there?" Theo asked, pointing at

Laura where she sat behind a partially folded wing. "Is she awake?"

Darren could clearly see Laura's face whenever Marbas folded back his right wing. He thought she looked totally stoned.

"She is entranced," said Marbas. "The spell I cast is very strong. Still, so is she. Very soon, she'll regain her senses. After that, we'll have just a few minutes before she's able to move again on her own. Once she can stand and move again, it won't be long before she regains her power. We have to decide what to do before that happens."

"We have to do something with her?" Eddie asked.

"Well," Marbas said, "we have to do something *about* her. I cannot let her go free. I believe I've learned enough to be comfortable with what must be done, though."

"And then we'll be okay, right?" Nick asked. "Once we figure out what to do with her?" He nodded toward Laura.

"I wish I could say yes." Marbas shook his head solemnly. "That's really the main issue we have to discuss. I've learned a great deal tonight. The very worst of which is that there is another, and she is coming. She may already be here, in the city. I don't know."

"Another what?" Theo gasped. "What other one?"

"She is a powerful demon," Marbas said, "known to men as Lilith. The Night Hag. The mother of all earthly demons."

†

Nick couldn't help but feel a horrible guilt. He was still very nauseated from the encounter at the house with Laura, and now his stomach was nothing but a solid, queasy pain. His legs ached and he couldn't get his lower lip to stop trembling.

He rubbed his hand absently across Darren's back, vaguely trying to comfort them both, as they sat listening to Marbas speak.

Marbas was talking to Eddie and Theo, answering as many questions as he could about the nature of demons. Mostly, it was stuff that he and Darren had heard before. Nick listened to his friends talk to the black winged lion. They questioned him casually, as though they'd known him in his demonic form all summer long. Nick was astonished at how easily they both seemed to be handling this staggering occurrence. He was also touched at how profoundly the sight of Marbas had affected Darren. Above it all, he couldn't help but feel that he was responsible for bringing them all to this day, where they were forced to discuss how to survive the arrival of still another demon, an ancient and malevolent force.

"Before we get into the particulars," Marbas was saying, "let me tell you about this person." He turned and folded his left wing to reveal the still unconscious man lying on the carpet near the wall. "His name is Bishop Robert Patrick. From what I understand, he is the protégé of Cardinal Nigel Matine. Cardinal Matine is the head of a very secret and very ancient order of the Church, charged with the care of Solomon's Vessel. That's the brass jar that Bishop Patrick had with him tonight."

"What was he doing with it?" Theo asked.

"From the Late Middle Ages until nineteen sixty-nine, I was sealed inside that vessel."

"Oh, my god," Eddie gasped. "Why? What happened?"

"It's a very long story, but I basically needed a place to hide. The secrets of my power had been revealed to men. Being so, I had to go where they could not summon me. I needed to be out of mortal reach until those secrets could be forgotten and lost once again."

"You were hiding in the brass jar?"

"Yes. Everything was working out just fine until the Vessel was opened. I don't remember anything about that event. Eventually, I came to understand that, despite being pursued by the Legions of the Beast, I was now also pursued by the Church."

"He was trying to put you back inside," Nick said, speaking just as the realization came to him. "That guy was trying to put you back inside the brass jar."

"Yes." Marbas nodded.

"But it didn't work," Theo chirped happily.

"The Church has forgotten so much." Marbas shook his head. "They have no idea what they're doing anymore. They're so confused. Over the centuries, they've laden themselves with so much of their own self-importance that the essence of divine nature is now quite beyond them.

"The jar isn't really magical at all. It's just brass. Although, I'm sure it's been blessed many times. The trouble is that it's an artifact of a very, very old legend involving King Solomon and the building of the Temple of Jerusalem. It was rumored that Solomon was able to force demons to do the work. The trouble with that story is just that, it's just a story. It never happened. Chalk it up to human embellishment. People have a fundamental need to explain their world to each other, and therefore themselves. In doing that, sometimes the tiniest fact can be interwoven with the most profound imaginings and, through the centuries, those imaginings will take on a very unique life of their own until they're indistinguishable from history."

Eddie chuckled. "So, this guy just crashed Karen's party and then attacked you with a metal jar?"

"Basically."

"What a goon."

"Perhaps." Marbas chuckled. "Though, he wasn't completely off base. Brass, for some reason, although not technically magical, is a substance that *can* hold a demon. It can hold anything, actually. Any supernatural entity may be contained within brass. There's no magic involved, however. Brass will simply hold a demon as long as it's sealed with lead. That's one example of a fact getting all mishmashed into a lot of fiction. But the trouble is getting the entity inside. That's where our friend here hadn't quite thought things through."

"What do we do with him?" Darren asked.

"Well, I don't really have anything specific in mind." Marbas shrugged. "Let's ask him." He turned to look at the man in the Armani suit. "Robert, it's time to wake up."

Instantly, the man opened his eyes. First, he shot a startled glance at Nick and the guys, then at Marbas. His eyes widened.

Marbas lowered his head and stamped his paw on the carpet. A distinct shimmer ran over the carpet and hit the man. His hair lifted, as though from a wind, and the bindings on his wrists and ankles flew off, striking the wall and falling harmlessly to the floor.

"Are you all right, Robert?" Marbas asked.

Armani Suit Guy — Robert — sat up quickly, then backed himself against the wall, still looking at Marbas with a silent though unmistakable panic.

"Robert," Marbas started again, "it's okay. No one is going to harm you."

"That guy punched me," Robert said.

"I'm sorry." Marbas shook his head. "That was unexpected. If you would like, I can —"

"Am I in Hell?" Robert blurted.

Marbas released a small sigh and closed his eyes. "That's such a personal thing, Robert. I couldn't possibly answer a question like that for you. You'll have to decide that for yourself."

"This isn't Hell?" Robert raised his eyebrows.

"Again, bishop…" Marbas sighed quite heavily this time. "Whenever we speak, it seems I'm forced to assume so much. Doing so now, I'll say that you're referring to the Christian definition of a literal location, a place of eternal torment. That being my assumption, the answer is no. No, Robert, you are not in Hell. Still, how interesting that you might believe so. This isn't Hell. This is Santa Monica. You're in my basement."

"You have a basement?"

"I know." Nick chuckled. "That's what I said."

Marbas grinned at Nick.

"What's going on?" Robert said. He wouldn't take his eyes off of Marbas.

"Would you like a chair?" Marbas swept his great head back toward Robert. The lion's enormous mane swayed in heavy, black waves.

"What?"

"You can't be very comfortable on the floor. Would you like to sit in a chair? There are plenty." With that, Marbas stamped his paw again onto the carpet and an empty patio chair slid across the floor and bumped into the wall next to Robert.

"Too cool," Theo chimed, shaking his head in awe.

Nick thought that Robert looked as though he was in shock. His breathing was very labored and he was sweating profusely. He just sat there for a moment and stared at the empty chair. Then, with a sort of stumbling motion, he got to his knees and twisted himself into it. He still didn't look very comfortable.

"You may take off your jacket if you like," Marbas offered him. "We could be down here for a while."

"I'm fine," said Robert.

"Suit yourself."

"We shouldn't stay here too long," Darren said. "I want to make sure that Karen is all right."

"Yes, of course." Marbas nodded at him.

"Where is the Vessel?" Robert asked.

"I have it," grunted Marbas. "I'm afraid I won't be able to give it back to you, though."

All the color drained out of Robert's face. Even in the almost nonexistent light, Nick could see his pallor become very pronounced.

"But I have to take it back to Rome," Robert whispered. "I have to take it back."

"Unfortunately, that is no longer possible." Marbas shut his eyes, shook his head. "I'm sorry, Robert."

"Vermin!" Robert suddenly burst, leaning forward in his chair, screaming. "Vile abomination!"

"That's enough, Robert," Marbas growled impatiently.

"Demon!" Robert went on shouting, shutting his eyes and spitting into the shadows. "Filthy vermin! Atrocity! Outcast!"

"Enough!" the lion roared.   A flash of hazy-blue heat knocked Robert against the wall, throwing open his jacket and buffeting his face. Robert clamped his eyes shut against the blow, turning his head and shutting his mouth.

"Whoa, Becky!" gasped Theo.

"That is all I'm going to take of that!" said Marbas, lifting himself onto all four legs and stepping closer to Robert. "I've shown you an enormous amount of tolerance so far, bishop. Ever since you so stupidly confronted me this evening. However, I am done. You are in my home. You are in my home and in my power only because you have proven yourself to be both shortsighted and horribly misin-formed. It's time for you to listen. It is now time for you to listen to what I have to say and to try and hear if there is a way for you to salvage some purpose for your life."

Robert didn't answer him. He just sat staring at the huge lion from his seat in the white plastic patio chair, panting in heaves of rage. Finally, with a cautious, labored motion, he leaned forward again.

"You are a liar," Robert hissed. "Nothing from the mouth of a demon is worthy of my attention."

Marbas just shook his head and sighed.

"Dude," Eddie said, "are you, like, mentally challenged? Are you a total idiot, or what?"

"Yeah, just shut up, man," Theo offered. "You fucked up. Okay? Just chill and we'll work it out. Like, comprende?"

"I think he may have just totally lost it, Scotty," Darren said.

"It's all of you who've gone completely insane." Robert squinted across the room at them. "Can't you see what's standing right in front of you? Have you so utterly devoted yourselves to the service of the Beast?"

"Well," Nick said, "you really don't know the whole story. There's a lot more to all of this than you think. A whole lot more."

"I know all that is necessary," Robert hissed at him. "I am a bishop of the Church and I will not be addressed in this manner by the vile minion of this beast."

"Hey, watch it there, pal." Darren almost rose out of his seat. "I'm just about thinking your head could maybe use another knuckle-knockin'!"

Nick, trying to stifle a smile, grabbed Darren by the arm and sat him back down.

"We were just discussing what to do next, Robert," Marbas said, sitting again. "We'd like your help."

"What?" Robert grunted at him.

"Do you know who this is, Robert?" Marbas folded his right wing, revealing the still-enchanted Laura.

Robert looked at her a moment. "What's wrong with her?" he asked.

"Do you recognize her, bishop?" Marbas repeated, more forcefully.

Robert looked back at him, making absolutely no effort to hide his contempt.

"No," he said. "I've never seen her before."

"This is Shehlá. She is a terrestrial demon in the direct service of the Beast himself. You see her in her human form. I've locked her there, for now."

"Shehlá?" Robert attempted the name.

"Yes." Marbas nodded. "Although, you would know her as Lamia. Or perhaps Lelia."

"Lamia..." the well-dressed young bishop barely uttered the sound.

"Yes," Marbas said again slowly.

Sitting back against the wall, Robert looked down at his lap. "That's Laura Shah then," he said.

"Do you know her?" Darren asked. He was leaning over his knees, listening to the conversation intently.

"I..." Robert started. "I... no. No, not personally. No, I didn't." He was still staring into his lap. "I had heard... I mean, I knew about a case, a couple of months ago... "

"Tell them about Alex, Robert," said Marbas. "Tell them about Alex Monroe."

"Alex?" Darren asked, looking surprised. "You knew Alex too?"

"Oh, my god." Nick suddenly had a terrible thought. "Scotty...?"

Marbas lowered his head, closed his eyes.

"Scotty," Nick went on, "did she...? Did Laura have something to do with Alex...?"

Eddie made a sudden gasping sound in front of Nick. Theo looked back at him. All of them had heard about the suicide, of course. Karen had told them. Nick remembered distinctly how much it had shaken her up, especially the part about the police questioning employees at the club.

"Tell them, Robert," Marbas said. He did not raise his head.

Robert looked up suddenly. There was rapid color in his cheeks and his eyes were damp.

"Did you know Alex very well?" Robert asked, looking at Darren.

Darren sat up. "Well, no. Not really. No. He worked at the club. He was one of Karen's door guys for a while. I thought he was a little young myself."

"He did not commit suicide," Robert said flatly. "She killed him. The Lamia killed him."

Eddie gasped again. Theo slumped into his chair.

"She what?" Darren said.

"This demon," Robert whispered, nodding at Laura, "she killed him. She killed Alex Monroe. I don't know exactly why."

"For his soul's power, Robert," Marbas said, raising his head and opening his eyes. He looked right at him. "She toyed with the boy for months, keeping him bonded to her. He would have been an easy source of energy, should she need him."

"But..." Robert croaked. "But he discovered her?"

"Yes."

"He knew."

"Yes, he did." Marbas nodded solemnly. "And so she took him. But not before forcing the boy to complete a task for her. She forced that innocent child to work a crucial part of her plan."

"What are you talking about?" Robert squinted at Marbas. "What task?"

"Laura killed Alex?" Nick could feel his eyes begin to burn.

"Yes." Robert nodded, looking over at Nick. There was real sympathy on his face.

"Everyone said he committed suicide." Eddie's voice hitched.

"He didn't." The bishop shook his head.

"There's more, Robert," Marbas said, looking down again, gazing somberly at the floor.

The bishop just kept shaking his head in quiet defiance.

"Someone else you know was at the party tonight, Robert," whispered Marbas.

"I didn't know anyone at that place," Robert corrected him. "I went alone."

"I was able to glean a great deal from this horrid demon tonight, while she was writhing beneath the power of my spell. I was able to take a great deal from her."

"What are you saying?" Robert repeated.

"This demon, Shehlá..." Marbas looked up at him. "Shehlá has been preparing for a very, very long time to stage a sort of rebellion. She's been trying to gain direct favor for herself from the Beast. On her own. She's been working on her own, despite the common belief among the Legions that she is one of Lilith's favored lieutenants. She's been amassing enormous amounts of energy for a very long time. Tonight, though... tonight she was presented with an incredible opportunity. Tonight, she shook hands with yet another bishop of the Church."

Robert just sat there, blinking back at Marbas, confused. The great lion was patient, though. He watched him with unwearied eyes.

"You can't mean..." Robert stammered. "You can't...!"

Marbas lowered his eyes once more, then his huge head. Great waves of dense black mane fell along his jaw.

"Oh, my God, no!" Robert burst into sobs. "Not Michael! Oh, my Lord in Heaven, what have I done? Oh, my dear God, what have I done?"

†

"Tell me what you need from me," Robert said.

It had seemed an eternity that he sobbed into his hands. Nick watched in sympathetic silence as the man heaved before them in agony. At one point, as they all listened, it became possible the sound would be too much for them. The man's suffering was so urgent, so crushing. Eddie had reached back blindly and Nick took his hand in both of his, rubbing his fingers lovingly, reassuringly.

Even after the expression of Robert's grief began to ebb, they'd all continued to sit in a sober, mute sort of containment. Marbas would not raise his eyes. Until he did, none of the boys were willing to speak.

"Marbas," Robert started again, "tell me what has to be done to destroy this demon."

"Do not speak with the voice of this temporary surge, Robert," Marbas said. "Already your anger has you seeking to destroy. You are now thinking of becoming a destructive force, something that was never in your plan for me, though, was it?"

"Tell me what needs to be done!" the bishop insisted.

"First..." Marbas raised his head, glaring at him. "First you must look into yourself."

"What does that mean?"

"This is not a choice of standing against a greater evil," Marbas explained. "There are clear intentions at work here. You have to know them, Robert."

"But there *are* two evils!" Robert huffed. "Why do you continue to lie to me, demon?"

"From what vantage do you think you're gazing upon us, priest?" Marbas blasted back. "The powers that move you are not innocent!"

"I am a delegate of the Church!"

"And as such you are branded!" Marbas hissed. "Do you believe your credentials carry any kind of trust, or some unquestioned purity? Do you think your hands are clean? Are you so dense to the world you believe the badge of the Church would clear your path without complaint? Is reality so lost to you?"

"You continue to speak with such a vile tongue?" Robert screamed. "Even with the lamia demon within your walls, you continue to rally your depraved deceptions?"

"Foul, stupid man!" the lion roared. "Open your eyes!"

"You can't rebuke me! You're standing amongst these addicts and heretics!"

"Self-righteousness is as addictive as any chemical, Robert!" Marbas huffed. "And you have gorged yourself upon it!"

"These are deviants at your side!" Robert roared back. "Vile, corrosive deviants, standing at the side of a demon! You're a mob of drug addicts and abominations!"

"Your words are swimming in the stench from your Scotch!" Marbas bellowed. "You've chosen your escape as well, as much as any one of these innocent men. You have chosen that which you would have soften the barrage of the world upon you. You cannot stand apart from them! Try as you might, you are shoulder to shoulder with them!"

"Liar!"

"*You* would only dare to believe so!"

"You are a liar! As all demons of the earth, you are a prince of liars!"

"Oh!" Marbas shook his head and glared at the ceiling. "The oldest and most convenient argument!"

"I was right about this city! It is teeming with the minions of the Beast!"

"There is a fifth demon at work here, Robert!" Marbas roared, lowering his head and leveling his eyes at the bishop. "It is not as ancient as Lilith, or the lamia, or even me, and yet it is by far the most foul."

"What are you talking about? Do you mean that servant to the lamia? I know all about him. Are you talking to me about—?"

"No!" Marbas shook his head furiously, sending waves of black mane cascading around him. "I'm not speaking of Lilith's imp."

"There was another demon at that club," Robert insisted. "I heard Alex Monroe describe him on a videotape. A short man working at the club with Alex—"

"Gillulim was the servant of Lilith," Marbas hissed. "He was the spy of Lilith, to report to her the actions of this lamia, Shehlá." He sighed. "I have seen to him."

"Then what are you talking about? What's this 'fifth demon?' "

"You know it well." Marbas squinted at him. "This demon has two heads, though it was born with only one. Doesn't that sound familiar?"

"A *fifth* demon?" Robert sat quietly now, looking perplexed. "Two heads?"

Nick looked over at Darren and he seemed to be just as confused. Scott hadn't mentioned anything like this to them during any of their many talks. No two-headed demon had appeared within any of their lessons.

"This demon," Marbas continued, "is not of the earth, as are Lilith and the lamia, but one of the Fallen. Fallen only from mortal grace, though. Not from Heaven, like me."

The bishop only gawked.

"In its infancy," Marbas continued, "this entity was not thought of as a demon at all. Just the opposite. It was thought to be something that would serve the good of humankind. Not long after its initial development, however, it sprouted a second head. Although the first head continued to strive to work for the divine, it was thwarted at every turn by the second. In fact, it seemed to be nearly blind to its own second head. Where the first would seek to spread love and peace, the second, out of arrogance and greed and ignorance, would sow lies, corruption, and cruelty.

"No one could believe the sudden and extreme duality of this monster. All were completely surprised. Its actions caused confusion and unrest wherever it moved. And it moved everywhere. For centuries it moved relentlessly across the globe, claiming to spread serenity and divinity, but dragging destruction and death in its wake, burning those who stood against it in an indifferent fire until its head of evil nearly overwhelmed its older head of mercy."

Robert huffed, leaned back in his lawn chair, crossing his arms.

"This demon does not exist."

"This demon is the Church," Marbas corrected him. "This demon is the body of men who believe they are working for a divine cause and yet are blinded by their misrouted piety. This demon is all those who stand atop the summit of their misinterpretations, their vanity, while they throw down ruin upon all who would confront them."

"Vile and putrid beast!" Robert spat. "May the flames of Hell consume you!"

"And so it may be," Marbas said. "Still, truth can be as wicked as any lie, reality as painful as any fabrication. How many souls were put to the torch, Robert? In the name of the Church, how many hands were bound together behind the stake so their flesh would be consumed by the blaze set around them? A blaze set by the wicked intentions of the Church, which you serve."

"That is not the church I serve!"

"No?" The lion's shining blue eyes bulged. "Your leader, wasn't it Urban the Second, didn't he begin a movement that sent wave after wave of the European faithful into the Holy Land where they would massacre men, women, and children, both the guilty and the innocent alike? Starting at the conclusion of the eleventh century, and not ending until the fall of Acre, it was the Church that ordered the destruction of city after city, household after household, life after life. And all in the name of, not God, but the Church itself. Was that not your church?"

"Those are the sins of a church long changed!"

Marbas huffed. "Old sins?"

"Old history."

"Historical sins?"

Robert spoke through gritted teeth. "*Forgiven* sins."

"Oh, great!" Marbas beamed. "How wonderful for you!"

Robert shook his head in disgust.

"You'll have to excuse me, then," Marbas said. "I hadn't heard."

"We have not been *that* church since..." Robert stopped, grunted, and gazed at the floor.

"That long?" The lion actually whistled. Nick almost laughed.

"Is that why you've brought me here, beast?" Robert squinted. "To discuss ancient history?"

"Hardly."

"Then get on with it!"

"I'm just so excited for you, though," Marbas chimed. "I mean, I really wasn't aware. I've been a little out of it, as you know. 'Out of the loop,' some would say now, about all this, the Church being completely forgiven, and all. You understand, don't you? You understand it's very, uh… chipper news."

"You're mocking me," Robert said blandly.

"Am I?" Marbas folded his wings, shook them once. A small gust stirred the lint from the carpet. "So, tell me, has the Church been forgiven for everything?"

"Forgiven for what?"

"For everything, Robert." Marbas again stood onto all four legs and approached the bishop. "This two-headed demon, the Church, this creation of man that has caused such suffering and deaths of such terrible agony for more human souls than the powers of Lilith and Shehlá combined, has the Church been forgiven for *all* of its 'historical' sins?"

"Of course." Robert's forehead burst with beads of sweat.

"Well," Marbas said, "if the Church itself might be forgiven, well… then maybe there's a little hope for the rest of us demons, after all."

Marbas folded his wings tightly, turned and strode across the floor, closing his eyes, sitting very close to the guys.

"Those were *holy* wars, Marbas," Robert called after him. He unfolded his arms, pressing his palms to his knees. "The Saracens took Jerusalem. They took the holy city, and so there were the crusades."

"You know…" Marbas cocked his head. "I've always said they were nothing but terrible instigators, those naughty Saracens."

Theo raised his hand and Marbas looked at him, suddenly grinning. Eddie laughed outright.

"Do you have a question, my sweet, sweet love?" said Marbas, just the slightest hint of mirth in his rumbling voice.

"Yes," said Theo, punching Eddie in the arm, who laughed harder. "What's a 'Saracen?' "

"It's what the medieval Christians used to call the early Arabian tribes."

"Those tribes had taken the city and were moving their conquests toward Europe," Robert said. He hadn't taken his eyes off of Marbas.

Marbas stopped grinning. "I thought you didn't want to debate history."

"They would have completely ravaged Europe."

"Europe was happily ravaging itself, Robert." Marbas shook his head again. "One of the demon's heads may have thought that the

Church was only marching toward Jerusalem to retake the holy city, but the other head knew perfectly well it was a scheme to unify the continent. The second head saw very clearly the sacrifice of so many innocent lives in order to save itself. The Church was raising itself up upon the death and suffering of the innocent."

Nick could see Robert gritting his teeth. The bishop crossed his arms and gazed into his lap.

"The second head of the Church watched the faithful march through their own lands," said Marbas, "destroying them on their way. It saw the devastation dragged across Europe before anyone ever reached Jerusalem. Finally, after taking the city, what, four years later, the demon's second head was not satisfied until the blood of every Arabian soul rushed through the streets in crimson rivers. Did everyone have to be put to the sword for the sake of this holy war then? I suppose someone thought so, because the crusaders literally waded through blood to their knees."

"They killed everyone?" Eddie had stopped laughing.

"Every man, woman, and child." Marbas nodded, his eyes locked to Robert's. "It was the second head's finest hour, was it not?"

"You are speaking of the Church and not a demon!" Robert spat.

"Indeed," Marbas said. "Call it whatever you want. You've accused *me* of killing children, though, and you're very stern about my label, aren't you? 'The Church, not a demon.' Hmm. Interesting. And we haven't even gotten to the Inquisition yet, bishop. Talk about tearing Europe apart —"

"The *Reformation* tore Europe apart!"

"Of course." Marbas rolled his eyes, shaking his head. "And the only possible answer to the turmoil was to toss about the label of 'heretic' upon the tiniest dissenting whisper. Must I go on? Must I list every atrocity enacted upon humankind in the great and infallible name of the Church? Should I name every scholar sent shaven and beaten to the fire? Do you want me to list the tortures performed upon those falsely labeled by the Church as blasphemers and witches? Perhaps I should start with the names of those who died under utterly fabricated accusations, for no more than the personal gain of one or other member of the clergy? Is that what you want to hear? I sincerely hope not, as that would be a very, very long list indeed. None of us have the time to hear it. Not the mortal or the immortal alike."

"You're speaking of masses of flawed and earthly people!" Robert spat. "The Church is not just a single being of one mind, one thought.

Not even a 'demon,' as you say, of two minds."

"What do you really know of demons, bishop?" Marbas growled. "I am not of the earth, as you've said. I am not a power released upon this globe by the wickedness of men, as is this silent being between us, Shehlá." Marbas swept aside his wing and revealed again the unconscious woman. "She is of the earth, this demon before you, Shehlá." Marbas paused and drew in a deep breath. "She was permitted existence through the wicked allowances of men."

Robert only gazed at the carpet, silent and obdurate. Marbas grunted in disgust. He shook his head and bared his lion's teeth, which were all the more startling and frightening because they were his; gleaming white daggers floating in the misty darkness.

"I am one of the Fallen," Marbas said. "What do you know of us? What do you really know of the truly Fallen? I am one of the Fallen, and not just from grace like your 'masses of flawed people.' I am one of that eternally wretched assemblage, the Fallen, from Heaven itself, and one of the last. You know nothing."

Robert leaned forward again, sweat dripping from his chin. "I know that Lilith is coming."

Marbas rolled his eyes again.

"And she's not coming for me, beast," Robert growled. "She's not coming for some imaginary two-headed creature either." He leaned back in his seat and smirked. "She's coming for you."

"I'll never understand how you're able to operate on only the barest fragments of information." Marbas stared at the ceiling, swishing his head, lobbing his words into heavy sighs. "Lilith, the Night Hag, is coming to Los Angeles, and you think it's me she is after."

"I've seen the signs of this demon all across the globe," Robert said. "Anywhere you've spent your time, any place between the poles that you've spread your wings, I've witnessed the attentions of Lilith." Robert squinted across the room at Marbas. "She's after you, my friend."

"I seem to remember you asking me not to call you that," said Marbas. "I said I wasn't going to eat you. That doesn't make me your 'friend.' "

"Just the same."

Marbas turned his back on the bishop and trotted the two steps back across the floor so that he could sit even closer to the guys. He sighed again and then looked Nicholas straight in the eye. "She is not after me," he said. "Lilith doesn't want me."

"Of course she's after you," Robert said behind him. "That's beyond question."

"You think you know so much, bishop," sighed Marbas, still looking at Nick affectionately. "But then, so did I. I suppose I shouldn't fault you. I thought she was after me too. I thought, perhaps arrogantly, that it was only me she was after. Me. I thought that Lilith wanted to present the body and power of Marbas to the Beast in order to receive his favor. I thought that, over all these centuries, I'd been just barely evading her grasp. Perhaps I should have listened to the imp the night he offered me a secret in exchange for his continued existence. Perhaps I should have allowed him to speak."

Nick reached next to him and took Darren's hand. "What's wrong, Scott?" he asked.

"She's never been after me." Marbas looked back at him solemnly. "Lilith has never wanted to capture me and present me to the Beast. That idea has been my most arrogant folly. It's been my most audacious mistake, my own unforgivable assumption." He turned and looked at Laura. "I was able to glean so much from this demon tonight. I was able to glean so much from the lamia. Lilith has never been after me."

"There is not any question here!" Robert erupted. "Lilith has been on your trail from the beginning!"

"From *your* beginning, yes," Marbas said. "Though, that is not important."

Marbas grunted, lowered his eyes. He slowly shook his mane.

Finally, he said, "She wants Nicholas."

†

"What do you expect me to do, Scott?" Darren roared. Nick was tugging on his arm, but he ignored him.

"I am absolutely to blame," said Marbas. "Your anger is justified."

"Darren!" Nick was pleading in his quiet-but-burly voice. "Stop this! Sit down. Please! Darren, sit down. Think about this!"

"What are you saying now?" Darren screamed at Marbas, all his former fear forgotten. Theo and Eddie were staring at him in shocked silence. "You're telling us that this Lilith-thing, this totally old, mega-bitch demon-thing, is coming here, here to LA, and she's coming to get Nicholas? What the fuck is that about? Huh? Some bitch from Hell is coming here and all she wants is Nicky? Are you crazy?

What the motherfuck have you done?"

"Darren!" Nick's burly voice was coming from between his clenched teeth now. "Please! Stop it! Sit down! Please sit down!"

"I did not know this," Marbas whispered, his head bent, waves of black mane rolling around his face. "I never knew this before tonight."

"Well, well," Robert huffed. "There is even deceit between you and those you claim to love."

"*Shut up!*" All four guys shouted at once.

Darren glanced nervously at Laura, but she was still totally comatose. They hadn't been that loud, apparently.

"Lilith isn't from Hell, Darren," offered Marbas. "I might be wrong but, actually, I think she's Sumerian."

"What-fucking-ever!"

"She's been following me for centuries, taking the souls I've enlightened," Marbas explained. "I always thought she was taking them to try and get to me, but it wasn't so. It was the enlightened human souls she was after, those souls most valuable to the Beast. She takes them and presents them to the Beast as trophies. He rewards her for them. After she brings him an enlightened human soul, he rewards her with more power than she could ever hope to attain on her own. It was this same power that Shehlá was after."

"What are we supposed to do now?" Darren asked. His head was beginning to throb.

Nick stood suddenly. "First," he said, glaring at Darren, "we *sit down!*"

Nick looked a bit upset. This couldn't be easy on him and Darren wasn't exactly helping to ease the tension. Darren ran his tongue along his teeth, took a deep breath, bit his lip, and finally sat back down.

Everyone held their breath for a moment. Nick exhaled loudly. "Scotty," he said, "I could smell her tonight, you know. Laura, I mean. The lamia."

"Yes." Marbas nodded. "I noticed that."

"She really reeked," Nick said. "It was awful. No, it was way past awful. It was completely unreal. It was like I couldn't breathe."

"Oh, my gosh," Darren started, rolling his head and slapping his knee. "That's what was wrong with you? I thought you'd, like, gone totally batshit on K, or something."

"Ever since that night with Gil," Nick continued, "I've caught very distant... I don't know, um... just very faint odors. Only at the club, though. Nowhere else."

Marbas nodded again.

"Then, tonight," Nick said, "when Laura, or whatever, came out of the back of the house…" He shook his head. "Man, it was like she'd fallen into a toxic dump and had to crawl through radiated sewage to get out."

"This is just the beginning, I think," Marbas said. "Something has changed in you, Nick. Since the night you first saw me as I am, since that night, something has changed and you're able to detect the scent of demons. Probably any number of other creature as well."

"Has this happened before?" Nick asked.

"Probably," Marbas said. He tilted his head a moment, thinking. "After we'd spent a lot of time together, especially after we'd moved to New York, Simon used to talk about smelling a campfire when he was around me."

"Yes!" Nick shouted, pointing at Marbas. Everyone jumped. "Karen said the same thing!"

"What?" Marbas looked puzzled. "Karen said that? Tonight?"

"Yeah, earlier." Nick nodded. "Right before you came back into the house, after you'd been fire-breathing out in the street."

"That's very odd." Marbas looked at the floor. "I was around Simon for years before he mentioned smelling a campfire. He used to mention the ocean too. He said it was like a beachside campfire."

"Yes!" Nick smiled. "That's exactly it. I noticed it the first time we met."

"In the alley?"

"Yeah." Nick nodded, absently rubbing his fingers together. "Yeah, in the alley. Right before I passed out. Right before I saw you looking down at me. The *Scott* you, I mean. Right before that, I smelled a campfire and the ocean. Then I don't remember anything until Darren called my apartment."

"Interesting." Marbas frowned.

"Karen said the same thing," Nick said. "I knew right away that it was you. I knew she was smelling you."

"I don't smell anything," Eddie said, pressing his eyebrows together.

"Me either," Theo agreed, squinting in concentration. "Maybe a little mold."

Marbas looked at him.

"It's no biggie," Theo chimed, giggling a little. "Why would the maid come down here? It's not that bad, though, really! I mean, you should smell my refrigerator. I brought leftovers home from Marix last weekend, and—"

Eddie elbowed him. "Would you just shut up?"

"I'm usually able to smell one of the Legions before they get anywhere near me," Marbas said. "They each have very strong odors, which are, as you've mentioned, Nick, quite, uh... distinct."

"You didn't smell anything tonight, huh?" Nick raised an eyebrow.

"No." The lion shook his head. "No, and that bothered me. But I believe I found the answer while she was first entranced. Shehlá said something tonight about me not understanding real power."

"Yeah, she did." Nick nodded. He looked up and saw Darren watching him with a smirk. "What?" he shrugged, smiling back. "She did."

"So, what does all that mean?" Darren asked Marbas, turning away from Nick and leaning back in his plastic chair. "Why are Nick and Karen smelling these demons? How come they're able to do it?"

"I'm not sure really," Marbas said. "Maybe it's some aspect to a type of clairvoyance."

Darren looked down at Nick, who smiled, shrugging. "That means 'clear seeing.' "

"Oh." Darren nodded, smiling back.

"It might be a sign of the development of clear sight, or 'clairvoyance,' " said Marbas, "that Nicholas and Karen can detect these scents."

"Okay," Theo said, "so, like, Nicky, you have, like, 'clair-smellance,' or some shit like that."

Eddie and Darren chuckled nervously, their arms crossed over their chests. Nick and Marbas smiled at each other, shaking their heads. Even Robert grinned a little.

"Karen too, I guess," Darren added.

Marbas stopped grinning and stared intently at the floor. "Perhaps," he said, then grunted. "Perhaps I should have looked for this."

"Looked for what?"

"I could smell Gillulim." He looked up at Nick. "But I never detected Shehlá. Tonight I think I've discovered why." He looked away, thinking.

"What does a demon smell like, Nick?" Theo asked.

"He already said that, stupid." Eddie smirked.

"Don't make me slap you in public," Theo whined. "What about that little imp thing? What did he smell like?"

Nick grimaced harshly at the memory, shuddering violently, shaking his head. "Bad!"

"Like Laura?" Eddie asked.

"No," Nick said. "No, totally different. He smelled like... oh, I don't know, like putrid snot."

"Eeeew!" Theo and Eddie sang in unison. Darren chuckled.

"And Laura..." Nick began. "Like I said, she smells like toxic sewage."

Theo and Eddie shuddered melodramatically, rattling their lawn chairs.

"Careful," said a slow, rasping voice.

Everyone froze. Marbas looked up from the floor and Darren saw his breathing stop.

The lion deliberately folded his wings tightly and turned around, backing a step or two toward Theo. Laura's eyes were open, though her head still lolled listlessly toward her shoulder.

"You're not being very nice," she said groggily. "You'll give a girl a complex."

Chapter VI

†

Demon Tongues

But the tongue can no man tame; it is an unruly evil, full of deadly poison.

- James 3:6 (KJV)

†

"Hello again, Shehlá," said Marbas.

Nick thought for an instant that Laura had zoned right back out because she just stared into space and didn't answer. Then, moving only her eyes, she slowly looked toward the giant, black lion.

"That's more like it, Marbas," she said. Her manner was calm, her voice a strained, thin rasp. "I like you better this way. I like you better as an animal."

"My form was not chosen to please you." He blinked and bowed his head slightly.

"No." Laura's voice ground out of her. "You had no choice, of course. Such a valiant effort. You've used your pathetic self right up. You blew your whole wad. I can still feel the coils of your spell sliding through my mind, you know. It's quite painful."

"I'm sorry," said Marbas. "The aspects of that charm are unfortunate."

"It gives me more reason to consider the many ways I will cause you pain," Laura said. "You look so big and scary right now, Marbas, but I'm not fooled." She still couldn't seem to move any part of her body, except her eyes, lips — which barely moved at all — and whatever components within her throat were necessary for speech. Simply whispering looked as though it took a great effort. Even so, she went on. "You're weaker than a kitten. I can see it in your eyes, you know. I like that look on you, kitty."

"Enjoy it while you can."

"You're pitiful," Laura whispered. Nick could hardly hear her. "You know this won't work. This spell will not last. I'll be up and about long, long before you've regained enough of your own power."

"That's true." Marbas gave another little nod.

"And you're going to need a great deal of strength, you big, stupid kitty." Laura closed her eyes into slits and glared at him. "You know you'll need more strength, and yet you haven't fled."

The two demons considered each other silently. Nick hadn't realized he was holding his breath, but when he finally took in air, he noticed a thin strain of odor, the odor of this demon who had just awoken before them. It was remote but unmistakable. She was like a frozen fish left on the counter to thaw. He knew the stench would build as she regained her strength. If he were caught down in this dank room when that happened, the reek of her would be unbearable.

Laura spoke to Marbas. The words came as though they were scraped from her. "What is it you think you'll be accomplishing here, you flying rug?"

The lion huffed and swayed his head. The sound of his massive mane was like dense wheat in a breeze.

"You really shouldn't have lost your temper, Shehlá," Marbas said. "It cost you a great deal. A very great deal."

"I'll be sure to think of that as I'm stretching out on your hide in front of my fireplace."

"Oh, that would be garish, even for you. I'd make a very poor floor decoration. You'd constantly be tripping over my head, for one thing. All your little friends would laugh at you. They'd call you 'Grace.' It'd be totally non-glam."

"You seem to be enjoying your time here in my little part of the world," she said. "You've taken to the language already."

"I like it here very much." Marbas grinned.

"You sound utterly ridiculous."

"You've adjusted to this age as well, Shehlá," Marbas said. "Through mortal contact, you've kept yourself from being touched by your solitude, just as the rest of us, just as those who also have the power to do so."

"I've done only what was necessary to take that which should have always been mine."

"Yeah, whatever." Marbas rolled his eyes.

"Maybe you would make a poor rug," Laura rasped. "Perhaps I should just have it mounted then? Your head, that is."

"Now you're thinking."

"And you're dodging me, cat."

"Not at all."

"You haven't answered my question." Laura's scratch of a voice held a hint of mirth. "I don't mind, though. Stall all you want. We can continue this conversation after your spell has failed and I'm tearing the hide from your body."

"That won't be happening, as you very well know."

Laura pressed her lips together and all their color disappeared. "Aren't we both a little old for these games?"

"Well, maybe *you* are," Marbas grunted.

"She's older than you?" Darren asked.

"Oh, yes." Marbas nodded at him. "By about three or four thousand years, actually."

"Who's that?" Laura rasped, trying to roll her eyes and gaze across the darkened basement toward Darren's voice. Her eyelids became spasmodic as the orbs slowly rotated beneath them. "Was that little Darren Jacobson? Oh golly, I hope so. Darren honey, sweetheart, oh my, but I owe you such a time, you have no idea. Before I'm through with you, you'll have screamed so much you'll likely drown in the drippings of your own bleeding throat."

"Now, now!" Marbas rumbled. "You know you're not going to have time for any of those sorts of shenanigans."

"Ah, well, there *is* a game then." Laura shifted her eyes back to Marbas. They still moved very slowly. "And it has begun, I assume?"

"Call it what you want." Marbas trotted over to her. He pressed his face so close to hers that Nick was sure she could feel the lion's long black whiskers brushing her cheeks. "Though... when *do* you expect Lilith to arrive?"

"Can't you just destroy her?" Robert said. He was standing up, his hands shaking. "Why can't you just destroy her now? Destroy this monster right here and now!"

"Aaah," Laura rasped. The sound made Nick's flesh ripple with chills. It was like crumpled paper being dragged across cement. "Bishop," she said. "I'm so flattered you're here. Is this party for me? Is it all for little, old me?"

Robert's breath hitched and he staggered on his feet.

"Robert, sit down!" Marbas grunted. He stepped back away from Laura and sat on his haunches, closing his eyes. He spoke in a rumble through clenched fangs, without turning to look at the bishop. "You're going to make matters much worse if you don't sit down right now."

"Destroy her!" Robert stretched out his arm, pointing at Laura, behind the lion's folded wings. Laura's eyes seemed to have found him anyway, picked him out in the darkness. "She took Michael! Destroy her!"

"Ooh, poor, poor bishop," Laura said. "How lovely of you to have come." When she spoke again, her mouth did not form the words. Laura merely parted her crimson lips and another voice issued from between them. It was a male voice, mocking and cheerful, with a faint British accent. *"Are all of you looking for little, old me?"* said the voice from Laura's open mouth. *"Why, I don't think I've ever been so flattered."*

"Oh..." Robert stumbled back to his chair. He nearly fell into it. "Oh, my God..."

"Don't listen to her, Robert," Marbas said. His eyes were still closed, his head lowered, resigned.

"Shall I summon him for you, bishop?" Laura rasped, her head bobbing listlessly at her shoulder. "Shall I call him? Brathwidth? It would be so easy. Wouldn't you like to see him again? I'm sure he—"

"Enough!" Marbas roared at Laura. Although the rest of the room jumped totally out of their chairs, Robert included, Laura didn't even blink. She didn't so much as blink, despite the fact that the demon-lion's breath had caused the sheet covering her to smolder.

"You really shouldn't loose your temper, Marbas," Laura said quietly. "It could cost you a great deal. A very great deal."

The blue eyes of Marbas burnished like the very belly of a butane fire. He stared at Laura for only a second before he turned and pushed his jaw almost into Robert's face, baring his bone-white teeth.

"Do not speak to her!" he hissed. Robert's eyes were nearly popping out of his head.

"I ..." Robert gasped.

"Stop now," Marbas grunted. "She knows all about you. Everything that Michael would have known, she knows. She took him. She knows him. She took every *essence* of him and you must steady yourself, father. Steady yourself for what is to come. If you are to survive, if you are to ever feel any kind of peace again, any peace at all after this moment, then you must stop now. Leave her to me. Sit down and keep your mouth shut while I do what has to be done."

"She has to be destroyed!" Robert heaved through his clenched jaw. His eyes were swimming in moisture and fear.

"I will not warn you again!" Marbas growled. "I will do what must be done to protect the ones I love. And you will not get in my way!"

Nick could see Robert grip the arms of his plastic lawn chair as he steadied himself. "She must be —!"

Marbas roared, "*You will not get in my way!*"

Once more, Robert's jacket flew open as the lion's breath assailed him. Again, he tried to twist his face away from the heat. Two of his shirt buttons flew off. Faint lines of smoke rose out of his breast pocket. It even looked to Nick as though Robert's belt was sizzling. A circle of thin, gray smoke was billowing along the cement wall behind Robert in a flat, widening circle, like the remnant of some minor explosion.

Despite all that, Robert's skin was untouched. He didn't seem to be in any kind of physical pain. His hair was windblown, though not yet smoldering.

Robert continued to press his eyelids together for another cautious moment, squinting harshly, keeping his face as far away from Marbas as possible. The giant black lion looked up at him, a low, threatening rumble emanating from deep in his throat.

Very slowly, Robert slid down along the cement wall and back into his plastic lawn chair. Marbas rocked back, away from the bishop. Robert's eyes did not open and his face remained averted.

The basement was completely quiet, except that Nick thought he heard the sound of dry, dead leaves being scattered over stones in a breeze. Nicholas stopped himself; there was no wind in the basement and certainly no leaves.

The faint, harsh sound was coming from Laura. She was laughing.

"I know Brathwidth quite well, bishop," she said quietly. "How interesting to have found that story within little Mikey's flesh."

Marbas continued to stare at Robert, but neither said a word. Nick was sure that Darren, Eddie, and Theo were as afraid to breathe as he was.

Finally, in a sudden, fluid motion, the lion snapped his wings in a single, narrow gesture. A quick but powerful gust hit Robert and extinguished whatever had been smoking in his jacket.

With a grunt, Marbas turned around and faced Laura again.

"Let's talk about the stories I found in *you*, Shehlá," he said.

"Oh, that would be a pleasure," she chimed, her voice less dry, a little more female. "Can we talk about Simon? Don't you want to hear him screaming? I know I do."

Marbas grunted again and lowered his eyes to hers. "If I hear you produce one more sound that isn't the natural voice created by this form, I will rip out your tongue."

Laura's lips slowly pressed themselves closed.

"You thought I'd overlooked your tongue, Shehlá?" Marbas asked softly. "I know you're surprised to still have possession of it. You're wondering, or hoping, maybe, if I might have totally forgotten to tear it out of your head?"

"Why would you rip out her tongue?" Darren asked. Nick was impressed that he sounded so calm. Maybe Darren thought he didn't have anything more to lose, since Laura already had it in for him so badly.

"Without her tongue," Marbas said, not looking back at them, "she cannot cast her own spells."

"Can't she just heal it?" Darren asked. "Like with magic or something?"

"Yes," Marbas whispered. "She could be healed with magic. Although not her own. There's only one entity under Heaven who has the power to heal a demon."

Nick distinctly saw Laura's eyes burn with hatred.

Marbas grinned. "And that would be me," he said.

Nick let out a silent breath of relief. Apparently, they did have some leverage. Whatever Marbas was planning to do, he would hold the threat over Laura, of ripping out her tongue, or worse, before she fully regained her strength.

Nick hoped whatever was going to happen would happen soon. He didn't want to see Laura turn back into that snake-thing again. Although he knew it was the power of Marbas that had locked her into mortal form, he also somehow knew that Laura—Shehlá—would take her true form if she could. She didn't need to cast spells to be a demon.

Still, Nick felt a bit better; his stomach was not so cramped and the nausea had abated a little. Marbas had a plan. He'd left Laura intact. She knew he could have done otherwise, and now she probably also knew that he wanted something in return.

"So, let's chat, Shehlá." Marbas sat back on his haunches again. "Let's discuss what we know."

"You know nothing," she hissed.

"Yeah, okay," Marbas grunted. "Let's start there. Let's start with the idea that you think I'm an idiot. I suppose that on one level, you're right. I certainly was an idiot to assume my escape from you five months ago hadn't been your intention all along. I was an idiot not to have realized that you dragged me all the way across this continent only so that you could get me away from Lilith. I was an idiot not to know, as I was hiding in that tiny, dark, little alley, that you knew precisely where I was the entire time and, in fact, were very, very close. You were listening to my conversation with Nicholas. You heard it all. You heard every word between us, from the beginning."

Fresh dread blossomed in Nick's stomach, instantly, as though it were freezing and expanding up into his throat, as though he'd swallowed a tiny canister of nitrogen and it had opened deep within his gut.

"I should have realized that you were watching me," Marbas went on. "You were watching and hoping I'd enlighten a human soul. You were the one who chanted the curse, causing the blood to flow from Nick's lungs. I should have realized it long before now. You were the one who forced the circumstances that bound me to Nick."

Laura didn't respond.

"But I've since begun to realize a few other things," continued Marbas. "Ever since you allowed that stupid imp to cross my path, I've started to put a few things together."

"I allowed him nothing," Laura said. "He was a servant of Lilith, always."

"You directed him so that he would encounter me," corrected Marbas. "Something I suspected then and confirmed tonight while you were babbling on the carpet beneath my charm."

Laura suddenly lifted her head straight up, away from her shoulder, and gazed at Marbas. His spell was weakening rapidly. She even twitched casually, swishing her hair farther off of her face. Nick had to stifle a gasp. Eddie wasn't as successful and Laura's eyes flickered to the four of them. Theo began to whimper.

Laura looked away again without saying anything. Then, staring at Marbas, she forced her mouth into a sneer. "You couldn't have taken very much from me," she said. "Not so quickly."

"I learned the most important thing," Marbas whispered. "I learned the key to it all."

"Your time is growing short," she hissed. She smiled at him this time, and it didn't seem to take her nearly any effort at all.

"Why can't I smell you, Shehlá?" Marbas asked. "Your power is coming back and I should be able to smell you. Nicholas can smell you. I can tell from his face. He's growing pale from your rising stench."

"The enlightened one will not have to suffer it long."

"Empty threat," Marbas whispered. "Why haven't I smelled you at the hub? You've watched that Hub of Influence for years now, supposedly on behalf of Lilith. Why didn't I detect you there?"

"Because you're a feeble, stupid—"

"Because," Marbas growled, "because you've cast one of the Spells of Anat."

Laura did not answer.

"You've cast one of the forbidden spells," Marbas repeated.

"Fool," Laura spit. "I would need a mortal to cast such a spell. I would need a sorcerer. Only a mortal voice will work with such magic."

"True," said Marbas. "But you needed something else as well. You needed more than a mortal voice to cast the particular spell you chose, the spell that would block your detection from a non-terrestrial demon. One that would protect you from me. To hide from me, from one of the Fallen, to complete the spell that would cover your scent from Marbas the Black... you would need something very specific indeed. You would need my *true* name."

Laura's chest was beginning to rise with deeper breaths.

"You've learned my name, Shehlá," Marbas said flatly. "I didn't need to crack open your thoughts to deduce that. Somehow, you've learned my name and were hoping to spirit me away from Lilith to a place where you could watch and control me, harvesting the mortal souls I enlightened, stealing from Lilith the power she receives by offering those souls to the Beast."

"I am a servant of Lilith," Laura hissed.

"Casting that spell for you was the last task of Alex Monroe, I assume," Marbas continued. "Did you promise him his life or just an end to his suffering? You came upon that innocent boy in his home and forced him to utter the charm. You forced him to chant a Spell of Anat. You taught him to pronounce my true name and then to chant the spell. You forced that innocent soul into the service of the Legions by tearing the living flesh from his face."

"I am a servant of Lilith!" Laura spat her mantra at him.

"Will she still believe that?" Marbas said quietly. "When she gets here, and she finds that you have been manipulating me, playing me, waiting to harvest the human souls for yourself, will she still see you as her faithful servant?"

Laura straightened her shoulders. She sat up against the white plastic chair. Nick was almost gagging from the stench of her.

"I am a servant of Lilith," Laura said again. Her voice rang with feminine tones. "What I have done, I have done in her name. What power is to be gained is gained for her, as it is, and was, and always shall be."

"Indeed?" Marbas looked puzzled. "I'm sure that would all seem just lovely to her. Really. I'm sure she'd be more than happy to hear that from you over a manicure and then maybe lunch at Chin Chin.

"I'm sure she'll forgive you, perhaps even neglect to mention your knowledge of Anat and her spells to the Beast..."

Laura's eyes began to burn with a sickening green light. Nick coughed, trying to cover his mouth and nose with the bottom of his shirt. Darren pulled him close, absently rubbing his back

"However," Marbas went on, "there's the little detail about knowing my name. Here, among these I love, I am called Scott, and I consider it, now, my truest name.

"Among the angels and the demons alike, all who speak of me with such inaptness, yet the name of Marbas is known to each.

"And still, there is yet another name. There is my name of power. There is that name through which I may be instantly summoned and by which I may be easily charmed. A name only known, supposedly, to myself and to the Divine. Would not the loyal servant of Lilith relinquish such powerful knowledge to her master? Would not Lilith's true servant bring such a powerful charm to her mistress should she stumble upon it?"

Laura did not speak.

"Five centuries ago," said Marbas, "I was summoned to the desert. I was called by a human voice that hardly expected the charm to actually work. Yet, there I stood before him. How did he learn my name? How did he come upon the spell that would summon me from the void when spoken along with the utterance of my name of power?

"I've considered that question time and again since my release from the Vessel all those years ago. I have a feeling that the answer will be just as interesting to Lilith as it was to me. You taught it to him, Shehlá. All those centuries ago, you taught my true name to that pathetic 'sorcerer' who stumbled into the desert with the priests. Even then, you'd planned to take me away and use me. But I disappeared, and could not be summoned back."

"You are a fool among fools, Marbas!" Laura screamed. "You've wasted your power, trotting across the globe, pretending that you still bear the wings of light!"

"How did you learn my name, Shehlá?" Marbas growled. "Then, after you taught the sorcerer to summon me, after you sent him into the wastelands beyond Judea with that band of priests from the Church, how did you plan to use me?"

"She fears you, Marbas!" Laura was moving her arms now. "Lilith fears you! You are one of the Fallen! She has very great power, though, powerful as she is, ultimately, she is of the earth! You could stand against her! I could stand beside you!"

"What will she think, Shehlá?" Marbas didn't raise his voice. "What will Lilith think when she learns you've taken me from her? What will she say?"

"The Fallen are so few now!" Laura leaned forward. "And you are one of the tiny few that do not stand with the Beast! With the Beast himself! You could easily take Lilith's place at his side! I could guide you there!"

"Was it Asmodeus?" Marbas asked. "Before he was destroyed by the Beast, did Asmodeus teach you to utter my name? Perhaps he even taught you to cast the Spells of Anat?"

"Marbas!" Laura pressed her fingers to her temples.

"It doesn't matter, Shehlá. Lilith will assume the worst. Lilith will assume that you've learned a new charm or two. She'll assume, having learned of the things you've done from Gillulim, the imp you expected me to destroy for you, she'll assume you've learned a charm that will reveal the true names of the Legions to you. All of them, perhaps. *Hers* perhaps. She'll fear that it will be her name that is next uttered within a spell cast by her servant, the Lamia Shehlá!"

"Kahstteká!" Laura shrieked. Her tongue leaped from her mouth, impossibly long. It was forked at its end. "Lil tah hah né—!"

"No excuses!" Marbas roared. "She will not listen to you! You know it is finished! She will fear for the secrecy of her own true name! Lilith will destroy you! Without hesitation, she will wipe your name off of the page of existence as easily as though she were brushing sand from her table!"

"Kahstteká, Marbas!" Laura was pleading. "Lil yātān? Lil ôr yātān, Marbas!"

"I can't help you." He shook his head. "You've made this. You have called this day down upon you and I cannot help."

"Qeteb lîlît, Marbas." Laura stood and pressed her face close to his. "Skotos, melek Marbas... Marbas, melek ti laylâ. Sah nu te... te laylé mi, Shehlá?"

The winged lion shook his head again slowly. "I can't hide you."

"Hah né kahstteká..." Laura said, but the strength had left her voice. "Lil... Lil tah hah..."

"Perhaps," Marbas barely whispered it. "There may be that, yes. There is perhaps one way, then."

Laura fell back into her chair and, for a moment, Nick thought that Scott had cast another spell on her. Laura's face lost all expression. Any light that may have been in her eyes was gone.

Marbas let out a breath and turned his head to them. "Nicholas," he said.

"Yes?"

"Take Robert and the guys with you upstairs."

"Scotty?"

"Take everyone upstairs right now!"

Without another word, Nick, Robert, and the other three guys stood and quickly headed to the stairs.

"Darren," Marbas called.

Everyone stopped. Darren looked back at the black lion, his face almost as pale as Laura's.

"Do you need me, Scotty?" His voice was trembling.

"No," Marbas said. "No, not for this. Go upstairs with everyone else. I may be a while, so try to get in touch with Karen, would you? Make sure she's all right? Go bail her out, if you have to."

"Of course," Darren said, nodding vigorously.

"And Darren," Marbas said. "Leave the brass jar with me. Leave the Vessel here."

CHAPTER VII

†

Preparation

Be silent before the Sovereign Lord, for the day of the Lord is near. The Lord has prepared a sacrifice; he has consecrated those he has invited.

- Zephaniah 1:7 (NIV)

Los Angeles, California
Inside a stretch limousine, idling outside the club on Highland Avenue

†

Not thinking about the spell was difficult, but it seemed very important at the moment. Nick could feel the terrible consequences of it eating at his resolve. If the time came, and the thing had to be done to save them all, there could be no hesitation.

He had to concentrate fairly hard to keep his focus on something besides the string of ancient words Scott had insisted he learn. Nick wouldn't have to say them, he kept telling himself. He wouldn't have to cast the spell. Everything would work out fine and there'd be no need for their last resort. No. Nick wouldn't have to cast the spell. It wouldn't come to that.

A limousine could be a very lonely place, Nick thought. The partition was up, closing him off even from the driver. The engine hummed, and the music of the time throbbed softly out of the car's many hidden speakers, more to provide a familiar, if subliminal, comfort than entertainment. Tiny lights beneath the plush seat-cushions illuminated the dark blue carpet in spots of brilliant color. Soft heat crept up through tiny vents to help blanket him from the crisp night. Nick hardly noticed any of it. Secluded inside his box of steel and darkly tinted glass, he was silently watching the entrance of the club and trying not to let his mind glide through the articulation of the ancient spell.

The words were both simple and somehow beautiful. They thrilled him in a small, secret way. But Scott had warned him about that. Scott had warned Nick about the feel of power.

"Isn't it, like, witchcraft, though?" Nick had asked when Scott first mentioned the need to teach him the spell. Nick was wholly against his learning it at all.

"A lot of people might think so, I guess," Scott had said. "But no, it's not witchcraft. Not this spell, anyway. Witchcraft uses ancient secrets to manipulate demonic power. You're not doing that. It's something very different, actually."

"How do you know it'll work for me when I say it?"

"There have been signs."

"Like what? The clairvoyant thing?"

"Yes." Scott had nodded. "The clairvoyant thing was a strong sign. But what convinced me the most was that you said you'd caught my scent the first night we met. I've only encountered that in a human once before."

"That sorcerer guy? That guy, the one who had control of you during the—?"

"Yes." Scott had nodded again quickly. He obviously hadn't wanted to visit the subject.

"Wow." Nick hadn't pursued it.

"Yeah, so you were a little bit of a shock, being able to detect me right off the bat and all. Apparently, whatever made detecting my scent possible was a part of you even before we met." Scott had looked at him and smiled. "And see, just now, you inexplicably picked up the connection to 'that sorcerer guy.'"

Nick raised his eyebrows. "I guess I did, huh? I didn't even notice."

"Yes," Scott had said, smiling, "the clairvoyant thing was a strong sign."

"Has this spell-casting thing worked pretty well when you've taught it before?"

"I wish I could say yes, but I can't." Scott shook his head. "Although, that's only because I haven't actually taught anyone to cast spells before."

"Oh."

"Still, there's a strong sign—"

"That it will work for me. Okay, I got that part." Nick frowned. "But it's still not a sure thing."

Scott only grinned. "What ever is?"

Now, in the limo, Nick was trying to keep his mind occupied by watching the line of hopeful partiers gather to celebrate the coming of the New Year. He'd watched the line along the building as it rapidly got longer and longer. Already it stretched around the corner, into the tiny parking lot, and far out of sight. Still they kept coming. Streams of people milled in from distant parking spaces and disappeared around the side of the building, searching for the line's end. The more ambitious/arrogant/stupid just marched along its length looking for a familiar face.

It'll take less than two hours to fill the club, Nick thought, once they opened the doors, and it'll be thriving well beyond capacity until very late tomorrow morning. That is, it *would have been* thriving, he corrected himself.

Even at this length, the line along the outer wall was a very familiar sight. Primarily men, young, observably muscled, bedecked in the most splendid adornments allowed them by the tame California winter and their prime Hollywood salaries. They grouped together in twos and threes, whispering, smiling, nodding, nudging each other playfully, rocking with their mirth and the unique night's anticipation. It was certainly the same, glorious, riveting, and familiar sight.

No doubt, some had already indulged in a little mood enhancement. By the way a number of guys held each other, caressed their bare arms, closed their eyes, smiled, and rubbed their faces against one another's, it was no doubt at all. Missy was among them. Missy was positively running amuck up and down their number.

Nick envied them. Had life ever been so simple? Had a night out with his friends ever brought so much effortless abandon, so much easy contentment? It was difficult to recall. When did everything become so enormous and imperative? Were all of life's simple pleasures connected so deeply to such colossal powers as those upon which he'd stumbled? Did such enlightenments wait for each of these revelers, these smiling, happy revelers that Nick watched, disconnected, through the car's windows? Would all of them, in turn, have to face the demons around them unmasked?

There was champagne in the limo's bar, but that was all. Darren hadn't hidden any secret compounds in there to enhance their evening. Not that Nick really wanted anything. Sure, it was New Year's Eve, but this wasn't a night for celebrating. At least not yet. Maybe the morning would bring cause for celebration. Maybe all this would work out. Maybe they'd all see another dawn and be allowed to go back to the simple celebrations in their lives.

Nick bit his lower lip and shook his head. Maybe he wouldn't have to cast the spell. Best to keep his focus clear.

He felt a little sorry for all the guys waiting in line. Most had paid a great deal of money for the tickets that would get them into the club before midnight. Nick felt bad because, if everything went according to plan, very soon all of those guys would be desperately looking for another place to ring in the New Year.

Not yet, though. Timing was very important.

All there was to do now was wait. Darren would be along soon and then Nick wouldn't be alone anymore.

Darren was busy with the task Scott had assigned him for the evening. Scott had given everyone special instructions to help prepare for this night. On the morning after the pre-party in Nichols Canyon, after he came up from his basement having done what had to be done with the lamia, Scott had tried to work out some actions that could be reasonably taken; basically how and who should do what and when.

Preparing the club itself was important, but of course only Karen and Darren were able to do any of that work without raising suspicion. The two of them worked extra hard, having also taken on a number of other responsibilities as well. Hopefully, Max hadn't noticed all the extra time they'd spent working together. Maybe he had, though, but merely chalked up that observation with all the other irregular happenings of the past few months, the sudden disappearance of Laura Shah, along with the revelations regarding her extreme criminal behavior, just being the most recent.

The fiasco at the private pre-party had certainly become a serious cause of chatter, however. At least Karen hadn't been arrested. She'd been detained at the house in the hills for hours and hours, but ultimately, the police bought the idea that Laura had been a major mover-'n-shaker in the Los Angeles drug underground. The fact that Laura had also been a peripheral suspect in the death of Alex Monroe helped to add substance to the idea.

Karen described for the guys, as they nervously laughed their asses off, the way she'd bawled and bawled in overblown feminine hysterics—not completely insincerely, mind you, just way out of character for her—as the police assailed her with questions.

Of course she didn't know anything, she'd bawled at the LAPD. *Of course* Laura had been working all these drug-shenanigans completely without her knowledge. *Of course* this whole mess came as an absolute and total shock to her: Laura, some kind of covert drug-hooligan? Karen's trusted long-time employee, Laura Shah, some sort of major player in the LA game of prohibited pleasure pharmaceuticals? Why, it was unbelievable and outrageous. It was astonishing and disgraceful. It was also the only remotely plausible explanation for the entire outlandish mess. Being so, the Los Angeles Police Department had fallen onto it like sumo wrestlers on an egg roll. Especially the ones who'd witnessed the magic demon-fire in the street, the fire that very effectively kept them from entering the house for a while, then just simply vanished. None of them wanted to focus on that at all. They only wanted to talk about drug-kingpin Laura Shah. That was rational. That was plausible. Yeah. Drug-kingpins, even tiny demure female ones with no previous record, were far more worthy of police attention than some phantom blaze, which suddenly no one could really remember seeing.

What fucking fire? Fire in the street that disappeared without a trace, not a single ash anywhere, not even a burn mark on the pavement? What fire? Who saw a wall of fire? I didn't, did you? Are you out of your mind? What fucking fire?

Eventually, the house had been cleared and taped off. The dead were collected in order to be studied by police forensics. Karen had called the families of Bobby and Glen herself. She'd felt she owed them that much. She said the conversations were pretty rough. Far beyond rough actually. Still, she felt better afterward.

As soon as the bodies were released, she planned to attend the funerals. Karen planned to mourn those who'd lost their lives because she'd trusted Laura. She only wished she hadn't bought the official report about Alex Monroe being crazy. Maybe then she wouldn't have been so uncomfortable at the idea of attending his service. That was a major point for her. She regretted having been so blind and allowing this devastation to continue right under her nose.

"You can't possibly blame yourself, Karen," Nick had said. "There's no way you could have guessed what was really going on."

"But I knew something was wrong!" Karen had insisted. "I never liked Laura. I kind of hated her, actually. I loathed her, even though I couldn't really pin down a reason why. I really couldn't stand her, but I kept her around because... I guess because..." She'd just closed her eyes and shaken her head, pressing her lips together tightly.

"You think that you kept her as an employee, despite your strong intuition not to, only because she was making so much money for the club," Nick had said gently.

Karen had clamped her eyes shut against her tears and nodded.

"You're the only one who has that harsh suspicion, Karen." Nick had gotten down on his knee in front of her desk chair so he could look her in the eyes when she opened them. "You're the only one who's being so rough with you about this, because the rest of us know that's not why you kept her around."

"No?" She hadn't sounded convinced.

"No. You're an amazing businessperson, but not from operating against your principles. Actually, I think you just now said why you never stopped contracting her. You couldn't pin down a rational reason. Even though she made your skin crawl, you were still nice to her and you still kept her working, because you weren't going to punish someone just because you personally thought they might be icky. So, you kept engaging her for events. It was the only fair thing to do, whether you secretly loathed her or not, and that's how you work. You're fair."

Karen had taken a deep breath and even managed a tepid smile. "My self-image as a flawed, though fundamentally good person sure hopes you're right."

"Well, your self-image can relax." Nick smiled back. "My own self-image as a reasonably precise judge of other people's intentions knows I'm right."

She'd shut her eyes again, this time in amusement and relief, and giggled.

"But Gil!" Karen's eyes had suddenly flown open. "Oh, that obnoxious motherfuckin' gerbil! Gil, from the moment I met him…" She screwed up her face into a very unflattering expression. "I could have wrung his little fuckin' elf-neck with my bare—!"

"I understand." Nick had chuckled. "Believe me, I understand. You're still not a bad person. As far as the little elf is concerned, I think it'd be impossible to find an opinion even remotely contrary to yours."

Nick had tried to keep Karen from letting any guilt eat at her over Laura. It wasn't easy. She wasn't the kind of person who just accepted that sometimes bad things happened. No, Karen felt that whatever took place in her life, good or bad, was either caused or allowed by her.

Karen would be along any minute too. She'd wait with Nick and Darren in the limo until they got the signal from Scott to come inside. First, though, she had to make sure Theo and Eddie were placed safely in their own stations to await the task that they were to perform.

While he waited, Nick looked around the empty limo and thought that he had never felt so alone. Across the street, the music of happy voices only deepened his pain. He was alone. He was alone but for the company of his own thoughts and his fears.

Nick pushed his cheek against his palm, imagining Darren's shoulder, imagining his arms holding him, his scent, his soft whisper, his lips as they brushed his ear. There was some comfort in such imaginings. He could almost hear Darren breathing, almost feel his hands as his fingers laced themselves behind his back, securing Nick to him.

And he thought of Scott too. Good-gravy-on-a-biscuit, there was certainly no keeping his mind off of Scott either. Nick sighed.

Tonight, Scott was very busy too. Oh, yes. The skotos was working at the devil's pace. The Gryphon of Greece had decided to make his permanent nest in LA. He therefore had much work to do.

Nick's thoughts turned to Scott with growing apprehension. Across the street, should any of the casual party boys decide to venture a glance at the stars, should any of them take advantage of the clear California sky, they might see something very peculiar. They might notice a wide shadow at some point in the evening, before their eventual admittance to the club. They might see what appeared to be a large black hang glider soaring silently over the rooftops. They might have a glimpse of a dark shape, a huge winged animal. They just might catch sight of it before it settled atop the very building into which they awaited entrance.

Although they'd worked there almost non-stop for the last several days, neither Darren nor Karen would enter the club today until they were signaled to do so from Scott. No one would go inside today, because *she* would be there. Lilith would be there, and she could have shown up at any time.

At first, Eddie and Theo hadn't really understood. Perhaps it was just a hunch, or maybe it was the developing clairvoyance within them, but both Karen and Nick had immediately made the connection between the demon Lilith's arrival in Los Angeles and the appearance of the famous European DJ, Lauren Isseroff. Darren certainly had a feeling about it, he'd said, even before Scott explained it to them. Even before he'd confirmed through Laura that Karen had actually hired the mother of all earthly demons to spin CDs at the club's New Year's Eve party.

Nick looked at the front door of the club, watching two new door-guys that he didn't know saunter through their duties. No doubt a number of the senior Security Guys had quit after they'd heard of the disaster at the private party. At least the sane ones, anyway.

It was nearing nine o'clock, which was opening time. Everything inside would be ready by now. Ms. Isseroff would be clicking open the CD cases of her first selections.

Lilith was in the house.

Karen had made some excuse to Max about why she needed to come in late. He'd been a little pissed—it was New Year's Eve after all—but he didn't make a huge issue out of it. Reluctantly, Karen chose Brad and Matt to be on hand instead of her. They'd be the ones available to help Lauren Isseroff when she arrived.

Karen's voice had shaken on the phone as she made the arrangements. She hadn't liked the idea of putting two more of her guys in the direct line of fire with yet another demon, but Scott had said there was no other way. Lilith must be kept at ease. Nor could the guys be warned at all; Lilith would know the moment she touched them. And she would certainly touch them.

Scott promised that he'd get the security guys out of harm's way well before any of the shit went down. Before he put his plan into action, he'd make sure that Brad and Matt were long gone. Actually, the plan was that everyone would be long gone.

Nick closed his eyes and took a deep breath. He tried not to think about the spell, that horrible spell. Scott had been very careful to make sure that Nick had it solidly in his memory. Nick wasn't worried about forgetting it.

So, Nick thought, witchcraft uses ancient secrets to manipulate demonic power. Well, the spell Scott taught Nick to cast, however, wasn't one that would manipulate him. No, no. Not one of those at all.

The spell that Nick reluctantly learned from Scott would destroy him.

If the ambitions of Lilith were such that Scott couldn't turn her away from Nick, then Nick was to cast the spell that would erase Scott totally from the realm of existence. Lilith would never have another enlightened soul from the actions of Marbas. The possibility would be utterly lost to her for the rest of time. No more goose, no more golden eggs.

Nick would be the mortal voice that Scott did not have back during the Middle Ages, back when he had so desperately wanted to destroy himself. He'd be the crucial mortal voice and cast the spell, if he had to, if it turned out there was no other way.

The ancient spell tumbled around Nick's mind, its completion missing only a single word: Scott's true name, his name of power. If the moment arose, and the decision was made, Scott would call it out to Nick so that the spell could be completed.

Maybe he wouldn't have to say it at all, though. Ever. Nick took a deep breath. Maybe he wouldn't have to say those terrible words or ever hear the articulation of Scott's name of power. Maybe something good could still come out of all of this. Best to concentrate on that. If he didn't keep his mind away from the possibility of what he might have to do, his heart would break, and he'd never be able to do it.

He'd kill himself first.

†

"Shh!" Karen hissed from behind Theo and Eddie. They were fighting over which one got to stand near the corner and be the lookout. "Would you both please just knock it off?"

"Sorry," said Theo.

"Sorry," said Eddie.

Fuck, but they were beginning to irritate her. Karen rolled her eyes. She was never going to have children. These two were plenty.

The three of them were sneaking around, trying to get behind the building without being seen. The problem being it was New Year's Eve, smack in the middle of a major American city, and duh, there were people abso-fuckin'-lutely everywhere. It still might not have been so bad, but Karen and her guys also had a large linen sack with them. 'Suspicious' probably wouldn't begin to describe what they'd look like to anyone taking notice.

Now add to all of that the fact that the Tweedle-Twins couldn't stop acting like the undisciplined mutant offspring of the Three Stooges.

Karen crossed herself and said the first line of the Hail Mary. She'd never been religious, so it was all she knew.

She was standing in dense shadow between the buildings, blocked from the alley behind the club by the Tweedle-Stooges. The two of them insisted they were far enough out of the light themselves that no one would see them. Karen didn't think that was the case. Still, maybe they had more experience doing who-knows-what in the dark recesses of Hollywood alleyways. Karen sincerely hoped not.

There were two ways to get onto the club's roof. One was a very convenient access door at the top of the stairs just above the third floor. That was out of the question, though, as it meant getting into position by going through the club. The second was a steel ladder bolted to the outside of the building in the back alley. That was the way they had to go.

The ladder on the back of the building was secured with a long steel plate against those who might scamper up its length. The plate was connected by hinges on one side and locked on the other. It fit completely over the ladder's lower rungs, quite effectively keeping people off of it. Karen had the key.

However, the back of the building was illuminated brilliantly by fierce halogen lights high atop thick telephone poles. The three of them would have to time their movement so that Karen could get the steel plate unlocked and the guys could get all the way up the ladder before another partier wandered through the alley on his way to the back of the entrance line. She'd replace the steel plate and then re-lock it. The guys would have to get back down from the inside of the building itself. That was the only way they'd have a chance of getting away with this shit. If they were seen coming off the ladder outside the building after doing what they were supposed to do, they'd be arrested for sure. No, Eddie and Theo had to get inside the club and pretend to exit with everyone else. That wasn't going to be fun. She didn't envy them.

Karen had given the key for the door on the roof to Eddie. At least the possibility that it would be lost was a little smaller than if Theo had it.

She was getting very nervous and wanted all of this to be over with. Still, the party people just kept coming. Karen thought that was really stupid. It was nine o'frickin'clock on New Year's Fuckin' Eve; whoever wasn't in line by now might as well just stay home. Anyone not already in line and within at least twenty feet of the front door had absolutely no chance of getting inside before four o'clock in the morning. Where they kidding themselves? Sheesh, stay home. Watch Times Square on television. It had to be better than listening to the celebration inside the club while they stood outside holding up the wall.

None of that mattered, though, she reminded herself. No one's evening would be going as planned. None of these party-boys would be inside the building when the clock struck twelve.

It hurt Karen somewhere deep in her heart, not to mention the pit of her stomach, to even ponder what they had to do, and what it meant to the club in the way of current and future reputation. Reputation which, of course, meant revenue.

She'd have loved to wait until after the party, or even after its prime, before going ahead with Scott's plan. She understood, though. If there was going to be a confrontation—and there was going to be a confrontation; it was inescapable—then it had to be on Scott's terms. There was only one time they'd all be sure of precisely where to find Lauren Isseroff, and that was before the after-hours DJ, Lauren's relief DJ, even got into the building. If they were going to act, it had to be while it was utterly guaranteed Lauren would be in the booth. It had to be when she was certain to be there and not even just outside letting a long track play. It had to be in the few minutes just before midnight.

There was no other way. It still made Karen sick, though.

"Is this the same alley where Nick and Scott...?" Theo whispered.

"No, dumb ass," Eddie quipped. "That one's two blocks up that way." He pointed around the corner.

"Get back here and shut the fuck up!" Karen growled. "I swear, you guys are going to totally screw this whole thing over and then what are we gonna do?"

"Sorry," said Theo.

"Sorry," said Eddie.

"None of this is going to work if we get arrested before we even get you guys up there!" she hissed. "Oh my god, they're going to think we're terrorists!"

"Sorry."

"Sorry."

Eddie's foot bumped the linen sack they'd set on the ground. Inside it, all the tiny canisters clinked together noisily.

Karen just shut her eyes and held her breath.

"Sorry," Eddie whispered, grimacing.

"*Please!*" Karen was growling now. "Pay attention! If even one of those things goes off, we're going to have pepper-spray all over the place!"

†

"It's not anywhere near what you're used to in Rome," Robert said, handing the cardinal a Scotch on the rocks, "but it won't make you gag, I don't think."

"Gag?" Cardinal Matine looked up at him, half grinning. "Believe me, after that flight, it would take a very bad Scotch indeed to make me 'gag.' "

With softly trembling lips, holding the glass with both hands, the cardinal drank from the crystal lowball, his eyes closed. After a heavy moment, he licked his lips, looked up and nodded briefly. "Thank you, Robert."

"Of course," he whispered, walking back to the wet bar.

"This is quite a marvelous view," the cardinal observed. "Breathtaking, I'd say."

The drapes of Robert's suite were pulled completely open, revealing the French doors through which the expanse of southeast Beverly Hills and the entire downtown Los Angeles skyline could be seen. Robert glanced back quickly, taking in the now completely familiar sight.

"Yes," he agreed, turning his attention back to the bar and pouring his own drink. "It's a true testament to this place. The view offers an intoxicating and seductive beauty. It's stunning whether it's day or night."

"Such beauty conceals much, I would imagine."

"That's quite an understatement," Robert said, turning around and walking to the sofa. "But it's the same with all such things. The deception only works from afar. One has but to venture a few feet from the doors of this hotel for the flaws of the city to be revealed. Up close, those flaws are more than evident. Flaws like open sores, gaping and infectious."

"Hm." Cardinal Matine sipped his drink again. Robert noticed that it was already nearly empty. He'd have to get up and freshen it almost about as soon as he'd sat down. It didn't matter. He'd freshen his own drink while he was at it.

"None of them would come?" Robert asked flatly. "None of my colleagues would venture out of Italy with you?"

The cardinal drew in a slow breath through his teeth, raised his gray and bushy eyebrows. "No," he said softly. "No, as soon as they'd heard that Michael was dead, they just went blank." He gave Robert a laden stare. "It was the final blow. They lost all their reason."

Robert pressed his lips together tightly. He hadn't been surprised that the cardinal himself decided to come. Nor had it particularly surprised him when the other members of the council abandoned him. Yet, somehow Robert still hadn't really expected it.

"They lost all their faith, you mean," he said, raising his glass to his mouth.

"Maybe not." The cardinal looked down at the ornate, antique coffee table. "If they didn't have any faith, of what could they possibly be afraid?"

The cardinal emptied his glass and set it down. Without a word, Robert stood and picked it up, heading back to the bar. The cardinal only nodded.

Matine was nearly seventy-five years old, at least. He may have already passed eighty, actually. Robert didn't know for sure. He was a shorter man, probably five foot seven, but stocky. He had a full head of thickly curled hair, coarse brambles of ash-gray with thin shards of white scattered throughout. Beneath his dark eyes he carried heavy bags of age, laden with living and exhaustion. His cheeks too sagged over the sides of his jaw. They shook when he spoke.

"I'll have much to answer for," he said quietly, "when I get back to Rome."

Robert refilled the cardinal's glass and touched up his own, thinking all the while that, if Matine was sincere about going along with him tonight, the idea of either of them ever getting back to Rome was, at best, optimistic.

He set the full lowball on the coffee table as though it had never been emptied, then returned to the couch. Sitting down slowly, he set his glass before him without making a sound as it touched the table. He'd lost count of just how many drinks he'd poured for himself that day, both while waiting for the cardinal to arrive as well as afterward. What did it matter, though? This night would bring a conclusion for everything. At least for him. The only issue now was to convince Cardinal Matine to remain as he had since the skotos first fled the Vessel: out of harm's way.

"You should let me go back to them on my own," Robert started. "You can help prepare me, but for both of us to face this—"

"No." The cardinal looked at him. Even in the dim light from the feeble bar lamp, Robert could see the rigidity in his gaze, his eyes adamant, his mouth set. "No, Robert. This is my mess. I've waited far too many years for the chance to finally clean it up."

"There will be more than just your single lost demon to deal with. The skotos will be surrounded by men. These men are beguiled by him, enthralled."

"I understand."

"These men are totally under his control," Robert repeated. "He's charmed them with both magic and the lure of material wealth. He's showered them with unthinkable riches and worldly comforts. They are utterly blinded."

The cardinal only shook his head. "Then they're to be pitied."

"Well..." Robert grunted, frowning. "I don't know how you're planning to handle them, Nigel. These are very young and virile opponents." Robert pointed to his still swollen lip. "If they become violent, you won't be able to pity them to death."

The cardinal took a deep breath. "I *am* going with you, Robert."

"But you know that's not the worst of it either." Robert leaned over the table toward him. "If the signs are correct, and if what the skotos said is true, then—"

"Yes, yes, I know." Matine nodded. "Lilith."

"Lilith will be there." Robert lowered his voice even further. "Perhaps with any number of servants. She could be commanding his minions, a host of the Legions. If Lilith has servants protecting her, they're not going to be human ones like those of the skotos. Pity will be of even less use against them, I'm sure."

"I doubt Lilith would require servants around her, much less tolerate them," Matine mumbled. "No, she'd not allow that."

"What are you talking about?"

"Nothing. Never mind."

"We've no way of knowing what she may have at her command, Nigel, what she would 'tolerate' or 'allow.' "

"Well, not the lamia, at least," said Matine. "You said she was destroyed?"

"No." Robert shook his head. "The skotos didn't destroy her. If my understanding is correct, she needed to hide from Lilith. Maybe even Lucifer."

"Yes. I suppose you explained that on the phone. Forgive me. It's just difficult to understand."

"I guess you could say that the skotos offered her sanctuary."

"Right, yes." Matine nodded. "You did say that. Sanctuary within the Vessel itself. I can hardly believe it."

"It's true."

"He didn't destroy her?" Matine shrugged. "That truly surprises me. It's ironic though, isn't it? Sanctuary within the Vessel."

"Ironic?"

"The demon chose to become the warden of the very prison that held him for so long."

"All that aside, Nigel—"

"You're sure that he got her inside of it?"

"I didn't actually witness the process, no." Robert almost laughed. "But I was there when he brought the Vessel up from the basement. It was sealed and…" he stopped.

"It was sealed and… what?" the cardinal pressed.

Robert took a deep breath. "It was moving on its own."

"What?"

"He couldn't set it down," Robert explained. "He could barely hold onto it. The Vessel twisted and shook in his hands. The demon explained that once the lamia's consciousness had finally settled into sleep, now that she was trapped within the Vessel, then it would stop moving. While he held it, though, standing right there in front of me, I watched it twist and shake as though it were alive. It contorted from the lamia's presence. She was still aware and restless. Probably even struggling."

Cardinal Matine continued to look puzzled. "The Vessel never did anything like that while it was in my care. Also, you know as well as I that no such report was made by any of its custodians before me."

"He said something else, too." Robert glanced out the window, ignoring Matine's confusion.

"Yes?"

"He said that, although it would not move after the lamia eventually went to sleep, as long as she remained inside of it, then the Vessel would be much lighter than if it were empty."

"Yes." Matine nodded slowly. "Yes, that's right. I'd almost forgotten about that."

"You'd told me several times about how it used to feel when you held it. How it felt while it still sealed the skotos himself inside, before he escaped."

"You mean before I released him," Matine said. He pushed himself against the back of the couch, tapping his fingers on his knee. "Yes, I remember."

Robert let the silence settle around them for a moment, then quietly leaned across the coffee table. "The skotos said that if there were enough demons sealed inside the Vessel, it would float in the air like a balloon."

"But…" The cardinal turned back to him, scowling. "That doesn't make any sense. If that were true, then none of the ancient vessels would have remained on the floor of the sea. None of the ones used during Solomon's time to capture all those demons would have stayed below the surface. Solomon would never have ordered that they be cast into the water if they had no weight at all. That would have been a silly way to try to be rid of them. I've never heard anything about the jars being weighed down or tied to anything to keep them below the surface."

"Neither have I," Robert agreed. "I don't believe there've ever been such details, either in the oral tradition or documented. Perhaps..." He stopped, bit his lip, stared down at the carpet.

Matìne exhaled loudly. "Go on," he said.

"Perhaps there's something wrong with all of this." Robert raised his eyes and laced his fingers together. "Perhaps there always has been."

"What do you mean by that?" The cardinal frowned and reached for his glass.

"You really must reconsider your decision to go with me tonight, Nigel," Robert said.

The cardinal grunted, looking away. "You insist on revisiting this subject, but my decision has been made."

"You know what might happen!" Robert huffed. Though, he'd wanted to say, 'what *will* happen.'

"Michael is dead and I am to blame." Cardinal Matìne did not look back at him, but his voice remained firm. "I am to blame, Robert. Michael is dead."

Robert wished the cardinal would quit saying that. The pain of Michael's death had only worsened with the passing days. It was a gaping and constant agony. Robert hadn't even liked Michael. Yet, even after the debacle on the island, even after losing Larry and all the rest, Robert didn't suffer in this way. They had all died horribly, but somehow Robert felt solely responsible for Michael's fate. Robert could have wept each time Matìne brought it up. He would have wept in an instant, but any tears were consumed now by his anger.

Robert pushed himself back against the cushion, shut his eyes, and clenched his jaw.

"Michael is gone and I am to blame for that," repeated the cardinal.

"Michael was killed by a demon, not by you." Even as he said it, Robert could hear the constraint in his own voice.

"He was only the latest, Robert," Matìne went on. "Only the most recent to die for my imprudence. You can count them as easily as I. Peter and Randal and Mark and Stephen... and Larry."

"That," Robert whispered, "is why I am here."

"You're here because of my arrogant mistake!" the cardinal growled. Now he did raise his eyes, lips pressed together until they were colorless. Obviously, nothing was going to divert the man away from his chosen course. Robert only wondered if the cardinal really understood exactly what was about to happen that night.

Because Robert understood. For the first time in his life, he understood.

After being knocked out, then kidnapped, confronted yet again by the skotos in his true form, and witnessing the exchange between the two demons, Robert figured that at least one thing he'd been hearing over and over again since he'd arrived in Los Angeles had to be true: He was missing a giant piece of the puzzle. Perhaps many pieces.

The inconsistency within the story of Solomon's Vessel was only the latest indication. First, Michael had warned Robert that maybe the two of them didn't know the whole truth about the skotos. Then the demon himself had made the same suggestion. No, that was not right; it wasn't a suggestion at all. It was a condemnation: Robert had wasted his life acting exclusively in regard to one side of the story. Then, finally and most cutting, one of the kids down in the demon's basement had casually observed that Robert's knowledge was lacking. It seemed even those enthralled by the powers of the Son of the Morning could clearly recognize the bishop's recklessness.

Robert should have seen it all on Cyprus. He should have realized that none of them knew what they were doing, the cardinal included. Such blindness was unforgivable. He should have seen everything clearly ten years ago, after his friends and colleagues were incinerated where they stood.

Perhaps Robert's knowledge was lacking. Yes, perhaps that was at the core of all his problems. Even so, what was now crystal clear was that such details had completely ceased to matter. Maybe his perspective was askew in regard to the complete picture. Maybe his beliefs were a bit tainted from years of hearing only flawed history and human ornamentation. All the same, by his own admission, the skotos was a fallen angel. He was an outcast from the service of God. For that reason alone, he had to be destroyed.

It was all so very simple. Demons were to be destroyed. All of them. Those fallen from the grace of God were demons. The distinction was black and white. That Robert should have allowed so many years to pass him by before the confusions of humanity fell from his eyes was a tragedy. There was no confusion now, though, because he didn't need to see the big picture anymore. There was no big picture. No. There was only here and now. The imminent was everything.

Oh yes, he understood. Robert's duty was no longer that which had been conceived by the Church, by those merely human and thus flawed. It was no longer to simply return the demon to his earthly prison, to the fragile confines of the Vessel. Robert's mission had changed. He would do whatever was necessary to fulfill it. He understood.

Robert also understood that he would not survive the task.

But what was his own life anyway? Without a doubt, Robert was no longer acting merely in the service of the Church. That earthly authority had fallen too, hadn't it? The revelation about the simplicity of his mission placed the truth beyond doubt and his human uncertainties. Robert was acting directly within the intention of the Lord God himself. The Almighty moved him now. The Creator of Heaven and Earth cried for the damnation of the skotos, the Darkness, and pressed Robert into the unencumbered service of light. For all the mistakes made in the uncertainty of youth and in the blind bidding of the Church, he finally heard the still small voice, the whisper in the breeze.

He had heard the very sigh of God.

All the lighted hours of his days and the solemn stillness of his nights were blessed now with the strength of *knowing*. The Divine had spoken and, with the recognition of that voice, Robert understood the confidence of a prophet.

He returned the cardinal's stare while thoughts of eternity gathered and stormed within him, as from the very breath of God.

Still, despite the tension, the older man's eyes did not waver. Robert was the one who finally looked away. He saw the night beyond his balcony deepening. Very soon he'd be expected at the club. The demon and his mortal associates were counting on Robert's 'help.'

"I'll have to meet them soon," he said. "There isn't any time."

"This is the end," said Matìne, "and I should be the one to finish it."

The cardinal's presence was a mistake. The call that resulted in his arrival should never have been made. What difference did Matìne's presence make now? Beyond this night, the whole idea of the council was useless. What difference would it have made if Robert had simply left the phone in its cradle and finished this business himself? Now he had this burden. The cardinal could only hinder him.

"He said things," Robert heard himself whispering.

"The demon?" Matìne nodded.

"Yes," Robert said. "The Vessel didn't consume him. It wouldn't take him back, and he stood there, mocking me. He mocked me, and yet, the power of the Church seemed stale and unwilling to touch him. He mocked me and he mocked the Church."

"You've heard his voice," Matine said.

Robert started for an instant, at first thinking Matine had somehow recognized Robert's enlightenment, somehow sensed the touch of God upon him. Then he realized the cardinal wasn't referring to Robert hearing the voice of God. He was referring to *exousia skotos*.

"The two of us are bonded by the true sight of him," Matine continued. "Yet, beyond that, you've heard his voice, actually spoken with him, as well as witnessed his human form."

"Yes."

"The very idea of such a thing humbles me," the cardinal said, staring out at the crisp evening darkness. "My glimpse was so brief and so long ago. Even so, that sight will never leave me. The giant, solid-black lion, spreading his dragon's wings across an impossible length, consuming the very room itself, it seemed. Even the walls had appeared to fade into blackness around him. I stared in a stone-silent terror while the world went dark from the shock of this demon's true existence. I don't know exactly how long it lasted, just a moment or two. Then it was the demon who simply shimmered away into nothingness."

"I've witnessed him," Robert said quietly. "He spoke to me."

"His voice?"

"Like boulders rumbling through a yawning valley." Robert embellished, indulging himself as well as the cardinal. "His voice is deep, like the roar of vast stone plates. It's the rumble of plates in the earth when they move."

"The Darkness himself."

"He denies that he is evil."

Matine stiffened in surprise, scoffing, pressing his mouth into a frown. "Preposterous," he grunted, jowls shaking.

Robert glanced calmly at the tired, gray-haired man. "The skotos claims that his evil works are the fabrications of imaginative, and malicious, mortal minds."

The cardinal shook his head again and gazed away, at the window, the fireplace, the wall, down into his drink. "A demon's tongue," he said, "is incapable of moving but to form the shape of lies."

"Or spells."

"What?"

"You're right, of course." Robert nodded quickly, smiling. "You're right to make that observation. Yes, only lies. That's exactly what's always been explained to me." He drew a deep breath, wondering why he'd even bothered with the subject at all.

"They don't speak but to deceive," said Matine.

"Yes, so the thinking goes. How convenient."

"What's that?" Matine squinted at him, pressing his white-gray eyebrows together.

"Nothing," Robert said and drained his glass.

Did the skotos lie? Maybe everything he said was true. Robert was close to believing that was the case. Even so, he reminded himself, it didn't matter.

One thing was confirmed by the creature himself: he was cast out from the presence of God. Such a creature, not worthy of the expanse of Heaven, could certainly not be allowed to share the place of men either, not when there was an opportunity to do something about it. Surely that was what had called to Robert's soul, changing him. Without question that's what had emblazoned his essence, carried to him within the voice of Yahweh, Elyon over all the earth.

"Where is the Vessel now?" Matine asked.

Robert shook his head. "I don't know," he whispered. "As I told you, the demon took it. He must have known how to use it to confine the lamia. There is no way to reclaim it. We'll be moving against the dark powers tonight unarmed."

The cardinal set his empty glass on the coffee table.

"Not entirely," he said.

†

The limo door opened suddenly and Nick turned to it, beaming a smile, only slightly startled. Darren leaned in with a sigh.

"Oh, man," he groaned, stumbling inside, shutting the door behind him, then falling onto the seat next to Nick. "I feel so bad, looking at all those people lined up over there."

"You'd feel worse if they got caught up in all of this," Nick said, scooting over a bit to make room on the long cushion.

"I know, I know."

"How did it go?" Nick asked.

Darren got up again and pulled the car's door shut. Then, stooping awkwardly, he moved onto the seat behind the limo's cab. "Well, I have to admit that I don't think the evening's exactly getting off to a good start."

Nick frowned. "You couldn't place the images?"

"It's not that," Darren said. They were seated very close to each other in the corner of the limo directly behind the driver. Although the wood-panel partition was raised, Darren still spoke very softly. "See, I thought the symbols Scott drew were easy enough. I mean, they were each just a couple of simple patterns laying over each other, right?"

Nick nodded, remembering the symbols, which had looked to him like hieroglyphic or cuneiform writing: simple geometric shapes, one on top of the other. Scott had explained that each symbol was actually the name of an angel. Some of the oldest and most powerful angels, to be exact, two archangels, five cherubs, and five seraphim. He said the images must be engraved upon tiny plates of silver that were about two inches square and an eighth of an inch thick. The guys were supposed to take care of the engraving. Scott obtained the silver himself.

"So," Darren continued, "I didn't think the engravers would have any problem duplicating the patterns onto the silver. But these guys have all had massive head trauma or something."

"They still weren't right?" Nick frowned. The work had been consistently inadequate. Darren already had the job redone with two different engravers.

"Nope," Darren shook his head. "I guess if it's not the usual award crap, like, 'For Best Total Dweeb Performance by An Utter Dork,' then these guys are completely useless."

"Oh, god." Nick shook his head. "If we'd only had more than a few days…"

"Don't get me wrong, there was significant improvement. But this last batch of plates still didn't have the symbols duplicated as precisely as all that. They're not as close to what Scott wanted as I think they'll need to be."

"You placed them anyway?"

"Of course!" Darren laughed nervously. "All twelve of 'em! That was the easy part."

Scott had instructed Darren meticulously in regard to the geometric pattern in which the icons had to be placed. They were to be secured at mathematical positions in an exact two-dimensional circle surrounding the club. Determining where they needed to go in the club's neighborhood hadn't been tough at all; the grid design of this part of the city helped enormously.

After they'd been properly placed, the symbols would hold Lilith within their circle. It all had something to do with a major confrontation she'd had with these angels thousands of years ago, but Scott hadn't had time to go into detail. Still, the icons couldn't be put into place until it was certain she'd already arrived and was inside the club.

"What did you use?" Nick asked. "Nails or something?"

"Oh jeez, no" Darren said. "I didn't want to fuck up the symbols any more than they already were. No, I stopped at Office Depot and got that double-sided spongy tape and some rubber cement."

†

Karen waited until Eddie had pulled the sack of pepper-spray canisters up over the lip of the roof before she swung the metal plate back into place over the ladder. Looking up as she re-secured the lock, she saw Theo and Eddie smiling down at her, each giving a thumbs-up. They must have been kneeling or laying flat on their stomachs. She giggled and shook her head.

Still grinning, frantically waving them away from the roof's edge, Karen ducked quietly back into the dark alley between the buildings. Once again concealed by the shadows, she waited a second or so to collect herself, taking some very deep breaths.

Fortunately, no one had wandered along and seen the guys scurrying up the metal ladder. They'd actually been surprisingly efficient, Karen thought with a smile. As smoothly as if they were Navy Seals, Theo and Eddie had effortlessly ascended the outside of the building, even managing to keep their bundle from making any noise. Of course, the higher they got, the more nervous and frightened she became. The building had never seemed so tall to her. The just-less-than two minutes it took them to scale the entire ladder would always lay in Karen's memory as a terrifying hour. She'd half expected one or both of them to fall and land on her at any second. She didn't kid herself that she'd be able to break their fall. Not even Eddie's. And Theo, no way. If that boy fell, he was going to crash straight through the pavement and into the sewer system. It'd be just like when Jack cut down the beanstalk.

They were safe for now, though. Therefore, the light was green to go to Phase Two. Maybe this entire psycho-mess was going to work out after all, Karen thought. Maybe sacrificing the club's revenue on this most profitable of nights, plus any possible liabilities and who-could-guess-what degree of reputation might actually turn out to be part of a greater and brighter good.

Suddenly sick again, Karen turned, and hurried through the darkness to join Nick and Darren in the limo.

†

"You're already up here!" Theo whined loudly. He wasn't worried about making noise; all the ventilation machines were going strong and would probably cover any banter from being heard on the street. He did wonder, though, if anyone on the third floor could hear them crunching across the loose gravel on the roof above them.

Scott looked up from his seat atop a humming vent. He was busy lacing his boots. "Well," he said, "this is the spot we decided we'd meet, isn't it?"

"I know," Theo huffed. "I just hoped we'd get here first. I wanted to see you fly."

Scott smiled and looked back down at his shoes.

"Did you just get dressed?" Eddie asked.

"Yeah, sorry," Scott said, still smiling. "You missed that too."

"Crap!" Theo barked.

"I carried everything up here with me in a paper bag," Scott said. "It's funny, I can phase from place to place and still have my clothes when I get there, but if I go anywhere in my true form, then I need luggage."

"Why didn't you just phase up here?" Eddie asked.

"That wouldn't have been possible. I've never been up here before."

"Oh," Eddie nodded. Theo gave him a quizzical look and shrugged.

"I could do it anytime from now on, though," Scott offered, eyebrows raised.

"Ah." Theo nodded back at him, despite having absolutely no comprehension of what Scott was saying.

"Now…" Scott finished with his laces and stood up. "This won't take long. I'm just going to cast a quick spell on you guys so that the pepper-spray doesn't affect you. Then I'm going to phase inside."

"Okay," Theo said. That made a little more sense. He and Eddie were supposed to release the pepper-spray into the air-conditioning vents in order to clear the place out. After that, they had to make their getaway through the inside of the club, exiting with all the gassed patrons, and then rendezvous at the limo.

Exactly why they needed to do this majorly insane thing was still a bit fuzzy to Theo. Something about Lilith and her revealing herself in front of people and therefore having to kill them all. So, Scott didn't want anyone to be inside the club who didn't absolutely have to be there. Just in case.

This chick must be seriously ugly when she was naked, Theo thought, if she felt she had to kill people after she revealed herself.

"Remember," Scott went on, "just sit tight until about eleven-thirty. Then get the canisters in place. Okay?"

"It's going to be so boring up here." Theo rolled his eyes. "And everyone is going to be so pissed off. They'll be talking about this shit for the next twenty years."

"Guys, it's very important that you're completely quiet before we have to empty the place out. Just do a little meditating."

"Oh yeah," Eddie said with a smirk. "That'll be much more fun than being downstairs."

Theo chuckled. "Meditate. Oh, my god."

"Oh!" Scott exclaimed. "I almost forgot. Give me your wallets."

Theo shot Eddie another quizzical look, but he didn't seem to understand this request either. Timidly, they handed their wallets over to Scott.

Their curiosity was deepened considerably as Scott opened the wallets and began licking them.

†

Enlightened one.

"What was that?" Nick looked up at Darren.

"What?" Darren said, pushing his eyebrows together.

"Did you say something?"

Darren shook his head. "Huh uh."

"Oh." Nick let out a breath. "I thought I heard something."

"I didn't—"

A loud knock on the limo door made them both jump. Nick screamed.

"Oh god, I'm sorry!" Karen said after she opened the door and poked her head inside. "I didn't mean to scare you!"

"That's okay." Nick was panting, but relieved. He looked at Darren and they laughed together nervously. "I think we're all a little on edge."

Karen ambled inside. "Well, I'm sure you'll be pleased to hear that I got the guys into position without killing either of them."

"That's good." Darren nodded, smiling.

"Hey, did Scott do that spell-thingy on both of you? The one so that the pepper-spray wouldn't affect you? He cast it on me yesterday. I guess now you could really say that I'm under his spell, huh?" She giggled.

"Yeah," Darren said, smiling. "He got us both back at the house and said that he'd zap Eddie and Theo when he met them up on the roof."

Enlightened one.

Nick snapped a look at Karen, who jumped.

Had she just spoken? It didn't sound like Karen's voice, but it wasn't a man's...

"What is it, Nick?" Karen looked more surprised than alarmed.

"Did you just say something?" Nick asked her sheepishly. The sinking in his stomach told him he already knew the answer, though.

"Honey, no... uh..." Karen looked over Nick's shoulder at Darren, probably for help.

"Babe..." Darren touched his arm. "Are you all right?"

A tingling, crystalline chill began to creep over Nick's skin. Gooseflesh rushed up from his wrists along his arms and across his shoulders. He exhaled loudly, feeling a rush of dizziness.

Angel or devil?

"Oh, my god..." Nick shivered and pushed himself against the seat cushion, rubbing his hands along the back of his arms as the chills rippled through him again.

"What?" Darren asked, leaning in.

Not really understanding how, Nick knew exactly what was going on. "You don't hear her, do you?" he asked.

Are you an angel or a devil?

"Hear who?" Karen said. "What are you talking about?"

"Oh no." Nick shook his head. Scott never even mentioned the possibility of anything like this happening. "Oh, my god..."

Enlightened one. Beautiful one.

"Nick, what is it?" Darren's eyes were the size of billiard balls. "Nick? What's happening?"

Nick looked back at him and tried to stay calm. "I can hear her," he answered quietly.

Another chill swept over him, raising the hair on his neck and sending tingles across his scalp. He arched his back and gasped. This wave of chills rushed all the way through his torso and clumped into icy knots just beneath his stomach.

Enlightened one. I can feeeeeeel yoooooooou...

"What...?" Karen was shaking her head, her face an almost

comical expression of bewilderment. Darren wasn't doing much better. His mouth was hanging open and, despite it all, Nick nearly giggled at him.

Enlightened one. Are you an angel or a devil?

Even the vaguest notion of what he should do about this was totally beyond him. Nick could only keep rubbing the backs of his arms as the chills began washing over him in more violent waves. He was certain now that only he could hear the voice, the soft female voice that seemed to be purring to him right there in the car.

How sweet of you to be here tonight.

Purring, sensual, and firm, the voice made him want to shut his eyes and whisper to her to go on. Keep talking. Keep talking to me.

"Do you mean Lilith?" Darren asked Nick quietly. "Are you talking about Lilith? You can hear her?"

Nick nodded. "I assume it's her. It's not my mother, I know that much."

"You can hear her what?" Karen asked, her look of puzzlement turning to unease. "She's what, like, talking to you? In your head or something?"

Nick nodded again.

Are you here for me?

"She's..." Nick started, then shivered violently as an enormous wave of chills blasted through him. He closed his eyes and could feel his lips trembling.

"Baby..." Darren reached over to him and rubbed his shoulders. "Talk to us, baby. Stay with us, okay?"

Beautiful one. I'm not sure you're ready for me.

"Oh, jeez," Nick stammered through chattering teeth.

"Are you cold?" Karen asked.

"No." Nick shook his head.

I want to see you. I've heard such things about you. I've heard such things about your beauty.

Nick's eyes were rolling into the back of his head. He couldn't help it. The chills were worse, violent and massive, though at the same time entirely pleasant and enchanting. He let out a deep sigh, feeling his limbs tremble.

I've heard such things about you. Enlightened one. Beautiful one.

"Hold on, okay?" Darren was rubbing Nick's arms too, pulling him closer. "Just hang on, all right?"

"What do we do?" Nick heard Karen gasp.

"Oh god, I don't know," Darren said.

I must see you. It's the only way.

"The driver's here, right?" Karen was fumbling around the car. "Where's the phone? I'll tell him to get us out of here."

"No!" Nick heard himself huff.

Are you an angel or a devil?

"This is totally insane!" Karen growled. "We've got to do something!"

He's with me now, you know. Marbas. Scott. He's with me now as before, so very long ago. Your Scott is here now, waiting for you, as I've been waiting for him.

"Oh god, no," Nick whispered.

"What is it?" Darren leaned closer.

Marbas. My beautiful Marbas. He enchanted all of Heaven first. Now all of us. His was always the heart of a lion, even before he fell.

"She has him," Nick said. "She has Scott."

Darren didn't answer. He just stared over at Karen, shaking his head, looking panicked.

You'll join us, won't you? Enlightened one. I've heard such things about your beauty.

Nick reached up and wrapped his hands over Darren's where they were clutching him. He shook his head, and with a little effort, focused on him.

"I have to go now," he said.

†

They told the concierge to get them a cab. Robert wanted to leave the Mercedes at the hotel. If either of them survived, they'd have enough problems without needing to cope with the car should anything happen to it.

The taxi that rolled to a stop in front of Robert was painted white with obnoxious stripes made with blue checkers along its length. One of the hotel's attendants opened the door for him.

Robert hesitated.

"Get in," the cardinal commanded. "Robert, get in right now."

Robert didn't want to get inside the taxi. Not with Cardinal Matine anyway. Robert didn't want to have anything to do with him anymore. For a split second he considered simply turning to the cardinal, punching him in the face as hard as he could, and then running away. Maybe, if he was lucky, he'd be able to deliver a punch with just half of the same power with which the formidable-looking blonde had flattened Robert himself just a few days earlier.

Maybe Matine would spend enough time knocked-out on the pavement to allow Robert to escape.

Robert was very confused. Within the past twenty minutes, his perception of the situation had been turned on its head. He didn't know anymore if the cardinal was someone who could be dismissed as useless or someone of whom Robert should be mortally terrified.

While he was still within the power of the demon, at the house in Santa Monica, Robert had agreed to assist the group in their ultimate move to protect themselves from Lilith. The memory of his cooperation was only so much hazy smoke to him now, but he knew he'd agreed to do what he could to help with the problem.

When Robert made the agreement, perhaps he'd meant it. Most likely he had, although he couldn't quite recall. The news of Michael's death had bashed his emotions around in his head viciously, like tissue paper in a hurricane. Then the exchange between the two demons was a bewildering mess to endure. Between those things, who could have expected him to retain any sanity, much less sincerity?

They'd asked him to meet them all at the club on New Years Eve. They'd brief him on what they'd eventually decided to do and how he could help. Robert had agreed, and was driven back to his hotel by the formidable-looking blonde.

It didn't take long, a day or two, before Robert's senses returned and he formed a plan of his own. He'd still go through with meeting them at the club, but then it was a matter of waiting for his chance to do what really had to be done.

However, the moment Cardinal Matine opened the single suitcase he'd brought with him from Rome, everything changed.

"We won't be facing the demons unarmed, as you thought," the cardinal had said. He stood and made a quick trip into the bedroom, returning with his single suitcase. He'd checked nothing onto the airplane and came back to the hotel with Robert in possession of only his single carry-on.

Moving both their drinks off of the coffee table, Matine had carefully set the case on top and opened it. The cardinal had packed no extra clothing, it seemed. At first glance, Robert thought the case contained some kind of lavish theater costume. He wasn't far from the truth. The case actually contained several very amazing things. As he recognized a couple of them, Robert's head began to ache, his palms to sweat.

Covering half the case was a clear plastic pouch containing a large, neatly folded, red garment. Robert had recognized it, despite the fact that it wasn't supposed to exist. With a trembling hand, he reached out to touch it.

"The Chasuble," he whispered.

Matine hadn't answered.

"Nigel…" Robert could only shake his head.

In the early fourteenth century, Saint Hippolytus had been rumored to possess a crimson chasuble that, when thrown over a demon while it was disguised in human form, would instantly force the entity into its true form and render it powerless.

Another plastic bag, this one much smaller—a Ziplock, actually, Robert noted—sat next to the Chasuble. In it was a dried and withered vegetable, almost black with age and dehydration. About three inches below its trunk, it split into two parts, each roughly the size of a small carrot, giving it a vague resemblance to the lower half of a child's doll.

Although he'd never actually seen one, Robert could tell what it was immediately: the cardinal had stuffed a mandrake root into a plastic sandwich bag and brought it with him to Los Angeles.

Lining the other side of the suitcase were three thin, antique boxes. They appeared to have been made by hand, from beautifully crafted, darkly stained, wood.

"What are these?" Robert asked, running his still quivering finger along one of the wooden seams.

"They each contain an athame," Matine answered simply.

Athame. A ritual knife. A witch-blade. The cardinal had packed three of them.

Moving one of the boxes aside to see what it concealed beneath it inside the suitcase, Robert saw a very old book. His breath caught in his throat. Before he could stop himself, Robert had reached down and opened it. Its pages were parchment. Its text was handwritten by quill.

"Nigel, this is the—"

"The Lemegeton," said the cardinal. "Yes. That's right."

Robert whirled around, barely containing his confusion. "How did you get this?"

"That isn't impor—"

"Don't tell me that, Nigel! You didn't just stop by Barnes & Noble and pick up one of the most ancient books of magic known to man!"

"You need to calm down."

"And don't you tell me to calm down either! You walk into this room carrying a mandrake root, three witch-blades, and none other than…" Robert stopped, rubbed his temples, took a deep breath. "Oh, my God, Nigel, the Lemegeton? How, under Heaven, did you ever get your hands on a copy of the Lesser Key of Solomon, the Lemegeton Clavicula Salomonis itself?"

"It's not the original, of course. That one, I'm sure, fell to dust long, long ago. This is a copy. And although it hasn't been dated, it's undoubtedly quite, quite old. Please don't touch it again."

"The Chasuble of Hippolytus?" Robert blurted, screamed really. The name of the mythical item flew from his mouth as though its significance had just occurred to him. "How long have you had that? Where…? How…?"

"Robert—"

"Why didn't you send it to me? Why didn't you send it here with Michael? Why didn't I have it along with the Vessel? Didn't you think I could have used the Chasuble against the skotos?"

"Stop it!" The cardinal grimaced. "I couldn't simply send every priceless artifact in the Church's possession out of Italy under Michael's arm as though loaning my neighbor a set of tools!"

"Nigel! I didn't even know you had it! I didn't even know the Chasuble actually existed!"

"I couldn't be sure of what you knew or didn't know! Frankly, Robert, I also had access to the hilt of the Sword of Paracelsus, but when I moved to acquire it, I discovered it was already gone. The theft of that artifact made me nervous enough about switching the Vessel with a fake."

"The Church was in possession of the Sword of Paracelsus?"

"Just the hilt. The blade itself has never been found, but yes, the Sword's hilt was also in the care of the Church. Let me reiterate, however. 'Was' is the operative word. That artifact has been stolen, and very recently, I might add."

"You're certain it wasn't simply 'borrowed,' by another member of the Church? Borrowed for some purpose, like what we've done with the Vessel and all of these?"

"Cardinal Bellotte was the custodian of the Sword of Paracelsus. No one else, outside of the papacy—"

"Wait a minute, isn't that our story too? And didn't you give regular dinners to entertain dignitaries, displaying the 'secret' Vessel for them?"

"Yes, that's true. Bellotte and I could have very similar circumstances. Whoever took the Sword's hilt, however, did not trouble themselves to replace it with a fake. What I'm saying, Robert, what's important is that you should understand my reluctance in attempting to acquire still more of the secret artifacts during that particularly important time. Getting the Vessel to you, the single artifact in my personal care, was difficult enough, as you well know. It took nearly three months. There has been a flurry of scrutiny since the Sword's disappearance. Very discrete scrutiny, yes, but a flurry of it."

Robert didn't understand. Just how many priceless pieces of divine history did the Church keep hidden and secret? The Sword of Paracelsus was said to have a magic crystal pommel. One of the crystal's properties was that it could imprison a demon within it, although only one, to be released, controlled, and imprisoned again at its bearers command. Even so, Matìne's charge of the Vessel would be held in much higher regard than Bellotte's charge of the Sword; according to myth, the Sword's magic crystal pommel was empty of any demonic entity, while the papacy believed that the Vessel of Solomon actually contained a true demon, *exousia skotos* himself.

"This is outrageous!" Robert yelled. "It's unthinkable that the Church would hide these things, even from those who would most benefit from them. Even from the simple knowledge of their existence!"

"Such is the challenge that could be leveled at me by every other bishop and cardinal within the Church!" Matìne rationalized. "What you have just shouted so insolently could have been bellowed by any member of the clergy anywhere in the world about, not only the Chasuble, but the Vessel as well! Have you forgotten the holy and secret charge of our sect, Robert? Have you forgotten the essence of that charge, that it is secret? Are you so steeped in the arrogance of this place to believe that each secret of the Church should be yours in the unbounded submission of all mankind to your great and sacred labor?"

No words would form. Robert was paralyzed by what Matìne had said, beaten into silence as surely as though he'd taken a blow to the gut.

The moment gathered between them, swelled and drowned them. The only sound was their livid breathing, firing in bursts from their noses as they clenched their jaws in tightly contained fury.

These artifacts were unbelievable. It was beyond Robert's ability to fathom that the cardinal had access to such treasures. Robert hadn't examined the athame, but he'd suddenly been certain that all three were made of gold or silver, encrusted with jewels, not to mention emblazoned with hieroglyphs, or Greek, or Latin words of power, and each infused with a long, remarkable history more intriguing than any epic fiction.

The content of Cardinal Matìne's suitcase, even without the Sword's hilt, was well beyond priceless. How the man had gotten past both the Italian and American customs officials was a mystery of staggering proportion, especially carrying three knives, priceless or not, in this age of terrorism.

"Nigel," Robert finally said, calming his breathing, forcing his fists to open, "these are the tools of a sorcerer."

"Oh, my son..." Matìne began, sighing, shaking his head, closing his eyes, slumping his shoulders in dejection. "Robert, there is so much to teach you. Our order has followed the minions of wretchedness for centuries across the very entirety of the globe. You think we have learned nor gathered nothing?"

The cardinal opened his eyes. Staring at Robert, he shook his head again in wonder.

Then, abruptly, the cardinal pushed past Robert and moved to the sink next to the wet bar. Grabbing a hand-towel, he turned on the faucet and soaked it with water. He wrung it out a little, then walked back across the room and handed it, still dripping, to Robert.

"Hold this," he said.

Standing back where he'd been, Matìne turned and gazed across the room. Apparently finding what he wanted, he nodded slightly, then crossed around the loveseat and picked up a small, cubed box of facial tissue. Coming around the couch again, he picked it up and set it on the wet bar.

"Nigel," Robert had started, "what are—?"

"Shh!"

Robert raised his eyebrows in surprise.

The cardinal stood again near to Robert, then turned and faced the box of tissue. He gazed at it intently, slowly raised his left hand, arm stretched out straight, palm down, fingers splayed.

Slowly, and with a noticeable degree of concentration, he'd rotated his hand until it was vertical. Then, with a quick and violent motion, he clenched his fingers into a tight fist.

The box of tissue burst into flame.

The explosion hadn't been at all large; more like a jack-in-the-box of fire popping up on the countertop. Although it was getting bigger, Robert had only been able to stare at it, his eyes unblinking, his throat drying out behind his gaping mouth.

"Robert," the cardinal had insisted.

He'd heard his name, but that was all. The flame danced before Robert's eyes, mocking him, growing taller.

His paralysis hadn't been something the cardinal could indulge, apparently. With a huff, the older man blew past him, snatching away the still dripping hand-towel and throwing it over the burning tissue box. Without waiting to see if the fire had been extinguished, Matine crossed the room and set the air-conditioning fan on high, and threw open the double French doors leading to the balcony, all the while glancing nervously up at the suite's fire sprinklers.

Somehow, somewhere along the line of his life and during his custodianship of the Vessel, Cardinal Nigel Matine had acquired the skills of a witch. Robert had not been able to form much thought. He could only stare at the cardinal and wallow in bewilderment.

Matine was a sorcerer, a witch.

The fire alarm had never gone off. Robert first noted a moderate amount of smoke, but the bulk of it had quickly flown out the window.

†

Darren really hated feeling powerless. Of all the feelings that put him in a bad way, powerlessness was the most potent. This was the second time in seven days that he'd felt utterly powerless to help Nick. He felt totally useless, yet again, and it was starting to really get on his nerves.

"You're not going anywhere," Darren said, holding Nick firmly by the shoulders.

Trying to maintain eye contact with him was very difficult, what with the boy's eyes rolling back into his head every few seconds. "You're going to wait here with us. You're just going to sit quietly here with Karen and me until Scott gives the signal that it's okay to go inside."

"I don't think that's up to me," Nick said softly. He kept turning his head slowly from side to side and his chest was rising and falling dramatically with what seemed like very labored breathing.

"Just let her say whatever she wants, Nick," Darren said. "Let her ramble all fuckin' night, if she wants to. You don't have to go inside yet."

"I'm not going inside," Nick said. "You don't understand."

"You're being entranced," Karen suggested. "I think that she's casting some entrancing spell on you from inside the club or some shit like that."

"That's got to be it." Darren nodded his agreement.

"What difference does it make?" Nick asked. "She has Scott."

"She could be lying, you know," Karen said.

Nick looked at her somberly, shook his head. "She's not."

"How do you know that?" Karen croaked, but all the fight seemed to have gone out of her voice. Darren shot a glance at her and saw that now she was rubbing the back of her arms too. That couldn't be a good sign.

"She's not lying, Karen." Nick smiled at her tenderly, still breathing hard, almost panting. "You know she's not lying. Scott's with her."

Karen pursed her lips and sighed, closing her eyes. "I know," she whispered, nodding.

Darren sat up very straight and took a long, deep breath. "What the holy motherfuck is going on?" he growled.

"Darren… " Nick started, but his voice was weak and his eyelids were beginning to flutter. He was going limp in Darren's arms as though he was passing out. "I'm not really sure, but… "

Darren pulled him closer, his hand behind Nick's head. "Nick!"

Nick managed to open his eyes. He tried to smile.

"You stay with me, okay?" Darren pleaded. "Don't you go anywhere!"

Still trying to smile, Nick let his head fall to the side so he could see Karen. "You'll stay with him, right?" he said. "Please just stay with Darren and wait for me, okay?"

This was not happening. Darren clenched his teeth and looked at Karen. He could feel panic start to quicken his own breathing.

Karen didn't look like she had any ideas, but was somehow much more calm. She gazed back at Darren sympathetically.

"Sweetheart…" she started.

"What's happening?" Darren almost shouted. "Karen, do you understand what's going on?"

"There's so much more to this, Darren," Nick said. "There's so much more than even Scott could have known. It's like what he's been saying all along, only we've been too wrapped up in ourselves to see it. There's so much more to all of this."

Darren looked at Nick, then back at Karen. "Do you hear her too?" he asked.

She shook her head. "But I can feel her. I can feel her pulling at Nick."

Darren just looked down at the carpet and closed his eyes. "This is so stupid!"

Karen moved across the car and touched the back of his hand. "Darren, honey, I think you've got to let Nick go. She's getting more insistent."

Darren looked down again at Nick. His eyes weren't fluttering anymore, but they were very droopy and unfocused.

Fighting a serious rage, Darren looked away quickly, trying to think. He was resisting a tremendous urge to burst out of the limo, march into the club, storm the DJ booth, and simply bash Lauren Isseroff's brains out with a mixing board.

She was taking Nick. Lilith was taking him. Well, his mind, at least, and Darren had no idea what could be done about it. Lilith was taking Nick. The thought sent spasms through his shoulders. Nausea erupted in his stomach and his throat tightened in on itself.

"Darren..." Nick had managed to reach up and touch his face. "I have to go now."

Not answering, not looking at his eyes, Darren just held Nick and forced himself to stay in the car. He wanted to say something, to offer some brilliant plan, but there was nothing. He would have simply shouted, shouted anything, if only to try to keep Nick awake, but Darren's jaw wouldn't move, his lips wouldn't part. Unable to speak, he just stared at the floor.

"I'm going to be fine," Nick whispered. "Please wait for me."

He sounded so relaxed, so resolved. Darren suddenly found his voice. "Oh, god Nick," he said, trying to stay calm. "How many times do I have to wait for you while you go off chasing your demons?"

There was a lot of noise outside the limo. Traffic on the street in front of the club had reached a near standstill as the city filled with cruising partiers, roaming with their windows down and their stereos blaring. Shouted exclamations and laughter echoed between the buildings, almost completely muffled by the car's tinted glass.

Karen put an arm around Darren. With the other, she reached over and ran her fingers across Nick's forehead, looking down and shaking her head. "What the fuck are we supposed to do?" she whispered.

"I don't know," Darren said.

"Don't..." Nick started, then closed his eyes.

"Wait!" Darren said.

Nick didn't answer. He was out cold.

CHAPTER VIII

†

The Night Hag

Thou shalt not be afraid for the terror by night.

- Psalms 91:5 (KJV)

†

Nick was standing just outside the limo's door. He could feel the cold steel of the car behind him and, looking around, everything else appeared normal enough, except for the little fact that all of the other people in the world seemed to have vanished.

It appeared as though the entire city's population had all heard of a much better party, and no one thought to tell Nick.

Nick didn't gasp or scream, but he couldn't help staring blankly at the empty and silent street, his mouth hanging slightly open, a little reluctant to venture forward into whatever was happening to him. There were other cars parked along the avenue, but nothing was moving on the street. The club was still there, right across the black pavement, but the entrance line was gone. Even the Security Guys had vanished from the front of the building. Although Nick was standing on one of the Hollywood's major, six-lane avenues, no one was in sight anywhere up or down its length. Only the long white limousine still parked behind him marked any familiar presence.

Nick knew he hadn't physically left the car. That meant, he guessed, whatever was happening, it was happening somewhere outside of the physical world as he knew it. It was happening somewhere... well, somewhere *else*.

Whether it was all in his own head, or even somewhere other than that, there was, at the moment, no way for Nick to make any sort of distinction. His own mind, another dimension, someone—or some*thing*—else's mind, or someplace his human brain could never imagine, wherever it was, it looked exactly like the street on which he'd just been waiting, inside the limo, with Darren and Karen. It looked exactly like that familiar street, sans any other people, though.

Nick thought for a second of simply getting back into the car, but sensed immediately that would be a mistake. The limo behind him was only an image of the real one, the one from his normal, physical world. He was standing next to a facsimile, which he felt with his mind. He felt that the limo was a fake, felt it quite easily, almost casually. Yes, Nick realized he'd just gotten a very clear psychic *sense* of the car next to which he was standing, sensed its nature with his mind, just as he saw its color with his eyes.

Most mornings Nick was awakened by Darren brewing coffee in the kitchen. Nick sensed the façade of this environment, this somewhere *else*, as easily as his nose distinguished Café Verona from French Roast. He made that distinction each morning by smell, even while he lay still half asleep in the bedroom, smelling the coffee in the kitchen, all the way on the other side of the beachside condo, hardly giving it a second thought. Now, he'd experienced this new mental sense just as easily. So easily, in fact, he nearly missed he'd done it at all.

Maybe 'new' wasn't exactly the right way to describe the ability. Nick also sensed that he'd had this talent for a long time now. Perhaps 'amplified' described it better.

Now, his newly amplified psychic voice told him, unmistakably, getting back into the limousine would not be a wise move. The people he loved were not waiting for him inside it. It would be a mistake.

Nick shrugged and smirked to himself, wondering if his new and improved intuition had any other options for him. Just by thinking of the question, he realized instantly that, *Yes!*, of course. Nick's psychic voice was practically screaming at him. It startled him a little and he jumped, steadying himself by clutching the facsimile-limo.

This psychic-thing might take some getting used to after all, he thought. How the holy heck did John Edward handle it?

There was only one option, his fully fueled and throttled sixth sense was roaring at him.

Go inside the club! it said.

"The facsimile-club, you mean." Nick chuckled, soothing himself. "Go inside, huh? Well, duh. That's a no-brainer."

Taking a deep breath, he started across the street, mentally attempting to calm himself some more. Nick shuddered anyway.

The first step was the most difficult, but after that, Nick felt himself shuffling somewhat briskly. It was an interesting feeling, moving around in this somewhere-else place. He wasn't dreaming, he knew that. He certainly wasn't exactly conscious, though, either. He knew that too.

Nick thought he should have been terrified. He wasn't, though. Not really. Maybe the wonder of it, the novelty of not only being somewhere-else but also experiencing his brand new mental, well... 'comprehension' of things, was keeping him distracted. He was grateful then, not to feel exactly how frightened he might actually be, for the moment at least.

Reaching the club's entrance, Nick first noticed the silence. He'd been at the club before when it was closed and empty, and he'd even witnessed a time when the lack of patronage had made it seem deserted. There'd always been music, though. The club always had a rowdy beat pulsing within its walls, like its life-blood. In Nick's experience, the club even played music while it was closed.

The club was dead silent now. Was there anything so un-inviting as an empty and silent nightclub?

"No," Nick answered his own thought. "I can't think of a single thing."

†

"I spy with my little eye..." Theo hummed.

"The Hollywood Sign," Eddie murmured, pressing his cheek into his palm, bored miles beyond his own personal threshold.

"Would you cut that out and just play it right, please!" Theo huffed at him.

"It has to be the Hollywood Sign, Theo. That's where we are in your pattern."

"Well it's not! It isn't the Hollywood Sign, Mr. Bitchy."

"Really?" Eddie tilted his head, nodding lazily. "Well then, I'm impressed because, for the last almost two hours, you've rotated, unwaveringly, from the Hollywood Sign to the Roosevelt Hotel to the El Capitan Theater to Darren's old apartment building, then back to the Hollywood Sign. Now, since we just covered Darren's old apartment building, I naturally assumed your little eye had again spied the Hollywood Sign, as it naturally would, according to the consistency you've demonstrated, as reliable as the grand rules of the universe, just as spring follows winter, just as the sun will rise tomorrow, just as the earth will loop the sun, just as the cosmos will go on cosmosing as it has since time immortal."

"Oh boy." Theo rolled his eyes. "Now you're done being Mr. Bitchy, so you're becoming Mr. Sarcastic Speech.   Talk about reliable."

"Are you now going to shatter my confidence in the very fabric of existence itself?" Eddie asked. He could hear that his timbre was rising steadily and knew Theo was right about the Mr. Sarcastic Speech thing. Eddie still couldn't stop himself. Alone with Theo, he never could. "Are you going to shatter me, Theo? Are you going to destroy my nice, organized, reliable world by telling me that your little eye has spied something other than the Hollywood Sign, such as the Capital Records Building, maybe? Because, if that's what you're going to do, then I think you really should give it a lot more thought because, you never know, giving voice to the fact that your little eye has spied anything else, anything other than the Hollywood Sign, might just shatter the fragile comprehension I have of all the conditions of what we call reality, thereby ripping my very world into ragged shreds of cosmic debris, shreds of the universe as we know it coming completely untethered and whipping all around inside my little head like loose fire hoses, mincing my sanity as quickly as a food processor. You're not going to do that, are you? You're not going to do that to me right now and make me spend the rest of my life humming and drooling on myself, are you, buddy? Are you going to do that? Are you going to bring existence as I know it to a sudden and violent end?"

Theo slowly crossed his arms. "Maybe we should just play a different game, Mr. Sarcastic Speech. I think you've taken this one a bit too seriously."

"It *was* the Hollywood Sign, though, wasn't it, Theo?"

"On second thought, maybe we should only sit here and just be quiet for a while, even. We could meditate, like Scott said."

"That'd be fine with me. But it was the sign. It's okay. You can tell me. It was, wasn't it?"

Theo rolled his eyes again. "Yes, but you think you're just *sooo* smart, and you're not, okay? Because if you even think about changing from Mr. Sarcastic Speech into Mr. Smug Stuck-Up Shithead right now, I'm going to pelt you one right across the mouth. Oh, and yes, it would be Mr. Smug Stuck-Up Shithead next, because that's where we are in *your* pattern! Right across the mouth, and I mean it!"

"Oh-I-am-so-scared."

"You should be, because remember the last time you became Mr.

S. S. Shithead, and I was forced to pelt you one? You remember that? Your lips got all swollen and everyone thought you had herpes. So, I'd think twice about my attitude right now, if I were you, dude."

"Your testosterone display is doing nothing to entertain me, you know."

Theo lifted his arm into the starting position of a mild backhand. "And who do I have the pleasure of addressing at the moment? Is it my good friend Edward, or is it Mr. S. S. S.? Hmmmm? We are not in public and I have no problem smacking you silly."

"It's kinda your fault, you know, that I'm ever Mr. S. S. S., because—"

"Fucking *what*? My fault?"

"—I never usually even *give* speeches, much less sarcastic speeches, you know. Ever! I'm not even talkative, and—"

"*My* fault? *Your* face flaps away and it's *my* fucking fault?"

"—so it's obviously got to be your fault."

"My goodness!" said a strange voice from behind Theo.

Eddie and Theo both jumped physically, scattering the roof gravel on which they'd settled. Theo almost landed in Eddie's lap from his effort to whip his enormous body around toward the voice. "You two are just like an old married couple!"

Leaning against the metal casing of one of the club's enormous air-conditioners, about ten feet from where the boys were sitting, was an incredibly good-looking young man. He stood there staring at them with a shameless smirk, openly amused with what he'd overheard, though not at all noticeably self-conscious, despite the fact that he was completely naked.

"I am, however, fairly positive you're not lovers," said the good-looking, naked, young man. "I've not been able to detect even a tinge of sexual energy between the two of you, which in itself is both telling and interesting." Neither Eddie nor Theo answered him or reacted so much as to close their gaping mouths. "Despite the fact that you're both really quite physically beautiful, neither of you feel the slightest sexual desire for the other. Only an outrageous amount of personal affection. I am correct, am I not?"

They sat stone still in their new positions, Eddie not even noticing Theo's hand pressing his own into the gravel in a way that should have been very painful.

The young man's smirk became a furious smile. "I do wish I could have stood here all night! I just might have, too. You both are such marvelous, unique entertainment. I might have simply stood right here and listened to your most charming and adorable banter. Really, I wish I could have."

Young and beautiful himself, the stranger had another characteristic that drew all of Eddie's attention, besides the obvious and quite major characteristic of his complete lack of clothing. Very short and ruffled in a highly fashionable way, the stranger's hair was the deepest, darkest shade of sheer black that Eddie had seen on anyone in the world. Anyone, that was, with the single exception of Scott. In fact, the young stranger reminded Eddie of Scott in some other way too, but he couldn't put his finger on it. Funny, Eddie thought to himself, that I should meet two people with such black, black hair, and both in the same year, and both white guys about the same age. That's very funny.

"Quite regrettably, I can't, you understand, just stand here and listen" said the Scott-like stranger. Eddie noticed the stranger had a slight British accent, which normally added a pleasant touch to a person's voice. It didn't in this case, for some reason. "I do not, unfortunately, have the luxury of merely standing here all night, or even for very long, in fact. You see, I've detected, although barely, mind you, that I have a moderate, personal interest in the events of this evening. Specifically, the events that are to take place here, within this building. Therefore, I've come to partake."

The naked stranger took a single step toward them and leaned forward slightly. Eddie felt Theo's entire body stiffen against him. There was something more about this stranger that bothered Theo too. More than the fact that he appeared without a sound, or that he wasn't wearing so much as a pair of thong underwear. There was something more than the fact that he'd somehow managed to gain access to a roof without an access. Eddie felt the hairs on the back of his neck rise with a rough, abrasive alarm as his mental defenses gave in, allowing him to accept what was brazenly obvious. The stranger reminded Eddie of Scott because the stranger had a great deal more in common with Scott than just hair color. After all, when Scott first gained access to this very same roof, he'd also done it without benefit of the access ladder, and he'd also been completely naked.

"I really don't have very much time, as I mentioned, so I won't elucidate," said the naked, black-haired stranger. He was still smiling. "Not that you wouldn't understand. I see you're both wearing expressions of stark terror, which is not the standard reaction to the sight of me, with or without clothing. No, somehow you've recognized my nature. I'm not yet sure how. Just a moment, though, I'll have it. Hmm." He cocked his head melodramatically. "What an interesting detail. You see, I've been hearing rumors for the past few years, rumors that a certain universal power is alive and well. Quite recently, I caught the strand of still another rumor, that this same celestial force had somehow ended up somewhere on the west coast of the northern American continent. If they contain even a modest amount of truth, these rumors, then I'll bet the presence of the two of you up on this roof is a very interesting detail indeed."

Although he couldn't see his face, Eddie was sure Theo must have reacted to the naked man with his usual I-Have-No-Idea-What-You-Just-Said expression, because the black-haired youth looked right at him, saying, "Well, perhaps I should help you with that little bit, at least. 'Elucidate' means, in this case, 'to make more clear or explain in further detail.' "

Theo nodded slightly.

The man went back to looking at both of them, each in turn, as he straightened his posture and clasped his hands behind his back. "This charming little mystery may have to wait, however. I really should be going. Still, before I do, I feel I must attempt to remedy any rudeness at my abrupt intrusion and introduce myself, as I should have done initially." He extended his right hand toward them, though not at either in particular. "My name is Brathwidth. However, you may call me 'Brad.' " The naked, black-haired demon-guy said. "Most do."

Neither Eddie nor Theo—good boy, Theo! Eddie thought with some pride—made the slightest move to shake the naked stranger's hand.

Brathwidth's grin disappeared. Without it, he was far less attractive.

"They're true then, I see." He let his arm drop slowly back to his side. "The rumors are true. He's here. Your expressions of fear, plus this little behavioral display, have added up to explain the situation nicely. You've been enlightened a bit. Not significantly, I imagine, not in any kind of harvestable way, but enlightened to some degree just the same. Well, that can only mean, then, the rumors are true. How surprising." He lowered his gaze to the roof of the building. "I really am genuinely surprised."

"Are you going to kill us?" Theo asked quietly. Hearing him, Eddie nearly cried. Those simple words spoken by Theo at that moment somehow carried with them all the innocence of his nature.

Once again, Brathwidth's eyes focused upon Theo alone, and he paused for a moment, seemingly also affected by the question.

"I'm not yet sure," he finally said. "You see, I've only just arrived, just now, this moment, and I've not had the slightest time to determine what is happening here, or about to happen here, at all, much less been able to decide, therefore, which actions might best serve my interests."

Theo lifted his hand from off of Eddie's and gently laced his fingers through Eddie's instead.

"It's not likely that killing you would be of very much consequence," said Brathwidth, looking down again, as though speaking to himself.

"Pfftht!" Theo spluttered. If Eddie hadn't been terrified out of his wits, and on the uttermost verge of screaming, he would have howled with laughter.

"It would, though," Theo said, nodding a little, his voice louder, very unlike his timbre of just a moment before. "It would be 'of consequence.' It would be, because he'd destroy you for it."

Brathwidth's eyes bulged. "Really?" He raised his brow, spreading his lips slowly from one ear to the other into a Cheshire grin. "You really think so?"

Theo nodded again. "And he wouldn't be gentle about it either, pal."

Brathwidth cocked his head and pout-smirked as though at a puppy.

Theo leaned a bit closer to the stranger. "You know that's the truth. I can tell."

"Don't be tiresome. Even you yourself don't know if that's the truth."

"Bullshit," Theo said. Eddie nearly fainted.

Theo slowly shook his head in clear defiance. "I know it's the truth. And I can tell that you do too. Yeah, I can tell."

"Indeed," said Brathwidth.

Theo turned his head. Eddie could just barely see his eyes as he did. Theo was squinting at Brathwidth with almost mocking suspicion. "Plus..." he started.

Brathwidth shrugged, closed his eyes; a child's gesture for appearing unimpressed.

"He'd do more, though," Theo said.

"More?"

"You also know he'd do more than just destroy you."

"Would he?"

"He'd hurt you first." Theo nodded slowly. "Yeah. He'd mess you up first. If you do anything to me or Eddie, before he destroyed you for it, he'd hurt you really bad. You'd suffer. A lot. It's not really in his nature to do something like that, but I bet it'd be just the thing to make him let out a lot of shit he's been holding back. The last straw, the bursting dam, shit like that. He'd unleash a whole lotta pent-up whoop-ass on your skanky butt, and I think you know that. Actually, I pretty well fuckin' *know* that you know that."

Eddie was just about breathless with shock and could do nothing but stare at the back of Theo's head.

"You know..." The naked demon's eyes lost their façade of mirth. "It was ridiculously obvious the moment I first heard you speak that you are someone who will never be mistaken for an intelligent man."

Theo didn't say a word.

"However," Brathwidth went on, "you clearly have a very strong sense of observation, which, you may be surprised to hear, is accurate to a startling degree. It's what people find most appealing about you, I'd imagine, although they likely aren't aware of it. You aren't aware of it either, as you believe people only tolerate you because you have such large muscles."

"Why are you telling us this?" Theo asked.

Eddie was beyond impressed, but not beyond alarmed, that his friend was able to speak at all, never mind what he was actually saying. He'd never, not in six years, seen Theo this way. It was staggering.

The eyes of Brathwidth focused only on Theo. Eddie, unconsciously shouldering the weakness that Theo was somehow temporarily pushing aside for each of their sakes, shuddered enough for both of them.

"There really is no reason for me to tell you anything at all, of course," said Brathwidth. "It's simply a little game I play with myself."

"Do you play with yourself a lot?" Theo asked.

That time, Eddie did laugh. It was a very brief laugh, stopped abruptly by an instant rush of terror, but still loud and ringing. Back down on the street, in the entrance line, several guys glanced upward.

Although he'd blurted out what Eddie thought was the zinger of his life, and to a naked, obnoxious demon no less, Theo did not so much as crack a smile. He stared right back at Brathwidth instead.

Another slow, patient grin spread across the demon's face.

"You'll never, not if you live to be very old men—which neither of you will—comprehend what just the simple passage of a single hour might mean to a creature like me. You'll never even glimpse the possibility of such a thing. Therefore, what games I use to color those ceaseless hours, and I have hundreds of them, will not seem significant to you at all. Nevertheless, it amuses me to glean from people everything I can without touching them. I test my own sense of observation and glean without gleaning, you could say. After that, there is a very entertaining way to determine exactly how accurate were my observations."

"That means you are going to kill us then." Theo squeezed Eddie's hand. Eddie felt his stomach cramp and his lips tremble.

"I didn't say that." Brathwidth shook his head. "I simply said that you wouldn't live to be an old man, which is obvious. I can smell the steroids ripping through your blood from here. Then there are all the other chemicals that have steadily eaten the years away from you. Neither of you will live to be old men whether I kill you or not. You passed 'too much' quite a while ago, I'm afraid."

"Whatever," Theo grumbled. Brathwidth grinned, probably thinking he'd struck a nerve.

"You are one who has a strong sense of observation, as I said," he went on. "So, it just might behoove me to take note of your warning, both because you very well may have accurately gauged the affection of the fallen one for you, as well as what would be the degree of my own power against him."

Even if this was their last moment on earth, it was Theo's brightest, Eddie thought. His friend didn't waver, didn't flinch or turn away, didn't cry or squirm, although he sat squarely beneath the gaze of what they both now easily recognized as a demon, a gaze that would have ruined Eddie's composure, if not his sanity, had it been settled upon him instead.

Theo had a strong spirit. Eddie understood that in a rush of comprehension and guilt. Guilt because he'd never recognized it before. Theo's spirit was as strong as his body, much stronger even, and here it was, Theo's buff, bulging spirit, flexing for all of them.

"That being the case," the demon said, "I'll let the question of your lives rest on the answer you give me now." Brathwidth leaned toward Theo, all pretence of charm stripped from his seamless face, and darn-it if Theo didn't so much as twitch. He just sat there like a gorgeous, Puerto Rican piece of granite.

"Tell me," the demon began, "what size are your trousers?"

†

They were just sitting there, like two old friends having tea on a Sunday.

The dance floor was empty, just like the rest of the club, the street outside, and indeed, Nick sensed, the rest of the entire world. It was empty but for a single cocktail table with three chairs around it. One chair had no occupant and stood slightly away from the table, awaiting Nick it would seem. In another chair, Scott was calmly seated, hands folded in his lap, an apologetic expression on his face. No fear or anger, no alarm or even irritation, Nick noticed. Just what he'd come to recognize as Scott's expression of modest shame.

Sitting in the third chair, beaming the grandmotherliest smile that could be possible for an ageless face like hers, pressing her fingers together in a halted position of applause was, Nick could only assume, Lilith.

Lilith. The beginning of the genetic line of all earthly demons. The curse of every child from the earliest of civilizations. The terror of the strongest men since the age of stone. The most powerful entity within the service of the Beast himself, deemed by medieval clerics from England to Israel as 'The Night Hag.'

Lilith was sitting at the cocktail table, right next to Scott, smiling across the bare expanse of dance floor at Nick as though she was his mother and he was about to recite the Gettysburg Address in front of his entire school.

Nick didn't know what he'd expected in the way of her appearance. Of course, he thought, he should have. Lilith was—certainly, utterly, and flawlessly—gorgeous. She appeared to be no more than twenty years old, if not nineteen or even younger, her childlike features delicate and captivating. Her skin was a silken, tranquil shade of cream—tranquil and yet unmistakably vibrant. She emanated her peaceful energy from a face with eyes as green as wild grass after a light rain. In wonderful contrast, her hair was a bounty of auburn, not-quite-red tresses. Thick and radiant, they wound in dramatic curls, much thicker and far longer than Scott's, falling behind her into a framing, complementing pattern as though each lock had been strategically placed by an artisan born for just that purpose. She was literally breathtaking, which Nick discovered immediately.

Someone gasped loudly and Scott chuckled a little at the sound. . Lilith giggled too. Nick realized the gasp must have been come from him.

"Nicholas, beautiful one," said Lilith, still giggling a bit through her blaring smile, pressing her steepled fingers into her chin, "you can't know how happy I am that you chose to come."

It was the voice from his head, the coarse though velvet pitch, smooth and rough at the same time, the one that purred to him so privately, so intimately back out in the car. Hearing it now, wherever he was, hearing that soothing voice come from her as she looked at him and spoke, completed something within him, bound time back into its natural circle, and he relaxed.

Enchanted — and realizing it — Nick smiled.

"I don't think I really chose anything, though," he said.

"You did." Lilith shut her eyes and nodded in a very motherly way, still grinning. "You chose."

Nick looked at Scott, who also grinned a little and nodded. Maybe it was Lilith's spell, the enchantment, or maybe just the sight of the two grinning, mirthful demons, but suddenly Nick wasn't afraid anymore. Not at all. He was just puzzled.

Actually, *confused out of his fuckin' gourd* would be a far more truthful phrase.

Lilith placed her hands, palms down, gently and deliberately on the table where Nick could still see them. She lowered her face at him. "Please come and sit down with us, beautiful one. Let not your soul be afraid."

"I'm..." Nick started, shaking his head. "I'm not afraid."

Turning her palm over in a gesture of invitation, Lilith motioned toward the empty seat. "Please."

Nick walked across the dance floor and sat down.

†

"Maybe I should try to find Scott," Darren whispered. He had Nick's head cradled in his lap, the rest of him lying along the length of the limo's side seat.

"You might find him," Karen said, "but he'll be just as unconscious as Nick." She was sitting on the floor of the car, facing Darren and gently brushing the tips of her fingers through Nick's hair. "But Darren, I really don't think it's a good idea, looking for him. Scott's fine for now. So is Nick. They're together, and everything's fine."

Darren sighed and shook his head. "What's going on, Karen? How do you know all that?"

"I'm not sure, exactly." She shrugged. "Well, that's sorta bullshit, really. What I'm just not sure of, I guess, is whether I can explain it."

"Karen, what's happening here?"

"He's okay, baby. He really is."

"Oh, yeah. He's just dandy. He's in a coma."

She couldn't help but smile. "No, honey, he's not. He's in a trance."

"Oh, thanks." Darren rolled his eyes. "I feel so much better."

"She called him to her and he went. I could almost hear her myself. Almost, but not quite. Something's happened to Nick and me in the last few minutes. Something big."

"Duh."

"I think something's happened to you too, Darren." She looked at him, tilting her head slightly. "But it's very different. Yeah, something's happened to you too, but not the same thing as with Nick and me."

"You mean, I haven't gone all loonie-toonie?"

"No. You've been affected by her too, but not like we have. See..." Karen bit her lip for a second. "Let's see if this makes any sense. I think that... or actually, I'm guessing that our spending time with Scott has affected us. I mean... well, I really don't know what I mean, but we've been changed... I think... somehow... I think."

"Karen...? Huh?"

"Being around Scott has affected parts of our, well, um... oh, I don't know, *being*, I guess."

Darren nodded slowly, willing to hear just about any explanation at the moment. "Go on."

"Well, the affect has been different for each of us, to a degree. But for Nick and me, it's caused a slow awakening of some kind of sixth sense. I think it's that, you know, 'clairvoyance' Scott was talking about."

"Right."

"We've all been hit, sort of, by Lilith being here in town and relatively close to us. I'm getting the feeling that being this close to Lilith has affected all of us in the same way as being around Scott, only much, much faster. When she reached out to communicate with Nick, it amplified all of these different aspects within each of us that have been developing recently because of our interactions with Scott, only much more dramatically."

"Each of us?"

"Yes." Karen nodded knowingly. "Yes, each of us. I can already sense that's the truth, just thinking about it. Each of us has been affected."

Karen was really giving Darren the willies. "Which means…?" he asked.

"Yup." She smiled. "Eddie and Theo have been affected too. They're probably having a very, very interesting conversation right now."

†

"I'm totally freezing!" Theo whined.

"How many canisters do you have?" Eddie asked, carefully lining up the ones for which he was responsible near the open vent. "I've got twenty-five."

"I'm not kidding, Eddie! I'm freezin' my buns off!"

"Don't worry, big guy," Eddie snorted. "You're buns are still there."

"Don't you start laughing!"

"I wouldn't dare!" Eddie looked over at Theo, quickly composing himself. "I swear, I am so impressed with you right now I can't—"

"Oh, my god, enough!" Theo rolled his eyes, and just about his entire head right along with them, ala Paris Hilton. "Would you shut up about that please!"

"No, really, Theo, the way you just looked right back at him and—"

"Eddie! Can we please just get this done so that I could maybe get to the coat-check or the lost-and-found or whatever and snag something a little warmer?"

"We're supposed to wait at least another fifteen minutes," Eddie said, grimacing, glancing at his watch.

"Oh, gaaawwwwd!"

"At least he didn't take your underwear!"

"Yeah. Whoop-de-da!"

"Or your wallet!"

Eddie patted his pants pocket where he was keeping Theo's wallet in trust. He really did feel sorry for Theo. He looked miserable trying to find a comfortable way to rest on the roof gravel. It sure couldn't be easy for a guy his size wearing nothing but a jock-strap.

†

"Lilith," Scott began, "I'd like you to meet my friend, Mr. Nicholas Reynolds."

Lilith winked at Nick. "We've met," she said. "I suppose not in person, technically. Only in dreams, perhaps. I know him just the same."

Nick couldn't stop staring at her. "It's a pleasure to meet you, ma'am."

Scott giggled.

"You are too adorable," said Lilith, stifling a hearty grin. "You may call me Lilith, if you like. But, since I've been addressing you with endearing yet descriptive terms, should you likewise think of any for me, I'm certain I wouldn't complain."

"I'd bet you'll blush, though," Scott said.

"Hush, you!" Lilith squeaked. Then, right in front of Nick's eyes, she blushed.

"You're blushing now in fact." Scott smiled.

"Again?" Lilith pressed her fingers to her cheeks.

Scott nodded, then looked at Nick. "That's the fourth time she's done it since I got here."

"It is not that many!" Lilith laughed.

"Not to worry. It's enchanting."

Lilith shook her head, grinning.

Nick leaned closer to Scott. "How long have you been here?"

"I'm not sure. Not longer than half an hour, I would think."

"And..." Nick glanced around him. "Where are we?"

"We're at the club, sweetheart," said Lilith. "I'm about to play Todd Fillamen's very cool mix of *Nebulous*, and you're reclining comfortably in the back of a limousine that's parked out front."

Nick took a deep breath. He was going to have to watch his words. If his questions weren't composed perfectly, he wasn't going to get any answers at all. Not helpful ones at any rate.

"Well..." He squinted, looking down at the table. "What distinction is there between my sitting at this table and my being—"

"You're not in the mood for some alcohol, are you?" Lilith asked.

"What?" Nick looked up at her, then over at Scott, who shrugged.

"Something alcoholic?" Lilith asked. "Scott was telling me... oh, and I think that's just immeasurably charming, by the way, that you call him 'Scott.' He told me all about that." She put her elbow on the table, resting her cheek in her palm. "He said you were quite horribly sick and had been vomiting in an alley when you met, which isn't really the most glamorous of circumstances. I'm sure you don't go around telling that story at pool parties. I do have to say, however, that I admire your decision not to allow yourself to be physically sick in public. So many people, I've noticed, don't have the same personal tenet these days." Lilith glanced at Scott. "It's even worse in Europe."

"It wasn't alcohol that made him sick, though," Scott said.

"I know, I know!" Lilith pursed her lips and waved a hand to shush him. "I was only thinking that we should order a round while we're sitting here and I wanted to know what he likes."

"I understand." Scott smiled. "Very considerate of you."

"I *am* the hostess, you know." She pressed her fingers against her chest and batted her eyelashes.

"All invitations having been willingly accepted, you are indeed," Scott said, giving Nick a wink. "And a lovely one at that."

Lilith turned abruptly to Nick. "What do you think?"

"Uh…" Nick looked at Scott, but he only grinned. "I think… um… I don't… I mean, about drinking something? We're going to order… are we even—?"

"You think I'm lovely too, don't you?"

"Oh! My gosh, yes!" Nick blurted. "You're stunning!"

Scott threw his head back and laughed, clapping his hands. Lilith was actually blushing again as she waved her hand across the table at Nick dismissively, beaming a lighthouse smile.

"I'm sorry." Nick smiled too. "I wasn't sure what you meant—"

"We won't be here all that long," Lilith said. "Not that it matters, though. Really, don't you think?" She was looking at Scott again. "Don't you think that time doesn't really matter?"

Scott glanced quickly at Nick, again wearing his mild expression of shame, then back at Lilith. "It would be a blatant generalization," he said, "but overall I'm sure I could agree with you."

"Maybe it still does to you, though." Lilith pouted. "Does it, Marbas? Time? Does it still matter? Isn't that very painful, though?"

Scott only smiled.

Looking behind Lilith, Nick saw the back-bar was visible beyond the edge of the dance floor. Glancing up, he saw that the B-crowd booths, though as empty as everything else, still held their familiar prominence. The silence was everywhere. The silence and the emptiness, they were the only alien elements. The silence, the emptiness, and Lilith.

"Iced tea!" Lilith nearly popped out of her seat and Nick nearly flew out of his skin. "I think we should all have iced tea."

"Yes, I'm very fond of it, thank you," Scott said.

Lilith turned her head and raised her eyebrows at Nick, who realized she also wanted his approval.

"Um, yeah!" he said, trying to will his heart back down to a normal rate before he had some kind of hemorrhage. "Yummy."

"I hope you like the sort flavored with passion fruit," she said, glancing down at the table in front of him. "Perhaps with a sprig of mint."

Following her gaze, Nick saw the tall glass of iced tea just in time to stop his downward glance before the straw went right up his nose. Topped with what was nearly a bushel of mint, the glass glistened with condensation as though it had been sitting before him for some time.

Looking up, he saw there were now identical glasses of tea in front of both Scott and Lilith.

"This is quite a treat," Scott said, giving Nick a quick nod, then sipping his tea. "Mm. And with just enough mint. Thank you."

Realizing what was coming, Nick quickly took a hearty sip of his tea as Lilith turned her grin toward him. He furrowed his brow, humming with loud satisfaction even before he swallowed. "Oh, my gosh," he said, setting down his glass. "I think that's the best iced tea I've ever had."

Lilith blasted him with yet another amazing smile, even blushing again just a bit. From the corner of his eye, Nick saw Scott's shoulders relax, heard him sigh.

"You are very sweet, you know," said Lilith.

"It's delicious." Nick lifted his glass again. All flattery aside, it really was very good.

"It's the mint that does the magic."

"I'll remember that."

Through a long and vivaciously purple straw, Lilith enjoyed a draught of tea herself, nearly emptying her glass, closing her own eyes and humming with satisfaction, wiggling the fingers of her free hand in the air, probably as much in a spirited gesture of delight as to show off her flawlessly French-manicured acrylics.

"Now," she said, finally setting down her drink, "you're all probably wondering why I've called you here." Lilith pressed her lips together tightly as her eyes darted back and forth from Nick to Scott. Then she threw her head back and laughed.

Risking a glance at Scott, Nick raised his eyebrows questioningly. Scott slumped into a silent sigh and mouthed, *Don't worry.*

"Oh!" Lilith reared back into a proper sitting position. "I never get tired of that line." She brushed at a tear with her knuckle. "I just crack myself up."

Nick couldn't help smiling right along with her. She was sort of cracking him up too.

"Unfortunately," Scott said, "there is business at hand, Lilith."

"Oh, yes, I know."

"And you don't mind that I need to ask you some questions?"

She leaned across the table again on her elbow, toward Nick this time, covering her mouth on Scott's side with an open palm, as though he wouldn't hear her. "He thought I was coming here to take you. Really, such paranoia. I've been through with all of that, over and done, finished, for just years and years and years."

"Then..." Nick whispered. "You're not? I mean, here for me?" He could have sworn that his heart stopped as the question was formed on his lips.

"Oh, my gosh, no!" Another dismissive wave. "I can't be expected to do the same shit, year after year after year after year after century after century after millennia after... oh, you get the idea, I'm sure. Don't you, doll-face?"

"I—"

"Time marches right along, on and on, as we're all really quite, quite, thoroughly aware. Not that it really matters to me anymore, but time does march on. On it marches, as they say. Things change. Shit changes, and so must I."

"Lilith," Scott said, "that really is wonderful news. But—"

"Shit changes, as time marches. Time changes shit. These are fundamental truths, guys. Remember that shit."

"Yes." Scott nodded. "We will."

"Do you remember Egypt, Marbas?" asked Lilith. The casual lilt in her tone was gone with her expression, her eyes suddenly out of focus.

Scott sighed. Then he leaned back in his seat, resigned. Grinning, he shook his head. "No. Not really. I put all of that away a long time ago."

"You know, fuck it all, I can't stop thinking about it," said Lilith. "I can't stop thinking about sweaty ol', fertile lil' Egypt. Can you believe that crap? When I do, when I think about it, though, I think about the really, really old Egypt. Ancient-ancient Egypt, I suppose. Just as men were starting to write. Way, way before the pyramids went up."

"You ruled there for a time, didn't you?" Scott asked quietly.

"Did I?" Lilith's eyes were shining, distant. "Oh! Yes! Yes, I did!" Lilith gasped, pressing her fingers to her chin. "I did rule. For a time, I guided them. I remember. I did."

"You remember. Time means nothing."

"I remember I wore so many jewels back then. Oh, sweet mercy me, such enormous stones of light, fuckin' big, glittering rocks of light, set, I shit you not, into bands of sunbeams shaped into gold."

At that, Nick heard himself gasp as well.

"Oh, I know it, doll-face!" Lilith said. "Get *that* shit on eBay!"

Scott seemed very relaxed. He was still smiling. "They loved you in Egypt, Lilith."

She paused, glancing back at him and taking in a long, melancholy breath. "Oh yeah. I was popular, baby."

"The Egyptians served and worshiped you."

She nodded silently, her gaze falling lazily to the tabletop.

"They praised and adored you," Scott said. "Didn't they?"

"And you know what else?" Lilith smiled, then stopped. Not speaking for a moment, she pressed her lips together tightly again, although this time not to await the reaction to a joke. Nick saw her lower lip was trembling and, as he watched, a tear spilled down her cheek. "You know what else, Marbas? The Egyptians... the early Egyptians... they spoke to me." Her voice hitched. Two more tears, one from each eye, streamed down her face. "They spoke directly to me. Knowing what I was, they sat with me, and listened to my wisdom. They laughed with me, they danced with me. They loved me and feared me. They thrived beneath me."

Scott nodded. "They knew you."

Lilith's eyes clamped shut, sending still more tears toward her chin. "Yes," she whispered.

"Lilith..." Scott just breathed her name. "You've allowed it to touch you?"

She didn't answer. For a moment she only sat there, pressing her lips together tightly, little streams of demon tears running down her cheeks. Then she nodded slowly.

Scott looked down at his hands. "Does he know?"

"I'm not sure." She tilted her head, shrugging. "Maybe. It's likely, I guess. Of course." She nodded again. "Of course. Yes. Yes, he must know."

Scott sighed and gazed down at the table for a silent moment. Then he raised his head and gave Lilith a gentle smile.

"They didn't know you as Lilith way back then, the Egyptians," he said. "Not you, anyway."

"Oh, that's true." She nodded, almost smiling with him. "At Gaza and Beth Shan, and in echoes throughout many centuries, and over thousands of miles, I was still called 'Beltu.' "

"Yes." Scott nodded. "Beltu. A goddess. Not a demon."

"What's the difference now, my friend?" Lilith lifted her eyebrows. "It's become very profound, hasn't it? What divides a goddess from a demon to these people?"

"Really, the particulars, those distinctions are lost to me as well," Scott said. "But you know the basic answer for this little dot on the map, don't you? You know the customary answer for these people. Whatever is not well within their strict comprehension of God is a demon. For most of them, there is no in-between."

"Perhaps," she whispered, then nodded slightly. "Yes. You're right, of course. Though, maybe we can teach them again, you and I? Maybe we can show them the lost distinctions?"

"No." Scott slowly shook his head. "What's the point in raging through the years fighting human language, human perceptions? I've stopped looking for the past."

"I..." She shook her head, exhaled in a trembling breath. "I can't seem to get far enough away from it."

"You'll eventually have to let all of that go."

She nodded.

"Lilith..." Scott whispered tenderly. "Time means nothing."

"You are an angel, my love." Lilith closed her eyes and cried softly. "You are an angel, still."

Nick didn't quite understand what was going on. He looked at Scott, who was watching Lilith closely.

"You've allowed yourself to be touched," Scott said, raising an eyebrow at her. "He knows and yet he has done nothing? He wouldn't forgive such a thing. It's not possible for him to do so."

"He... " she whispered, licking her lips, looking away, off toward the entrance hall. "He ignores me."

"I'm sorry, but I'm really lost," Nick whispered. "Touched by what? What happened?"

With a gentle sigh and a motherly grin, Lilith tilted her head toward Nick. "A demon may not allow themselves to be lonely, beautiful one," she said. "Once an entity under the command of the Beast allows themselves to be touched by their solitude, it's an open door for all manner of compassions to tempt the demon until they're useless to him."

Nick shook his head. "Touched by their solitude?"

"That's the expression, yes," Lilith whispered. "Compassion can be tempting to a demon, as choice is to an angel."

Lilith didn't speak for a time. She wouldn't look directly at Nick or Scott for what seemed like several minutes, only sitting quietly. Nick got fleeting images of dancing bodies, heard the din of many voices from far away, felt the brush of a passing hand. The dance floor on which they sat sipping their magical tea was packed with people, mirth-filled and riotous people, celebrating with enthusiastic abandon. It was packed, and the reality of it was slipping in upon them, through cracks that were widening, creeping through into their quiet place. It was creeping through into Lilith's secret Somewhere Else.

The world was calling. Nick heard it clearly. Lilith's refuge was weakening and the world was calling them back.

She suddenly smiled, glanced up at Nick, and lightly slapped her open palms onto the tabletop. "It's like talking to a celebrity, you know."

"To Scott?" Nick smiled back at her, glancing at Scott.

"My dear boy," Lilith said, "he is one of the Fallen, and one of the last."

"I knew that."

"He has wings, you know. In his true form, that is."

"I knew that too."

"Even I don't have wings. Only the Fallen have wings."

"I don't think I knew that."

"I'm thousands of years older than Marbas. I'm…" She tilted her head toward Scott and pressed her fingers to the base of her neck again. "Sorry about this, but it's true." Back to Nick. "I'm far, far more powerful than he is, and yet he has wings and here I sit, wingless."

"That's gotta suck," Nick whispered.

For some reason, he felt a profound sort of pity for her. Lilith was suffering. A loneliness lay upon her, the depth of which Nick didn't want to comprehend. He could hide his pity, of course, in a purely mortal way, although he sensed such a thing would be nothing to her. He wondered if she took notice of his pity and was offended.

"Oh, it's not the biggest deal in the world," she said. "Wouldn't that be a kick in the pants, though, having wings?"

"Yes." Nick nodded. "I have to say I agree with you. That would be 'a kick in the pants.' Not to mention a pretty fuckin' major shock to just about all of my shirts and jackets too."

Lilith looked at him for a second with a startled expression and then abruptly laughed again. Nick and Scott laughed right along with her.

"You are a charming, charming, beautiful man!" she finally said. "I must say, I understand the path Marbas chose more and more with each passing day."

Nick glanced at Scott, but said nothing.

"Do you know why I chose to be a DJ?" asked Lilith. "In the nightclubs, I mean. Why I became a club DJ?"

"Well," Nick said, "no. I could only guess."

"Guess then."

Nick glanced at Scott quickly, then took a deep breath. "I'd have to say, well... I guess, well... You know, Lilith, I don't really know, but I'd just have to say because it's simply... a lot of fun?"

She stopped smiling and a bit of flush disappeared from her face. Nick's stomach immediately cramped.

"Nicholas," she said.

"Yes, ma'am." He licked his lips.

She grinned. "Please, again, call me Lilith."

"Yes, m—" Nick caught himself. "I mean Lilith."

"Nicholas, enlightened one, beautiful one, you are exactly correct."

"I am?"

"Yes, lovely man, you are." She nodded at him, raising her eyebrows. "Some of these places, these massive parties, some of them still hold the spirit of many of the ancient festivals that have been the hub of humanity back through every millennium. A few of them do, at any rate. A few of them hold that same, timeless spirit."

Nick nodded.

"Sometimes..." Lilith brushed at the moisture on her glass of iced tea, glancing down at it, through it. "Sometimes it's the very big ones, the grand and opulent ones, though not always. I feel it when they come together, that echo of the ancient days, the spirit of the festival, the soul of those forgotten gatherings. I feel it from the ones who come to truly celebrate. Not so much from those poor lost children who are simply seeking the easy desires of their flesh or the comfort and luxuries of this time and this culture. Still, even today, there are those who are almost free of such things. When those people gather, when the enlightened ones seek to be together and the spirit of the festival is alive, there is a true celebration. That's when the others might learn. That's what the enlightened ones can give them.

"They'd come to be a part of the spirituality, back in the ancient times, at the festivals of man. It was worship, you know. There was no distinction between the celebration and their religion. The celebration *was* religion. Worship was a celebration.

"That is the soul of these gatherings, my dear. Even today, dancing beneath a glittering, mirrored sphere, bellowing laughter and abandon within the glow of a thousand electric stars, they still worship. The celebration is a religion and those with the eyes to see it and the grace to feel it gather together to delight in one another and to revel in the spirit. That's what moves them to dance. It's not the rhythm, the pulse of so many electronic drums, but the spirit of the festival. When it lives, when it thrives among them, as it does tonight, they gather together in worship and contentment and move in delight together. They gather together, feel the spirit, they feel it move them... and so they dance."

A fleeting shadow of light, the flash of a burning image, assailed Nick's eyes. There were dancing people, packed together, pressing into a throng of energy and delight. He heard laughter and the din of many voices, raised to land on just the ear of one, gathered together to add to the music its crucial core, its human meaning. It was a flash in his face, an instant of light to his eyes, like the burst of a bulb set into a camera. Then it was gone.

It was the sight of the dance floor around them, the dance floor not suspended within the spell of Lilith, caught within her special place, her Somewhere Else.

Or was it?

Perhaps it was the sight of a gathering from long ago. Millennia ago. Perhaps the voices came to him from across centuries and out of her memory to remind him, to teach him, to show him that the jewel of human existence was the dance. The gathering.

Perhaps it was a vision of both. Perhaps there was no distinction.

†

"What are we going to do?" Darren asked. "It's nearly time."

Karen shook her head. "There's only one thing we can do, Darren. We're going to wait."

†

"Can't we just start?" Theo asked, shivering.

"No," Eddie said. "You're all set up, though, right? You're ready to start clamping the triggers?"

"Yes! Jeez, you wanna ask me that one more time and make it an even ten?"

†

"If it's not to harvest Nicholas," Scott said, "then why are you here, Lilith?"

She dropped her eyes at that, glancing away from him.

While Lilith had been speaking to Nick about the ancient festivals of man, her voice took on a subtle weight. She sat up straighter, held her chin higher, her expression shining with the calm of ultimate understanding, ultimate confidence. Now, at the simple mention of her purpose in Los Angeles, she almost slouched. She wouldn't look either of them in the eye and picked at one of her fingernails nervously.

Once again, a vaporous vision flashed around Nick; dancing bodies, a suggestion of music brushing past and through him as though he were a dandelion. It was a bit stronger this time, an instant longer, enough so that Nick was sure the image was contemporary. He saw the crowd adhering to the features of the club, assuring him it was his own time he was seeing.

Very likely also, was that Nick wasn't the only one who'd detected the cracks in Lilith's spell, the magical Somewhere Else. Scott was patient, though. He allowed Lilith the silence, letting her have whatever time she needed. Eventually, she straightened a bit, answering his question in a delicate breath. "I need you, Marbas."

With those words, Nick's new sensitivities perked up even more. He didn't get another vision of the dance floor, though. Instead, he felt the weight of a new burden, the bond of fresh responsibility. With it, or being concealed by it, he sensed there was a danger as well. Nothing direct, nothing imminent, but for the first time since falling into Lilith's entrancement, real fear touched him.

He looked at Scott, who had closed his eyes.

"Lilith, please," Scott said, "you must know that I'll give you any reasonable help I can, but—"

"It's your power alone that can help me now."

"Again, please, Lilith…" Scott looked down at the table, slowly shook his head. "To ask such a thing of me…"

"We don't have much time left, Marbas, and there's something else you should know."

"I—"

She raised her hand, silencing him. "There will be a convergence within this hub tonight," she said. "I'm sure you've felt it gathering power. You couldn't have missed it."

Scott sighed very heavily. Then he sat up straighter, pushed back his shoulders, and allowed still another abrupt change of subject. "Yes, Lilith, I've felt great power gathering here. Although, I naturally assumed..." He held out his hand palm up and briefly waved it in front of Lilith.

"Oh!" she squealed, looking slightly embarrassed. "Yes, of course. How could I not have guessed that? Well, you naturally assumed it was *my* impending appearance that you felt. Just me alone."

Scott nodded.

"No, no, darling." Lilith closed her eyes, shaking her head. "A convergence has been brewing here for many, many weeks. I believe the catalyst was your own abduction from New York. That set things in motion. It alerted the forces that will confront each other here tonight."

"Forces?"

"Yes, dear. All have gathered. The foreseen and the unforeseen. Each of them is already here, already within the Circle of Twelve."

Scott went pale. "I hope you understand about the Circle, Lilith. I had to at least try to protect Nick—"

"Don't worry about that," Lilith said, waving him off again. "It's not a very *good* Circle, sweetheart. Several of the icons were so poorly reproduced you could hardly have expected it to actually work."

Scott grimaced. "That bad, huh?"

"Oh yeah, honey," she said, nodding, a sympathetic frown on her face. "I have to admit, at first I was confused as to why this time you'd arranged to have the Circle constructed, but now I guess I just wasn't thinking clearly. I don't believe I've been thinking all that clearly for quite a while." She turned briefly to Nicholas and gave him an embarrassed grin.

"I made the arrangement for the Circle," Scott said, "because this time I didn't plan to run."

"No," she said, looking at him with an expression Nick was almost sure was one of envy. "No, darling, of course you wouldn't run. You'd assumed I was coming to take this beautiful man from you, to take Nicholas away. You thought that it was me you'd perceived as the approaching threat. It makes sense, though, since you couldn't have known that I'd been touched. You couldn't have known I haven't harvested any souls in years."

"You've kept that secret very well. Neither the lamia nor the imp knew."

"Only the Beast himself."

"And he's been ignoring you."

"Yes." She nodded. "Although, I don't know how much longer he can continue to allow me to wander unchallenged. I'm not sure how much time I have left before he begins to perceive even me as one who might eventually betray him."

"Which," Scott said, "is why you've never stopped following me."

Nick frowned. "I don't understand."

Scott looked at him. "Lilith has allowed her solitude to touch her, Nick, to change her. She's continued to follow me because I'm the only one who can heal her."

"Oh." Nick nodded slowly. "I see."

Lilith tilted her head and sighed. "Marbas, this isn't easy for me, as you must know. It is not a simple thing for me to beg for your help."

It was Scott's turn to look away. "You haven't begged," he said.

"And I know now that you would never have subjected me to such humiliation." Lilith turned back to him. "Although, merely following you all of these years, I couldn't be sure. I had to meet with you again. It has been many centuries since we've stood within sight of each other, and our powers have been at odds ever since your own enlightenment. I know the path that you chose hasn't been a simple one, to say the least. To say the very least."

Scott didn't answer for a moment. Then he blinked, tried to grin a bit, and pulled his chair in closer to the table. "Tell me about this other force that has been drawn here tonight."

"There is more than one, though, as I said…"

Scott was silent for another moment, then, "Can you help?"

"My own understanding of this event, unfortunately, is not very comprehensive. Actually, it's downright thin." She took a deep breath. "And we all know what that means."

"Um…" Nick said, raising his hand. "I don't know what that means."

At that, Lilith smiled, shaking her head. "Nicky, my luscious-lolly, I really think that you do."

"I do?"

Scott nodded. "Yes."

Lilith cannot perceive the details of this convergence, Nick's amplified awareness told him, *because her own fate is woven within it.*

"Marbas," Lilith said, turning to him abruptly, "I won't ask you to decide now, here, about whether or not you'll help me. We have a little time at least. Save your strength for whatever's coming tonight. I'll do what I can to help, of course."

Scott looked quite visibly relieved.

"However," Lilith went on, "I would like to take this very last moment we have here together to thank you for your most thoughtful gift."

Scott looked confused for a second, then grinned, nodding. "You're quite welcome, Lilith. It was the least I could do."

"What gift?" Nick asked.

You know the answer to that too, his psychic voice said, beginning to irritate him. *Scott sent it to her quite a while ago.*

"Oh, I have it right here." Lilith reached beneath the cocktail table and pulled out what Nick first thought was a huge metal cross. It appeared to be a heavy, silver cross, about two and a half feet long. Lilith just whipped it out from under the table as though it had been on her lap the entire time. Nick knew better.

When she set it down on the table, Nick saw that it was really the hilt of an old broadsword, a medieval-looking relic. Nick's focus was immediately drawn to its pommel, which appeared to be a smooth, crystal sphere, just a little larger than a golf ball. The crystal, though, wasn't what made Nick's breath freeze in his mouth or his heart hammer against his ribs.

Within the crystal pommel, Nick could clearly see a single eye. Blinking and aware, it settled on him and, as it did, the pupil began to blaze with fire. Nick instantly sensed the hatred within that single eye's stare. He just happened to know the prisoner of the hilt's magic crystal pommel.

It was Lilith's imp. It was Gillulim.

†

They sat in the taxicab, which was parked opposite the entrance to the club, directly behind the long, white limousine. Robert wondered what kind of plan the skotos had derived. Was the group's staple white limo empty? Perhaps one of the demon's children were gazing out the darkly tinted rear window at that very moment, watching Robert, wondering why he was just sitting there, wondering who the other man might be that was sitting next to him.

"I should check inside," Robert said.

"No," Matine answered. "There will be a sign for us. We'll know when it's time to leave this car and go inside."

"What kind of sign?"

"I don't know. I've only been able to detect that there will be a sign, but what kind I can't determine. The sign will come, though. That much, at least, is very clear."

"And how did you get this information, Nigel? Do you have a familiar I should be aware of? Maybe you've hidden a speculum or two? Are you sporting some crystal balls?"

"My patience with your disrespect has come to its end, my boy. You will remain with me and you will remain silent. Please don't make me bind your tongue. It's not a complicated spell, but I'd really rather save my strength."

†

He was a little embarrassed at needing to make the request, but Lilith didn't seem to mind putting Gillulim away when Nick mentioned that it would make him more comfortable.

"What about Shehlá?" he asked after the sword hilt was again out of sight. "Would you really have destroyed her if you got here and found out what she was doing?"

"Without hesitation," Lilith said.

"But Scott took care of her. So, you don't need to do anything, right?"

"He did what was correct for all of you at the time," she said, her tone again reverberating with the confidence Nick found so soothing, so comforting. "Although I can sense that she's not completely out of the picture. Shehlá is not easily dispatched. Also, I understand from my conversation with Marbas prior to your arrival that she's grown quite strong. No. I'm afraid we will see her again. Somehow, we'll see her tonight."

Nick sighed. "That so really fuckin' sucks cheese, man."

"Indeed."

"She's no match for you, though, right? I mean, she's still in pretty deep shit with you, isn't she?"

"Nicholas, beautiful one, let not your soul be afraid," Lilith said. "As it is, we really don't have the time to discuss this."

"Why? Why don't we have time?"

"Well, darling," she said, raising her eyebrows, mock frowning, "you know the answer to that perfectly well."

"Oh, no…" Scott lowered his head.

"What?" Nick whispered, trying to contain his growing panic.

"You are about to end my party a bit prematurely," Lilith said.

Eddie and Theo, said Nick's irritating little psychic sense.

Nick's stomach sank directly into his balls. "Oh shit."

†

"Now!" Eddie screamed.

Theo and Eddie flung themselves into their appointed task. The roof of the club was a flurry of activity. Safety clips flew. Triggers were clamped so the valves would remain open. Pepper-spray streamed in between the slats of the ventilation ducts in tiny jets as though from air-pump squirt guns. First only two, then four... eight... fourteen... twenty-two... forty...

Finally, fifty pepper-spray canisters were discharging jets of the chemical irritant directly into the club's air-conditioning.

Theo turned to Eddie. "I sure as shit hope that Sean's not here tonight."

†

At first, Darren couldn't be sure if the plan was working. It was already ten minutes to twelve. Eddie and Theo should have started five minutes ago. Fifty canisters should have been plenty to do the job. The plan was to make being inside the club just uncomfortable enough that the partiers would want to leave, not to debilitate them. For additional insurance, though, Darren had decided to take an extra measure, something he considered devious but necessary. Just before dawn on a Tuesday morning—one of the only times the club was ever completely empty—Darren and Karen had removed a few strategic filters from the club's ventilation system.

Oh god, Darren thought to himself, sitting in the limo, waiting for some sign that their plan was working, *now I suppose I'm technically a domestic terrorist.*

Only a few people were exiting. They didn't look to Darren as though they'd been gassed, but they did seem irritated and a bit huffy. Still, he had to wonder why anyone would leave the club just twenty minutes before the New Year Eve countdown. The pepper-spray had to be having at least a little effect.

That was when Nick sat bolt upright in the limo. Darren and Karen both screamed.

"We have to stop them!" Nick shouted.

"Oh, my god," Darren said, trying to catch his breath. "You scared the fuck out of me!"

"Stop who, Nick?" Karen asked, grasping his shoulder. "Who do we have to stop?"

"Eddie and Theo!" Nick looked a little sick. He looked very panicked and a little sick.

Darren glanced out the limo's window again, across the street, and took in the significantly changed view.

"Oh, baby," he said. "I'm thinkin' it's way too late for that."

†

"That's the sign." Matine opened his door and got out of the cab.

Robert quickly looked over at the entrance to the club. He couldn't believe his eyes.

He'd noticed a trickle of people exiting just a minute before, but now a wave of them was pouring out of the front exit. The crowd was still moving in a rational manner, but appeared as though they might not be too far away from real alarm. Enough of them were already jaywalking toward their cars in singles and small groups that they stopped the auto traffic completely. Judging from the rapid growth of the crowd outside, Robert guessed that every emergency exit was being used as well.

A great many members of the exiting crowd were coughing, or rubbing at their eyes, or both. Robert was also relatively sure he could hear more than just a couple of them swearing, if not all that creatively, quite loudly.

†

Karen couldn't help it, she burst into tears. The sight on the street was simply too much for her. The terror at the house on Nichols Canyon hadn't brought her to tears, but seeing this, on the party night of all party nights, the patrons of her club filling the street in a state of explicit rage, or overwhelming disappointment, or an evident combination of both, mercilessly tore her heart to shreds. They looked devastated. Most of them appeared completely overcome by this obviously intentional act. It was either competitive sabotage by another club, or senseless mischief by some incredibly detestable asshole, or, the worst possibility of all—once they realized it was just a moderate dose of pepper-spray and not anything like anthrax—outright betrayal by the club itself. She'd heard about such things before; large clubs setting off stink bombs on the dance floor, or using similar tricks, to thin out the crowd during a key part of the evening. Once the crowd had been thinned, the unscrupulous management could refill it with freshly charged patrons.

Darren and Nick were doing their very best to console her, bless their sweet little hearts, but she was pretty far beyond that now. She got onto her knees on the limo's floor, then sat back on her heels, pressing her nose to the window beside the limo's bar. There, she sat and watched helplessly.

The loss of revenue was no longer even a peripheral concern to her. Stories would be told, gossip would be spread, rumors would be created and believed. The variations on the events of this night would be coming back to her from every sort of witness, genuine as well as false, first, second and third hand, for years to come.

Of course, in the time since the plan was developed, she'd imagined what going through with it might really mean to the club, especially after the fiasco at the pre-party. She'd known what she was doing, but seeing it actually happen turned out to be much, much worse than she'd ever allowed herself to envision.

And no one would ever know the truth. Perhaps the version that ultimately gained the most supremacy would not be one that branded the club with a fatal reputation. Perhaps she hadn't just mortally betrayed the man who'd saved her from a trailer village lifestyle, ruined Max's very purpose in life, the center of his existence. Perhaps she hadn't just ended her professional career for all time, blacklisting herself from comparable employment all around the globe. Perhaps she didn't have to move to New Zealand, dye her hair, and change her name to 'Gerta.'

As Karen watched the street through the limo's glass, as she witnessed the crowd become thicker than a midnight marijuana giveaway during Mardi Gras, she sobbed long and loudly. Tears ran down her face that were so heavy she could actually hear them splash onto her blouse. Her nose and splayed fingers made eleven pathetic streaks across the inside of the tinted window.

One day someone might discover that she'd allowed this to happen. One day someone, maybe a great deal of someones, might be able to look at her and know the truth. They would despise her. They'd hate her with all the vehemence of children dragged out of Disneyland after only a brief, tantalizing taste.

Even so, no matter what they eventually knew, or thought they knew, not one of them would ever understand that Karen had made this choice because she loved them all. She loved them, and she made a choice to save their lives. In a very real sense, Karen had sacrificed her own life for theirs.

She laid her forehead against the window's cold glass and cried as though all of Heaven had fallen.

†

"Okay, I think we should be concentrating on pants," Theo said. He and Eddie were frantically rummaging through the enormous lost-and-found room on the now deserted third floor. "If you find a nice big, long coat, preferably one with a little style, that'd be fine. Some boots, I think, would be a miracle. But mostly what I really think we should be looking for are some pants."

"Right!" Eddie whipped up and down the rows of hanging garments in a whirlwind search. Theo shook his head. He didn't think Eddie would be able to spot anything useful until he calmed down.

When Eddie ran right smack into him, Theo was going to make just that suggestion. Before he could, though, a third voice entered their conversation.

"There's a very large box here in the back," the third voice said. "It's got a bunch of pants and shoes in it. Some shirts and stuff too."

Staring at each other, their eyeballs the size of wall-clocks, Theo and Eddie were only terrified for the briefest of instances, which was the amount of time it took them to recognize the voice.

"Scotty?" Theo said. "Is that you?"

"Yeah," Scott called out from the back of the coat-check room.

Eddie and Theo exhaled.

"I think there are some boots here that'll fit you, Theo," Scott called again. "But I'm just a little curious as to why you guys are looting the coat-check." He walked around a row of hanging coats and stopped, his own eyes bulging, presumably at the sight of Theo.

"A demon stole all of my clothes," Theo whined, sighing.

"Oh, sweetheart, I'm so sorry." Scott tried to stifle a grin, but failed. "Nice jock, though."

†

Why had Matine stalled him in the cab if he wanted to go into the club alone? As Robert watched the street fill up with people, going from relatively sparse to elbow-to-elbow in an astoundingly short amount of time, he happened to catch sight of the cardinal making a beeline for the side of the building. The older man was shoving twenty-somethings out of his way as though he were a star of the WWF, his case of magic do-dads dangling absently from his arm.

Robert, apparently forgotten, opened his own door and began to follow. He was immediately stopped, however, by a very irritated and somewhat wigged-out taxi driver, and therefore further delayed while he paid the guy.

†

"We should get in there," Darren suggested. He really didn't want to leave Karen, but he didn't want to abandon Scott to whatever was going on inside the club either.

Nick shook his head. "Not yet."

"Why not?"

"Well, I don't really know for sure. Actually, that's sort of bull-shit, really. See—"

"Oh, dear lord, not this load again!"

"Wait a second," Nick said, and pointed out the limo's rear window. "Take a look at that."

Darren saw what Nick was indicating right away. The guy in the Armani suite, the one Darren had punched out after Karen's tragic private party, the very one who was supposed to have met up with all of them hours ago, seemed to be in the middle of a verbal altercation with a cab driver, who was parked right behind them.

In the next instant, the Armani Suit Guy—Robert, Darren remembered suddenly—simply tossed a couple of bills at the taxi dude, turned, and disappeared into the milling mob.

Better late than never, Darren supposed.

†

"Almost right after I'd phased inside," Scott explained, "I realized I needed to quickly find an out-of-the-way spot where I could safely be unconscious for a while."

"Why?" Theo asked, pulling on a pair of pants he'd found in the box. They fit him surprisingly well.

"Lilith had cast an enchantment that caught me as soon as I appeared. It was more of an invitation, actually. I could have refused, had I really wanted to. She didn't really seem to be herself, though. I couldn't sense any kind of threat. So, I crawled into this lost-and-found box and allowed her spell to overtake me."

"Totally wicked," Eddie chirped.

"No. Actually, she's completely different from the way she was the last time I encountered her. You see, she has something of a major problem. Or, rather, what would be a major problem for a demon such as her."

"No," Eddie said, shaking his head. "When I said 'wicked,' I didn't mean that in a bad way. I was saying it was cool. Ya know, like—"

Theo nudged Eddie.

"Yes, thank you, Edward, my love," Scott said. "I'm just messin' with ya."

"You dork." Eddie laughed. "Well, what happened then?"

"We had a lovely conversation over some tea."

Theo smirked. "You're fuckin' with me." Eddie nudged him.

"No." Scott shook his head. "Nope. Nope. She, um, 'invited,' Nick too. He showed up about twenty or thirty minutes after I got there. We all had iced tea and talked about stuff."

"Is he okay?" Theo asked. "Is Nicky all right?"

"Just dandy, I hope. He should be out in the limo with Karen and Darren at the moment, which is right where I'd like the two of you to be as well. If you hurry, you can cut them off at the entrance to the club and get all of you back inside the car."

"Right," Eddie chirped.

"First, though, I need to know about this demon you two encountered."

"Oh, yeah!" Eddie nearly shouted. "Scott, I swear, you should have fuckin' *seen* Theo! Holy shit, I nearly —!"

"Shh! Shh! Shh! Shh! Shh!" Scott pressed a finger to his lips and patted Eddie on the chest. "Both of you, just give me one of your hands."

†

"She's not evil," Nick said.

"I knew it!" Karen blurted, still sniffling uncontrollably.

"What does she want with you then, babe?" Darren asked.

Nick looked back at him and nearly cried, he was so glad to see him. He didn't, though. He knew it made Darren uncomfortable, so he kept a lid on it, which wasn't easy at all, what with Karen ballin' her frickin' eyes out.

"Nothing, Darren." Nick smiled. "It's all been a very big misunderstanding. There's so much more to all of this than we knew, like I said before. She doesn't want anything from me. She's sick. For a demon, I guess, she's really sick. And since Scott is the only entity who can heal a demon, she needs his help. It really was him that she's been trying to get to, not the souls he enlightened. At least for the last few years, anyway. She's sick and she was just trying to work up the nerve to ask for his help."

Darren looked right into Nick's eyes throughout his entire explanation without even blinking. After Nick finished, Darren didn't say a word.

"That's what happened, Darren," Nick said. "I swear."

Darren only nodded. Then his lower lip suddenly pressed into his upper, which was an expression Nick had never seen on him before. He had just enough time to notice the tiny wells of tears forming in Darren's eyes before his boyfriend pulled him close, lay his head on his shoulder, and cried like a baby.

†

"Brathwidth," Scott said, letting go of Eddie and Theo's hands, "is a very powerful incubus. Though, I've had no direct dealings with him myself."

"What's he doing here?" Theo asked.

"He's finishing a game." Scott gazed solemnly at the floor. "Nothing more."

"Can you believe Theo?" Eddie smiled. "I was shittin' in my shoes and he—"

"Eddie," Theo said, nudging him. "He knows."

Scott put his hands in his pockets, took a deep breath, and shook his head.

"What's wrong, Scotty?" Theo asked.

"I'm not completely sure."

"Did I screw something up?"

"Oh, no, big guy." He looked up at them. "It's just this change in both of you that has me concerned."

"I don't think there's been much change in me, Scott," Eddie chirped. "But I still can't get over—"

"Eddie!" Theo nudged him again, this time with a bit of real irritation. "Listen. He's trying to tell us something."

"Okay, okay, shovey," Eddie whined.

"Theo," Scott started, "you remember, while we were in my basement, we spoke briefly about a clairvoyance that's been awakening within Nick and Karen since they've been around me?"

"Yes." Theo nodded.

"Well, the presence of Lilith has boosted that awakening immeasurably. I was even a little taken aback when Nick appeared within the space she'd enchanted for our meeting. It takes a strong metaphysical capacity to navigate such places. Perhaps Lilith awarded him that extra boost for some reason. I doubt it was simply to meet with him. Though, with the way she is these days, I can't really be sure."

"So, now, after that, Nick has very, very clear sight, right" Theo asked.

Scott nodded. "As well as Karen."

"What?"

"We don't have to go into much detail about this, but Karen's clairvoyant ability has been boosted too." He stopped, took a breath. "But that's not all."

"You mean..." Theo started. "Oh, my gosh."

"Yes. You and Eddie, as well as Darren, have also been affected, but in different ways. Lilith has affected everyone around me. Everyone within my circle. I don't know in what way Darren's been touched by her, but with you two... well, there's been a sort of... well... cosmic balancing, I guess, is probably the best way to put it."

Eddie and Theo looked at each other quietly.

"Theo," Scott said, "you're powers of observation have been enhanced, yes, but that's just the tip of the iceberg, I'm afraid."

"There's more?" Theo raised his eyebrows into his hair.

"Oh yes." Scott nodded again. "With the boost you've gotten from Lilith, you've become something of a soothsayer."

"Say what?"

"A soothsayer. It's a bit different from a clairvoyant. You'll notice your ability growing as you learn to trust what you see, but very soon you'll be able to sense the patterns within events and behaviors to the degree that you'll predict future events and behaviors with significant accuracy. You'll see the past as well. You're going to have a very clear understanding of the truthful elements that have contributed to any number of things as they are today."

Eddie had slowly stepped away from Theo while Scott was talking, an elfish grin spreading on his face. "Dude!" he said.

"Oh, and Edward..." Scott shook his head. "You've got to be very, very careful now, my friend."

"Scotty, whatever's happened to Theo, it's his, and he frickin' rocks with it. I never felt any change, and it's not a big deal at all. I'm still just Eddie. You don't have to worry about me. I'll let my big, bad, baby say all the sooths for both of us."

Theo laughed. "Eddie, you're being a total goob, you know —"

"We don't have time for this!" Scott nearly shouted, silencing them both. They gazed at him with open embarrassment.

"Sorry," said Theo.

"Sorry," said Eddie.

"You have also been affected, Eddie."

"But..." Eddie shook his head. "I haven't felt anything. I haven't noticed anything at all."

"You will, my love. Oh, you will." Scott blew an anxious sigh. "In the interim, however, Eddie, please, *please*, from now on, it's extremely important that you be very, very careful at whom you bat your eyes or send a flirtatious grin. You're going to find those simple things will likely have a result that's far more profound than you've ever seen before."

†

"It's time," Karen said. She closed her compact, relatively happy with the job she'd done fixing the mess her tears had made of her face.

"I'm not sure you should come," Nick said.

"I'm fine. Really. You guys don't have to stress. It's just something that I had to get out of my system, I suppose. It's over. I'm ready."

"That's not what I mean and you know it."

She leveled what she hoped was her most stern stare directly into Nick's eyes. "They can't stop me. They won't."

"Who?" Darren asked.

Karen flipped her hair off her shoulder. "The guys in the street. The second I step out of this car, they're going to recognize me."

"And have an awfully clear target for their very justified irritation," Nick said. "We'll never get you through the crowd."

Darren nodded. "I think he's right."

Karen dropped her compact into her handbag and snapped it shut. "Foolish mortals."

†

"Why is she affecting all of us?" Eddie asked, quickly lacing one of the boots they'd found while Scott helped find Theo another shirt. The first one out of the box that could possibly have fit him barely earned a passing glance from Theo and a, "I wouldn't wear that if I were dead."

"It really isn't her," Scott explained, "not in a manner of speaking. I think it's because of me, actually. I'm not entirely sure, though. I've never been in a position like this before."

"What position?"

"Well, you've all been accepted by me into a specific group, one that carries my favor, which... well, the favor of a demon placed upon a specific group has very ancient implications, I'm afraid. If I'm right, you'll be affected in some way by every demon you ever encounter, even if it's just that you can detect them."

"No way!"

"I highly doubt you'll encounter many more, but don't freak out. You'll never be affected so severely again. See, Lilith is quite powerful. Second only to the Beast, really. I really think she's pretty much boosted you guys as much as possible."

"Unless we run into the Beast?"

"Even in that exceedingly unlikely instance, he'd still have to grant the power to you."

"I still don't get it," Eddie said. "I don't understand why our whole group got buzzed. I don't understand why she gave all of this to us."

"It seemed appropriate to her," Theo said. "Didn't it, Scott? It was the polite thing to do, right? She assumed you'd have expected as much."

Scott gave him a sheepish smile and nodded. "That's what I'm guessing, yeah."

"Theo, you're really gonna spook me somethin' serious pretty soon, buddy," Eddie said.

"That's what threw me off about all this though, Theo," Scott said, still smiling. He appeared to be a bit embarrassed though. "If what I'm thinking is true, then Lilith made something of a massive assumption, I'm afraid. Actually, for her, I suppose it's a very reasonable assumption that's she's made about our little group, you, Eddie, Darren, Nick, and Karen. The poor thing might have been giving away power because she thought it would be something I might want from her in return for my help. Something I'd ask her to bestow on my… " He stopped.

"On your what?" Eddie prodded.

Scott sighed. "On my 'coven.' "

†

"Oh, my god, what's going on?" Karen screamed as she stepped out of the car. "What are you guys doing out here?"

Darren watched and listened. He tried to play along, tried to pretend that he, Nick, and Karen had just arrived, but his real concern was just to keep Karen moving and make sure no one got too close. He suddenly remembered that he had to watch Nick too, making sure he didn't reach out and touch anyone. There was that little rule as well.

The crowd, so far, was behaving themselves. With as much force as he dared, Darren tried to act as though he were Karen's own private Secret Service Agent, propelling her through the mob. With one hand on the small of her back, and the other in a posture of possible threat, he moved Karen briskly along, toward the other side of the street.

They didn't have to go very far—just from the limo to the front door—but moving through the crowd was like wading through butter.

Karen shocked and surprised Darren yet again. He was completely baffled at how she managed such a convincing degree of alarm as she was regaled with the saga of the evening again and again. Then there were the more, well, 'discourteous,' patrons who wanted answers concerning their due financial compensation.

It was these latter individuals that got Darren steamed. One particularly bulky man, who stood at least an inch taller than Darren, and whose shoulder width outdid his enough to be visibly discernable, planted himself firmly in Karen's path and demanded to know what she planned to do about "this bullshit."

"We need to get by, please," was what Darren chose to say. He thought it sounded professional yet vague.

"Not until—!" was all the discourteous man was able to articulate, because Darren had not allowed Karen to stop. Not for the tiniest of instances.

Acting as a human barrier, Darren positioned himself in a manner that allowed a small space for Karen to move behind him. Doing this, anyone attempting to get to Karen would need to bypass Darren, which would involve touching him first, which would technically frustrate any assault charges any individual might level at him at a later time should he just happen to 'touch' them right back. Yeah, maybe he'd just touch them right back down onto their ass.

It was a slim legal consideration. Darren actually had no idea whether or not it was sound. Still, it was what he kept telling himself. It made him feel better.

So, when The Guy Who Was Bigger Than Darren tried to adjust his stance in the street to keep Karen from simply walking around him, he tripped Darren's legal safety system: he pushed Darren. So, technically, The Guy Who Was Bigger Than Darren had instigated things.

Darren was just going to give him a moderate shove in response. He only intended on raising his arm in a sort of non-threatening manner, and employing enough of his considerable muscular prowess to physically convey to The Guy Who Was Bigger Than Darren that Darren meant business; the guy needed to step back.

The guy didn't step back, though. He flew back.

When Darren shoved back a little with his arm, the six-foot-four, discourteous bodybuilder was lifted completely off the ground and hurled several feet. He flew parallel to the pavement, knocking quite a few of his, um, 'associates,' hither and thither like shirtless, muscled bowling pins.

No more acting was required from Karen. No more briskly compelled movement from Darren and Nick. Still watching The Guy Who Was Bigger Than Darren as he moaned in his now horizontal position on the pavement, their jaws hanging nearly to their sternums, the crowd kindly parted and allowed the trio a path into the club without further hindrance.

†

Nick found himself once again at the entrance to the club. Under somewhat opposite circumstances to the last time, however.

The street behind him was far from empty; it was a carpet of bodies, aimlessly milling with growing impatience and agitation. Nor was the club at all silent; music continued to pulse through its chambers in a steady, rhythmic flow.

And the spell. Nick thought of the terrible spell with a relief that was numbing in as much as it was invigorating. He would not have to say it. The ancient magic would remain harmlessly locked away within his memory, incomplete and useless.

"Graham," Karen called to the only security guy in sight. "What the heck happened?"

"I don't know." Graham shook his head. "We think someone set off some tear gas or some pepper-spray inside the club. Something like that."

"What?" Karen shrieked. She was really getting into it. "I thought they were all kidding!"

"Nope. The place is deserted. I wouldn't go in there if I were you, not for a while anyway."

"I'm just going to check it out for myself," Karen said. "If it's still bad, I'll let you know, but I'm getting to the bottom of this."

A little cheer went up behind them. Nick turned with Darren and, smiling, they watched as the crowd immediately around the entrance grinned and clapped. One aspect of the plan was not going as they'd expected; no one was leaving. It appeared as though the entire throng that had occupied the club only moments before still waited just outside it. They were waiting, apparently, for word it was all right to go back inside.

No doubt hearing the cheer herself, Karen turned back to the crowd.

"This is total bullcrap!" she called. Another cheer went up, louder this time. Karen smiled.

"Oh, saints in heaven, save us all," Darren chuckled under his breath.

"Don't any of you worry for one little second!" Karen yelled, stepping toward the street slightly. "I'm going to find out what the holy fuck happened and get this party back on its feet! That's where it belongs, motherfuck it all! Dancing on its feet!"

The crowd roared. Arms flew up in praise and applause.

"In the meantime, my precious, precious loves," Karen screamed as best she could, but her voice still cracked with emotion. "Happy New Year!"

Nick thought he'd never before heard a more deafening roar of joy.

CHAPTER IX

†

The Language of God

The mountains quake before him; and the hills melt away. The earth trembles at his presence; the world and all who live in it.

- Nahum 1:5 (NIV)

Los Angeles, California
The side alley immediately north of the club on Highland Avenue

†

Not more than four feet into the club, Robert had to turn and run right back out again. He would have had a much easier time breathing, once he got back into the fresh air, if he'd been able to keep himself from laughing at the same time he was trying to cough.

Pepper-spray. The demon and his gang had decided to clear the club using pepper-spray. Although Robert was forced to admit the tactic was effective, he still found it comical.

The fact that the club had been gassed, so to speak, meant that whatever magical strength Matine had reserved for himself by not binding Robert's tongue must have been spent getting into the club without being affected by the chemical. Robert didn't have any such resource and so would have to wait.

Robert had watched the cardinal as he passed around the crowd pouring out of the main entrance, then headed toward the north side of the building. Following him, Robert swept through Matine's wake, through the coughing party-people retreating from the side exit, all of whom seemed barely aware of either of them.

Once around the corner and inside the thin north alley, Robert held back and just watched. Matine made his way like a salmon upstream to the emergency exit on that side of the club. Both doors were wide open, secured nearly flush to the building's thickly painted brick. A steady flow of exiting patrons streamed out and into the tiny alley. Once arriving at the open doors, and with a discernable disruption to the exodus, the cardinal disappeared inside. Therefore, Robert assumed Matine had either cast a spell that enabled him to tolerate the pepper-spray, or he had a gas mask hidden in his suitcase somewhere beneath the Chasuble.

First, the parade of exiting party-people had lessened to a drip. Then it abruptly ceased. The place was, supposedly, empty. That's when Robert had tried to go into the club himself.

After his retreat, Robert's coughing fit didn't last all that long, but he still had to spend several minutes standing a few feet away from the open doors, covering his face with the lapel of his jacket. His eyes were watering and difficult to keep open, but the irritant couldn't have been used in very large quantities, as the effects were relatively mild and quickly wearing off. It was nothing like being hit with a direct blast of the stuff, he knew. That was a completely debilitating experience, which was something he'd learned while being certified to carry it himself.

No one lingered with him in the thin alley. A long chain link fence, topped with curling razor wire, ran its entire length, dissecting the width of the alley by half. Whoever owned the building to the club's immediate north sure didn't like having the club sitting right next to them. The fence effectively corralled any wandering nightclub attendees away from the immediate neighbors and out to a much more conspicuous area.

At the alley's west end, near the club's façade, Robert could see a wall of people as they milled about on the main avenue. No one seemed to be paying any attention to him, but that didn't matter. He'd prefer not to be noticed going inside, but overall, he really didn't care.

They didn't appear to be too upset, the people at the end of the alley. As Robert watched, they all stopped moving around and seemed to suddenly share a single point of focus. They were smiling too. Robert could tell from halfway down the alley that the people on the street were smiling. Despite their so-far tragic evening, the displaced party-kids were standing on the street in front of the club and smiling. Then, as he watched, they suddenly cheered.

Robert shook his head. He would never understand this city. Never.

Deciding to ignore the crowd out on the avenue, who were all obviously overwhelmed by some incredibly serious drugs, Robert gazed into the club. He had never seen it from this angle. The entire empty dance floor stretched out from the open emergency exit, underneath and just to the left of the DJ booth, to the open hallway leading through the main bar and then to the front lounge. The music was still blaring. The lights over the dance floor were still flittering through their synchronized, computer-designed patterns.

Glancing up the inner west wall, Robert could see about a quarter of the DJ booth fairly clearly. From this angle, it appeared empty, which really meant nothing. In fact, he couldn't see any movement at all inside, anywhere. There was no sign of activity within his view.

He knew, of course, the halogen streetlights were doing serious harm to his ability to gaze into the dark club. To make any useful observations, he'd have to go inside and allow his eyes time to adjust.

Across the dance floor, he could see the telltale glow of another set of open emergency doors as more halogen light filtered into the main bar from the front lounge area. Those other exit doors emptied into the south alley, just a foot or two from the front of the building. No doubt, they were also wide open.

With both sets of emergency exit doors standing open, the pepper-spray wouldn't remain at an effective level for too long, unless its dispersal was still ongoing.

Risking another coughing fit, Robert stepped back inside the club, but could tell immediately it was too soon. He scampered back out, quickly covering his face with both of his jacket lapels.

It appeared as though he would have to wait outside a bit longer.

†

"Don't look back," Nick said to Darren. Karen was just closing the front doors behind them. "If we walk quickly, maybe we'll leave enough doubt about the conditions in here that they'll all stay outside a good while longer."

"I told Graham not to let anyone back inside," Karen offered, rushing up to them.

"How long do you think your new door-guy'll be able to keep them out there?" Darren asked. "What if someone suddenly decides that there's no problem any more?"

"I'm not going to think about that," Karen said. "Let's just pray the boy has enough sense to get out of the way."

†

"There isn't much time for the two of you to get to the front doors," Scott said. "Do you both have your wallets?"

"Yes," Eddie and Theo said in unison, patting their butts.

"Good. Get going. I'm going to find Brathwidth."

†

The crowd had cheered two more times while Robert was waiting. The last cheer had been ridiculously loud and long, as though someone was giving away thousand-dollar bills. After the cheering stopped, the crowd's mood didn't seem to diminish at all. They hugged, kissed, and generally carried on just as if they were still within the building's privacy.

Once again, Robert turned his back on them.

He could lean inside a little now, but still felt the sting of the gas. It was a bit too soon. Just a few moments more. He could wait. It wouldn't do him any good to wander around inside for only five or ten minutes before he was forced to seek clean air again.

A breeze was blowing into the south emergency exit doors and out the north. Robert stayed where the pepper-spray caught within the exiting draft wouldn't affect him and bided his time. It wouldn't be long now.

†

"Where do you think she is?" Karen asked.

They were standing in the mini-lounge just outside of the empty DJ booth. Since the booth itself was a unique architectural feature, jetting out over the dance floor between the first and second levels of the club, it had its own access hallway. A door from the second floor near the club's west wall led to what the regulars called "the secret passage."

The secret passage was really only a thin hall that ended in a half flight of steps leading down to a tiny, private lounge. The space held two old loveseats and a cheap pressboard end-table. There, the entourage of the currently spinning DJ could watch the activity through an open archway leading into the booth itself.

No one sat down, and Karen had only leaned into the booth long enough to determine that it was vacant. Although, a rather good CD was still playing.

Nick shook his head. "I don't really know," he said. "I can only sense that she's, um, well…"

"That she's near." Karen nodded.

"I can't tell how near, though, or even if she's still in the building."

"You guys are gonna make me feel like a third wheel sooo quickly," Darren whined.

†

As they opened the doors, Eddie saw that, so far, only two police officers had arrived. The Security Guy was doing his best to keep the crowd appeased while at the same time explaining to the cops what he thought had happened.

There was no sign of Karen or the boys. They must have gotten inside the club before Theo and Eddie could get downstairs to head them off.

Well, he and Theo would just have to do this thing right. Couldn't linger.

Eddie watched as Theo went right to work.

"Gentlemen," he said, pulling his wallet out of his borrowed pants, "I'm very glad you're here. We need your help for just a bit while the building is being secured."

As Theo reached for his wallet, instant alarm burst onto the faces of both the police and the new Security Guy. A second later, though, Theo had his wallet open and was flashing its demon-licked contents.

Holding it up for all three of them to see, Theo appeared calm and professional. "I'm Agent Ramon," he said, "and this is Agent Thornton. FBI."

Eddie couldn't help it; he had to sneak a peek at the inside of his wallet. Scott had licked it for several seconds while they'd still been up on the roof. Sure enough, in the slight instant Eddie dared glance, risking appearing as though he'd never seen his own badge before, he glimpsed the incredibly credible-looking identification. The famous abbreviation, FBI, jumped out at him long enough to nearly pop a stupid grin on his face before he was finally able to mimic Theo and hold the wallet up. He didn't know who he felt more like: Moulder or Scully.

Both cops, as well as the new Security Guy, were barefacedly stunned.

†

"There are more here," Nick said. "I don't think we can afford to wait around much longer."

They hadn't moved. Since the DJ booth was empty, the secluded mini-lounge behind it allowed them a small level of comfort, what with it being so seemingly secluded.

"What do you mean?" Darren asked.

"I mean Lilith and Scott aren't the only ones here," Nick said. "Lilith talked about a convergence of power. She said there were more coming, that they were already here, actually."

"I can sense them too," Karen said.

"There's Scott." Nick sighed with relief, pointing up through the DJ booth toward the second floor.

Darren glanced out and saw Scott as he briskly passed the B-crowd booths. He made eye contact with him. Scott pressed his hand through the air to indicate he'd be with them in just a moment and that they should stay put. Darren knew that, with the building empty, Scott would be there in just a couple of seconds.

"At least we found him quickly," Karen offered.

"That's swell, guys," Darren said. "Now we just need to find Shaggy and Scooby."

"They're at the front doors." Scott's voice echoed down the secret passage. He'd covered the distance between the door and the mini-lounge with astonishing speed. "They're buying us some time."

†

"Impersonating a federal agent is a very, very serious offense, son," said one of the policemen.

"So," said the other policeman, crossing his arms and frowning, "how long have you two prodigies been out of the academy?"

Eddie stepped up before Theo could answer. "Officers," he said, "let's not get off on the wrong foot."

Then, remembering what Scott had just explained to him, Eddie smiled.

The result of Eddie's grin was obvious and instantaneous. It took all of his personal will not to allow his knees to buckle and to fall to the ground in a fit of laughter violent enough to rupture his larynx: both police officers immediately popped identical smiles onto their faces in crisp unison.

"Right," said the first cop.

"Sure," said the second cop.

"You guys don't look stupid to me," Eddie said, still smiling. "And you certainly don't look like assholes." He lowered his head a bit, still gazing at them from beneath raised eyebrows, morphing his smile into a playful smirk.

"No!" said the first cop, shaking his head. "No, we're not!"

"Definitely not," said the second cop. "Absolutely not. No way.

Not assholes."

Both policemen were now nervously shifting their weight from foot to foot, alternating their glances from Eddie to the ground to each other and back to Eddie. They were even elbowing one another.

"I could tell." Eddie nodded, smiling brightly again. "In fact, I could tell right away that you two are consummate examples of the very high standards expected of law enforcement officers within this dangerous city."

Willing himself to keep eye contact, Eddie had to hold back another major belly laugh. It was the toughest thing he'd ever done; both policemen were blushing.

If even one of them said anything that remotely sounded like "Aw shucks," Eddie was going to lose it totally.

"We're not asking for all that much," Eddie continued quickly. "We just wondered if you'd mind keeping this entrance clear while we secure the building and wait for backup. Most likely, what's happened here tonight was just a prank, but we'd be pretty derelict these days if we didn't follow a full protocol, don't you think?"

It felt a bit weird to do so at this particular moment but, going with what seemed to be working, Eddie blasted them with another smile.

"Absolutely!" said the first cop.

"No problem," said the second cop.

Both officers crossed their arms, threw their eyebrows together in a blatantly obvious attempt at a stern, professional expression, and nodded their heads as though they were a pair of plastic novelty puppies.

"Just fifty to sixty minutes," Eddie said. "That's it. It's no big deal. By then, more agents will be on site. Any questions or concerns you have will be immediately handled to your satisfaction, I'm sure." Eddie smiled even brighter at them. "That's not too much to ask at all. I can tell that you two are remarkably reasonable and rational. Keeping this entrance clear for us for the next hour or two, or possibly as long as necessary, is completely reasonable and rational."

The two cops nodded vigorously, each speaking right over the other.

"Sure is."

"Isn't a big deal at all."

"That's very rational."

"We'll handle it for you."

"As long as necessary."

"No problem."

Eddie didn't hesitate another second. He grabbed Theo by the wrist and pulled him back into the club.

†

While it could no doubt eventually become a pretty useful attribute, having a super-enhanced psychic sense was nothing more than confusing at the moment. Nick was lost in the land of sensory overload. He could detect other active forces within the club, something he equated to the electronic hum from a computer or other high-tech appliance, the kind of which most people didn't even make note until the device was turned either off or on while they were in the same room. Even so, he found that interpreting any specifics was fleeting and near unachievable.

Nick tried to pinpoint locations, or movement, or anything that might help them assess what was happening inside the building. Although he could tell such detections would not ultimately be impossible, the skill was currently beyond him. Maddeningly so, unfortunately. Nick needed practice. A whole, heck of a lot of practice.

"This is driving me a little nuts," he said.

"Me too," Darren huffed. "Do you guys mind if we turn this off for a bit?" He stepped into the DJ booth and flipped off the music.

"That's not what I meant," Nick said.

The club went silent. Nick shuddered.

†

When the music stopped, Robert knew he couldn't wait any longer. Abrasive environment or not, he had to get inside the club. Steeling his resolve, he pulled up his jacket lapel and walked briskly onto the dance floor. His shoes made so much noise, though, he slowed down right away.

That was when he heard the chanting.

†

"What's that?" Karen asked. "Do you guys hear that too?"

Nick, Darren, and Scott stopped moving, cocked their heads, and listened.

Karen could tell that, indeed, the guys heard it too. All three of her friends rapidly became visibly pale.

†

"Robert?" The voice came from the corner of the room.

Robert had made it across the dance floor and into the main bar. He'd realized the chanting was coming from the VIP room behind the back-bar. So, naturally, Robert decided to walk in the opposite direction until he figured out what should exactly be his next move.

Maybe some Scotch would help. His nerves were on fire. The main bar was bound to have an open bottle or two.

The worst thing was that the chanting voice was obviously Cardinal Matine's. While Robert had been leaning over the main bar, searching for an open bottle of Scotch, Cardinal Matine was across the dance floor, behind the back-bar lounge, in the VIP room, chanting very loudly in a mishmash of old languages and dialects. Robert couldn't make out what was being said.

It was while Robert was wondering if he really had time to pour himself a little Scotch that the other voice had called to him. It came from the far corner, below the level of the bar. Some guy was calling Robert by name, and he was sitting on the floor.

Robert swallowed. "Who's there?"

"Robert? Is that you?"

The voice was so familiar. It was a young man, much younger than Robert. He knew that voice. Robert knew it very well. The name was right on the tip of his tongue. Robert knew this young man sitting in the corner. It couldn't be who Robert first thought it was, though. It just couldn't.

"Robert, come here," the voice called again. "Please come here. There's something I've learned. Something you have to know."

"Who is it? Who's there?"

"She wrote the word on my face. I can't do anything about it. With her own blood, she wrote the word on me. So, when he called I had to bring it to him. You understand, don't you? Even though I knew him by then, I still had to bring it."

Robert rounded the bar and saw the young man sitting in the corner, his chin in his hands, elbows propped on his raised knees, looking bored silly. Robert finally saw him. The corner of the main bar offered no refuge from the light, but it was still darker than the rest of the room. Even so, the business's normal illumination was quite sufficient. Add the bit of street lighting filtering in from the front lounge and even the floorboards could be seen.

Robert recognized the man in the corner without any difficulty. There could be no more denials. He would have screamed, but the sight of the man sitting there completely shocked all the breath from his body.

It was Michael.

†

"It's an incantation," Scott said.

"Who's chanting?" Nick asked. "Can you tell?"

"It's not a demon." Scott squinted and lowered his head. "It's a man. There's something very strange about him, though. I can't quite tell what it is. I know his voice. I know his voice, but..." Scott stopped.

No one pressed him to continue. They all just listened to the unknown man's voice and his melodic articulation of the strange language.

"Nīr hes ŕeth, ahs cas līlīt," the unknown man chanted. "Il mara', tēch il molēch. Corá hes ŕeth, bas cas līlīt, eśēru il mara'. Ahs cas līlīt, il mara', eśēru il mara'."

Nick was chilled by the chant. He couldn't understand what the specific words of the incantation meant but he sensed that, all together, it was a type of summons. Specifically, a summons for a demon.

Very quickly, Nick understood that there was a man in the building using an ancient incantation to summon forth a demon.

Rapid footsteps in the passageway made Nick jump. Darren put his arm around him just as Eddie and Theo came into the mini-lounge.

"I asked for two hours, but I think we've got about twenty minutes, tops," Eddie said. "And I think there's some freak behind the back-bar trying to sing something in Spanish."

"He's inside the first floor VIP room," Theo said. "And I don't think it's Spanish, baby."

"Whatever."

†

"Oh Michael! Oh, my God, please forgive me!"

Robert couldn't stop crying. He didn't remember falling to his knees or when he'd put his face into his hands. He also didn't remember exactly when he'd started sobbing, but there he was, on his knees, still needing to lean the bulk of his weight against the outside of the bar, sobbing stridently.

"No, no, Robert no," Michael said. "Don't grieve."

His voice was closer. Without looking up, Robert realized Michael was crawling over to him.

"It's all my fault, Michael," Robert said.

Whether or not the creature that had been sitting in the corner like a third-grader at recess was really Michael Sigovia, Robert didn't care. Even if he did, even if Robert allowed the terror within him to attempt to animate his limbs into flight, any fear would have been easily overwhelmed by the anguish that now crippled him. "I should have listened to you. I should have heard you."

"You always were so arrogant Robert," said the maybe-Michael thing. "It wasn't the choices made by you that ended my life."

"I should have kept you with me!"

"Oh, so powerful, are you?" The voice was right next to him. Robert was sure that if he glanced up from his hands, he would be nose to nose with the corpse.

"Bishop Robert Patrick," Michael went on, "by whose whim the faithful are fortified with life and by whose disdain the wicked are left defenseless within the shadow of death."

Regardless of his fear, Robert looked up. Sure enough, Michael's face was inches from his own. Robert didn't flinch, though. He didn't so much as whimper.

Michael looked beautiful. He had the radiance of youth and his eyes shone with strength and... something else. Robert thought it might be disappointment.

The only element out of place with Michael—and it was a considerable element—were the crimson symbols written across his forehead, אמת.

It was 'emēth.' If Robert remembered his Hebrew correctly, it meant 'truth.'

"God sent me here," Robert said, tears pouring down his face. "Michael, it was God. I was sent here by Him to destroy the skotos. But the cardinal... Michael, the cardinal is a witch."

The Michael-thing smiled.

†

"He's summoning a demon, isn't he, Scott?" Nick asked.

Scott nodded. "Yes."

"That's not everything that's happening, though," Karen said.

"Yeah." Theo nodded too. "There's definitely more. Tell us the rest."

"Oh no, Thelma," Darren whined. "Not you too."

"Oh yeah, believe it baby," Eddie sang. "He's a soothsayer now. A genuine sayer of the sooths."

"What?"

"I told you," Karen said, smiling. "Lilith affected us all."

"Right." Darren nodded.

"Don't act all innocent, Blondie." Karen laughed. "It wasn't a heavy wind outside that threw that guy across the pavement."

"You did what?" Eddie's jaw dropped.

"Oh yeah, boy!" Karen turned to Eddie, nodding and smirking. "It was like a scene from *X-Men*. The guy was a frickin' mountain, too."

"Wait a minute," Darren said. "What about you, Eddie? Are you going to be joining the clairvoyant crew, manning the phones for Psychic Psychotic's Looney-Line?"

"No." Theo shook his head before Eddie could answer. "But he's been touched, though. Oh, good-golly, he's been touched. You should have seen him handle the cops outside. I nearly got a boner myself, just from standing next to him while he did it."

"Shuuut uuup!" Eddie laughed.

"What did he do?" Nick asked, smiling.

"We don't have time to get into it now," Theo said, "but just don't flirt with him. You'll only end up washing his car."

†

"The word is written in the demon's own blood, Robert," Michael said. "That's what you're looking at. The demon marked me with her own blood so that I might be called forth later to work her will."

"Witchcraft."

"The very thing."

"She couldn't have called you forth, though. Not one of the Legions, anyway. A mere terrestrial demon can't ..."

Robert stopped.

"Go on," Michael said. "You might be arrogant, but utterly ignorant, you are not."

"I always understood," Robert whispered, "that is to say, it was always my understanding, that terrestrial demons have somewhat limited abilities when it comes to spells and magic, casting in particular, especially if chanting is required. They're able to cast certain spells, but the powerful ones, the spells with any real..." He stopped again.

"Yes, Robert." Michael nodded. "That's right. The real shitkickers require a mortal's help. And not just any mortal either."

Robert thought he understood what Michael was trying to tell him. "Who called you, Michael?"

"Oh, Robert, Robert," Michael said, smirking. "I just told you that you're not completely ignorant. I just gave you a bigger stroke than you've ever even given yourself. Don't prove me wrong so quickly."

Robert's throat closed up on him. He knew what name was correct, the only name that *could* be correct.

"He's been with me since he got off the plane, though," Robert heard himself explain.

Michael smiled again. It broke Robert's heart to see it. Michael looked so young, so very much younger than he'd appeared during the last days of his life, the days during which Robert had held him in such contempt.

"No matter," Michael said. "It was him. He called me, as she taught him to do."

"But why?"

"It had always been a small part of their plan together."

"To call you forth from the dead?"

"Yes," Michael whispered, nodding. "And you as well."

†

"What is it, Scott?" Karen asked. "What are we missing?"

"I know the man who's chanting downstairs." Scott took a deep breath "I know him."

"Is that important?" Darren asked.

"I'm really not sure."

"He's very old," said Theo.

Scott nodded. "Much older than you're sensing, though, I think."

Nick stepped to the archway leading to the DJ booth. He looked through it, watching the disco lights as they swept silently over the dance floor.

"I wish we had more time," he said. "We have to get down there before he stops chanting, don't we, Scott?"

"His incantation isn't going to work."

"Why not?"

"He's trying to undo a charm that's well beyond his power."

"What are you talking about?"

"He's trying to call forth the lamia to serve him."

"The lamia?" Nick said. "You're talking about Laura Shah, aren't you? She was a lamia demon, right?"

Scott nodded.

"He's summoning Laura back?" Karen looked a little green. "He's summoning Shehlá? Are you sure that he won't be able to do it?"

"But..." Eddie said. "She's sealed inside that brass thing, right?"

"Yeah." Nick nodded. "She is."

"It's here," Scott said. "The Vessel is here. I can sense that it's downstairs, but the incantation he's using won't be enough to break the charm that sealed it, the charm I placed myself. The sorcerer downstairs doesn't have the power. He can't free her."

Listening to Scott, Nick got the sense that, although he wasn't lying, Scott was somehow unsure of what he was saying.

"He won't be able to free her," Scott repeated softly. He crossed his arms and gazed at the carpet. "He can't free her and so she won't be able to cast any spells. Neither of them are a threat."

"Oh, thank God." It was lucky Karen had been standing in front of one of the love seats; she landed in a near sitting position as she fell back.

Scott frowned and Nick felt queasy.

"How did the Vessel get from your house to here?" Nick asked.

"I don't know." Scott shook his head, then looked up at Nick. "That sort of bothers me too."

†

"I brought it to him," Michael said. "The word is written on my brow in her blood. When he called, there was nothing I could do. I brought it to him."

"Matìne has the Vessel?" Robert's stomach froze inside him.

Michael nodded. "You can hear him this very moment, chanting for the lamia's release."

"He's a sorcerer. A witch."

"Oh, yes."

"And he's powerful enough to open the Vessel? Even though it was sealed by the skotos?"

Michael shook his head. "No sorcerer on earth, not one who is living or has ever lived, has the power to overcome a charm that's been put in place by one of the Fallen."

Robert's stomach thawed a little. "Well, that's good then. We're okay. He won't be able to open it, right?"

Michael shook his head again. "The cardinal doesn't know it yet, but he's going to have help."

†

"Shh." Scott pressed his finger to his lips.

"What's wrong?" Darren whispered.

"There's another voice downstairs now."

They all stopped and listened. Sure enough, in the empty club, without the music playing, they clearly heard a second male voice echo up to them as it interrupted the first.

"No, no," said the second voice. "You'll need to roll your Rs much more. Especially when you try to pronounce 'feth.' It's a very important detail."

The first voice responded, but Nick couldn't make out what he'd said. The door to the first floor VIP room must have been left open. Even so, the first guy's voice was only perceptible while he'd been chanting.

"Do you want to release her or not?" the second voice said in answer to the question Nick hadn't been able to hear.

Nick looked at Scott. "I think we need to get down there now."

Scott nodded.

The booming second voice drifted up to them again. "This is an extremely ancient dialect, remember. Simply keep in mind, if you can, that, back then, the structure of a comprehensive language was still relatively new. Even those who could accomplish it to some degree, as well as those with a modicum of legitimate skill, still could not keep themselves from occasionally tripping over their own tongues."

Nick didn't exactly catch the first voice's response, but it sounded like, "Fine. I'll start again."

At that, Scott turned, bounded up the half flight of stairs, and strode hurriedly out through the secret passage. One by one, as silently as they could, they all followed him, Nick and Darren, then Karen, with Eddie second to last, Theo's hands resting upon his shoulders.

As they exited out onto the second floor catwalk, they heard the louder voice again. "There is one little problem," it said.

Scott turned to his group and, while glancing tensely down from the catwalk toward the back-bar, he put his finger to his lips, then indicated with his hands that they should all walk more slowly, in order to move as quietly as possible.

The sound of the first voice wafted to them from behind the back-bar, though the words were not clear.

Adopting Scott's pace, Nick and the rest of them followed.

The second voice responded to the first. "This work will require more power than you have at your command, witch."

More unintelligible sounds from the first voice.

"I suppose I could," said the second voice. "However, you know of course that, should you choose to utilize my support, you would be required to articulate the request."

"He sounds British," Karen whispered up to Nick.

Theo and Eddie exchanged a glance.

Scott stopped, turned back to Karen sharply and, with a touch of anger on his face, pressed his finger to his lips a second time.

Karen grimaced violently, clenching her teeth and raising her fists into a very dramatic oh-crap-I-fucked-up expression.

Sorry! Karen mouthed silently, then nervously pressed her fingernails to her lips as though she were biting them.

†

"Robert," Michael said, "listen carefully."

Robert nodded.

"There is a word you must remember," Michael continued, "so that you may whisper it to the enlightened one."

"Who?"

"Robert, listen."

"I'm listening."

"I know the single word that names all demons. A word spoken in the language of God, the Lord of Creation. I know the very word the Divine would use to refer to every demon in existence, all of them, every entity within the Legions and the Fallen alike. I've heard the name of power, that which holds command over every creature of celestial relation not upheld within the angelic spheres. In referring to them all, when casting His mighty hand through the range of Heaven to indicate the entirety of the horde of power against him, the word He would use is 'seriyima.' "

"Seriyima," Robert repeated. As the word fell from his lips, the very sound of it numbed him.

Michael nodded. "'Seriyima.' It's the name He would use, the one for all demons. Where you would say, 'demons,' the voice of God would say, 'seriyima.' "

The voice of God, Robert thought. A brutal shudder racked through him.

"Tell the enlightened one," Michael said. "He will know what to do. Give the enlightened one the name of all demons. 'Seriyima' is the key. The enlightened one will know how to use that word. It is a name of power, plucked from the language of God. The word, through the enlightened one, may open the very doorway to redemption itself."

†

The first challenge was going to be getting into the downstairs VIP room without being seen. Nick followed very closely behind Scott, his heart racing faster the closer they came to the main stairway.

If the group could somehow get to the far wall of the back-bar lounge, they could each flatten themselves against it between the open doorway and the room's corner. There'd be plenty of space along the wall for them to stand that way for a while, shoulder to shoulder, out of sight from the open doorway as well as through the two-way mirror. The fact that they'd also resemble ducks in a shooting gallery was something on which Nick decided not to dwell.

Still, once they got to the bottom of the main stairway, there was only about eight feet of wall to conceal them before they had to walk onto the dance floor. They'd have to get across the dance floor and through the back-bar lounge before they'd be out of the VIP room's line of sight. It was a long way to walk and crouch. Nick supposed they could crawl, Special Forces style, but that might take too long. Besides, Karen was in a rather tight skirt and Nick was sure she wasn't going to be enthusiastic about any complicated *Charlie's Angels* maneuvers.

Finally, they reached the top of the main stairs. From there, the conversation behind the back-bar was easier to hear.

"I'm sure you will be well compensated," said the first voice, "once the charm is broken."

"Even so," said the second voice, "rules are rules. If I am to apply any power at all, you'll have to articulate the request yourself."

Scott had stopped at the top of the stairs and the group gathered behind him. Nick tapped him on the shoulder and was about to ask a question when Scott turned back once more, his finger on his lips.

There's no need to speak aloud.

Nick's eyebrows jumped and his jaw dropped. He pressed both hands to his mouth and squelched the peel of delighted laughter that nearly flew from him. It was primarily nervous laughter, considering their circumstances. All the same, not since Scott had popped magically around Nick's pre-dawn living room had he been so elated. It was like finding a secret button on his stereo that turned the speakers into go-go boxes.

Nick tried something. *Can you hear me too?*

Of course.

Pressing both hands onto his mouth again, Nick actually bounced up and down a little bit, bearing all of his focus on keeping himself from laughing out loud.

What about Karen and the guys? Can they hear us?

Scott gave Nick a quick downward nod to indicate that he should look behind him. Glancing back, Nick saw that all four of his friends were gazing at him as though his head had just fallen off.

Guess not.

†

"Who is this 'enlightened one?' "

"You'll know when the time comes, Robert," Michael said.

This was not at all the way Robert had thought the evening would play out.

Michael cocked his head at him. "Don't tell me the chosen prophet of God is here, in the midst of the battle of the righteous, only to find himself void of confidence."

Robert's stomach knotted and he nearly gagged.

"I'll give you a hint at least," Michael said. "The enlightened one is the favorite of the skotos, the leader of his coven."

"They're not a coven."

"Aren't they?"

"No, no." Robert shook his head. "They don't control the demon. It's not witchcraft. The demon is with them because… they're…" He looked at Michael. "They didn't summon him. He hasn't been bound."

"Really?" Michael smiled. "What an interesting situation that no one could have predicted."

"Don't do this to me, Michael!"

"Why shouldn't I?"

"How could I have known these things? I couldn't have possibly seen all of this!"

"You don't say."

All the feeling left Robert's face. He stopped crying and his mouth went dry. He wanted to close his eyes, to squeeze them shut, lay his head upon the floor and weep. Michael's eyes held him, though.

"Although it might give me some final mortal satisfaction to sit here and revel in your weaknesses, Robert, I can't. You have a duty before you. I can't help you any further."

Robert wiped at his face.

Michael moved closer. "You can help me, though," he whispered.

"What do you mean?"

"You can set me free."

"What?"

"Release me from the cardinal's summons. Break the demon's charm."

Robert looked back at Michael. There was desperation on his face as clear as the Hebrew word.

Robert swallowed hard. "That would mean... I'd have to..."

"You know how to break the charm."

"That's ridiculous."

"Please stop hiding. You cannot hold yourself so high and help me at the same time."

His head shaking back and forth in tiny tremors, Robert could barely draw a full breath. His chest felt as though it had been bound with steel, his lungs tied to prevent them from expanding.

"You would really leave me like this?" All at once, Michael's voice was strained with fear. "I never truly believed it of you. Not really. You would leave her blood on me? Robert? The cardinal commands me only because his demon bound me with her blood! You would leave the demon blood on me?"

"Michael... my... witchcraft is not... I am the one He spoke to... I'm the one sent to..."

"Oh!" Michael gagged pathetically. "I hoped I'd seen real mercy in you. I thought you would not be so lost in your dreams as to prevent you from reaching down to give me your hand."

"It's witchcraft, Michael." Robert gazed at the floor. His jaw ached and his breath hitched. "I am the one He spoke to..."

Michael's eyes clenched shut, his mouth drawn into a scowl. He slowly bent forward until his face was near the floor as a low, anguished moan droned from his throat.

Robert's eyes blurred. He raised his hand and placed it on the back of Michael's head. "Oh, no, Michael, shh. No. Don't. Please. Of course I'll help you. Michael..." Robert's eyes were watering more and more. He wiped at them with the back of one hand, stroking Michael's hair with the other.

Michael raised his head. There were tears on his face too. "You are the one He spoke to?"

"I..." Robert tried again to draw more than a shallow breath. He couldn't. His head was still trembling and he could feel his jaw quiver as well.

Another tear rolled down Michael's face. "You are... the one... You're the one who has truly heard His voice?"

Robert reached out and brushed a tear from Michael's cheek. His body allowed him a single, deep though trembling breath. Finally, Robert shook his head.

"I am no one," he said.

Looking up, he gazed at his friend's forehead, at the crimson Hebrew word, 'emēth.'

"Thank you, Robert." Michael closed his eyes with a shivering sigh of relief. Two more tears ran over his cheeks. "Go with God."

With the sleeve of his jacket, Robert rubbed one of the symbols off of Michael's forehead, leaving only מת, the ancient Hebrew word 'mēth,' which meant, 'dead.'

"Be at peace, Michael."

The youthfulness in Michael's face was gone instantly. His eyes became sightless, gray orbs.

Turning away, he guided Michael's head to the floor, not wanting to let it fall and strike the hardwood. He looked at the ceiling, also not wanting to witness the wounds left from the demon's torture as they were revealed once charm was broken.

†

Theo and Karen, after a moment or two, appeared as though they understood. Darren and Eddie, on the other hand, had the look of children standing in the middle of a busy department store desperately trying to spot their mother.

Nick relaxed, though, as Theo and Karen each took hold of one of the clueless ones and retreated with them back down the hall in order to whisper an explanation.

Nick turned back to Scott. *That second voice downstairs, that's a demon, isn't it?*

Scott nodded.

Nick took a deep breath. *And, together, they'll be able to open the Vessel, won't they?*

Scott took a breath then nodded again.

Nick felt the promise of some massive anxiety. *Well, we have to do something then. Right now. Why are we still waiting up here? That demon can sense us too, can't he?*

Shaking his head slowly, Scott grinned at Nick. *Nope.*

Scott pointed to the bottom of the stairs. Squinting a little in the darkness, Nick looked and was stunned to see the outline of a woman sitting lazily on the steps, leaning against the wall, hands clasped in her lap.

As he watched, the figure waved at him.

Hi, doll-face.

It was Lilith.

†

He was staggering, and he'd never even gotten the chance to pour himself some Scotch. He really needed some Scotch. Wanted some Scotch. Craved it. He was requiring Scotch.

After some Scotch, he wouldn't have to think about leaving Michael's mutilated body lying on the floor of a disco in Hollywood. He wouldn't have to remember that he'd spent his entire life in the service of a man who'd bonded his soul to a demon in a partnership to achieve a wickedness he could not fathom.

After some Scotch, he wouldn't have to fathom any wickedness.

So, then. That was the plan. Find a bottle of Scotch. Drink it. Find another bottle.

Perhaps, during this process, he might seek 'the enlightened one.' If finding the enlightened one didn't hamper the Scotch, then maybe he'd whisper the word to him. Maybe he'd whisper the magic word to the enlightened one, like Michael wanted. That would be a good thing, he thought, if he could do what Michael had wanted. First, though, he needed some Scotch.

Find a bottle of Scotch. Drink it. Whisper the word to the enlightened one. Find another bottle.

After all that, if he did what Michael had wanted, and he followed his plan to the letter, followed all the complicated criteria, then he would let himself rest. He would close his eyes, lay down near his empty bottles, he would lay down quietly and calmly, and he would keep his eyes closed.

Maybe if he did everything well enough, then he would never have to open his eyes again.

†

Nick left Scott and the gang at the top of the stairs and tiptoed down to Lilith. She was grinning at him.

Smiling, he sat down on the step just above her. *Where have you been, young lady?*

Lilith stifled a giggle. *You are so darn cute, I could just lick you!*

I wouldn't if I were you. Nick shook his head. *My boyfriend is really, really strong.*

Lilith pressed both of her hands to her mouth, ala Nicholas Reynolds, and silently kicked her four-inch sling-back pumps into the air. *Stop it! You're gonna make me pee! We'll fuck this whole thing over if you bust me up.*

Nick smirked at her. *Sorry.*

You should be happy that you have a really, really strong boyfriend, doll-face. You'll be thanking me every time you need to move any furniture.

Nick shrugged. *I wasn't worried about that. When it comes to moving furniture, I was thinking I'd just get Eddie to wink at some college wrestlers.*

Lilith started kicking into the air again, covering her face and shaking her head. Then she gave Nick an affectionate push on the knee.

Nick nodded toward the back-bar lounge. *Shouldn't we be doing something about that?*

Lilith shook her head. *It isn't time.*

Why?

I really don't know, doll-face. It just isn't time to do anything yet. I'm keeping the forces inside that room from detecting us until I'm sure it's the right time to take action.

Nick nodded. *Well... okay, I guess.*

Lilith only grinned at him.

So, really, Lilith, where were you? We went to the booth to pick you up, but you were gone. I wanted to introduce you to my friends.

I was outside, fixing the Circle of Twelve.

Nick sat up straight, raised his eyebrows. *You're kidding.*

Lilith shrugged. *All right, I guess I wasn't 'fixing' it exactly. I was, um, 'altering' it a bit.*

Nick stared at her.

She rolled her eyes. *Fine. I was altering it so that it would actually be useful. I changed the icons so that they would contain demons. Any and all demons.*

Nick didn't understand. *But that means Scott too. And you! You and Scott won't be able to leave?*

Lilith nodded. *That's right. None of us are leaving until this whole mess gets worked out. This ends tonight.*

†

The bottle was already more than half empty when the chanting started again. He stopped drinking. Something was different.

He took a deep breath and looked around. He'd made sure that, when he went back into the main bar area, he stayed on the opposite side from where he'd left Michael. He didn't want to see Michael again. Well, not here anyway. Not... well, he hoped he'd see Michael again, someplace better.

He hoped there really was a Someplace Better. After all this bullshit, there'd better be.

He laughed.

He drank again from the almost half-empty bottle. Goodness, but he felt better. Not great, really, but better. His chest didn't hurt anymore and the brick that always seemed to be sitting in his gut had gone away.

Sure, there were tears just streaming down his face. Two wide open faucets, it seemed, were sending constant rivulets of tears down his cheeks to join into a steady drip from his chin. He couldn't stop them. He was leaking.

He laughed again.

There were two voices performing the chant now. He nodded. That was it. That's what was different. Two voices. One was the voice of The Wicked Cardinal of the West.

He pressed the back of his hand to his mouth, laughing, spitting warm Scotch over his wrist and fingers. It dripped down and mingled with the tears on his chin.

That was funny. The Wicked...

He stopped.

The other voice stopped his laughter. The other voice made his throat hitch. Scotch burned back up into his mouth.

He spit.

The other voice. The other voice.

Now, he thought he should find the enlightened one. Through him could be gained redemption itself. Tell him the word. Tell the enlightened one the word plucked from the language of God.

He drank again from his bottle, washing away the taste of Scotch and bile.

The brick was back in his gut.

†

Who's chanting in there? Nick gestured again toward the back-bar. *Do you know?*

Lilith nodded. *Yes, and I never could stand either one of them. Until now, they've both had the good sense to stay out of my way. At least for the past few hundred years or so.*

Nick scowled. *But, Scott said one of them is just a man...*

Resting one arm across Nick's knees, Lilith leaned onto him and made herself comfortable. *That's right, he is. Unfortunately, he's one of the last true witches in existence, what with bonding himself to Shehlá so that she'd keep him alive and young. He must have really pissed her off, though, because she sure hasn't been following through on the 'young' part of the deal. I think he's a bozo either way.*

Smiling broadly, Nick leaned his elbows back and relaxed a bit more himself. Sure, maybe they only had fifteen or twenty minutes before the whole city came storming back into the club on top of them, but how often would Nick have a biblical entity older than the city of Jericho resting across his knees as though she were his high school girlfriend? Sometimes, ya really had to quit sweatin' the small stuff and just laugh.

Nick almost did laugh, but managed to control himself.

Flipping her gorgeous hair over her shoulder, Lilith smiled at him. *What's so funny?*

Nick smiled back at her so hard his cheeks hurt. *Oh, golly, I dunno. Maybe the fact that I'm lounging here in the dark with someone who actually told the very first man on earth to go fuck himself.*

Oh! Lilith shook her head and stuck out her tongue. *Talk about bozos!*

Nick had to stifle another laugh. *You are too much!*

You know, doll-face, technically he wasn't anywhere near the very first man on earth, but that's just a whole other tree of figs.

So, who's the other chanting guy? The one helping the witch-dude?

Throwing her fingers in the air like she'd just touched something slimy, Lilith frowned and wrinkled her nose. *He's what you'd call an incubus. Just the smarmiest motherfucker this side of the Great Wall.*

Nick sneered. *Will he be a problem?*

Don't insult me, doll-face.

Nick suddenly sensed another presence getting very close to them. He stiffened, sitting up very straight.

Lilith yawned and patted him on the leg. *Relax, pretty boy. Don't ask me why, but it's very important that he stumble over here fairly soon.*

Can you tell who that is?

Funny you should ask. Um, I'd have to say 'yes' and 'no.'

Relaxing back onto the stairs, Nick frowned. *You lost me there.*

One problem with being so wrapped up in all of this is that my objectivity's been corrupted. Lilith sighed. *I sense things, but I can't really trust what I learn. All I know for sure is that the man tottering over here has no idea where he is anymore, he's so drunk. Oh, and one other very, very interesting detail, the yes and no thing, well… he has no name.*

Nick squinted down at her. *How can that be?*

She frowned, shrugged. *I dunno. But I'm really quite sure of it. The guy about to stagger around that corner has no name. He's no one.*

†

He'd been in this room before, hadn't he? Was that today? He had to get a grip on himself. He had to pluck the word from the enlightened one.

The chanting was moving him. The chanting. The chanting. Matine was chanting with …

The very doorway of redemption was plucked from the language of Scotch.

He'd not been very careful putting the bottle to his lips and now he also tasted blood. There'd been blood on Michael's forehead. It had said 'truth,' but he'd remembered the old legend and wiped off some of the blood. Then there was no more truth. Only death.

God was here, though. God was sweeping his mighty hand through the air and chatting it up about the seriyima.

Seriyima.

The chanting was getting louder. Matine was chanting loudly with a seriyim. It was the same seriyim that …

The pluck was from the word of the almighty redemption.

He very quickly tried to take another drink and this time broke his tooth.

†

Are you two having a good time? Without making a sound, Scott sat down next to Nick.

Looking back up the stairs, Nick saw Darren and the gang. He smiled up at them. Darren smiled back, crossing his arms and shaking his head. Karen grinned and gave Nick a little wave.

The reality of the situation settled back onto Nick. He took a deep breath. *Are they all okay, Scotty?*

Lilith suddenly stood and brushed off her skirt. *You two stay here. I'm just going to run up there, introduce myself, and get them someplace safe. The seal on the Vessel won't last much longer. It'll crack pretty soon.*

Listening for a moment, Nick thought the chanting was quickening a bit, perhaps with growing enthusiasm.

Scott nodded up at Lilith. *Thank you.*

His stomach doing a couple of flip-flops, Nick glanced up at Lilith too.

She gave him another motherly grin. *I'm not going far, doll-face. You have to stay here, though. You have to be here when what's-his-fuck finally hauls his loaded ass around the corner. I don't know why, but it's important.* She cocked her head and gazed upward. *I think it is, anyway.*

Nick steadied himself and nodded. *Don't be long, okay?*

Lilith stood there for a couple seconds. Then, *So, you trust me with your loves up there, enlightened one?*

Of course. Take care of my family for me, okay, good-lookin'?

Lilith pursed her lips and nodded, her lower lashes glistening a bit. *As though they were the very pupils of my eyes, beautiful one. I will protect them.*

†

Which way should he go? Back toward the room with the weird light, or upstairs?

He was not moving. Well, not walking, anyway. One hand gripped the neck of the bottle, the other pressed against the wall next to which he swayed like a metronome.

There wasn't much left in the bottle. It would be completely empty soon.

The chanting stopped.

Silence surrounded him for a long moment. He couldn't even hear the sound of his own breathing. Then, he heard the sound of shattering glass.

He had dropped the bottle.

†

"We're out of time," Nick whispered.

†

Sweat burst onto Karen's face. She cramped and doubled over, coughing. Vaguely, she could hear Darren saying something to her, but couldn't make out the words very well. Eddie was trying to help Theo, who'd fallen too. He was crouched near the wall where he was throwing up.

They'd been trying to get to the third floor VIP room, where Lilith said she could cast a spell to protect them. They didn't have to worry, Lilith had said. There were no powers at hand she couldn't easily overwhelm.

Although Karen couldn't make out anything that Darren was saying, she heard Lilith quite clearly.

"Il nā' lāh." Lilith's voice rang in Karen's ears. *I heal her*, Karen sensed.

"—feel sick?" Darren was saying. "I'm just going to lift you back to your feet, okay?"

Karen nodded. She felt fine all of a sudden, but let Darren help her up anyway.

Turning around, she saw that Theo was standing too. He was pressing his fingers to his temples, nodding at Eddie, who looked a little pale himself.

"I'm so sorry," Lilith said.

Karen turned to her. "It's not your fault."

"What happened?" Darren asked.

"They were much faster than I'd thought they'd be," Lilith said, biting her lip. "Karen and Theo felt the blow of the seal breaking open on the Vessel. Shehlá is released."

†

Nick heard the snake's hissing breath, as well as the familiar sound of a painter's tarp being dragged across the floor. Before that, though, he smelled her.

Shehlá's voice echoed through the club. "This had better mean you have what I require."

"Of course." It was the voice of the man.

"Whisper it."

Hearing this, Scott stood. When he glanced back at Nick, Nick thought Scott looked worried.

Nick shook his head. Boy, that was just a wonderful sign. Scott looked worried. Fuck it all, what had they just gotten themselves into?

"Now write it down." Shehlá's voice rang out. "Not there, dolt! There!"

His heart hammering, Nick got up and stood next to Scott.

"Because you left the door open, moron!" Shehlá's voice rang out to them. "Was it your intention that they overhear everything?"

Nick heard the man's voice again, but he must have been mumbling; not a single word was discernable outside of the VIP room.

"No!" Shehlá screeched. "They're here!" She was silent a moment, then, "They've been concealed from you beneath a mask set in place by Lilith. Marbas himself sits with the enlightened one just outside."

Scott walked toward the dance floor. Nick followed him. Staying out of sight probably wasn't an issue any longer. Though, hopefully, they weren't jumping the gun. Nick didn't think so. He had a very solid feeling that the proper time to act, for which Lilith had been waiting, came the instant the lamia popped back out of the brass jar.

They passed the boundary of their visual concealment and walked onto the hardwood dance floor. Jeez, but it looked enormous when it was empty, like a polished, mahogany soccer field.

Scott stopped and faced toward the back-bar lounge. Nick stood just behind him.

They waited in utter silence for nearly two full minutes, which seemed to stretch out like days. Nick was just wondering to himself what kind of score walking over and going into the VIP room would get on the Stupid Meter, when the lamia appeared in the open doorway.

She'd made no attempt to conceal her demonic form. Rising up briefly, Shehlá swept the room with her eyes. Instantly spotting Nick and Scott, she smiled, and then dove toward the floor. Her sleek body, all seventy or so feet of it, slid between the many cocktail tables, slithering with frightening speed, like leather lightning.

Nick couldn't help gasping and taking a step back. Though, he promised himself it would be his only retreat. At this point, any thought of escape was, of course, absurd.

Reaching the dance floor, the snake demon rose up again, much higher this time, at least ten feet or more, coiling a mass of her tail beneath her in a mound of writhing, incandescent loops. Nick remembered the metallic-looking brown and green color of the creature's scales from the encounter at the house party, but under the club's still-dancing illumination, she glittered like a kaleidoscopic anaconda.

"You don't even look surprised, Marbas," she said. "You're no fun at all."

A very well-dressed, older gentleman appeared in the doorway next. He strolled casually around a few cocktail tables, but stopped well before he left the back-bar lounge itself, staking out a position next to the bar. He carried a suitcase with him. Placing it upon the bar, he opened it.

The older gentleman was followed by a strikingly good-looking, young man. It was the other demon, Nick sensed. He was wearing a highly fashionable ensemble, which was clownishly too big for him. The shape of his body was utterly lost in the folds and billows of his outfit.

The demon-guy stopped in the doorway, grasped his pant legs, one in each hand, pulled them up to flood level, then walked rapidly between the tables. He stopped near the edge of the dance floor. Nick thought the guy might have kept coming, maybe even choosing to face them while standing right next to the lamia, but a fair length of her tail continued to whip around, resting for just a second in a single spot before slapping toward another. The lamia's tail occasionally took out a chair or two, some barstools, and once even cast an entire cocktail table into the wall. The demon-guy wisely chose to remain where he could see it.

Scott and Nick faced them. So, Nick thought, maybe this was how Wyatt Earp had felt. He was trying to relax himself. It wasn't working.

"You're not honoring our agreement, Shehlá," Scott said. "Your mistress won't like that very much."

"No, she won't," said a stern, velvety voice from behind Nick. He turned to see Lilith striding angrily onto the dance floor. She winked at him as she took up a place next to Scott.

The lamia raised herself higher. Now, her head was at the same level it would have been were she standing on the second-floor catwalk in her human form.

"Things have changed," Shehlá said. There was not a hint of trepidation in her tone. Nick sensed a clear intention: Shehlá knew something.

"Be careful, you two," he said. "She's hiding an ace somewhere."

The lamia smiled down at him. "It appears, Nancy Boy, that you've been touched by Lilith, as well as enlightened by the fallen one. My, what a prize you've become."

Lilith turned around and faced Nick. "Sorry, doll-face," she said, "but like I just told your friends upstairs, this is for your own protection."

Before he could even raise his eyebrows in surprise, Lilith produced a small, black sphere—it looked to Nick like a tiny marble—and lobbed it at him. It would have struck him clean on the center of his chest, but when it came within a foot or two, it burst in a mini-explosion of white-blue light.

Nick heard a sort of *Whomp!* sound as the air around him rippled with energy. He felt dizzy for a very brief moment, then glanced down and noticed he'd drifted about a foot and a half off of the floor. He was floating, suspended above the spot on which he'd been standing just a second earlier.

"What did you do?" he squealed.

"Relax." Lilith turned back around and faced Shehlá, though she still spoke to Nick. "You'll be fine. Nothing can touch you for a few minutes. Not bullets, not magic. You're Superman, kiddo, enjoy it."

Scott turned his head to Lilith, smirking. "How in the name of the Almighty did you get your hands on gremlin eggs?"

"Don't insult me, Marbas."

Abruptly, Lilith stepped forward. She raised her right arm, pressing her fingers and thumb tightly together as though she were working a sock puppet. Pointing her fingers at Shehlá, she popped them open and, as she did, the air before her rippled violently. A circular wave of clear energy tore across the dance floor.

It struck the lamia first. The creature shrieked and flew backward, slamming its head on the second floor railing. Her coiled body, lifted in its entirety, was buffeted by the blow as well, wildly flipping over itself, curling and snapping as though the giant snake was no more than a strand of pasta.

The wave of force knocked the good-looking demon-guy in the way-oversized suit right out of his shoes, sending him flying backward, and slamming him into the back wall of the lounge. He thudded noisily off the painted plaster, then fell face first onto the floor.

The older man had tried to duck. He was on the ground when the wave hit him. It slid his body back across the floor, mangling him painfully within the legs of several chairs.

It appeared Lilith's blow was only intended to toss about animated objects. Nothing without its own pulse, not even a cocktail napkin, had been moved by it.

Dazed and tottering, the bulk of her serpent body strewn haphazardly all over the lounge, Shehlá appeared to be struggling to keep the human-ish portion of herself vertical. She failed.

In a slow, agonizing arch, Shehlá fell, her arms spread, her thick, serpentine body whistling through the air. It was a good two seconds between the time Nick realized she was coming down to the time he turned his eyes away, not particularly interested in witnessing the snake-skin covered skull shattering on the dance floor in front of them like a porcelain globe.

He might not have seen the impact, but he heard it. Nick didn't think it sounded like a head bursting open, not that he was familiar with such sounds. No, he thought instead that it sounded like a bowling ball had been dropped onto the dance floor from the B-crowd booths. Puzzled more than anything else, he turned and looked.

Shehlá's head had landed mere inches away from Lilith's feet. Amazingly, it was still perfectly intact, at least what Nick could initially see. The dance floor, however, now sported a crater the size of a fruit basket. The lamia lay facedown in the crater, her body stretching back across the floor in a straight line like a downed telephone pole with scales.

Nick was about to call out to Lilith when Shehlá raised her head, right out of the dance floor crater. Her face appeared to be completely unhurt. It should have been flattened beyond recognition, but the bitch's makeup wasn't even smeared.

The smile on the lamia's lips made Nick sick to his stomach. Never mind her stench. Just seeing her whip her head out of that hole in the floor, grinning up at Lilith, peering at her with an expression of complete triumph, Nick wanted to vomit on the spot.

Then, Shehlá began to laugh. The sound was wet and guttural, like an old, old man, watching the orderly who'd just called him 'Gramps' slip and fall on his ass.

Nick sensed fear. Although it was mild and somehow unfamiliar, the feeling was clear enough to recognize. It washed over him like ice water. Then, Nick realized it was not his own fear that he'd felt. It was Lilith's.

Shehlá spoke. "Elit donc, Beylèhya!"

With a piercing shriek, Lilith flew backward faster than a cannonball, her body tearing right through two wooden support beams separating the dance floor area from the main bar without even slowing down. Nick heard a final explosion of splintering wood and shattering plaster, and then nothing. Lilith had been propelled right out of his line of sight, if not the building itself.

Just about then, Nick made a tentative deduction as to why Shehlá had not been harmed by Lilith's power, as well as why the mother of all terrestrial demons herself had succumbed to the lamia's words. Tentative, because the deduction scared the living fuck out of him.

Just after she was released from the Vessel, the man had given Shehlá exactly what she 'required,' the final bit of leverage she still lacked while she'd been in Scott's basement and seemingly helpless.

Whoever the older man was, he'd given the lamia Lilith's name. *Beylèhya*. Lilith's true name. The name intended to be known only to her and the Divine. Her name of power.

What Nick could not sense, however, was how that man had learned it.

†

Twice the creature had called out in reference to the boy who'd been standing with the skotos labeling him as the enlightened one. The boy was also 'touched by Lilith,' whatever that meant.

There was nothing left to do. The time was now. Everything came to this. No more big picture. The imminent was everything.

Leaving his hiding place, he slowly walked toward the dance floor. He would do what Michael had asked of him. There was nothing else.

†

"You have all you require, Mistress," the older man said. He'd picked himself up and limped out toward her. Blood poured down his face from a terrible wound just above his hairline. "I acquired the name of the Fount, as you wanted. And this creature," he gestured toward Scott, "was named for you long ago."

The demon serpent, still slithering in a great, sweeping circle around the floor, pulled the rest of herself out from between the tables and chairs, bringing her extensive body into the open. During it all, she retained firm eye contact with Scott.

"Yes," she hissed. "I've known his name for centuries."

"We are reconciled, then," said the older man. "He's been reclaimed."

"He has."

"Then, you may restore me, may you not?"

Still without looking away from Scott, Shehlá gave voice to another spell. "Cehs ahs mohevēh, il nā' loh."

Nick glanced over at the older man, only he wasn't older anymore. The wound on his head was gone, but that was the least dramatic change. Standing in the gentleman's now slightly oversized suit, was a fair-skinned boy of about twenty-five. Where the man had course, gray curls of hair, the boy's was so blonde it was nearly white. Even his eyebrows were white, sitting below loops of soft, pallid curls, like a crown of cotton.

"Hello, Daniel," said Scott.

†

"Are any of you getting any closer to the floor?" Theo asked. "I think I'm getting higher."

The four of them were floating together in one of the second floor common areas. Every wall in the room was nearly covered with mirrors. It was sparsely furnished with carpet-covered boxes and platforms; not a very interesting feature of the club, to be sure. Simply a place for fatigued party-kids to gather, chat, and cool down.

"Did she think we'd get in the way or something?" Darren shook his head.

"I don't think so at all," Karen said. "She honestly thought she'd be able to handle everything very, very easily, so she just popped us up and out of harm's way."

"This is kind of cool, though," Eddie said, swinging his feet through the air. "I wonder if we could get our own gremlin eggs. Do you think gremlins have, like, nests, or something?"

"I don't think they're real eggs," Theo said. "They're seeds, I think, poppy seeds or something. They've been rolled up with some other stuff, you know, rare, like, weird ingredient type stuff, like witchcraft stuff, right? So, they're not really eggs. They're just little balls of weird witch stuff that's been enchanted by magic."

"Thelma?" Darren said.

"Yeah, babe?"

"When this is all over, you and I are going to take that new soothsayer talent of yours and do some serious damage on the game show circuit."

†

"How long did it take, Daniel?" Scott asked. "How long before you betrayed me, not to mention the Church, which you'd sworn to serve?"

"You don't know me, demon," Daniel whispered. "We talked together once. Once, in the belly of a hot, dusty cave nearly eight hundred years ago. Together, we tried to hide from the inevitable, but that's all. You don't know me."

"But I did know you. You offered me your hand. I touched the skin of your palm and knew you far better than you imagine. I knew you far outside of one afternoon in a desert cave."

"My life before that day is one thing. I couldn't have foreseen the consequences of what we did any better than you."

"There was no need for either of us to look at the future. Your heart was clean."

"Yeah." Daniel nodded, chuckling bitterly. "And I was left alone with it. Left alone with my clean heart and the Vessel. I was alone, because I was tending an item that only I knew had any legitimate value. What difference does it make how many years passed while I gazed at it, knowing what immense power it contained, unable to prove anything to anyone else? I would always be that marvel's only witness."

"Daniel, you had a leader—"

"What?" He squinted at Scott, frowning sarcastically. "My 'leader?' His Holiness?" Daniel shook his head. "Oh, no, no. That's a road you don't want to take. Yes, you are correct, Urban left you and your prison in my care. However, not because he genuinely believed, but 'just in case.' "

"What were you—?"

"Don't you understand?" Daniel screamed. "You slept! I was forgotten and you slept! The sun rose without you, demon! You hid yourself away from the world while the Vessel became little more than a target for increasing ridicule. As did I."

"I see." Scott nodded, lowering his eyes to the floor. Nick thought he'd never seen him so wounded. "I made yet another mistake it seems. You're right. I couldn't have foreseen the consequences. I failed you."

Daniel glanced away, sighing.

Scott looked up. "And so you became a witch?"

"I only studied the craft, I didn't practice it," Daniel explained, turning back to Scott. "I was looking for a means by which I could reveal the true nature of the Vessel without disturbing you. I found none."

"No. Instead—"

"Instead, I found Shehlá!"

Scott winced.

"She was there!" Daniel pointed at the demon serpent, who tilted her head and grinned complacently. "She came to me while you slept!"

"And offered you youth? Acknowledgement? Contentment?"

"I was aging," Daniel whispered, turning his hands over in what looked to Nick like a plea. "I could see nothing before me but misery. You were sealed away from time itself. You were sealed away, sleeping, while I faced years filled with nothing but dejection and obscurity."

Scott closed his eyes and sighed. "And you believed her?" He shook his head sadly, looked up at Daniel, distinct pain in his expression. "You believed Shehlá when she said she had the power to change that?"

"I didn't have much to lose."

"Wasn't it also Shehlá who, as punishment, allowed you to resume aging when I was released and then lost?"

"I..." Daniel shook his head, squeezing his eyes shut. "I released you, and you were gone so quickly. I stumbled. I was supposed to—"

"Daniel!" Shehlá snapped. "Don't bore Marbas with the details of your weakness. He doesn't care."

Shaking his head in disbelief, Scott squinted at him. "Daniel, you must know what you've done! You serve Shehlá in return for youth?"

"Oh, demon," Daniel sighed, "you have to know that, now, I am so much more than merely young."

"In exchange for which you've allowed her unchecked claim over the power of your soul."

"As well as assistance with her own ambitions, yes."

"You're talking about harvesting other souls, Daniel, innocent souls. You're talking about Shehlá's 'ambition' to harvest human souls. You would actually assist her in such a betrayal of the Almighty?"

"She has already amassed redoubtable power."

"Enough to reach her end? Enough to destroy Lilith and take up her name? Enough to become the Fount herself?"

"You know nothing!"

"And so I am asking you!" Scott's eyes flashed. "Why have you stood with her? When did power become such a prize to you?"

"You can't judge me! You abandoned me!" As his voice broke, nearing sobs, Daniel leveled an accusing finger at Scott. "You left, just shut your eyes and went to sleep, leaving me to carry you back over the desert and face a lifetime alone! That's a long time to have expected me to endure when the only acknowledgement I was to receive was laughter!"

Still slithering around the dance floor, Shehlá rose up and smiled. "You're going back into the Vessel, Marbas. You've done what we intended you to do."

"She showed me power!" Daniel ranted on, spittle flying from his lips. "Power I soon discovered was feeble compared to what was possible! Shehlá knew how to attain real power, though. Through you. It took us centuries to attain what we needed." He forced a weak smile, wiping at his chin. "It took us centuries, but we have it now. We have it! Through you!"

Scott sighed. "You offered me the sanctuary, Daniel."

"You begged me for it!"

"And what would have been different if I'd stayed with you? Would you have loved me?"

"You don't know me, demon!"

"Had I stayed at your side, would you have quietly allowed the time to pass? Would knowing me have slowed the seasons? Would you have been so content?"

"You don't know me!"

"Or would you have eventually sought *my* power? Would you have panicked at the passing years and sought anyway that for which you've become so willing to trade your own soul?"

"What I have traded was mine to do with as I wish!"

"Liar!" A very familiar, male voice shouted.

Nick looked behind him in time to see Armani Suit Guy — Robert, he corrected himself — stumbling onto the dance floor. He looked like shit. Really, the guy looked like he'd been beaten up and then run over by a bus. Twice.

There was blood trickling out of Robert's mouth, over his swollen bottom lip, and down his chin. His clothes were saturated from his collar to his pant cuffs. Plus, he was obviously drunk out of his mind.

Nick squinted at him. With his regular, mortal eyes, Nick could see that the guy was Robert, the bishop-dude. With his new, enlightened sense, though, Nick didn't recognize him at all. He was a total stranger. This was the man Lilith said had no name. He did have a name, though. It was Robert... Robert Somethinger Something Something.

"Robert?" Daniel squinted at him too. "Is that you? What happened...? I can't..."

"Daniel," Shehlá said, slithering to the opposite side of the dance floor, away from the man she couldn't identify, "who is that?"

"You are a liar!" Robert screamed. He took a step toward Daniel, shaking his finger at him. "You've sacrificed more souls than just your own! You are a hypocrite!"

"What is he?" Shehlá swept back and forth, her human torso sliding through the air like a kite on a string.

"You know him!" Daniel barked back at her.

"No! He is strange to me!" The demon snake rose higher, shaking her head. "I am blind where he stands!"

Daniel paused, squinting toward Robert again. "Yes," he said slowly, nodding. "I don't understand it, but his soul is somehow nameless."

An angry moan rose from the lounge behind them. Even Shehlá turned and glanced back toward the far wall. There was another frustrated grunt.

A cocktail table popped up and out from the wall, crashing down again noisily a few feet away. The good-looking demon-guy stood up.

"Is she gone?" he asked.

"Brathwidth, come here," Daniel said, watching Robert, but waving back to the demon. "Tell me if you recognize this man."

At the sound of Brathwidth's name, Nick watched Robert take two steps backward. He heard him groan.

Scott stepped forward, turning his eyes onto Brathwidth. "Stay where you are, worm."

"Why are you still here, Marbas?" Shehlá said. "You should be back inside the Vessel. Must I cast the spell?"

Scott lowered his head and growled. It was an animal's growl, a livid warning from the giant, demon lion.

In the next instant, enormous, black wings burst from Scott's back, each one stretching to its full length, nearly reaching the walls. Scott leaned forward and stomped his left foot onto the floor. Nick sensed a surge of energy rushing across the wood.

As if to bolster the punch, Scott flapped his dragon's wings in one, immense and sweeping movement. The air in front of him undulated, rolling toward Shehlá like a tide.

Even as Scott was casting his strength at her in a magnificent sweep of his massive wings, Shehlá dipped through the air, the end of her tail whipping behind her, and splayed out the fingers of both her hands, throwing her arms out into wide, opposing circles.

Scott's power met Shehlá's. Thin streaks of fire flashed over the dance floor in vertical spires, blazing nearly white-hot in seemingly random spots before becoming dark, gray and black tubes of smoke. The collision of energy lasted just a second or two, but it was clear Scott's attack had been diffused.

"I'm so glad you chose to do this the hard way, Marbas," Shehlá said. "You might prove to be some fun after all."

Another animal-sounding growl echoed through the room. Nick

couldn't tell from where the sound was coming, but he knew it hadn't come from Scott.

Folding his wings behind him, Scott took a deep breath, shaking his head as though to clear it. Nick saw Scott's wavy hair twist and pulse, growing an inch or two longer as he watched.

The demon guy—Brathwidth—had ventured out of the lounge a bit. "I don't recognize that man, Daniel," he said. "Why would—?"

"Don't look at him that way." Daniel shook his head. "Look at him with your eyes."

Brathwidth glared. "I was looking with my eyes. I like to observe things. I looked at..." He stopped, his jaw dropping slowly, even as a smile bloomed on his lips.

"Yes." Daniel sighed. "You remember."

"You were on the island," Brathwidth said. "You were my storyteller. I allowed you to live so that my work might be known."

Robert was swaying on his feet. It was not at all subtle. Nick thought the poor, drunk bastard was just seconds away from falling down. Robert only stared back at Brathwidth, not speaking, blood and drool spilling over his chin. His breathing was loud and labored.

"Yes, yes," Brathwidth said, smiling, holding out his hand, palm up, as though he was giving a presentation. "I allowed two of you to leave the island. Your companion went insane, though, didn't he? I was quite sure he would snap very quickly. I was correct, wasn't I?"

"Your... your 'storyteller?' " Robert stammered.

"Frankly," Brathwidth said, "I'd fully expected that you would lose your mind as well. Although my guess had been it wouldn't happen so suddenly as to prevent you from creating a little buzz for me, getting me some credentials. It's one of the games I play, you see. I love to hear the stories about myself. Call it narcissism, but I love to hear the form the myths eventually take, to hear the stories as they ultimately settle. I watch the details as they weave themselves into various works of fiction. Nowadays, I get to watch events that I set into motion as they blossom within the theater and cinema too. Maybe these are rather tedious distractions; such novelties are trite, I know, but they do pass the time."

"Pass the..." Robert staggered backward.

Brathwidth began to laugh. "I'm sorry," he chuckled. "But... well, look at you! It really is rather funny."

Robert staggered again, backward then sideways, toward the west wall. He was shaking his head, squinting back at Brathwidth as the demon made a feeble attempt to conceal his mirth.

"This is very discourteous of me, I'm sure," Brathwidth said. "It's just so rare that I'm served such a treat like this. It's utterly fascinating! Don't you understand? Your very soul has lost its face! I've never encountered such a thing."

"Are you hearing this, enlightened one?" Robert said, keeping his eyes on Brathwidth. "Do you see now what kind of creature you've been skipping around with?"

Nick didn't answer. Brathwidth laughed even harder. Shehlá kept back a bit, watching silently, a contented smirk on her face. Daniel gazed at the floor.

"Do you hear this, enlightened one?" Robert asked again.

"Scott's not like that." Nick shook his head.

Robert turned toward Scott, gesturing angrily, palms up. "Look at him! He is seriyima!"

At the sound of that word, Shehlá stopped sweeping across the floor. Scott turned his face away from Brathwidth. He stared at Robert, his mouth slightly open.

"He's what?" Nick raised his eyebrows.

"Seriyima," Robert repeated. "It's the language of God, you know. His name for them, the evil ones. Seriyima."

CHAPTER X

†

Demon Blood

The joy of our heart is ceased; our dance is turned into mourning.

- Lamentations 5:15 (KJV)

†

"I'm coming down," Theo said.

"Me too." Eddie was still swinging his feet, but now they were just an inch or two above the floor.

"It's wearing off, I guess," Darren observed. "Okay, whoever hits the carpet first needs to jet downstairs and find out what the heck is going on."

†

"Destroy him!" Shehlá screamed, pointing at Robert while at the same time rising higher and slithering away.

Immediately, Daniel turned around, quickly retreating toward the back-bar. Robert lumbered after him. As he did, Brathwidth bent down and screamed. Nick knew what he was doing, as he'd once been the target of another demon's incinerating breath.

Ripples in the air shot over the dance floor. A streak of blackened hardwood ran beneath it as the heat of Brathwidth's blast raced to cremate Robert.

"Scott!" Nick yelled.

Before the word was out of Nick's mouth, one giant, black wing had snapped open between Brathwidth and Robert, shielding him from the blast. In the next instant, Scott swept his wing toward the opposite wall. The heat was blown back at Brathwidth instead, knocking him through the air—it was apparently this guy's day to be tossed around like a football. Brathwidth sailed backward, caught in the wave of his own power. His oversized ensemble burst into a roaring blaze.

As Nick watched, Scott continued to change. His clothing tore away from him in flashes of white-blue light, replaced by heavy, jet-black fur.

A raging, guttural growl echoed through the room. Nick looked up, thinking it was coming from Shehlá, but the serpent demon was also scanning around. She didn't know where the sound was coming from either.

A blinding flash of white-blue light brought Nick's attention back to the dance floor. Now, though, Marbas the Black stood where Scott had been.

†

He could see that the suitcase was already opened. The cardinal had set it on the bar earlier, separating its contents into neat stacks; easier to snatch up and put to use.

The man the skotos had called Daniel was running straight to it. When he got to the bar he didn't stop to catch his breath—a young, healthy kid like that wouldn't be winded by such a short sprint. Instead, he quickly grabbed one of the old, wooden boxes containing an athame.

It was while Daniel was fumbling with the box's latch that he reached him, wrapping his arms around from behind, closing his hands tightly over Daniel's wrists. He pulled Daniel's hands apart so that he couldn't open the latch, but merely hold the box with his left hand.

Daniel fought him, trying to pull his right hand close enough to flip the tiny metal latch and draw out the athame.

"You are a liar and a blasphemer," he said to Daniel, his face right next to the kid's ear, fighting to keep the now-younger man's hands apart. It wasn't too difficult. Daniel might be younger, but he was also shorter and thinner. "Your own soul wasn't the only one you've sacrificed! How many souls have you bound away from Heaven? How many? I know Michael's wasn't the first."

†

Marbas issued a low growl, then he spoke, his voice rumbling like a rolling bass drum. "Nahš chē 'bn, rūah ištēn chē 'bn."

While he spoke, he moved his right paw in a slow circle, repeating the phrase again and again in a steady, rhythmic chant.

Shehlá screamed, staring suddenly at the floor and clawing at the air as though she were in terrible pain.

Nick looked down and saw that the coils of the serpent were changing color, beginning where its skin touched the wood and progressing gradually upward. The snake was changing from brown-green to a dark gray. The dark gray portion stopped moving.

Marbas was turning Shehlá to stone.

Shehlá gritted her teeth, grunted loudly. After a very brief moment, she took a deep breath, pressing her hands slowly downward through the air in a controlled fury.

She began her own chant. "Haus cēsh tres, evah cēsh natāya!"

Nick watched as the air around Shehlá's coiled body rippled and swelled as if she was out of focus. Again, spirals of white-blue fire snapped in random spots above the floor, becoming cylinders of smoke.

Behind him, Nick heard a squealing kind of grunt. He turned his head. Writhing on the floor in the front bar area where he'd been thrown, Brathwidth ripped at his burning clothes. Nick saw that the incubus was nearly consumed by flame, but was managing to tear giant pieces of material off of himself and hurl them away. The torn clothing flew in blazing chunks, deeper inside the front bar area and out of sight. Nick knew the walls in that room were covered with plush, hanging drapes. They'd ignite instantly.

Nick couldn't see the actual fire or feel any heat, but the flickering light that came from around the corner became intense very quickly. The alarm began to scream and the sprinkler system snapped on, but the firelight did not diminish.

Lilith had told Nick he'd be protected from bullets and magic. He sensed he'd be protected from fire too, but Nick wondered if the gremlin egg's magic would wear off before the fire reached him. His fear was that it would wear off afterward.

†

He watched as Daniel flipped open the box's latch with the thumb of his left hand. The lid flew open as they struggled, and the sparkling, silver athame fell out, thudding loudly onto the lounge's thin carpet.

While he was trying to see where it landed, still holding Daniel's arms tightly, the fire alarm went off and the overhead sprinklers snapped on, startling him. Daniel's right elbow slammed backward, knocking him sharply in the ribs. The force of the blow winded him only slightly, but it was enough for Daniel to tear his right hand loose and bend down toward the knife.

Adrenaline flooded through him, overpowering his confusion and anger, not to mention nearly three quarters of a bottle of Scotch. He shoved Daniel, and the kid went over like a bowling pin. The athame lay between them, glittering in the disco light. He bent to grab it while Daniel scrambled to get up again.

Before he could reach the knife, Daniel raised his arm toward him. "Noh a'k tē!"

The handle of the athame turned toward Daniel. It slid a few inches, then flew into his outstretched hand.

"I'm sorry you had to learn all of this, Robert," Daniel said, standing up, holding the witch blade's handle in his left hand. "You were just supposed to find him. That's all."

"Bullshit."

Daniel grinned. "I've never heard you speak that way. You've really let this place get to you, my son."

"Shehlá was supposed to kill both of us, wasn't she? She was supposed to prepare Michael and me both before you arrived, so that we could be called back from the dead."

"Well," Daniel shrugged, "it's the only chance there is to discover a demon's true name. We searched, believe me, but it's the only means we ever found. Sometimes a name of power may be revealed from the lips of the dead."

"God forgive you, Nigel. What did you think you were doing with your life? With mine?"

"Please don't call me Nigel anymore."

"You've only been masquerading as a man of God for all these centuries. All this time. Do you really think it will never end? Do you really think that you'll never have to face the Beast?"

"You're an idiot!" Daniel snapped. "I was only the Vessel's first custodian. I left the Church. I enjoyed my skills, living as many men, under many names. Only after I learned how to use the power of the skotos did I come back, to be the Vessel's last custodian."

"You still know those things that are truly eternal. It is that which is of Him, and Him alone."

"We'll see."

"You are flawed!" he screamed. "As are all of us! You couldn't even truly bind your demon!"

"Shut up, Robert!" Daniel bawled. "You don't know anything! If there's one epiphany I ever heard come out of you, it's that you are truly missing the big picture!"

"Maybe that's true," he nodded. "Maybe it's my folly, my sin."

"Oh, enough with the sin crap already!"

"But I know you tried to use the skotos without telling Shehlá! That's how he got away from you, wasn't it? That's why she punished you! You might look young, but you're just as frail as any mortal. Shehlá's punishment will not be your last!"

Daniel lunged at him, but the kid was either way too slow or not at all used to his new body. Even schnocked out of his gourd, he was able to step aside, catching Daniel's wrist again, pushing it and the knife safely away.

Daniel turned. With both hands he fought to push the blade away from himself and back toward his target.

"You must yield, Robert," Daniel huffed, straining to press the athame forward. "You cannot kill me. It is His law."

"You can't tell me what to do anymore. You don't command me."

"But He does! Yield and I will make it quick. Yield and I promise not to bind your soul."

He held Daniel's wrists firmly. The boy had very little strength and would not be able to overcome him. Holding the kid's wrists steady, he quickly moved his right hand, covering Daniel's fingers with his own.

Daniel's eyes bulged. "You cannot kill!"

One quick thrust and he had the athame's blade pointing in the opposite direction, toward Daniel.

"Robert!"

" 'Suffer not a witch to live.' "

A single, final thrust, and the athame's blade was buried in Daniel's throat.

†

Another animal growl rumbled through the club, but it didn't come from Marbas. He was still chanting loudly. Although his rhythm didn't falter and he continued to move his paw in a repeating circle, the collision of his power with Shehlá's was becoming more severe. Tiny tubes of flame flashed more often and then sizzled out in the mist from the sprinklers overhead.

From behind Nick, Brathwidth issued a high shriek, which rose to a deafening pitch. Nick turned again, and screamed himself.

The burning clothes had all been torn away. Shreds of smoldering cloth lay everywhere. Brathwidth was standing in their midst. Along with his oversized outfit, though, Brathwidth had also been forced to shed his human form.

His face was the same, with the exception of a fresh burn, blistering horribly across his cheek and under his chin. Rising just above Brathwidth's hairline were two jet-black horns. Nearly straight, only curving very slightly backward, they were at least seven or eight inches long, very thick at their bases and each tapering to a deadly point. Unlike Gillulim's cracked and bark-like horns, Brathwidth's looked heavy, solid, and smooth as polished onyx.

Brathwidth had the face and torso of a man, but his hands ended in incredibly long, curving claws. This demon, Nick saw, also had a feature that was strikingly similar to Scott. Below his waist Brathwidth was completely feline, covered entirely with black fur. Because of the similarity to Marbas, Nick thought at first that Brathwidth was half lion, but his long, waving tail was more like that of a panther.

The most vivid distinction from Marbas, of course: Brathwidth was wingless.

Shrieking again, Brathwidth stepped back onto the dance floor. His chest and back were very badly burned, as well as the left side of his hip. Blood poured from wounds on his torso, dripping over still-smoldering fur between his waist and knee. Tottering on his panther's legs, he limped a few steps, then fell forward, his clawed hands digging into the wood of the dance floor. He tried to push himself upright, to stand on his panther legs, but the burns he suffered along his side aggravated the awkwardness of his feline limbs, forcing him down onto all fours. Nick could tell the position irritated him. Brathwidth hated succumbing to his true form.

The demon grunted loudly and shook his head. The wounds on his back appeared to be very harsh, bleeding and blistering in a wide area across his shoulders and down his side.

Brathwidth looked up once, watched the battle between Marbas and Shehlá for just an instant, then turned his attention to Nick.

†

Ding dong, the witch is dead.

He couldn't help cackling at the joke, but by the time he put the back of his hand to his lips, trying to stifle his laughter, it had already become sobs.

He howled with grief, doubling over, wracked with horrid, painful bursts. They shook him, knocking the air from his lungs.

One on top of the other, the sobs came, and he quaked as from enormous hiccups. He sobbed for Michael, for Larry, for everyone he'd known and loved whose lives had been destroyed by Matine's ancient deception. He cried for his lost faith. He cried for his lost name.

The adrenaline in his system began to abate, along with his lucidity. His head throbbed. Even so, he knew a wonderful and soothing void was waiting. He had but to lie down and allow it to swallow him.

He couldn't, though. Not yet. There was one more thing. One more thing he needed to do before he could rest.

One more thing.

†

Brathwidth smiled at Nick.

If he hadn't been exposed to Gillulim, prepared for the horrors of the earth by the stench of that corpse-gray imp as he bound Nick to him with his demon's claws, the sight of Brathwidth's smile would certainly have driven Nick very close to crazy. No more man's square and rational teeth; the smile of the incubus was a show of impossible fangs, glistening ivory razors. Had Nick been subject to the demon's stare much longer, one could likely have predicted a good deal of Thorazine in his future. However, a sharp, cracking sound startled them, Nick and Brathwidth both.

Looking past Marbas, Nick could see that Shehlá had won. She was not turned to stone. Beneath her, the mahogany floor had split in several places, either from her weight before she'd been able to conjure herself back into flesh, or from the collision of her power with that of Marbas, or a combination of both. Whatever it was, the dance floor had been shredded. Not that it made much difference. Karen was going to have a lot of explaining to do anyway, seeing as how the place was burning down and all.

Nick glanced behind him. The fire hadn't left the main bar area; the sprinklers were doing some good at least. Judging from the still flickering light, though, the fire was far from going out.

Marbas must have been exhausted. Nick could hear him panting and it broke his heart.

"Scott?" he said, turning away from Brathwidth and the fire.

"You have to cast the spell, Nick." The winged lion didn't look at him as he spoke. "I cannot stop her, and she knows my name."

"Oh, Scotty, no." Nick's throat closed as he shook his head.

Slithering toward them, Shehlá swept her arm in the direction of the DJ booth. With that, Marbas was lifted into the air, thrown nearly twenty-five feet, and battered against the low-hanging platform. He growled once, then fell to the floor, his legs crumbling, his jaw slamming down with a sickening thump. His eyes were closed.

Shehlá turned to Nick. "Speak even one word of magic, Nancy Boy, and I will cast him into the Vessel."

"Shit-load of good that'll do you, bitch!" Nick screamed. "Get away from him!"

"Oh!" Shehlá cocked her head, slithering slowly across the floor toward Nick. "Do not take what I say for nothing, enlightened one. I hold the true name of Marbas the Black."

Brathwidth began to chuckle.

"You still need a mortal voice." Nick could hardly speak. The stench of the serpent made him cough and gag as she came closer. "You need a mortal voice to use him."

Shehlá stopped. She squinted her eyes and appeared to be listening. Nick knew she was trying to locate her newly restored witch, Daniel.

Another animal growl, loud and terrible, rumbled through the room. Hearing it, the serpent-demon rose up. From her high vantage, probably thirty feet or so in the air, she swept the room with her eyes.

"It will be easy enough to reveal you, Lilith!" she said, raising her arms and closing her eyes. "Tet'ka donc, Beylèhya!"

"Tsk, tsk, tsk." The voice came from the second floor landing, in front of the B-crowd booths, just behind Shehlá's head. "That was a mistake."

Nick saw the arm that reached out of the darkness clearly enough. Huge, with a defined musculature, it moved with classic femininity, even though its fingers ended in claws as sharp and black as Brathwidth's horns.

The clawed hand found the top of Shehlá's head in an instant, talon-nails ripping into the serpent-demon's eyes, as well as the sides and back of her head.

Shehlá didn't even have time to scream. The giant hand snapped her head backward and her mouth open. A second arm appeared just as quickly as the first and, with the black claws jetting from its thumb and index finger, it tore the tongue from Shehlá's mouth as deftly as though it were shucking an oyster. The entire process took only about two seconds. Although the muscled arms were nearly twice as long as any normal arms, pretty or not, that Nick had ever seen, and its demon-fingers clicked and snapped their dagger nails, every movement was sleek and graceful; the practiced, swimming gestures of a prima ballerina.

Blind and tongue-less, Shehlá shrieked. As she did, the arms that had disabled her disappeared back into the shadows.

†

It was God's will, of course. He watched as the lamia bellowed, slithering aimlessly around the room, blood pouring down her face and torso.

Across the floor, he saw that Brathwidth had revealed himself.

One more thing to do. One more.

He moved deeper into the back-bar, toward the cardinal's open case and the fabled, magical, red, red robe of a long dead holy man.

†

"Nick!" Darren's voice was coming through the burning front bar. "Are you okay?"

"Yeah!" Nick called back to him. "But don't try to get through! The main bar is on fire!"

"No shit!"

"Darren, get out of the building!"

"I'm gonna go around to the other stairs! You hang on!"

"No! Darren, get out!"

There was no response.

"Darren?" Nick yelled.

Nothing.

He turned around, looking hopefully toward Marbas, but the giant lion hadn't moved. His eyes were still tightly closed.

"Was that your little boyfriend?" Brathwidth paced right in front of Nick, keeping a very watchful eye on the gap between the floor and Nick's shoes, which was visibly diminishing. "I can't wait to meet him."

"You just better keep your mouth closed, dickhead. If you cast your demon breath again, I swear, I'll see you destroyed."

"Do you kiss your mother with that mouth?"

Behind them, Shehlá roared, tearing across the room, splattering blood everywhere as she clawed uselessly at the air.

Nick pursed his lips and looked the incubus in the eye. "I am not fuckin' around, dumb-ass!"

The panther-demon growled.

"Ever hear of the 'Spells of Anat?' " Nick asked.

Brathwidth's smile faltered.

"Well," Nick went on, "I just happen to know one of them!"

"Indeed? Perhaps you should cast it then. You should cast the spell right now, before your feet find the floor, and my teeth your throat."

Nick smiled and Brathwidth growled again.

"You think I'm bluffing?" Nick squinted at him.

"He is quite the impressive power, I agree." Brathwidth nodded. "But Marbas the Black was—"

"Was one of the ten, you idiot! He was one of the ten fallen who'd banded with Linos!"

"The Beast himself destroyed the ten—"

"Only five of them, shit-for-brains!" Nick locked eyes with Brathwidth, not daring to turn to the stairs and alert the demon if Darren arrived. "I am not bluffing, seriyim. Do not make this mistake. It is crystal clear to me, with only a budding skill of clear sight, that Marbas the Black must have been one of the original ten. Why can't you see it? What's wrong with you? Something must be wrong with you. You don't want to try and call this one. You need only see my eyes to know the truth. Use your powers of observation." Nick pointed toward the shrieking snake-demon. "She can't help you anymore. The wisest course for you would be to flee. Believe me, dumb-fuck, at this time, running would be the only thing to best serve your 'interests.' "

Brathwidth didn't answer. Listening to Nicholas speak, all the blood drained from the demon's face. It was a sufficient answer.

†

The fire in the main bar had been slowed by the sprinklers, but not stopped. Darren could only wonder what had started it.

"We can't go that way," he said, turning to Karen behind him. Theo and Eddie were still a bit elevated, but would join them soon. "I'm going around to the other stairs. You have to take the guys and get them out."

"Darren..." Karen squinted, tears welling in her eyes.

"Honey," he said, grabbing her shoulders, "Nick's okay for now. You heard him. I'm gonna go get him."

"No, it's not Nick!" she sobbed. "It's Scotty!"

†

You have to cast the spell.

Scott's eyes were still closed, but Nick could sense him easily.

It's time.

Nick shook his head and covered his ears. *I can't.* He could see Brathwidth below, pacing and frowning up at him suspiciously.

Doll-face, Lilith whispered in Nick's head, *it's all right. Cast the spell and name us all. Marbas is right. It's time.*

Can't you help me? Lilith, isn't there anything you can do?

There is a great deal I could do. But...

Nick! Marbas opened his eyes. *She can't continue this way, and I don't think she wants to. The Beast will come eventually and she'll be destroyed. Unless I heal her.*

Still howling, Shehlá groped at the dance floor railing. Her face was covered in blood, running freely off of her chin and onto the floor.

Brathwidth turned away from Nick and, seeing the blood, sprinted suddenly across the room. At first, Nick assumed it was to help Shehlá, but he was wrong, of course. Demon blood was a very powerful substance. Brathwidth simply took his chance to lap it up. Shehlá certainly wasn't going to see him do it.

Oh, doll-face, Lilith's voice, though only in his head, still enchanted him, still made Nick swoon, *just look at that.* She meant Brathwidth, he knew. *You don't want Marbas to heal me back into... back into...*

Screaming, Shehlá tore the dance floor banister from the wall. Blind as she was, she obviously had a good idea of where she'd thrown Scott and began to slither his way, leaving a slimy, smeared, red trail.

Scotty! Nick glanced downward and saw that his feet were just about back on the ground. *I don't think I can do it!*

Nicholas, the lion fixed his eyes on him, *you are the only one who can do it.*

With a nauseating howl, Shehlá took a massive swing, arcing the torn-out dance floor rail, connecting with splintering force on the bare hardwood only a few feet away from Marbas. She howled again.

You're asking me to kill you! Nick could feel the tears streaming down his cheeks. *I can't kill you! I can't!*

Marbas closed his eyes again, as though he didn't have the strength to keep them open. *Nothing can kill me, Nick. I'm asking you to let me go, that's all. It's time, my love. Let me go.*

Scotty, I can't! Nick sobbed.

Nick... Scott sighed and Nick sobbed even harder. *Think of what you'll be doing. You've been given the divine name for all demons. You must cast the spell. Name us all, each and every one of us. Cast the spell.*

Nick could only shudder, swiping at his tears.

You have to know what you've given me, Nick. Scott's familiar voice floated within Nick's head. *You've let me love you, and more. You've let me bring Darren to you. I've seen miracles born in Theo's devotion and in Eddie's peace.*

"Scott!" Nick sobbed out loud.

Shehlá turned to his voice and threw the steel railing like a spear. It struck Nick's chest and, had he not still been held within Lilith's charm, would have flown through his heart, tearing it completely out of his body. Instead, it crashed into the magic barrier, which was fading, but still completely effective. The rail hung vibrating for an instant, humming a low, metallic pitch, then fell to the floor.

"Oh!" Brathwidth exclaimed. "So close! Just give it a couple seconds, babe, and you can have another go at him. He's just about down."

Brathwidth went back to licking up Shehlá's pooling blood.

The snake-demon wailed, slithering away from Scott and toward Nick.

Marbas raised his head. "Nick!"

Shehlá stopped, turning back toward the voice of the great lion.

"He's about thirty-five feet to your left, precious," Brathwidth said, pawing at his now-crimson face.

The black lion took a deep breath. "Chant the spell Nicholas. I am but a shadow, cast by the consent of your own soul. I am yours. I live for you and will perish for you. I've always been yours, to allow, or to put aside."

Shehlá turned toward the voice of Marbas and yowled. Rising up, she clawed the air and slithered toward him.

Nick raised his hand, splayed his fingers, and began to chant. "Kās melek, kās Khonsu, tes nac tama kās Amun, kās tes logos tes mara', kās Dynamus tres seriyima."

The words seemed to take shape on their own, forming their pronunciation behind Nick's lips. They flew from him like stones and his arms quivered from the rise of their power.

Shehlá stopped. Beneath the trails of gore, her face turned white. She whipped her head toward Nick, slinging huge drops of blood in a wide, cherry mist.

Brathwidth stopped licking the floor but did not raise his head.

Only his eyes turned back to look at Nick.

Nick stopped chanting. The room was silent but for the crackle of the fire, which was slowly growing in the room behind him, despite the sprinkler system. The demons, one and all, were holding their breath.

"Goodbye, Scotty." Nick blinked back tears. "I wish I could touch you. If I could just touch you, you'd know how much I love you."

Marbas could only close his eyes. Tracks of demon tears glistened down his face.

Nick raised his hand again and chanted the Spell of Anat. He chanted the spell over and over, louder and louder, until the spell's ancient magic had overwhelmed both the righteous and the wicked alike.

†

He heard the word of the Lord spoken by the enlightened one and gasped. The very air began to shudder, snapping sparks here and there as though the atmosphere itself was suddenly uncomfortable, whipping back and forth, seeking a chance to escape.

He saw when Brathwidth leapt toward the distant doors and the night outside. But he was ready.

Dashing along the back wall, he threw himself onto a cocktail table, at the same time throwing the crimson Chasuble ahead of him, covering the demon's path.

Brathwidth ran right into it.

The shriek that issued from the incubus was searing and sharp. The red cloth billowed down over the feline half of the demon, covering his burned and bleeding fur. Beneath it, the demon's legs were as still as stone, frozen to the floor. The rest of him, the uncovered part of Brathwidth, still screamed and struggled, clawing at the floor frantically, huffing between cries. He was like a bug, trying to tear its still-living half from beneath the finger of a cruel child.

Finally, he thought as he watched the creature struggle, an artifact that actually worked.

Even watching the demon writhe beneath the Chasuble, seeing its skin tear and bleed where the material ended, holding the creature to the floor as solidly as a slab of cement, even witnessing this end, he could not be glad. He took just a moment to wonder at it, but that was all. He could allow himself joy, but not from the destruction of the demon. He could allow it because now he could rest.

Brathwidth bayed like an animal. "De Montleon," the Demon of Cyprus, so composed, so confident in his power and his stature, thrashed and roared like a common beast. After taking Larry, after consuming innocent and prolific lives to satisfy his boredom, the demon revealed himself truly. A common beast. One such as this killed and moved and, in the end, meant nothing.

He turned his back on him, though the demon's agony still echoed. There was a comfortable booth in the back room, he remembered. Perhaps he'd find the Vessel there as well, empty once again. Maybe he could hold it while he sat down. He'd hold the Vessel, sit in his favorite booth, and close his eyes.

†

There was just so much smoke, even though Darren knew the club very, very well, he still got a little turned around. By the time he'd found the north stairs and bounded back down, it was all over.

A blinding white flash made him think that something had blown up, maybe something big and electronic and dangerous. There hadn't been any sound, though, no report at all. In fact, still at the top of the stairs, the room below sounded strangely silent and empty. Darren didn't hear anything for a moment, then, just as though a switch had been thrown, he heard the faintest crackle from the fire in the main bar, then the patter of the falling water, then the alarm, then the noise from the ruckus out front. Any second, there'd be men bursting in with axes and hoses, water and people everywhere.

Darren went right to Nick, who was lying on the carpet, just off the dance floor's west edge. Nick was out cold and drenched from head to toe. Forcing himself not to panic, Darren felt for Nick's pulse. It was very strong. Darren sighed, smiling.

Looking around quickly, Darren was extremely disturbed at how much smoke had gathered just since he'd gotten back downstairs. It was very black and quickly filling even the three-story center of the enormous club.

There was no sign of anyone else, not another person or demon or whatever. The dance floor was an appalling mess, the hardwood actually shattered in spots.

No sign of Shehlá or her minion. No Lilith either. No Scott.

Darren picked up Nick, who seemed almost weightless. Darren frowned for a second, until he remembered.

"Oh yeah," he said to himself, turning toward the far exit.

CHAPTER XI

†

Demon Tears

I will both lay me down in peace; and sleep: for thou, Lord, only makest me dwell in safety.

- Psalms 4:8 (KJV)

Santa Monica, California
A condominium on the shore side of Pacific Coast Highway, two miles south of Sunset Boulevard

†

They hadn't been home for more than half an hour when one of the Security Guys from the parking garage buzzed them.

"There's a woman here to see you, Mr. Jacobson. She says her name is Lauren. Lauren Izzerloft."

Darren heard a woman speaking in the background.

"Oh, no..." the Security Guy corrected himself. "It's Ibberoft. What?" Pause. Some speaking away from the mouthpiece. "Izzerompt? Izzer...?" Pause. Ruffled movement. "Her name is Lauren something-or-whatever."

Lauren Isseroff, Darren thought. It's Lilith.

He was too shocked to think much about it. "Send her in," he heard himself whisper.

Nick was in bed, still out cold.

Back at the club, everyone had just gotten the hell out of the building. Karen and the guys were waiting when Darren got back to the condo with Nick. Theo had insisted on carrying Nick inside. He and Eddie took one look at their unconscious friend and both started crying.

"I think he'll be fine," Darren had told them. "Eddie, I'm gonna call that doctor you dated, though, and see if he'll come over here, just in case. If he says we should take Nick to the hospital, we will."

Karen placed her hand on Nick's forehead. "He's fine, Darren. He's safe."

Theo nodded, tears streaming down his face. "Yeah, man. Don't call anyone. I've got him."

They'd all walked silently to the elevator, into the condo, and watched as Theo gently laid Nick onto the bed. Karen had grabbed some towels and Darren took off Nick's shoes.

They hadn't said another word the whole time. Darren didn't think any of them had realized that they were just standing there, all four of them, looking down at Nick. It wasn't until the call came from the garage that he noticed.

A couple minutes later, there was a knock at the door. Lilith was standing there, radiant, beaming her solar smile.

"Where is he?" she said.

"He's out, Lilith," Darren said. "I mean, he's unconscious."

"'Lauren,' Darren honey." She nodded at him. "Just call me 'Lauren.'"

"Oh. Okay." Darren shrugged. "Um... Nick is unconscious, Lauren. He's, ah—"

"Well, of course he is, handsome!" She patted Darren on the cheek, stepped past him politely, and took off her coat.

Darren noticed Lilith—Lauren—had been wearing a very large, old windbreaker. She had a huge black T-shirt on underneath, which covered what Darren thought might be a pair of men's khaki shorts.

Darren raised an eyebrow. "What happened to your clothes?"

"Nick will be out for quite a while yet, I'm certain," Lauren explained. "I just wanted to get here to make sure he's okay, and to take care of him until he comes around."

"What's wrong with him?" Darren asked, absently taking Lauren's windbreaker from her and hanging it up.

"He's in the bedroom, right?" she said, pointing and walking to the back of the condo.

"Yeah." Darren rushed after her.

"Hi, you guys." Lauren grimaced as she entered the bedroom. "I'm so sorry you had to go through all of that. Apparently, I was a little out of the loop on some things, and so, well, it kinda got out of hand a bit."

"What happened?" Karen asked.

"Well, first, let me just tell you that I saw Max standing outside watching while the club burned down."

"Oh, my god—!"

"He was so happy!"

"What?"

"Well, I had to introduce myself, of course, 'Mr. Hertz, I'm Lauren Isseroff, nice to meet you. Blah, blah, blah. Lovely fire, don't you think? Blah, blah, blah.' But it worked. He shook my hand."

"Did he say anything?"

"Well, no, he was really smart about that. His alibi is tight as a clam's ass, honey, you don't have to worry. But let me tell you, he was happy about two things. First, that his insurance was current and, second, that he'd had someone like you in charge, someone who'd gotten just about everyone out of that death trap."

"Just about?"

"Yeah, well, see... the firemen found two bodies before they had to get out of the building themselves." She turned to Darren. "The whole thing is totally gone. There were club-kids outside with marshmallows and *every*thing. It was an event."

Lauren turned back to Karen. "Anyway, apparently there's a little mystery now, because neither of those people were killed by the smoke or the fire. One of them stabbed the other one, then walked into the back-bar, sat down, and died. Someone mentioned something about alcohol poisoning, but I don't know."

"Robert," Theo whispered, shaking his head.

"That bishop dude?" Eddie asked.

"Yeah." Theo nodded. "I think so."

"He got stabbed?"

"No." Lauren shook her head. "He was the stab*ber*. But, really, don't worry about the 'victim.' " She made a quote gesture with her fingers. "Live by the witch blade, die by the witch blade, I always say."

"He just died then?" Darren asked. "Robert just... died?"

Lauren turned to him. "Yeah, I guess. He was just sitting in a booth in the back-bar. I'm glad you guys know who he was, because I couldn't tell, and he didn't have any ID on him. He's a John Doe at the morgue right now. Actually, it's the same story with the other body too. No ID."

"I'm gonna have to answer for them anyway." Karen sighed. "Two guys in my club without ID end up dead, and you can bet it's my door the police'll come knockin' on."

"You really should get down there soon, Karen," Lauren offered. "They're wondering what happened to you."

"I know. I'll go in a few minutes. Tell us about Nicky."

"Oh!" Lauren exclaimed, smiling, covering her mouth with her fingers. "Oh, my doll-faced hero! He cast the Spell of Anat, you know. The little shit cast his first spell, and it was none other than the flagship work of one of the mightiest powers to fall from the grace of Heaven for the duration of time itself. He chanted the Spell of Anat with the command of a prophet and the force of an earthquake."

"He actually cast it?" Darren gasped, shaking his head.

Darren had known, of course. He'd known about the spell and when he hadn't seen Scott, well...

Lauren nodded at him, grinning. "Yup. Like a pro. He just raised his hand and bellowed as much authority as I've ever heard. I was so proud! Well, terrified, but proud just the same."

"Terrified?"

"He used a divine name in the spell."

"Scott's?"

"Oh no!" She shook her head vigorously. "No, he used the divine word for all demons. The word that, used in a spell like that, would destroy all demons, everywhere."

"Oh, my ..." Karen gasped.

"Uh, huh." Lauren nodded, smiling. "What a champ, huh?"

"But, Lilith..." Darren squinted at her. "Something about that doesn't make any sense."

"Oh no, Darren, sweetness, please..." She turned back to him, bit her lip.

"What?" Darren didn't understand. Lilith suddenly looked like she was going to cry.

"Darren, please..." she whispered again. "I'm not..."

"What?"

"Please don't call me Lilith." She closed her eyes, shook her head. "I'm just 'Lauren' now," she whispered. Darren could barely hear her. "Please call me Lauren."

"Oh, right," Darren said, confused. "Yeah, I'm sorry. Of course. Lauren."

She nodded, pressing her fingers to her lips, grinning behind them. Even so, a tear rolled down her cheek.

"I'm sorry, Lauren," he repeated.

She nodded again.

"Lauren," Darren said," please tell us, though—"

"The spell destroyed all the demons in the whole world?" Eddie asked. "Even the Beast?"

Lauren turned to him. "Well, yeah, it shoulda done that, but um, well..."

"What happened?" Darren touched her arm.

"The thing is, the reason it didn't work as, well... comprehensively as it should have is sort of my fault. Well, actually, you could sort of say Marbas had a hand in it too." She took a deep breath, grimaced, and bit one of her nails. "Guys... I fixed the Circle of Twelve."

"You mean the icons?" Darren crossed his arms, cocked his head and raised his eyebrows.

"Yeah. I fixed 'em. I fixed them so that they'd contain demons, but what it ended up doing was limiting the power of Nick's spell to just within the circle. But that gave it quite a whollop, let me tell you. Shehlá and Brathwidth were destroyed horribly and totally!"

"But..." Eddie shook his head. "What about... ?"

Lauren smiled at him. "I don't know, sweetheart. I should have been destroyed too. Actually, I felt the spell, and it sort of tickled a little bit. I don't know why I wasn't destroyed."

Eddie turned his palms toward the ceiling. "What do you mean, you don't—?"

"What about Scott?" Darren blurted.

"Oh!" Lauren turned to him, eyes wide. "Honey, I don't know about Marbas either. About Scott, I mean."

"What?"

"I can sense the destruction of Shehlá, Brathwidth too, but as for Scott..." She shrugged.

Darren stared at her. He crossed his arms, licked his lips.

"Darren, sweet-face, I'm sorry." Lauren frowned, shook her head. "I simply don't know."

"What was the word Nick used?" Karen interrupted. "The word for all demons."

Lauren cocked her head, grimacing. "Now that's funny. I... my goodness, I don't remember."

"Well, Lauren..." Darren said. "Can you help Nick?"

"Oh, good glory, yes, doll!"

Lauren immediately went and sat next to the still-sleeping Nick, placing her hand on his forehead as Karen had done.

"Anyway," she went on, "I suppose the Spell of Anat *did* affect me. I know it affected me, actually, part of me, well... because I can't change."

"What?"

She turned back to look at Darren. "Demons always have a true form, something hideous that reveals their nature to human eyes. I have one. At least I did. I thought that, during the whole fiasco, I'd lost enough strength to keep me in that form for quite a while, but when I passed a mirror on the way out, I saw that I was, well, like this." She raised her arms in the air and looked down at herself. "I'd have been here sooner, but I had to find some clothes. I can't even phase anywhere."

"How'd you get here?"

She looked up. "Oh, I'm not completely powerless." Lauren stopped. She closed her eyes, licked her lips, took a long, slow breath. "I honestly don't know all the details." She opened her eyes, spoke slowly. "Even so, whatever the spell did to me, I can still work magic, it would seem. So, I was able to get here. That was easy, really. As far as I know, actually, I just can't... I can't phase anywhere and..." She stopped again, glanced down at her hands, shook her head. "I can't phase anywhere, I can't look like a demon anymore, and... and I can't find Scott."

No one spoke for a moment. Darren sighed, nodding.

"Well," Karen said smiling, "we're glad that you don't look like a demon, Lauren."

"Oh, good glory, me too!" Lauren looked up at her. "Ain't it a kick in the pants? You wouldn't have wanted to see my other form anyway, let me tell you, it was nine and a half feet of ugly!"

"Lauren, please..." Darren walked past her. He reached down and brushed some hair off of Nick's face. "Can you wake him up?"

She tilted her head, smiling at Darren sheepishly. "No. I'm sorry, handsome. But he'll be back soon. In the interim, I mean to take good care of him. In fact, he made me promise to take care of his whole family, and so I'm here for all of you. Anything you need. Anything at all. And I'll sit here with you and watch him and make sure no power touches him. No matter how long it takes, we'll all sit here together and wait for him to come back to us."

†

In his dream, Nick sat quietly and thought. There was a rhythm in the air. It wasn't quite music, though.

He thought about the Spell of Anat and was awed. Such power was overwhelming, even to consider. He remembered his chanting, the face of Shehlá as she realized what was happening. He remembered feeling a great sense of relief, of a decision long ignored and now mercifully made. The sense of relief, he knew, had not been his own, but Lilith's.

Nick remembered his desperation not to cast his eyes toward Marbas, not to see the fallen lion, the demon who had saved him. As Nick chanted, the image of his ancient friend, the tumbling tufts of his mane, the total blackness of his fur, the glacier blue of his eyes, haunted Nick. Instead, he watched Shehlá, taking strength from her pallor. He knew if he'd glanced at the majestic, black lion, he would not continue. He couldn't have completed the spell. All would have been lost because, powerful as they were, even on their own, even seeming to leap from his mouth by themselves, the magic words of the Spell of Anat would have been halted in his throat. The sight of Marbas the Black, of his friend Scott, lying prone and lifeless, disco light reflecting from the paths of his demon tears, would have muted Nick in an instant.

In his dream, he could consider these things. He was sitting alone in an alley. He leaned his shoulder onto a very heavy, steel dumpster, which was somehow warm, somehow comfortable. He could consider the spell and his potent chanting. He could almost see the flash of light that signaled the end of his memory. A blinding flash had silenced him. There'd been an impossibly brilliant light, he'd turned his head and now... now he sat, not in memory, but in dream.

There was a rhythm in the air. Nick closed his eyes, wrapping his arms about his legs, listening and feeling the pulse of the night. It wasn't a real night, he knew. It was a dream. Still, he smiled.

How long had he been there? That, he couldn't fathom. His dream gave him no sense of time passing, no hint at how long it had contained him. He heard a rumbling far down the alley. The washed brick brightened as he opened his eyes. Maybe he should get up. Maybe he should walk away.

"I think you'd better stay where you are," said a deep and familiar voice.

Nick turned his head and grinned. There was an angel in his dream too. An angel was sitting across the alley, his knees pulled to his chest, his arms wrapped comfortably around them, his brilliant locks of black hair tumbling across his cheek.

The angel flicked his head and smiled. His hair flew back, off of his face.

Nick sighed and the angel giggled. It was a wonderful sound, the giggle of an angel.

"You are Marbas," Nick said.

"Yes." The angel nodded. "I am Marbas of God. I am an angel, a messenger of the Lord."

"I think I've been waiting for you."

"I'm sorry I'm late." He grinned again.

"You're supposed to be with me in my dreams, you know."

"That's true. And also while you're awake, but you won't see me so well."

Nick was beaming a smile. Around him, the air lived with its rhythm. "I still have clear sight."

The angel nodded. "Yes. From now on, you will always see clearly. You are the enlightened one. Still."

"But I won't see you."

The angel smiled. "Only in your sleep. Only when I can kiss you and not disturb your love."

Nick took a deep breath. "That's okay then. I guess, even though I did magic, I'm not really a witch. So, it's still okay for angels to kiss me while I sleep."

The angel nodded, smiling.

Nick smiled back. "You can kiss my love too, you know. He misses you."

"And I miss him. I miss all our loves, Nick."

"You'll see him then? When he dreams?"

"He'll know me. As he listens to you breathe, as he watches your eyes while they move behind your lids, he'll know me."

Nick nodded.

The dream sat around them. Nick thought for a moment that they weren't speaking. He didn't know how long they'd been together, not speaking. It didn't matter.

"Demons can't shed tears," Nick said. "Seriyima are not capable of crying. Their natures will not tolerate the essence of compassion to any degree. It's just not possible."

"And so it is." The angel gave a bow of his head.

"I met a demon once," Nick whispered. "But he could weep. And I found out later that it meant—"

"That he was not a demon at all." The angel cocked his head. A wavy lock of his hair, his black, black hair, black as blindness, swept across his lips. He was very beautiful, the angel.

Nick smiled.

Coming Halloween 2007

Joshua Dagon is a novelist,
playwright, and columnist.
He lives in Las Vegas, Nevada.